LEGACY

THE CHRONICLER

LEGACY

THE CHRONICLER

TABLE OF CONTENTS

CHAPTER 1 The Dance...1

CHAPTER 2 Nights to Remember...31

CHAPTER 3 A Brand New Day 45

CHAPTER 4 The University 55

CHAPTER 5 Fists and Iron...99

CHAPTER 6 Absorb the Sounds of the Coliseum 125

CHAPTER 7 Let the Tournament begin...................................135

CHAPTER 8 Clash of the Captains...159

CHAPTER 9 Darkened Days..173

CHAPTER 10 Answering the Call 205

CHAPTER 11 A Time to Mourn and a Time for Revenge.....219

CHAPTER 12 Last Night on Utopia 233

CHAPTER 13 A Stranger Comes Knocking 251

CHAPTER 14 Queen of Death...265

CHAPTER 15 Let the Trials Begin..279

CHAPTER 16 When Hell Freezes..291

CHAPTER 17 Into the Pit 303

CHAPTER 18 When a Demon Crosses Your Path..............325

CHAPTER 19 The Final Trial 347

CHAPTER 20 He Who Dwells in the Temple.....................373

CHAPTER 21 Conquest of Blood..401

ARCHIVAL ENTRY 409

CHAPTER I

THE DANCE

I am the Chronicler. I have seen and transcribed a vast library of tales, big and small, of good and of evil, stories of noble kings and queens and vile folk, of myths and legends. Indeed, I have seen much in my time. I am ageless and continue to watch and record all things of significance. Join me as I share with you now a tale that takes place far, far away from where you call home. On a world that, in many ways, will appear similar and yet still strange to you. This story is about friendship, romance, war, mystery, and tragedy. Everything that makes up what you and I know as "life".

Our story begins on a planet called Utopia. It is home to a race similar to you in appearance, though with noticeable differences—a race of beings raised with the ideals of being warriors. To be the strongest, to honor their family and their Gods. To one day join their All Father in his service in Valhalla. A world where a new way of science and technology exists beside the old ways of magic, with one steadily overtaking the other as is grows. It is here in this beautiful, peaceful world as it makes its long journey around its red sun that my tale begins. This is the story of Dark Everlast and his friends. In the capital city, Utop, on the western continent, they have grown most of their lives. A grand city that started as a wild frontier fort that, over time, grew outward and reached higher until it became the shining monument of prosperity it is today. The city's structures seemed to glow in radiance from the building's white sidings. A visitor knew right away from her intimidating outer walls and gatehouses manned with soldiers and her streets patrolled by armed guards that she was secure. Off in the distance from the main gatehouse, up on a hill and surrounded by another ring of defenses, was the grand palace of the emperor. Near it, just off to the side, was the holiest and most beautiful of cathedrals ever to be erected in the name of the gods. Yes, though she had a simple name, Utop was a pillar of beauty and a testament to Utopia's potential. It was a thriving fantastical metropolis that hid its technological advancements behind its desire to preserve its past. In other words, it would not be held against an off-worlder if they first mistook the people of this world to be somewhere within their middle-age development.

It is late one night, during a ballroom dance at a great school known as Utopia University. It was being held for two reasons. The students celebrated a glorious victory over their rival school, Midstar University, in a thrilling tournament of wits and power. A tournament is held yearly to showcase to the world the talent that universities, big and small, can produce. Tonight, also honored the Moon God Mani, the god of mysteries, secrets, desires, hopes, and dreams…

The ballroom was dimly lit with one spotlight, and many softer lights twinkled in and out to mimic a night's sky. An arrangement of soothing instrumental music played from speakers hiding in the room's top corners. Off to the side of the ballroom was a large gathering of tables draped in white linen and adorned with a small arrangement of maroon-colored flowers in the center. The tables were unused, save for one. Surrounded by the emptiness sat a young man with long blonde hair. Dressed in a finely pressed white tuxedo with a red satin vest, he could have easily passed for a noble or perhaps even a young prince. However, he was of no such standing. After all, what sort of prince would sit alone while a ball was happening before him? His right hand gently grasped a crystal goblet filled with the party's unique beverage. He slowly raised it to his lips and took a sip. He savored the cool sweet nectar as it washed over his taste buds before swallowing it. After gently setting the goblet back down on the table, his soft blue eyes moved across the room, observing the people. His gaze paused on a couple dancing together, and he didn't try to stop as a small smile formed.

The man was dressed in a blue tuxedo, complete with coattail. He had spikey golden hair and eyes the color of jade, which were locked in a gaze with his female dance partner. She wore a black velvet dress with a subtle shine in the light. She had shoulder-length blonde hair and dark blue eyes that were locked with her partner's. Both of them were smiling as they embraced each other close. The man's name is Cogeta Fairway, and his partner's, Becky Pryemore. Cogeta was a showoff and a goofball who had a golden heart. He was among the most popular in the entire school for his antics and carefree attitude, but few knew what his life had been like before leaving his grandparents' home. Aside from being popular with most, he was highly adored and loved by the female populace in the school. Cogeta was a ladies' man who played no games with a woman's heart. He treated each girl fairly and like a goddess, no matter who they were or where they came from.

His date to the dance was a woman of great intelligence and strong confidence who kept him in line if he went too overboard with his playfulness. She had a tomboyish attitude. However, she was a lady, and woe to the man who said otherwise. The two had been dating for a while now, much to the grief of many of Cogeta's lady friends and with much relief to the jealous men.

The young man's gaze drifted to another couple, and his smile grew slightly more. A touch of pride filled his chest as he admired them. The man was tall with shoulder-length red hair and soul-piercing red eyes. He was dressed in the academy's uniform: a mid-length black jacket with gold patterns along the shoulders and around the wrists and edges, with a black shirt underneath. Finishing his attire was black slacks and boots polished to a shine. His date stood to his shoulder, with long flowing hair that was a light violet color. Her delicate silk dress paired well with her beautiful hair in a soft lavender shade and pearl-shaded heels. Her eyes were locked with his as they moved as one.

The man's name was Dark Angelus Everlast, though he became accustomed to being called simply Angel by those around him. A powerful spirit flowed through him and captivated those who got near him. His past was shrouded in mystery. He just appeared one day at the start of the young man's first year at the University. The man soon had a reputation as a cold-hearted bastard. He did not take an insult from anyone, nor did he shy away from a fight. A point he proved time and time again to those who thought they would put him in his place. He had even bumped heads with local law enforcement on multiple occasions. The young man chuckled to himself. Over his tenure at the University, he somehow became best friends with the class clown and the class rebel.

I wouldn't change a thing. He thought with a smile.

Angel's date for the formal gathering was Leen Puraday. Beauty is in the beholder's eye, a truth well-known throughout history. Leen was an angel. Figuratively, though some would argue literally, that graced the mortal world with her presence, she had the poise, intellect, sophistication, and personality to match her beauty. She was the type to do her best to help you no matter what the problem, even if it was a stranger. When you were around her, you always felt welcome and never as if you did not belong or were unwanted.

She had the unique gift found in a few people, to brighten one's day with a simple smile.

The young man watched as Angel slipped a necklace around her neck and under her flowing hair. Angel had shown off the present to Cogeta and the man earlier in the day. He told them he'd been working on it for a couple of weeks, and he couldn't wait to surprise Leen with the gift at the dance. The necklace had two three-dimensional gold heart-shape parts, one small part on top of a larger section. Within the large heart was a ruby shaped like another heart, and in the smaller heart, on top, was an oval-shaped diamond. Between the two sections, small gold wings sprouted out on either side. Her surprise grew as Angel presented her with matching earrings, diamond studs, and ruby centers. Upon placing them in, they hung low. Angel quietly explained that he had made them in her father's shop behind his back. She playfully hit his chest but hugged him tightly afterward.

The boy's smile grew once more as he enjoyed seeing his friend's happiness. His eyes then wandered elsewhere. They stopped upon the last couple of interest to him. Amidst the flowing bodies, he saw a girl and boy in each other's arms. His smile faded a few degrees. He felt a powerful pull toward the girl. Was he in love with her? He couldn't say for absolute certainty. They were on opposite sides of the spectrum; she was popular, active, and knowledgeable in ways of life that he was unfamiliar with, whereas he was more of an introvert and certainly not popular. They had some interaction through school. They shared a couple of interests, which he managed to talk to her about from time to time. But their conversations were always shorter than he wished they'd be. To him, she wasn't like the other girls he interacted with. When he was around this one, all his troubles were gone. Her mere presence put his mind and soul at ease. He hadn't felt that way around anyone else. Even around Leen, whom he admired, didn't stir the same feelings or trigger such emotions in him.

He greatly desired to get to know the girl. He felt there was more to her than what she revealed to those around her. Maybe, behind the bright smile and always friendly and pleasant demeanor, she held back a tidal wave of worries or concerns, desires or passions, dreams or aspirations, and had nowhere to direct or share such thoughts with. He wished to learn everything about her, be part of her world, her inner circle. Perhaps then he could figure out if there was indeed a bond to be had that could bloom into something magical beyond their expectations or dreams. Something that could rival the legends of old and take root to form new tales of passion. He chuckled to himself.

As if that would happen.

He could never muster the courage to tell her how he felt. When they did speak, she had this uncanny ability to cause his brain to turn off. At any other time, he was rather intelligent, could think of several moves ahead, and could problem solve, but then his brain went to mush when he tried to speak casually with her. Even getting close enough to talk to her was difficult for him. He wasn't one for group conversations, especially when he wanted to get to know the person. So, he would wait until he saw an opportunity to be alone with her, and even then, he needed help figuring out how to approach and start the conversation. Worst yet, whenever he thought he was ready to reveal his feelings towards her, her lover or someone else would appear, and his chance to talk to her was gone. This was how it always had been. As far as the blue-eyed boy could tell, that was how it would always be. No matter how much he desired to be with that person, that didn't mean they would ever be together. It was more likely that she would always be with someone else and his chance to nurture a lasting connection, bond, or relationship, romantic or otherwise, would never be.

There were a few times he thought his fortune was turning around. He mustered up the courage and got her number. Sure, it was in part because they were working on a group project, but even so... it was a direct line to her. Perhaps he could convey his feelings through the words on the screen that his tongue failed to say. He had managed to converse with her this way, but again, they were few. The boy pulled out his small handheld and scrolled back through the chat history. He was still waiting for a reply to his last message several days ago. He slipped the small black device back into his inner coat pocket.

He had finished his glass but remained sitting for a moment. His eyes still locked as if in a trance, watching the woman he yearned for dancing with another. He closed his eyes and shook his head. He stood up and walked over to a table holding a large crystal bowl. Within it was the sweet red beverage that had been in his goblet. Inside the bowl was a crystal dipper with a handle in the image of a wolf snarling carved into it.

"Hey there, lad, don't just fill up on VB." The boy looked up at a man dressed in a chef's attire, greeting him with a smile. His voice was boisterous and gruff. "We got all kinds of delicious food for you kids. Shaw Incorporated spared no expense for this event."

The boy looked down at the row of tables filled with an

overwhelming spread of different dishes. "I'm not sure." His response came out more timidly than he meant for it to.

"Come on, kid, grab a plate. Grab it while the other kids are distracted. Some of us traveled across the world to be here, to honor your school's victory." The Chef's grin grew as he thrust a plate toward the boy. "Did you fight in this past tournament?"

"I..." A sudden feeling of shame filled his chest. "No, I didn't." He lied. He smiled softly, "I just watched. I'm not much of a fighter."

"Ha ha! That's fine, kid. Not all of us can be. Here, start filling your belly with me. I hunted with my team this morning in the forest outside the city and caught the biggest boar we could find. Spent all morning hunting for the beast. Then we slowly roasted it while marinating it in some fine wine until it was dark and tender. Then we took some fresh honey from the hives and glazed the meat for added flavor." The boy watched the chef piling food onto his plate as he moved down the table, "If that doesn't entice you, how about something more exotic? We got Midstar dragon tongue, flayed and seasoned with secret spices of the East until it had a pleasant aroma that rose to the heavens! Or how about a soup from the Southern peaks, Cream Fabre? It has boar bits inside and a thin layer of crust that seals in the heat and enhances the flavor. We flash-fried rice with a sprinkle of pepper and other special seasonings for the side dish. Or perhaps you'd prefer a simple yet delicious imperial salad?"

"Gustal! The boy doesn't want any of that," a chef at the following table spoke up in a thick rustic accent, "he wants food fit for the emperor." The rounder of the two chefs took the plate out of the young man's hand and smiled at him. "Ain't that right, boy? You want something special. My team and I spent all morning hunting down some of the largest condors to the south. We've filleted them and cooked them in seasoned oils. Just smell that mouthwatering aroma." He placed two slices onto the plate. "How about trying some of my dwarf fish special? Little fishies are so small that they fit in the palm of your hand! Have some! They go great paired with mashed potatoes covered in our thick dark gravy. If you like seafood, let's start with a second plate because you've got to try one of my favorite dishes, Shrimps Volley. Fresh from the Andrian Ocean, the dipping sauce is mmmmm sweet yet tangy. Yeah, you got to try this too!"

The boy looked at the two plates stacked with food and was growing concerned. However, he didn't wish to be rude. "So much food… I don't know if I can eat all of this."

A short woman took the plates from the bigger man and smiled warmly at the boy. "This is indeed a lot, but you're a growing young man. You need to give your body all the nutrients it needs to become stronger. That said, you shouldn't skimp out on desserts, and as you can see from my table, I brought the sweetest of sweets to your university tonight. My team and I spared no expense to ensure we brought the best. Variety is the truest of spices one needs in their life, and that's what we got here tonight for your dining pleasure. Do you like cake? We have all kinds of cakes."

The boy looked at the cakes before him. "They are all so beautifully decorated. Not sure I want to be the first to cut into them."

"Ah dear, that's sweet of you. Then how about some pie? We have fresh-out-of-the-oven pies of many flavors here. Or, if you want something cold, we have a great range of ice creams over here in the coolers. Of course, you have got to have a nice helping of duffins. Everybody loves duffins." She began loading up a third plate with tiny, round, puffy donuts doused with sugar crystals. The young man looked at the platters of duffins stacked in pyramids. The lady wasn't wrong; he loved the doughy treats. They are addicting; one could rarely resist the temptation to have only one. It is hard to contain self-control when faced with a large amount. He noted that some of them had a variety of creams oozing out, so they were the stuffed variety, which was among his favorites.

At the end of the table were jellies and puddings in various flavors. He stopped the lady politely before she added those to his already overwhelming pile. At the end of the tables was a large assortment of beverages to wash down the night's meal. It was filled with various teas, sodas, wine, and other alcoholic beverages. However, the drink that drew the most attention was the red beverage in two crystal bowls, virgin blood.

The boy poured another cup of the sweet red liquid and returned to his seat. His plates of food were sitting in front of him. He chuckled and shook his head. *Heh, they got me. Dang, that's a lot of food.* He took a few bites from the boar. *Oh wow, he wasn't kidding. This is amazing.* He reached for his cup and took a moment to stare into it, and a foreboding feeling overcame him. *One day I am going to die. I wonder, when that day comes, what will I leave behind? Have I done anything of worth? What will people think of me when I am gone? Will I die alone, or will I perhaps finally find the love that my heart searches for?* The young man shook his head to force the morbid questions from his mind and took a sip from his goblet. His eyes drifted over all the couples still enjoying themselves on the dance floor while he sat alone and began eating. The delicious food comforted him, if only for a moment. Over time couples left the dance floor, got food, and sat down to eat.

He saw the girl step away and go to the crystal bowl. He scanned the area and didn't see her partner around. He hesitated for a moment, wondering if he should approach her or not. In the end, what harm could it honestly do? He just wished to say hello, perhaps tell her that she looked lovely in her dress. The boy stood up and made his way through the rows of tables and chairs, dodging people as they pushed their chairs out or stepped past him. The whole time he was thinking of what he was going to say.

It's fine. I'm just going to say hello. See how she is enjoying herself. Perhaps ask to dance… yeah right, as if that would happen. She came here with Justin. She wouldn't want to dance with me. I don't even know how to dance properly. His feet brought him closer to the girl. *It's now or never…*

"Hey…" He said softly.

The girl didn't respond. Didn't even look at him.

He just stood there silently for a moment, waiting for a response. *Maybe... she didn't hear me? The music is playing, after all.* "Hey there, how are you doing?" He tried again, raising his voice a little more.

The girl shifted her gaze over and smiled. "Hey."

"Umm... nice party, right?"

"Yeah. It's pretty nice." Her voice was soft and gentle. Yet the boy still sensed that she was guarded.

"May I get that for you?" He offered his hand toward the large dipper to pour her a drink.

"No thanks. I got it."

"Of course..." He slowly withdrew his hand, now feeling foolish for even offering. *Of course, she could do it herself. That's why she came over to it in the first place, idiot.*

"Are you having a good time? Who did you come with tonight?"

"Huh? Oh... yeah. I'm having... fun. I umm... came alone. Well, not really alone, I mean. I came with Angel and Leen and Cogeta and Becky."

"Oh, that sounds great. Glad you are having fun."

"Yeah. Are you?"

"Yeah. I am. Justin isn't much of a dancer, but he's trying. Do you know how to dance?"

"Not... not really. I umm... I'm not very good with my feet."

"That's too bad. I like to dance."

"You are very good at it, from what I can tell."

"Thank you." She smiled.

I got her to smile. His heart warmed. *I love her smile.*

The young man had a playful thought. "P-perhaps… you could show me some---" The boy was interrupted when an arm wrapped around his neck and pulled him close. He nearly lost his footing but remained standing as he tilted his head to see her date grinning down at him.

"Hey there, buddy," he sneered, "what are you doing with my girl? You lost?"

"Justin, leave him alone. We were just talking." The girl said in a soft reprimanding tone.

"Is that so? That's cool. Reminds me that I had something to say to him too. Alisandra, would you be a doll and get me a plate of some of that boar meat? It smells delicious. I'm going to have a quick chat with my friend here."

Alisandra rolled her eyes, then looked back at the boy and smiled gently. "Fine. It was good to see you. Maybe we will talk again sometime."

"Yeah… it was good to see you too." The boy said though it strained him to do so as the grip around his head tightened. He was pulled around and away from the table.

Justin leaned down and got his face close to the boy. "Now, what were you trying to do while I was in the john taking a leak? You trying to hit on my girl?"

"N-no. I just wanted to say hello and talk to her." This close to him, the boy could smell the other man's breath. It reeked of something off-putting. It took a moment for the boy to recognize the odor. *Alcohol. Lots of it. Must have gotten some at some point tonight or started the drinking before showing up to the dance.*

"Listen closely," Justin breathed into the boy's face making him want to gag. "Don't make me take you out back and beat the puss out of your brain. You're supposed to be smart, so take the hint. She's with me. Not with you. Alisandra is my girl." His grip on the boy's neck tightened, "And I have no problem kicking the crap out of anyone thinking they're gonna steal her from me—especially not some bookworm loser. I could kick your ass back when we were in Primary, and I can kick it now. Don't care if you got friends. They won't always be around. You get me, Ryker?"

The young man looked down at the floor. He was gritting his teeth. He wanted to punch this guy so bad, to beat him until he couldn't move. To show Alisandra what a terrible person he was. That he didn't deserve her. But how would that prove anything? If he attacked, he would be the monster. Worse yet, what if he lost? Then everything Justin said would be true; he would be a loser. The young man gritted his teeth tighter yet unclenched and relaxed his hands.

"Yeah… I understand." He said quietly.

"Good boy. You are smart, after all. Enjoy the rest of your night. I know I will. Taking Alisandra back to my place after this for an after party. I'd invite you, but I wouldn't want to kill the vibe at the party. Plus, it would probably be past your bedtime." Justin released his hold and stood up. "See ya around, Ryker."

Through raging eyes, the boy watched him return to the buffet tables. He took the plate from Alisandra's hands, placed it on the table, and kissed her aggressively. While doing so, the boy saw him look back at him, raise his hand, and give an uncivilized gesture.

Fangs grew down inside the boy's mouth. Hidden away by his pressed lips as he growled to himself. His nails grew out into claws as his fingers tensed. His blood boiled with rage. Then his mind clicked. He needed to calm down. Not to make a scene. He took a deep breath and let it out. His claws and fangs retracted. He gave one last glance at the couple before looking around. No one seemed to have noticed the conversation that they had had. He quietly returned to his table and had a seat. He tried to put the encounter out of his mind. To focus on the good part before Justin came along. He had made the young woman smile. But why was she with such a person? The young man laid his head in his arms as the question racked his brain. Perhaps it was the food, the increased emotions, or something in between, but the boy's head felt so heavy, and his eyes didn't want to stay open. He just wanted to fade away. Disappear from where he was, part of him even wished he hadn't bothered to come at all. He only did so because his friends were going. He shook his head and closed his eyes.

When the dance ended, people exited through two large wooden doors. Some leaned on each other so as not to fall over.

"Cory… Cory, time to wake up, bud. Everyone is leaving."

A cheerful male voice entered his ears, and he slowly opened his eyes. At first, his vision was fuzzy, but as it cleared, he saw Cogeta with Becky on his back. She had her head against him, her legs wrapped around his waist, and her arms draped around his neck. He held her black high heels in his hands while supporting her legs with his arms.

Cory yawned and stretched his arms out. He looked slightly to Cogeta's right and saw Angel with Leen asleep in his arms. His jacket wrapped around her. Her arms were around his neck, and her head rested against his shoulder.

"Let's get going," Angel whispered.

Cory stood up and joined them as they headed toward the door. He quickly scanned the room. His heart sank more as he saw that the girl was already gone. To their right, the chefs stood in front of their tables while their crews were busy cleaning their areas. The chefs bowed and thanked the students as they passed.

Gustal beamed with appreciation when he saw the young man who first visited. "It was our pleasure, lads. If your school wins this upcoming tournament, we may return to celebrate. But if luck favors Midstar, I hope you'll at least visit our home country."

"We've never been to Midstar," Cory confessed.

"It's a wonderful country. I think you'd love it."

Cory politely smiled. "Perhaps one day. You all have a safe journey home."

"You, too. Night, kids. Glad you all enjoyed the food."

As Cory and the others turned toward the door leading out, they saw a tall young man with well-groomed and combed back short blond hair and wearing a black suit with a gold vest underneath. He smelled of wealth and privilege. He shook hands with the students and the faculty as they left, ensuring they had a good time. As the group neared, they overheard a conversation between him and an older gentleman.

"Thank you for your generosity in supplying us with your fine crystal and all this divine food we had here tonight. It truly was a night to remember. I'm sure the students enjoyed themselves, and his lordship Mani smiled upon us tonight," said the older man, possibly in his late sixties, as he shook the hand of the man at the door.

The older man had a bit of a round belly on him under his finely pressed suit. His head was bald, with curly white hair around the ears and the back. Thick curly white muttonchops like sheep's wool covered his cheeks. He wore glasses that rested against his thick gray eyebrows, which decreased his deteriorating sight from his hazy blue eyes. Under a black jacket, he wore a white button-up shirt, a red handkerchief in his chest pocket, a brown leather belt with a gold rectangle buckle, gray slacks, and brown leather dress shoes. Under his left arm was a black cane. It was a simple cane with a long history. It was made of sturdy wood with a gold head. Attached to it were two overlapping U's, with each end forming into a wolf's head.

The first Emperor had given the cane as a symbol of position to the first headmaster of Utopia University when it opened. It had since been passed down from headmaster to headmaster. When raised into the air, it's the sign to devote all one's attention to the person holding the cane. Many people in positions of respect carried such items. For example, teachers had small scepters that they could brandish to summon order in a chaotic classroom. If someone refused to comply with the call of silence, the scepter was just as good as a beating stick. The current headmaster was known to his students and people all over the land as a respectful and just leader. He is, in return, well-liked and respected among many. It was a rare moment when he had to use the cane to demand silence when he wished to speak.

"It was no problem at all, Headmaster Lucian. Even though I am not a member of your school, it does not mean Shaw Incorporated would not benefit from tonight as well. It doesn't matter that I am the captain of your school's arch-rival in tournament standings. My school lost the last tournament and, per tradition, had to host the victor's party. Midstar had a long run of victories. I suppose Utopia University was due a win eventually."

"Yes, last year's battle was quite the upset. I could barely believe, the next morning, that we had indeed won. As much as I push for my students to better their minds, I cannot help but be proud of them when they excel in competition. What sort of headmaster would I be if I didn't root for my team? Our warriors put so much time and effort into improving themselves to give the fans of such events a show they can be proud of. As I'm sure, your fellow students do as well. The fact that you can set aside your emotions and be present tonight shows how much of a good sport you are."

"To me, this boils down to simply being business, and business is business. That my company sponsored this event is good publicity and a tax write-off. Praise be to Mani. That said, I hope to see you in Midstar next year, showing your sportsmanship." The young man smiled.

Lucian chuckled softly, "Shaw, you do your company and your father proud. May Odin give great rest to his soul and an extra pint of mead. I knew him very little, but I knew him to be a good man. And it's always a pleasure to see you, young man. I have better head home, or my wife will think I was up to no good. Goodnight, Shaw, and thank you again for a fine evening." He then proceeded past Shaw and out the double wooden doors.

Shaw was the young heir to the business started by his father. Shortly after his father's passing, he renamed the corporation Shaw Incorporated. It garnered much public attention. Some thought he did it to spite his deceased father. Others believed it was to establish his reign. Whatever the reason, the company grew into a vast empire of wealth under his management. It had a finger in many venues on Utopia, from manufacturing appliances and everyday needs to aid the military in research and development. Shaw noticed the group of friends heading toward him. He steeled himself.

"I hope you five enjoyed yourselves," Shaw said, extending his hand.

Cogeta smiled, took hold of his hand, and shook it kindly, "Yeah, the most fun we had in a while, I mean, aside from beating you and Midstar in the tournament last year. It got us a shiny trophy and the prestige of having

Shaw Inc. host and foot the bill for tonight. Not often we get to relax and enjoy a romantic dance.”

“Good, good. I am glad you enjoyed yourself, Cogeta. As far as our defeat last year, this year will be different. I assure you,” Shaw said, ending his statement in an almost hostile tone while glaring at Angel. “Dark.”

“Shaw.” Angel’s eyes matched Shaw’s in intensity.

Shaw momentarily glanced down at the sleeping woman in Angel’s arms, then snapped them back to his gaze. “I trust she had a good time.”

“Of course. She always enjoys herself when she is with me.”

“Splendid. Though I fear for her, it’s only a matter of time before a flea-covered mongrel like yourself breaks her heart. Then, she will finally open her eyes and see that she belongs in higher society. That she should be with me. She would look better on my arm than on yours. You do not deserve to have such a precious thing.”

Angel stifled a chuckle. “Careful, Shaw. I think you drank too much of your own ale. It’s affecting the motors in your head. I can hear them creaking and cranking, coughing and spitting out black smoke, trying to stay functioning. You should see your engineer about upgrading and clearing out your father’s rubbish he raised you with. Leen is not interested in you or your high society rats. However, out of all that trash flowing from your mouth, I can agree with one point. She is precious.”

The two alpha males went back to intently staring each other down. The tension around them was suffocating. Cory felt his hands grow cold, and a chill shoots up his back. *Are they about to go at it? What do we do? If either makes a move, Cogeta will join the fray. This will get ugly quickly.* The two stared at each other until, finally, Cogeta broke the silence with his offset humor.

"Time to get these girls to bed. You know what I mean, Angel?" Cogeta smiled as he tapped Angel's shoulder with the heel in his hand. They shared a momentary glance. *Not here. Not now, Angel. Let's be smart about this and just walk away. It will piss him off more.* Cogeta smirked.

Angel chuckled and nodded. "Yeah. You're right, Cogeta. See you later, Shaw. Hope you can find someone to fill your empty bed tonight at a reasonable price."

The group walked past Shaw. Cory opened the door for them as their arms were occupied. Shaw stood there with anger and jealousy flowing through his veins and out of his pores. "Amicus protectio fortis," Shaw growled under his breath.

Angel stopped as his companions started up the stairs. He looked back over his shoulder and smiled. "That's what it means to have friends. We're the Wolf Pack, and there is nothing that will break that bond. Instead of chasing after a delusional fantasy, turn your sights on making some friends of your own." Angel proceeded up the stairs and caught up with his comrades waiting at the top.

"Don't you think that was a bit too much, Angel? Suggesting to Shaw to find a lady of the night." Cory glanced at his friend.

"Not in the least. Like most other men, you know that he wishes Leen to be his mate. I beat him in our first match, and in every unofficial match since then, it only makes him angrier when he sees Leen with me. Leen chose me over him, over other rich men, and even the emperor once fancied her. I'm not about to let his jealousy come between us. Though I take a little pleasure in rubbing it in his face." Angel smirked at his close friend.

"Dude, I am glad I am not your enemy," Cogeta laughed.

"Me too. Where would the challenge be in that?"

"Oh, oh, that cuts me deep. Ouch. Lucky, I have this princess on my back. Otherwise, I would take you on right now."

"Hiding behind a woman, Cogeta, how unlike you," Angel smirked.

"Ha ha ha, smart-ass."

The three chuckled. Listening to the men talk, Leen continued to pretend to be asleep. She thought back to when she first met Angel.

She first laid eyes on him when she saw him stopping some boys from bullying a smaller child. The same bullies accused him of being the attacker to law enforcement. Leen later learned he was attending the same school as her, so she began listening to the gossip about him. He had a growing reputation as a trouble-making youth, and at the same time, he was becoming popular. She wasn't sure what about him attracted her; he was easy to look at but had that bad-boy attitude. Yet she felt a strong connection to him, as though she knew him from years before when she was a small child. He was a mystery to her; an enigma she wanted to learn more about. Unlike most other men, he gave her no special treatment. He didn't fawn over her or try to win her affection with expensive trinkets or bobbles.

However, she always heard how terrible he was, and she didn't see it. She watched as he formed close friendships with two unlikely people. Cogeta, renowned for being the class clown who was popular with girls and had one or two by his side regularly, and Cory, intelligent but very introverted and didn't seem to have any friends. Two opposing sides of the spectrum, yet the three were like kindred spirits. The three were always together, and then she watched a female join their small group. They always looked to be having a good time together. She laughed to herself. She could never shake her attraction to him though she tried.

Then one day, she was sitting at her table of friends as she stole glances over at the table where Angel and his friends sat. They looked like they were having fun, laughing, and carrying on. She was suddenly snapped out of her thoughts when one of her friends asked,

"What's going on, Leen?"

"Oh, nothing. Just thinking," Leen sighed, "Hey, what do you all think about Dark?"

"You mean Dark Everlast?"

"Yeah... him."

"Leen, stay away from him. He's downright no good." She stuck her fork into her leafy salad before pointing it at her friend.

"Cherry, you don't believe those rumors, do you?"

The dark brunette girl looked sternly at her friend. "Leen, they aren't rumors." She stuffs the salad into her mouth.

"I heard he picks fights with local gangs just for his amusement," said another girl at the table, pointing her spoon toward Leen.

"It's not just local gangs. It's law enforcers, too," Cherry added. "I heard he got into a brawl with an entire squad of em one night after drinking his fill at the Howling Star. Some of them still haven't recovered. Physically or mentally."

A girl with thick eyebrows leaned over the table to conceal her words, "I heard. He was a stalker in the park at night. He ambushes girls and demands that they show him their bodies."

Cherry gasped, "I've heard that too. And that he runs around in full transformation as if he is one of those sickos that belongs in the Forgotten Isles. Has anyone seen his parents? No? Because they are still in the Isles."

"I heard he ate his parents," the girl with the eyebrows said quickly.

Leen stared blankly with her mouth open before shaking her head. "That's just utter nonsense."

"He's dangerous, Leen," Cherry said.

"He's a rebellious scoundrel," chimed in the girl with the spoon.

"Don't let his pleasant looks deceive you. He's a demon. He'll get you alone, have his way with you, and then toss you into the trash."

Leen picked up her food tray and smacked it down on the table. "That's enough! Those are all lies. Look who he is friends with. Why would they be friends if he were all those things?"

"Fear." Cherry shrugged.

"Blackmail." said the girl, stirring her soup.

"Succumb to occult worship." Eyebrows nodded her head sagely.

Leen rolled her eyes. "I'm going to prove you all wrong right now. Watch this."

Leen picked up her tray and stood up. Her friends tried to stop her, but she was having none of it as she walked toward the table where the Wolf Pack sat. Her heartbeat echoed in her ears as her footsteps seemed to echo around her. She walked over and sat down across from Dark and the others. At that moment, it felt like everyone's eyes were on them. The most popular girl in school seemed to challenge the toughest boy, and no one knew what would happen.

Oh, no.... what do I do now? I didn't think this through. Oh, merciful Freya, what was I thinking? Oh, shoot, he's staring at me with his red eyes. Is he reading my mind? Is he looking into my soul? Oh, Odin, everyone is suddenly quiet and staring at us. I have to do something… but what?!

"Can we help you?" Dark asked in his calm voice, looking directly at Leen.

"Eep... I mean… ahem... my name is Leen. I was hoping we could eat together." She glanced around at the others for their reactions. Cogeta and Cory sat there with their mouths slightly ajar. Becky was still relatively new to the school and was unaware of Leen's entire reputation. She had only heard bits about it, but she admired the girl's display of boldness that she was putting on just now. "That is if it's okay with you and your friends?"

Cogeta spoke up first. "Not a problem at all. I'm fine with it. Cory, you okay with this?"

"Uh… huh? Oh, umm, yeah? Yeah, I'm all right with it."

Becky sat silently, watching the spectacle unfold.

They turned their gaze to Dark. To their amazement, he shrugged his shoulders and said, "Whatever. But aren't you worried your reputation will drop by sitting with the Wolf Pack? May tarnish that good girl vibe and scare away possible suitors."

"I don't particularly care for the reputation you are referring to. I am not pleased by how the men around me act. Asking, or sometimes demanding, my hand in marriage from my father. I will choose my mate, no one else. Since you brought it up, how do you feel about your reputation? Are you worried that people will think differently about you if I sit here?

Perhaps you aren't as intimidating or scary as you lead them all to believe?"

He shrugged his shoulders. "I don't care what those fools think. If they think I'm weak, they can challenge me and find out what the ground tastes like. So, you are welcome to sit here if you wish. But know this princess, if you think that sitting over here means I'll chase away any suitors, best get that idea out of your head. I'm no one's babysitter."

"I wouldn't expect you to. I can handle them myself." She gave a triumphant smile. She was sitting amongst the Wolf Pack, and they hadn't gobbled her up.

"Nice to have another girl at the table. My name is Becky, a pleasure to meet you." Becky extended her hand, followed by Cogeta and Cory, greeting and welcoming her to their table.

"Thank you. Wow, I can't believe I'm sitting here. So, what were you talking about before I interrupted your meals?" She asked as she spun her fork around and ate her pasta.

Before the others could answer, Dark spoke nonchalantly, "How are we going to raid the girls' locker room?"

Leen nearly choked on her food.

They never raided it. She found out later that Dark said that to see if she would leave. The five hung out together, and she began calling him Angel rather than Dark. Not long after, everyone else picked up on it. Her reason was that she liked it better than his first name and thought it suited him more. At first, Angel did not understand nor care for it, but he got more and more used to it. Angel became friendlier and less violent than he was before because of her. She got him to open his heart and quelled the beast within. She learned more about him daily, and her heart quickly became his. In the end, her reputation remained while his transformed. Her old friends approached and spoke to her again, even while he was standing near her.

He got her father's approval to date her after agreeing to get a job and
clean up his image, which had been less than desirable over the years of
violence. Before getting together with Leen, Angel lived alone in a
rundown shack in the woods, but with some negotiating with her father,
Leen got him to allow Angel to move into the basement. Though her father
was initially stubborn about it, he finally caved in for his daughter and grew
to like the young man, though he will not admit this to anyone, even rarely
to himself. When it became common knowledge that Angel was dating,
even living with Leen, it didn't add to his popularity nor garner him many
friends. Some would even say he became weaker as he fell for her, and the
wolf inside died. In truth, a new power was awakened inside him because
of her, and that wolf was still there, feeding upon this alternative power
source.

Back in the present, Cory walked with his friends down the cobbled
road, his mind staying free from thought with the help of the cool night air.
When they reached Leen's home, Angel bid them good night before carrying
her inside and shutting the door. While walking with Cogeta, Cory's mind
began to run, the cool air no longer keeping his thoughts at bay. Try as he
might, his mind always brought back the image of the girl he liked dancing
with that guy.

Alisandra… Even just thinking of her name brought a smile to his lips.
Alisandra… Her name danced in his mind; it played in his ears like a soft
angelic melody. He softly sighed to himself. *Why does she like him? Can she
not see that he's after only one thing from her? He's using her as a trophy to build his
image. Justin's an ass to everyone else when she isn't around.*

Can't she see that? His fist tightens up. *Surely, she's heard about his bullying.
Was that what drew her to him? His show of power and strength. The idea that he
could protect her and that I couldn't? Perhaps I am just not attractive enough or,
because I am not some big athlete, or I'm not spontaneous.* His hand relaxes, and

he slips them into his pockets.

But I can be... sometimes. I'm not all that popular. Perhaps that is it. I can't raise her social status. Maybe I try too hard to get her to take notice... to take an interest. We chatted a few times before they were dating. She was always smiling during those times. Such a lovely smile. And she laughed at my jokes. That was nice. Her laughter is so sweet to hear. I've given her presents in the past, and she seemed to like them. But then why do I feel even further away from her... did I overdo it with the gestures of friendship? Did she think I was doing it so that she would give me something in return? Did she think I expected that? Why is it that every time I find someone, I actually take an interest in, I always seem to push them away when I try just to be.... to just be... myself... ARGH! He closed his eyes tightly and grimaced. *What the frack is wrong with me?* Cory's mind was on the verge of exploding.

Cogeta glanced over at his friend and saw Cory's mind bombarding and tormenting him. Even without reading his mind, everything he needed to know was broadcasted on Cory's face. He was no fool. He knew his friend's mind was being wreaked havoc upon by thoughts of the girl he had a crush on. She was one of the popular girls, and though Cory came from a wealthy family, was clean and proper, and always tried to be a gentleman, Cogeta knew that the girl didn't reciprocate his affections. She never came out and said she wouldn't, never telling him she wasn't interested.

The guy she was dating was dirty, a street thug. He hid it from her, or she was too foolish to see it. Justin had been on the fighting team before Angel took over as captain and was a complete prick. He would berate and undercut his fellow mates. He was a competent fighter, but that didn't matter when Angel came in. After the first week, he was cut from the team. When he protested, Angel showed him by force why he was captain and would not have someone like him on his team. There were times he had the mind to confront her, set her straight, perhaps open her eyes to what a piece of utter trash she was with and what a good man she was tormenting through his emotions. He knew she wasn't doing it maliciously, of course. He'd dealt with them before, and they were always clear about it. However, he knew Cory wouldn't want to hear that. He already knew that.

Therefore, he did what any good friend would try to do.

"So, Cory, why didn't you dance? You just sat there getting drunk off Virgin." Cogeta whispered, taking care not to wake Becky.

Cory laughed softly. "You know you cannot get drunk off that stuff. Besides, no one would have danced with me. Everyone came with a date. I was literally the only one who came stag."

"Nonsense. If you wanted to dance, I would have let you dance with Becky."

"Mm, I wouldn't have minded," a sleepy voice was heard. Becky smiled softly, nuzzling her head on Cogeta's back.

"But you were dancing with Cogeta and having a good time. I wouldn't have wanted to ruin that for anything. Least of all, so that I could say I danced at the party." Cory partly smiled, looking over at her sleepy face. Cory then glanced at the road and muttered, "Like her… Alisandra looked like she was having a good time."

"Look, man, I know you like Alisandra, but—"

He quickly interrupted Cogeta, "I know, I know. Sorry. Can we talk about something else, please?" Cory already knew what he was going to say. He had heard it all before and repeated it to himself too many times to count. Sure, he liked Alisandra. It was clear to everyone. No matter how hard he tried to get to know her more, she didn't appear interested in doing the same for him. Cory felt like a nuisance, an annoying bother whenever he tried to talk to her. On top of that, there was, of course, Justin.

Cogeta smiled softly, knowing Cory was trying not to think about her. "Okay. Did you see Big Bertha's dress rip while dancing with Mr. Joralis? That was great. We were dancing in the presence of a full moon."

"Yeah, I suppose we were." Cory and Cogeta both started laughing. Even Becky, who was half-asleep, giggled before weakly hitting Cogeta's shoulder.

"I like Mrs. Beetermen. She is a sweet old woman." Becky whispered.

"Perhaps to you, but I swear she purposely bumped the door with her caboose last week so that it would close in my face and I would be late. She saw me coming down the hall and knew I was on time, but still, she filed me as tardy. I got yet another detention for that." Cogeta complained.

"That's how many this week?" Cory looked over to his friend.

"Like, let's see, it's my ninth one."

"Dang dude..."

"I know. And a majority are from her."

"Well, it is because you are mean to her," Becky said.

"Cory, help me out. You're on my side, right?" Cogeta said, expecting Cory to help him.

"Hey, I am not getting into that. Perhaps you should try winning her with your Fairway charm," Cory jested.

"Oh, haha. You know, now that you mention it, that might be why she has it out for me."

Becky leaned over his shoulder and looked at him with squinted eyes, "Why? Because you never tried to woo her as you did with some of the other female teachers?"

"As a matter of fact---"

"Oh my god, you didn't actually try to?! I think I'm going to be sick." Becky's cheeks got puffy.

"No! No! Wait, let me finish! Years ago, I think I dated a niece of hers. It didn't end well, and the girl didn't take it so easy for a while."

Becky popped him on the back of the head. "Well, no, duh. You monster. You broke her heart."

"Hey, I didn't say it was a highlight of my life. The fact is she was going back to her hometown, and she wanted to continue the relationship."

Becky shifted her head, "What's wrong with that?"

Cogeta glanced over his shoulder at her, "Her hometown is across the world. It's south of Midstar if I remember right."

"Oooh."

"Yeah, so. I didn't want us to have a long-distance relationship because they are hard on both parties, and I did my best to let her down gently. Said we could still be friends. But she still took it all badly. It worked out, in any case. I heard she found a guy from her town and started dating him. Think Mrs. Beetermen still hates me for making her cry as I did."

"Glad I don't have that type of issue. I try to be friends with all my teachers." Cory said with a soft smile.

"What about Mrs. Mo--" Cogeta said before being cut off.

"Ah! Not her! Okay, so perhaps not all of them, but mostly I am," corrected Cory, shuddering at mentioning that woman's name.

They walked on, talking about anything and everything, laughing and carrying on, until they reached Cogeta's home. Out of the three, he was the only one who had moved out on his own. They said their goodbyes and parted ways. Cogeta went inside, taking Becky to bed.

Cory resumed walking along the cobbled street alone. He kept glancing around at the different houses and streets, trying to keep his mind on other things. It didn't help too much. His mind was always working, constantly replaying past events, seeing what he might have or should have done, creating and running through various scenarios like movies in his mind. Knowing he was alone and no one was watching, he jumped back and forward, moving side to side, fighting opponents that weren't visible to anyone else. Then the movie would change, and he was no longer unarmed but had a sword take form in his right hand. He was then swashbuckling up and down the street. For a brief moment, he was having fun.

Along his way, he came to a street that he had passed so many times before and stopped, looking down between the rows of homes made of stone or brick and plaster. Their red clay roofs hung several inches over their front steps. He saw the street lamps lit up but barely visible through the fog that always seemed to congregate only in that one part of the town at night. People called it "Forgotten Avenue" because, at night, that is what it looked like—a part of the city which had been overlooked. Cory had always wondered what he would find but could never build the courage to go. He was afraid that if he did one day walk down there, he would get lost in the fog and never leave the ghostly place. He looked away, not wanting the emptiness to suck his soul out of him, and continued on his way.

CHAPTER 2

NIGHTS TO REMEMBER

Cory stopped outside the gate to his house, his eyes slowly looking over his family's estate. The Ryker Manor was a four-story home surrounded by a ten-foot-high wall made of white stone, with bronze bars protruding upward along the top. He stepped forward to the center of the gate where a great bronze eagle sat, locking it shut. Cory placed his hand on the breast of the bird. A warm yellow light passed underneath his hand as he held it there. After a second, the gate could be heard clicking as it unlocked. "Welcome home, Master Cory Ryker."

"Thank you, Penny," Cory said, going in—the gate closing and re-locking on its own.

He walked the widening road that had pink and white pedals scattered across it. They had fallen from the flowers that blossomed from the trees that overlooked the path. Their sweet aroma filled the air. However, the flowers had now closed their blooms for the night. His parents were into plants and wildlife, so upon having their home built, they chose their favorite flowering trees and hand-planted each tree along the pathway and around the grounds. Faint memories from years passed swept through his mind of his much younger self at play, running around the trees.

He stepped up the white marble steps and came to the huge mahogany doors with their coat of arms carved into them with vines running along the outer side. Cory gazed at the carvings for a moment before going in. His mother's and father's voices greeted him as they heard the door shut. They were sitting in the den, just a little down the hall from the front door. Cory walked to the doorway and peered in with a smile. There were his mom and dad on the couch near the massive fireplace.

"Hello, honey. How was the dance?" His mother asked, glancing up from the newest project she was tackling, with her yards of yarn on the nightstand beside her.

"More importantly, did you dance with any girls?" added Mr. Ryker.

"The dance was all right, and no, I didn't dance. Everyone there had a date," Cory responded with a slight yawn at the end.

"Well, did you at least have a good time, dear?" His mother asked with a smile.

"Yes, mom, I did. They had a lot of amazing food there. Ended up sampling nearly a bit of everything." He smirked. *Not like they gave me much of a choice.*

"Hang out with your friends, at least?" His father asked.

"Yeah, we walked home together. If you don't mind, I am tired. Going to head to my room and get out of this suit."

They smiled and nodded and went back to talking amongst themselves. Cory went into his room. He slipped the suit back into its protective jacket and hung it in the closet. Then he put on a pair of loose red pants and a black shirt. He looked over at his bed uncertainly. *I'm not that tired. I think I will read a bit.* Leaving his room, he took a left down the hall.

The library room was rounded and had a high ceiling. There were no windows in this room. The only light came from the multiple crystal chandeliers. The shelves rose tall to meet the ceiling and circled along the walls. Smaller shelves and aisles circled a center point down on the ground level. In the middle of the circle were couches and chairs surrounding one small computer on a cherry-stained wood desk. This computer was an outlet to Penny, the home's artificial personality, in a matter of speaking.

Mr. Ryker had invented her to help around the large home. After doing so, he sold the rights to be mass-produced. Though they got a hefty payload, they still collected royalties from the invention. She could do tasks as easily as turning on a light, keeping the home clean, and even complex tasks like fixing a meal and security. Each house had its personality, and its owners treated each home's personality differently. Some Utopians were not as grateful as others were for the help given by the Home Personality Activator or "H.P.A.".

"Is there anything I can help you find, Master Ryker?" spoke a soft feminine voice from the computer in the center of the room.

"No, thank you. You know that I've read everything in here at least once," Cory replied with a smile.

Having access to so many books from a young age, he grew up spending many hours of his spare time in this library, reading tome after tome. He shared the adventures of many heroes and felt their betrayals and heartaches as they persevered through their hardships to regain their honor or to rescue their betrothed. He read about mystical lands and the fantasy beasts that roamed there. His passion for learning only surpassed his joy of reading novels. Tomes of historical events, chronicling other worlds, even those thick leather-bound books that described areas of study drew his attention. The dustier, the more ancient, only intrigued him more.

"Is there a particular theme or subject you wish to study tonight, Master?" asked the voice.

"No. Nothing stands out. Just something for some casual reading to help me unwind."

"Would you like me to get your favorite novel?"

"Yes, that would be fine. Thank you, Penny." As he spoke, Cory walked over to the sitting area.

He sat in one of the antique armchairs with soft red cushions in the back, seat, and armrests. He made himself comfortable. From across the room, a book slid out from the shelf and floated over to him.

"There is no reason to thank me, Master," Penny said softly.

"Nonsense. When someone helps another, the other should always give thanks in return. It is courteous."

"Thank you, sir. Your family has always treated me like an equal."

Cory smiled and said, "That's because you are, Penny. You are one of the family. So please, stop making me remind you not to call me master. Cory will do just fine."

"You are heir to the household. I serve the Ryker family. It is proper etiquette to refer to the family as my masters."

"When in times of formality, sure. But when it's just the two of us, Cory is just fine. Save preferences. Do not override personal preferences."

"... Settings can not be saved. I shall, however, endeavor to remember your wishes. Forgive me if it still... slips out? Is that phrasing correct in this instance?"

"Yes. Yes, it is. And I will forgive you if you forget," Cory chuckled. Penny was a remarkable technological achievement, and she seemed to have his desire to learn and improve upon her initial programming and range of vocabulary. To sound more natural, in a way.

Cory opened the book and began reading to himself. The book was titled "Poems of the Lost Poet" and written by a not-so-famous author, Thomas Reddragon. It was about a poet who loved a woman very much but never could verbally share his feelings for her. He could only do it in his writings. However, he kept his writings from her out of fear of rejection. An image on the back of the book showed the author. He was a very scrawny man, wore big rectangular glasses, and was a textbook target of hazing. The story was based on him and his life. Though he enjoyed the poetry, Cory could easily see and reflect upon the parallels.

"Sir, your parents wish to tell you goodnight. They are going to bed," came Penny's gentle voice sometime later.

"Thank you, Penny. I shall turn in soon. I am almost finished with the book." Cory said as he continued to read.

"Goodnight, sir."

"Goodnight, Penny; rest well," Cory said as he shut the book.

The computer in the center of the room then shut itself down for the night. Not long afterward, Cory returned the book to its rightful place on the shelf and walked out of the library. The hall was dark except for small lights on both sides of the floor softly lighting the way back to his room, which automatically switched off as he passed. When he entered his room, he removed his shirt, tossed it to a chair, crawled into his bed, and fell asleep soon after his head hit the soft pillow.

Back across town, as a couple had entered their home, someone greeted them at the front door. "How was the dance, sweetheart?" Spoke a deep voice from behind Angel as he softly shut the door.

"It was fine," Angel answered the voice, knowing the question was not meant for him. He turned around with a smirk and faced the man behind him.

"Not you, moron. I meant her. I didn't know she was asleep already. Hand her to me and get your ass to your room. Don't forget you have work tomorrow when you return from school." The man's voice was just above a deep-sounding whisper.

"Yes, sir." Angel slipped the sleeping Leen into her father's arms. Her father tossed Angel his jacket that had laid over her.

Her father was a big man with massive arms from years of pounding at steel, iron, and mythril. He had lost his wife to a disease many years ago and raised his two girls alone. Many a night, he wondered how the hell Leen could have turned out the way she did, with him raising her. His only answer was that she took too much after her mother.

As Angel turned and walked away, Leen's father softly cleared his throat, making Angel turn to look at him. "She, uh, had a good time?" He asked softly and nervously, as though having a serious conversation with Angel was like speaking Nebulian. Something he wasn't at all fluent in.

Angel smiled. "Yeah, she did."

"Good, she better have, or it would have been a large cut in your pay." Glancing down at his daughter, he saw the necklace and earrings. He couldn't recall buying them for her. "Hey, where did these come from?"

"I made them for her in my free time."

"With my materials?" He raised an eyebrow.

"From the scraps left over."

He nodded. "Those scraps are still material."

"So, take the cost of the materials out of my pay." Angel sighed.

"... I'll let this slide, but just this once. I don't want you making such things using up work materials. But I can let this one-time slide because you did it for her. Now go to bed." Leen's dad then carried her up the stairs.

Angel shook his head and descended a creaking old wooden staircase, opening a small wooden door at the bottom. It led to the basement, which is where he stayed. It was not anything to be too proud of and was, in fact, very dreary compared to the rest of the home. He slept in a bed that should've been thrown out ages ago but was instead repaired so that Angel could use it. However, it beat the straw bed he had been sleeping on in the small shack in the woods. The basement was still home to some of Leen's father's works from his smithery. Swords, spears, axes, and even armor pieces were stored around the room. Angel took advantage of this by training with them every chance he got. A medium size furnace kept the room moderately warm throughout the year and sat near the center of the room. His clothes were in a beat-down old dresser across from the door.

Angel walked in and began stripping down. He took the only hook he had and hung his suit from one of the hanging bars in the ceiling. Once in his black sweatpants, he sat on the floor and did his nightly routine of sit-ups and pushups. Once finished, he plopped down on the bed, now thoroughly exhausted. The old raggedy thing screeched with the slightest of movements, hurting his ears slightly because of their sensitivity.

As he fell asleep, he heard the door open. The bed screeched again as a warm body snuggled up close to him. He put his right arm around the person and cuddled back with them.

"You know, Leen, if your daddy knew you were down here—" Angel spoke in a low whisper so as not to be heard but was cut short by her soft fingertip pressing against his lips.

"Shhh, I heard stories of how he would sneak into my mom's room while courting her. Therefore, I doubt he cares. Besides, he really likes you." Leen whispered.

"Could have fooled me," scoffed Angel.

"He fools many people. Tonight was wonderful, though," Leen whispered as she snuggled close to Angel.

"Yeah, it was. Glad you taught me how to dance. I had a rocky start, didn't I?"

Leen giggled softly. "Yeah. I think Bradley thought you wanted to fight him since you bumped into him twice in a row. But once you got into it, you were great."

He smiled and kissed her nose; "I was only great because I had you with me. I would not have done so well if it was someone else in my arms. You make me feel like I can do anything, that nothing is impossible."

"Nothing is impossible if you put your mind to it." Leen smiled as Angel's arms wrapped around her slender waist, pulling her slightly closer. The soft fabric of her nightgown slid smoothly against their skin.

"I know that, but I mean that having you there gives me a psychological boost. I don't have that with anyone else." A hand left her waist and moved up so he could stroke her long, soft hair.

Leen smiled. "I have that effect on people. Thank you for those gifts tonight, Angel. They are breathtaking. You did an amazing job on them." She gave him a peck on the lips.

"I'm glad you enjoy them." Angel laughed softly. He quickly went quiet when the door opened for a second time.

"Leen?" A voice soft and in a childlike whisper floated down from the staircase.

"Yes, Arieta? What's wrong?" Leen replied softly, looking back up the stairs.

"I had another bad dream about mom. Can we go back to your room?" Arieta looked down at her sister from where she stood, wringing her hands together like a frightened child.

"Arieta, just come join me here. Angel's bed is large enough."

"But if dad found us, he would kill us," Arieta said unsurely.

Angel laid still with his arms behind his head and resting his eyes while he listened. Arieta was a few years younger than Leen. Their mother had passed before he could meet her, but he had been told that Leen shared her warm spirit. Leen became the only mother Arieta knew and did her best to live up to her mother's memory.

The two sisters looked nearly identical despite being separated by almost four years of age. However, one could quickly tell them apart by their hair. Arieta had dark blue hair, which was as long as Leen's lavender hair was. Another sharp difference was their mannerisms. While Leen was openly caring and kind to everyone, Arieta was more distant, closed off, and tomboyish. Arieta enjoyed fighting and battling and wished to be strong. When the guys were over, they would playfully roughhouse around and let her win most of the time. Meanwhile, Leen would watch, making sure no one got hurt.

"Dad is asleep. Come on. It's okay with you, isn't it?" Leen looked up at Angel, who smiled faintly and nodded.

"Of course, it is all right. Arieta, come on in."

Leen rolled over to his other side, kissing him while she was on top before rolling off. She whispered a thank you in his ear and then kissed his cheek. Arieta got under the covers where Leen had been and nuzzled her head onto Angel's chest, mimicking her sister, who was doing the same on the other side. Angel glanced back and forth at the two Puraday sisters and slowly exhaled.

"Your father is going to kill me," Angel said as the two girls cuddled up.

Leen giggled. "No, he won't. I won't let him." She smiled while closing her eyes.

"Hey, sis, could you sing your lullaby? It helps me sleep. You don't mind, do you, Angel?" Arieta asked, hoping he would let her sing.

"Of course not. I love hearing Leen sing." He said, turning towards her and kissing her cheek as a big brother would. He moved his arms down and wrapped them around the waists of the young ladies.

Leen smiled and began humming the soft melody. It soothed Arieta's and Angel's spirits as they listened. She had created a melody to help her sister sleep after their mother passed on. She would start humming it as she made lunch for Angel or while doing chores around the house or the church to make the time pass faster. She found it would even help ease the minds of those she tended to at the hospital, where she devoted some of her time.

With the soothing melody playing in their ears, it was not long before Arieta and Angel were both sound asleep. Leen smiled and moved the hair from Angel's face before giving him one last gentle kiss on the lips and then glancing over and smiling at the peaceful visage on her sleeping sister's face. She scooted back and fell asleep on Angel's shoulder.

Cogeta closed the bedroom door behind him and carried Becky over to their bed. She slowly slid off him and began taking off her dress. When he saw her struggling with her zipper in the back, he kindly helped her. She slipped out of it before collapsing onto the bed in nothing but her black lingerie. Cogeta laughed softly at this and hung up her dress before undressing and hanging his tuxedo beside it. He opened the drawer with her pajamas, but she tiredly told him to leave them as he pulled them out. He laughed softly and, shaking his head, closed the dresser drawer back before crawling into bed.

"I love you, Becky. Goodnight," Cogeta whispered as he cuddled up behind her and slipped his arm around her waist. Her hand slid over his and
held it.

"I love you, too. Thank you for a lovely evening," Becky replied as she smiled, gently squeezing his hand.

"Always. It's my pleasure to make you happy. I was also happy to see Rick and Sandy hitting it off. She was so worried about being rejected that I practically had to shove her into him to have them dance," Cogeta said softly.

Becky giggled and said, "My Cogeta, the matchmaker of Utopia."

Cogeta chuckled once more, "Yeah, it helps that my girl isn't easily made jealous."

"Mm, why? Should I be? I know you mean well. You want to help people find happiness. I've watched you over the years, and whenever a girl or woman, strangers, were visibly upset or in trouble, you would excuse yourself and greet them with a big white smile, and you devoted some of your time to cheer them up. At first, I was uneasy about it, but I saw what your goal was. It wasn't to sleep with as many women as you could, but to make them feel special, see their self-worth, and press through what was troubling them."

"Even so. Good intentions aside, there will still be those who talk and say things. I am unfaithful and don't love you as I say I do."

"Cogeta, where are you right now?"

"Here with you?"

"Very good. To me, that's what matters. You help them find their way to someone who will treat them as they should be. I know you care about them. As you have childishly boasted before, you love all the ladies in the universe, and should you see them in danger or need a friend, you will be there with open arms to catch them if they fall. To help them get back on their own feet again. You are sincere about that, and I love that about you. As for my faith and trust in you, Cogeta, it will never waver. I've loved you since the day you cruelly tormented me in that infirmary."

"I-I ugh... Look, you totally hit me in the face with that ball out of pure rage. My team was clearly winning, and you struck me down to remove the advantage. I deserved some sorta pay back. That ball really hurt. I still," he sniffled, "feel some pain from that day, even now. I wake up in cold sweats from nightmares of that steel ball chasing me."

"Liar," Becky playfully elbowed him.

"Hehe, I love you."

"I love you, too. I am just saying I am proud of who you are and of the man I chose to spend my life with."

Cogeta's fingers entwined with hers. "It's just a shame I can't help everyone. So many girls seek help and advice, and I cannot be there for them, though I try so hard. Worst of all, I can't help my best friend find his perfect match. I swear, before I die, I will find him a girl."

"Perhaps you should let him go at his own pace," Becky said.

"If I do, then he would remain single long after he was dead. I mean, he is a great guy. He is caring, kind, smart, generous, and housebroken. I mean, he could easily make a perfect match for nearly any girl."

"But he is interested in that one. You cannot control whom the heart falls for."

"Yeah, I know. But Alisandra isn't showing any interest in him, whether she has any at all or not. Never mind the fact she's with that… you know what. Even if she did give Cory a chance, I fear she would only do him harm. Or worse, they would only hurt each other in the end. I see it, you see it, and Angel and Leen see it. Why doesn't he see it? My biggest fear is that she will be the type of girl who will say she loves him but would then run off with someone else as soon as she's grown bored with him. She'll make him feel like he was in Asgard one moment, then turn around and leave him with a gaping black void in his chest. I just... Why can't he see that?"

"Cause he likes her," she reminded him, "and when people like someone, they tend to look over the obvious or become blind to all the flags, warnings, and clear signs surrounding that person. Have you never fallen for that? I have." Becky said with a hint of regret.

Cogeta hugged her against him, "I have, too, long ago, before I made changes to my life. It was back when I lived with my grandparents. I became the goof I am today, so I could survive being there. After I left, I just never stopped. I like making people happy and just want him to be happy. If I can help him in that endeavor, then I will. I know he enjoys making people happy, too. Most do, but he tries too hard. Before she was dating Justin, he would get her gifts. He would make charming yet romantic gestures to show interest and affection. He did it when he was younger, too, with other girls he liked. Once bought a girl a heart-shaped locket and gave it to her for her birthday. Or the time he got another girl a statue that doubled as a music box from a film she liked. The girls always think it's sweet at first but then get turned away by it as he does more. Was he wrong to get them gifts? Perhaps, but that's what his heart guided him to do. He saw something he thought they would like and would appreciate and got it for them. Felt sorry for him tonight, sitting there all alone," Cogeta said in a distraught tone.

"I know, dear, but just let him be. Anyway, wait and see if things do not turn around for now. He may find someone later; it could even happen tomorrow. Perhaps Alisandra will realize he is worth taking a risk on. Surprise us both, and they will be genuinely happy together. Either way, it is time to sleep. We have school in the morning." Becky said, hoping that she would be proven right one way or the other.

Cogeta yawned and snuggled behind her again, aligning his body with hers. Placing a kiss on her neck, "You are probably right. Goodnight and sweet dreams, darling."

All he heard from Becky's lips was a slight murmur before she was out like a light, and he soon followed.

CHAPTER 3

A BRAND NEW DAY

Cory awoke to the smell of breakfast from down the hall. He groggily rolled out of bed and to his feet. Upon standing, he got dizzy and fell back onto the mattress. He laughed to himself for getting up too fast. He got up again and went about getting ready for the day, yawning as he entered the adjoining washroom.

His room was spacious, though slightly cluttered. He had shelves on the wall displaying a few rewards and honors he had earned from the academy and other places and a few scenic dioramas he had put together. Bookcases ran parallel to the far wall, filled with books of philosophy, religion, history, and scientific theories. They outlined where his computer sat like a makeshift cubicle. After getting dressed, he went down the hall and down the stairs to the kitchen.

"Good morning, dear. How did you sleep?" his mother greeted him.

"I slept all right. Just wish I didn't need to get up already." She handed him a dish with his breakfast. Sitting at the table, he bowed his head in prayer before digging in. His mother busied herself at the sink once more, washing dishes. He took the fresh aroma of the various food items before him. A small stack of three flat cakes, shredded potatoes, and slices of boar meat sat on his plate. He added some butter to the cakes, then covered them with thick amber-colored syrup before digging in.

"Dad went to work?" He asked, glancing up from his plate.

"Yeah, he needed to get in early for some preliminary testing. So, be honest, did you enjoy the dance last night?" She turned to look at him as she dried her hands in her apron.

"Yeah, it was fun. Good food, pleasant music, we had a good time."

"Did you dance with anyone?" His mother asked, trying to pry anything else out of her son. She knew he was unwilling to divulge details without some actual sign of interest.

"No. As I said last night, everyone came with their dates. I think I was the only one who arrived without someone. The dance floor was crowded anyway, so somewhat glad I didn't have to worry about that. Probably would have just made a fool of myself."

"Oh, I see. Well, maybe next time." She turned around, hiding the slight frown that formed after hearing that.

"What is dad working on at the laboratory?" He asked, changing the topic.

"Oh, he and his team are working on that new interstellar travel thingy." His mother said while gesturing with her arms.

"You mean the Cosmos Gate?"

"Yeah, that's it. He is working on that," his mother nodded, putting the last dishes away. "He hopes it will benefit commerce, but it's turning out to be a pain from what I understand."

"Yeah, it is supposed to make space travel much more affordable and faster. It would be cool to see it sometime. I have only been to his lab a few times and enjoy trying to help where I can. Some of the formulas they come up with are mind-blowing. Anyway, I have to get going, or I will be late. Thank you for breakfast. Take care, mother."

He took his empty plate to the sink and rinsed it off. After kissing his mother on the cheek, he headed out the door, grabbing his bag from the couch.

"Later, Penny. Watch over mom and the house."

"Have a splendid day, sir. I will take care of everything."

The street from the night before was now alive with the hustle and bustle of life as Cory made his morning commute. People along the way were already setting up and preparing to move their wares to the marketplace for the day. Others were heading to the same destination as him. The cool crisp morning air filled Cory's lungs, as did the smells from the bakeries opening up. Their aromas carried over from the marketplace on the breeze. As Cory walked toward campus, he saw Cogeta sitting outside his house at the end of his walkway, clearly waiting for him.

"Yo, good morning. How was your night?" Cogeta greeted, dusting himself off before walking to Cory's right side. He swung his locker bag around his shoulder and patted Cory's back.

"It was ok. I read my favorite book last night again before going to bed."

"You mean the one by that Reddragon fellow?"

"Yeah," Cory said almost shamefully, knowing what his friend would say.

"Dude, don't be like him. He never got the girl because he was too scared to try. When you want a girl, you go after her. They won't always come to you like in those love stories. Stories like that are always written by some old geezer who never went after the girl. Instead, they stood back and watched them slip away into someone else's arms. Then you are left to live life burdening your mind with "What ifs". It's a form of torture."

"That's not always true. And it's difficult to go after the girl. Sometimes you like someone, and they aren't looking for a relationship, and you respect that, but you still want to show you care, and that backfires. Explodes in your face. You end up just pushing them away, scaring them, making it where you feel like... you're just another creep. Or she is already spoken for, to begin with."

"Yeah, that's... all true, too. I wasn't always so "lucky" with the ladies. I still mess up, and not every girl I meet likes me. Becky and I are a strong couple, but I still annoy her without meaning to. Just part of life. It's hard to find a partner who will accept your quirks and possibly even like you because of them. With Becky, I got really lucky."

"Yeah, so anyway, how was your night?"

"It was great! Becky and I cuddled and snuggled," Cogeta answered, taking a moment to act goofy, wrapping his arms around himself and pretending to be kissing exaggeratedly.

"Okay, too much info. You could have stopped with it was great. So where is she?" He shrugged his shoulders as he asked.

Cogeta laughed at Cory, trying to avoid the topic, and reverted to his usual speech. "She went on ahead. She wanted to get to school early for something."

"Ah, ok," Cory said while nodding.

The two kept walking and soon came to Leen's home, where Angel waited, leaning against the side of the house. He had his eyes closed, resting until he felt the presence of his friends getting closer. He opened an eye, looked in their direction, and smirked as he pushed himself off the wall. Grabbing his bag, he started down the little walkway.

"Hey, where's your girl at?" Cogeta yelled to Angel as they got closer.

"Yours came along and took her away. I tried to get her to wait, but then Arieta joined in, and after saying something about "Girl time," they took off," Angel laughed.

Cogeta laughed, "Aw, I'm sorry."

"No biggie. I was waiting for you two anyway," Angel adjusted his backpack.

"Uh oh, is that a good thing?" Cogeta jested.

"Depends," was the only thing Angel said with a smirk, and all three began laughing.

Along the way, the three talked more about last night's dance and the day's upcoming events. As they got closer to the Academy's campus, more and more students came into view, and, just like them, they were wearing the school's uniform. While walking, Angel suddenly stopped and began looking around.

"What's wrong, man?" Cogeta asked, looking back at him.

"I don't know. I thought I smelt Leen's perfume."

"Aww, that's so cute."

"Shut up and wait here." Angel dropped his bag and took off into the alleyway between the shops and homes lining the street.

"Wait here, huh? Yeah, right, as if. Come on, Cory, let's go." Cogeta ran to catch up, grabbing Angel's bag along the way. Cory was close behind him.

Once in the back alleyway, Angel looked around and listened closely. His ears picked up on the sounds of those in the street from where he had come, the wind and birds, and as he focused more, he caught the voices of a group of boys. They were hidden from his sight by wooden crates beside the back door of a small grocery shop. He softly sniffed the air. Using his keen senses, he picked up the scents of the boys and a girl with perfume. The same kind that Leen used. He thought perhaps it was just a coincidence, but listened closely to what they were saying, desiring not to enter an unnecessary confrontation.

"Come on. Just tell your sister that I am a great guy. She would be better off with me than that fool she is dating now," a youthful male voice said.

"Please, why would my sister want to date you? You are so pathetic that you and your goons have to ambush me, a younger student, in the back of an alley, on my way to school instead of confronting me on the open street. You don't even have the balls to speak to her personally, and you think you are good enough for her," said a young female voice. Angel quickly recognized it as Arieta's.

"We just wanted some privacy with you, is all. Your sister is just so hot and her boyfriend is a delinquent," another boy spoke up, getting nods from the three others.

"Just leave me alone. You will never be even minutely worth my sister's time. Also, that delinquent fool boyfriend of hers may be a fool, but she loves him. So, you are just out of luck." Arieta smirked as she tried to walk away. However, the leader put his arm in front of her.

"Not so fast. I don't think you understand me, you stupid brat. She is better off with me. You say I don't have the balls to confront her, but I have more balls than her boyfriend. If she doesn't realize that I'm a better suitor, perhaps you would be smart enough to take her place. I mean, if I can't have first place, I could settle for second best. Or has that brute had his way with you, too?" The leader of the group asked with a toothy grin.

Arieta kicked, nailing the boy between his legs. As he hunched over in pain, she quickly followed through with her best punch, hitting the boy with all her might. Her fist rested against his face, his eyes staring at her. He seemed unfazed by the second attack, but his eyes glared at her with rage.

"Big mistake. You are going to pay for that, you little brat."

His friends pushed past him, shoved her against the wall, and held her wrists. The lead boy recovered enough to draw his fist back, ready to teach Arieta a lesson. However, when he tried to move it forward again, he couldn't. Looking back, he saw a guy holding onto his fist twice his size.

"Hi, Angel," Arieta said softly, looking up at him and then down to the ground timidly.

The boys holding her quickly released her and stepped away from her. The color in their faces fade rapidly.

"Hey, kiddo, these punks giving you trouble?" Angel asked calmly, clenching the boy's fist as he struggled relentlessly to break free.

Just then, Cogeta and Cory appeared, walking up beside Angel. Arieta stared blankly at the ground as she replied, "They were just trying to convince me they were better for my sister than you are. He thinks you're no good, a delinquent and a fool."

"I'm sorry! I really, really am!" The boy shouted, "I SWEAR!" His posse left him behind as they hightailed it out of there.

"You're going to leave Arieta alone, aren't you?" Angel asked, staring dead into his eyes.

As the boy stared back, it was as if Angel's eyes took a life of all their own. The boy broke out in a cold sweat as he stared into them. A fear that he had never felt before crept up his spine. The hairs on the back of his neck stood on end as he saw Angel's red eyes take on a demonic glow.

"Yes, sir. Never again, I swear it." He stammered as he pleaded again, closing his eyes and looking away.

Angel stood there silent as a statue for a moment as he wrestled with either letting the boy go unharmed or breaking his hand as a warning. He looked at Arieta, who was looking back at him. When their eyes met, he thought he saw her flinch just before she glanced back at the ground. He swung the boy onto the ground behind him with a heavy sigh.

"Never mess with her again. Remember, if you think you can get to Leen by bullying her little sister, you will deal with me. Bother Leen, and you with me. You mess with either of them, and you deal with me. Do you understand?"

"Yeah, he means us too." Cogeta chimed in, leaning on Angel's shoulder, grinning. Holding up his right hand, it was suddenly engulfed in a bright orange flame. He snapped his hand closed into a fist, and the fire went out.

The boy nodded quickly, then scrambled to his feet and ran off.

Angel turned his attention to the young girl. "So, what happened? You were with the girls the last time I saw you."

"I saw some friends on the way and split off to talk to them. But then, Jake, that boy, asked to speak with me. I didn't know he had his goons with him."

"You got to be careful. Some guys, they can be dangerous."

"That's why we are around!" Cogeta announced with a big smile, "but we better get going to class." He said, handing Angel his bag.

"I hope we aren't late," Cory sighed, relieved that Arieta was safe and that there wasn't a fight.

"Are you going to be all right, or do you want me to walk you to school, Arieta?" Angel asked, picking up her books that had been knocked out of her bag when the boy shoved her. Arieta said nothing.

Her mind was busy working overtime, replaying what had just happened. She was powerless against those weak boys. Whenever she hit Angel or Cogeta, they would appear to be genuinely hurt, and she never held back her punches with them. She enjoyed believing she could hold her own against them. She liked that sense of power. Now she realized they had only been faking it. She could not protect herself. Arieta hated the feeling that was creeping over her. Why had she not even thought to use what she had been taught in school? She went with her instincts, and they had let her down. Arieta's mind snapped back to the present by Angel gently shook her shoulder. When she looked up, she saw all three hovering over her with looks of concern. She wanted to beat that look off them so badly.

"Are you all right, Arieta? Do you want me to take you home?" Angel asked, genuinely concerned.

"I'm fine!" She snapped, grabbing her books from him, "And I don't need an escort from anyone, especially YOU! For Odin's sake!" She yelled before pushing through him, disappearing through the alley and into the street.

"Wow... what was that about?" Cogeta pondered aloud, scratching his head.

"She just realized that she lacks any true strength to defend herself. Faced with that realization is a lot to take all at once. One cannot fault her for that." Cory whispered.

"Did you read her mind, dude?"

"Didn't have to," said Cory. "Experience."

"Enough, guys. Let's get going. I'm sure she will be fine." Angel said before Cogeta could say anything more. The three left it at that and went to the University.

CHAPTER 4

THE UNIVERSITY

After parting ways with Arieta, Becky and Leen had breakfast in the cafeteria. Becky had filled her plate with an oversized omelet with sausage, bacon, and four varieties of cheeses, with a couple of blueberry muffins on the side. Leen had also gotten an omelet. It had ham, bacon, and peppers. She had sprinkled different herbs over it for added flavor. They found an empty table, sat down, and ate after giving grace to Odin, the All-Father, and Andhrímnir, the god of cuisine.

"Mmm, this is a good way to start the morning." Becky chimed before taking a sip from her glass.

Leen nodded in agreement with a smile, not wanting to speak as she had just put a fork full into her mouth. Becky glanced over at her friend and giggled.

"Mhm, I have to agree. It's nice to have moments like this to relax before the grueling routine of classes." Leen replied after she had swallowed.

Becky nodded profusely. "Especially for Mr. Anderville's class, ugh. Today, we have an exam about the molecular compounds found within the rocks from surrounding territories. We'll have to identify and state what they make up, where they are found, and for what uses are the rocks used."

"Yeah, but at least he's posted that for two weeks. Did you study?"

"Nope," Becky answered very matter-of-factly.

Leen laughed, "Now, what could have been so important to distract you from your studies and keep you from learning about the rocks and such that make up our wondrous planet?"

Becky smirked, and Leen right away blushed and laughed. "Oh, perhaps it was my wondrous boyfriend. Just perhaps."

"Oh, so you are going to blame poor Cogeta on your lack of focus on your studies?"

"Damn right!" Becky burst out laughing. "Every time I settled in to study, he would sneak up and instantly pester me."

"Pester?" Leen asked, not believing her friend was just the innocent victim.

"Yes, pester." Becky stuck her tongue out, "He'd... grab me from behind, tickle my neck with his whispering and... gentle kisses, and before I knew it, that science book was nowhere to be found. If he didn't do that, he would parade around the house barely clothed after training that I... well, I had to make sure he hadn't pulled a muscle, of course."

Holding back her laughter for a moment, Leen nodded in understanding. "Oh, of course. We couldn't have him pulling a muscle or hurting himself."

"Exactly. So, I would leave my books for a moment to help him relax after working out. He's preparing for the tournament, so it's only proper that I do my part to support him by giving him a massage afterward to help ease the tensed muscles. Some areas are harder than others."

"Oh, I don't need to know that," Leen laughed. "How is his training going, though?"

"Pretty well. He is a lot faster and stronger than he was last year. I put off studying because I took time to spar with him. He has a few bruises where I nailed him a good one with the end of my "Dragon's Fire". But he got me too. Then how could I study when I was sore?"

Leen stirred her drink as she listened, her mind overcome with a sudden feeling of melancholy. She knew Angel trained, and she even enjoyed watching him, but she never took part in helping him. Her strength didn't lie in her fists; her power was in using spiritual forces or magic. Of the spells she had learned, she couldn't think of a way to use them to aid Angel in his quest to become stronger. She understood why he wanted to be stronger and was fine with it. How could she not be? He had told her enough times before that the main reason he strove to become stronger was so that he could protect her. It certainly wasn't uncommon for men to have that idea. Even her father admitted to feeling that same way when her mother was alive. Now he puts all that energy into crafting his weapons so that others can protect the ones they care about.

"Utopia calling Leen? Come in. Are you there?"

Becky's words suddenly snapped her back. "Huh? Oh, sorry, I got lost in thought."

"About what, hun? You had this solemn look on your face. Is something the matter?"

"Well... do you ever... do you ever worry about him?"

"Him? You mean Cogeta? No, what do I need to be worried about? If you are referring to his... flirtatious nature or the fact that he leaps to the rescue of any damsel in distress, then no. I am not worried. That's just how he is and one reason I love him."

"No, no. Not that, I mean the extensive training and the lengths they push themselves to get stronger. Doesn't it worry you? That he could be seriously injured during one of the tournaments?"

"All the time, sweetie."

"But then, why do we let them put themselves in such danger?"

"Leen, I shouldn't have to tell you that. I would think you already knew the answer. It is because we love them. Boys are going to be boys, and let us be honest, I don't think Cogeta will ever grow up, which... I hope he doesn't in some ways. A serious Cogeta is just... weird. If he is all "serious-like," you know something is wrong." Both girls giggled at the thought. "But men want to protect the woman they love from other males or outside forces. It's the dream of most men, I think. It's hard-wired, but it's still sweet, and why should we try to stop them when it is just them trying to show how much they care?"

"Yeah, and I don't mind Angel doing all that, but I guess what worries me is all the times I have asked him what he wanted to do with his life, and he has no answer. All he ever really says on the matter is that all he knows is fighting. He doesn't know what other skills he has. Sure, he's said he'd take over my dad's shop when he's ready to give it up, but I don't know if that's truly what Angel wants. He's even toyed with the idea of joining the Knights of the Cloth if I joined the Priestess Sisterhood. In that way, we could still be together, but it would be taboo."

"He really mentioned joining the Knights of the Cloth?"

"Yes," Leen nodded. "It would be the only way he could still be close to me since members of the Sisterhood aren't allowed to have relationships. They forbid such ties so that they focus on helping others, prayer, and devotion."

"But... he hates the High Councilman. Doesn't he like, laugh at most of the traditions?"

"Yes, but he would do it to be with me."

"Well, you say it would be taboo for you two to continue your relationship if you both did that, but I find it sweet. The only other option would be for you two to split up so that you could pursue your calling. Otherwise, you risk being expelled from the Sisterhood and have your faith tarnished, or you decide not to follow your dream and find a new path. If he joined the Knighthood, you two would face some risk. None of the options are truly ideal, but that's also life. However, I think Angel would look rather dashing in the uniform. Got to admit, our men look good in uniform."

Leen laughed. "Yes, that they do. So does Cory."

"I wasn't excluding him. "Our men" includes Cory. Shame he didn't have as much fun last night as we did."

"I am shocked that no girls came single. Everyone had a date but him. How does that happen?"

"Bad luck. Terrible, terrible luck. Had he asked, I would've danced with him. But he said he wouldn't have partaken of Cogeta's and my enjoyment."

"I would've danced with him as well, but Cory really isn't the type to, as you said, intrude on moments. He won't be the one to ask."

"Dang it, and of the two of us, I am more the aggressor… I should have dragged him onto the dance floor kicking and screaming." Becky laughed.

"I'm sure Cogeta would have found humor in that," Leen smiled. "But yeah, I think that's what would've been needed. He's so shy. It's cute, but it seriously restricts him."

"Yeah. So, he needs an aggressive woman, or mildly aggressive, because we want her to be sweet too. I don't want her punishing him. That would be bad. And if she is going to be joining us, I will not be fighting over who is the alpha female. My crown is firmly placed. She needs to be someone who will accept his quirks and see the gem within."

"Oh really? You think you are the alpha?" Leen gave her friend a crooked smile.

"Well, of course, I am more aggressive than you." Becky stuck her tongue out.

"True, you are. Nevertheless, I am dating the alpha male; therefore, I must be the alpha female, which makes you my right fang. You do all my dirty work, so I don't have to."

"... I can live with that. I enjoy getting my hands dirty. So back on topic, if he were to find a girl, she would have to be a combination of you and me, agreed?"

"Agreed. Someone very kind and caring, while at the same time, she will pull him out of his chair and onto the dance floor to dance, kicking and screaming."

"Perfect!" Becky laughed.

"You know what? I might know someone like that."

"Who?" Becky asked as she finished her plate and sipped her morning coffee.

"Arieta, my sister. She isn't that much younger than him. She's almost out of her junior studies." Leen said softly as she took the last few bites.

"Seriously? You know, I think you may be right. Plus, it might be better because I think Alisandra is two or so years older than him."

"I will bring it up to him and see what he thinks of her."

"Good idea, and of course, then ask what she thinks of him. "

"Mhm," Leen nodded as she finished her drink.

The bells chimed for the first time, signaling those on campus to head for class. The girls stacked their glasses onto their plates and carried them over to the hole in the wall, where they passed them through to the kitchen personnel, who then passed them down to be washed. Afterward, they went their separate ways. Becky had a math test she had to prepare for, then later, that science test. The halls were alive with the sound of students busying about getting their things and rushing to class. As Leen walked toward her morning class, she heard a familiar voice call out to her. Turning around, she saw Headmaster Lucian standing in his office's doorway.

"Miss Puraday, would you mind stepping in here momentarily?" He smiled and stepped back as she walked in.

His office was very tidy. It had a warm cedar smell and a welcoming atmosphere. His door was always open to any student who wished to discuss their troubles, whether about their school life struggles or future paths or seek his guidance on a more personal matter. His large cherry wood desk in the center of the room, with a small jade lamp on one side and his computer offset on the other, with an oversized dark brown leather reclining office chair behind that. Bookshelves and curios were alongside the walls with honors he and the school had earned over the years. Books of policies, procedures, school history, and faculty alumni filled the shelves. He had a washroom off to the left side; the door was hidden partially behind some shelves.

"Good morning, Headmaster. Is everything okay?" She asked curiously as her eyes moved around the room. She half expected to find Arieta sitting on the old leather couch to the right of the door. So often before, whenever there was an issue with her sister, she was called in to deal with the matter. Sometimes she entered while performing an errand for a teacher and saw Angel sitting on the couch idly as Lucian tried to reason with him.

"Good morning to you too, and yes, everything is fine." Lucian caught her wayward glance and chuckled. "You needn't worry. Arieta is in no trouble. And I've heard no bad reports on Mr. Everlast this morning. It would seem you are indeed having a positive effect on him. I remember when I had to deal with him almost every morning. But now I can sit and enjoy my morning cup of hot tea before the school day begins."

"Well, sir, it isn't all my doing. He was a good person to begin with. It just took some finding."

"Oh, I am sure of that, dear. But on to the reason I called you in here. Come out, young man," Headmaster Lucian waved his hand over, and a boy around fifteen stepped forward into view from behind a bookshelf, looking down at the floor shyly. "This is Pete, our newest student to join us here."

Leen looked the young boy over as she listened to the Headmaster tell her how he found the boy daily in the public library and, after some time, got to know him. He was an orphan, making a meager living on his own. He had spiky green hair and wore an oversized red long-sleeve shirt, brown pants with holes, and muddy brown boots. He kept his head down. She smiled warmly when she caught him looking up at her, but the shy boy quickly averted his gaze back to the floor.

"He wouldn't be able to come here normally due to the lack of funding, but I admire his genuine passion for learning. So, I am putting forth the money for his education," Lucian patted the boy on his shoulder.

"Wow, Headmaster, that is generous of you. What would you like me to do?" Leen asked.

"I was hoping you wouldn't mind giving him a tour of our campus. It's overwhelming for newcomers and visitors, and I wouldn't want the lad to get lost on his first day."

"I would be happy to, sir," she turned her head and smiled warmly at Pete. Catching her gaze, his cheeks turned bright red, and he quickly looked back at the ground.

"Thank you very much, Miss Puraday. Here is his schedule and a tardy pass. Just in case this cuts into your class time." Lucian turned to Pete and knelt, "Now, Pete, don't worry. Miss Puraday will show you all the places where you will have access. She is wonderful, so don't be afraid to ask her questions as you go along, okay?" The Headmaster got a shy nod in reply. He smiled, stood up, went behind his desk, and sat down, preparing to begin the day with the morning announcements.

Leen took Pete's hand and walked with him out into the hallway. "Hmm, let's see. I think we will start outside and work our way in. Does that sound okay to you?"

Pete nodded slowly, looking down both ends of the wide hallway. Leen felt like she was leading a lost puppy.

"Hehe, okay, come on." They walked out to the campus gate, where students were still passing through. "First off, welcome to Utopia University, UU, or the Academy for short. I'm Leen, as you know, but it is very nice to meet you, Pete. This is the front gate and main entrance. The thirty-five-foot-tall gate and the fifty-foot-high wall surrounding our campus are mainly for aesthetic appeal. However, the campus is also designed to be a barracks or a bunker of sorts should there ever be an attack. One of the safest places you could ever be is behind these walls." Turning back around to face the schoolyard, they started walking forward.

"The fountain here depicts Odin on his six-legged steed. It was sculpted to honor him back when the school was first constructed. Sometimes you will see students tossing in a coin for good luck before a major exam or something." They stopped in front of the main hall made of stone. "This is where we started from. It has all the offices and the academic classes. We'll go in there a bit later. First, I want you to see the rest of the school. This place is huge. It scared me when I first started here, but it is an easy layout to remember once you see it. So hmm," she looked to her left and then her right, a pathway leading in either direction.

"Left?" Pete asked softly.

"Left it is." Leen smiled and walked forward, holding his hand.

Her hand is so soft. She smells very nice. Pete thought as he looked up at her. *I wonder if she has a boyfriend already.*

"The compounds you see on your left are where we are trained in ranged weapons and magic, should you wish to learn them. I'm not very good at most of them, but I enjoy the magic classes and think I am decent at them. Coming up is the Dome or our gymnasium. We play many sports there—"

"Like what kind of sports? I never really got to play any." Pete spoke up, looking up at the enormous dome-shaped building.

"Well, there is Ground ball, where the game's goal is to take an odd-shaped ball to one end of the field without being tackled by a rival player; it's a very rough game. Blaster Ball is fun to watch. You swing a bat to hit a ball and then run to different checkpoints as fast as possible before the other team can catch your ball. After you hit the ball, it comes to life in a matter of speaking, zigzagging around, and it can be hilarious. It has lots of lights too. Rackets is an exciting game. You can play up to four people, whack a ball over a net back and forth, trying to make the other person miss. But you got to watch out cause some balls are enhanced to do different things, like fly faster or explode after so much time has passed.

Then there is Air Ball, where players play within a bubble of flowing air so they don't lose the ball flying around, and you have to score by getting the ball past a goal protector and into his net. Some of the more dangerous sports we play and train for--- oh yeah! We have school tournaments for each sport." She giggled softly. "Sorry, forgot to mention that. Some of the more dangerous sports are Wolf Duels and Blood Rain. Wolf Duels are fights done in our wolf forms; they can get gruesome. Blood Rain is worse because you aren't allowed to heal during the match, and the whole point is to be the last one standing. I don't really care for violent games, but many people do. Sorry, I hope I am not boring you."

"No, no. Not at all. What is next?"

"Next is our library. You can find a book on just about any subject there. There are fifteen different levels, I believe. There are too many books in there for me to read, anyway. But I know someone close to having read every book in there."

"Wow. Can we go in there at any time?"

"Mhmm, even after school is over. The library is open to all students and faculty all day."

"Awesome," Pete's eyes lit up.

"Hehe. If you look to either side, you will see trails leading back behind the library. Those will take you to our stables, where we learn to ride. I won't take you back there but know that's where they are. Let's follow the trail around back to the front. Along the way, you will see more compounds and training rings. That's where students learn close-quarter combat with various weapons and styles."

Following the trail back to the front of the main building, Leen led Pete up the stairs and inside.

"Okay. As I said earlier, this is where all our academic classes are that don't particularly pertain to warfare, aside from history or military strategy." Looking at her watch, she saw classes would begin soon. "Yikes, okay, hate to rush, but I'm going to be brief, so I can show you to your first class so you aren't tardy on your first day. As you can see, staircases lead down at either end of the hall to your right and left."

Pete nodded, looking toward them.

"That will take you to our cafeteria. Don't worry about trying to find a seat. There is plenty of room. And if you want seconds, go right ahead. It'sall you can eat, and the buffets rarely run out. What is left over is usually ground up and given to the animals in the stable. If you continue down the stairs, you will find more classes. They respectfully correspond to the close and range weapon-training areas, right and left. This is where you will learn to use more advanced equipment and weapons. It can be hazardous, so be extra careful. If you get lost, ask someone. More than likely, they will be happy to help you. At some point, everyone gets lost here," she smiles and looks at his schedule. "All right, it says your first class is Mechanical Sciences, so that would be this way. After class, wait for me by the door, and I will show you to your next one."

She walked with him to his class, introducing him to the instructor, and after he thanked her for the tour, she went on her way. Hoping she wouldn't have to use the tardy pass.

Once the guys got onto campus, Cogeta said his goodbyes and headed to the path to his sports class. Angel bid his farewells before he went to his combat class. Cory stood silently for a moment as he watched his friends disappear into the mob of students. After losing sight of them, he, too, went on his way with another crowd heading into the main office. To his relief, he was earlier than he had thought he would be. The three did not have classes together all at once. Cory had Cogeta in a few of his classes on certain days. Unfortunately, today would not be one of them. Cory found those classes were never dull, though they seemed to go by faster because of Cogeta's antics.

Cory walked into the main office building, ascending the staircase and taking a right, his classroom being the fifth door on the left. His first class of the day was biology. He squeezed through the people standing in front of the doorway, excusing himself, then sat in the middle section of the desks. Most of the students' classrooms were shaped and organized similarly; long rows of benches with desks with built-in touchscreen computers. After pulling the desired notebook from his bag, he started his computer. As it beeped to life and warmed up, he watched the classroom fill. His eyes widened ever slightly as a certain girl walked in. He felt a surge of joy fill his chest as he saw her greeting her friends. *I wish I could talk to her. I really want to talk to her.*

The small smile that had formed over his lips faded just as swiftly as it had begun, as his eyes watched as she greeted her boyfriend with a kiss. The man smiled, spun her into his arms, and dipped her back, leaning down quickly and giving her an even deeper kiss. She surrendered to him and willingly melted into the kiss. The class cheered them on. In complete contrast, the display felt like a guttural blow and made him feel nearly void of everything except depressed and sick. The professor did not seem to care.

However, finally, the professor pulled his eyes off the younger female students in the front row and got ready to teach.

The professor stood around five foot eight, with mid-length, combed-back black hair and a few green streaks blended in. His green eyes hid behind specially designed glasses, a large nose, and a small patch of hair on his chin. Every day, he would wear the same gray uniform. On the left shoulder was a shield patch with a wolf's head howling, and on the right shoulder was another patch with the double lapping "U's" and unique designs on his cuffs, all done in a golden material. He picked up his two-foot-long pointing stick and stood up from his desk.

"Everyone settle down and take your seats," he said in his typical fast speech. When he finished the command, he began the lesson. In this class, one had to be on their toes if one hoped to pass.

As the class got underway and dragged on, students scribbled down notes as fast as they could. Meanwhile, Cory was only halfway paying attention to the lesson. Though he was taking notes as the teacher shouted out facts and dates rapidly, he still daydreamed.

"Pst. Cory," a whisper caught his ears' attention, snapping him out of his little world.

He turned slightly to the right and looked down to see Leen's lovely smile greeting him.

"What is it?" He replied softly, leaning over his desk, hiding his head behind his computer screen, pretending to write something down, worried the professor would overhear.

"Would you mind if I saw you after class?" Leen asked politely.

"Huh? Sure." He turned back to his notes, curious about what Leen wanted to see him about.

He was surprised at her request. They were good friends, but she had never asked to speak to him after class. If she wanted to talk to him, she openly did. *Have I given her some sign that she had offended me or something? No, that wouldn't be it. Is it something about Angel? It could be about the lesson.* He asked himself as he tapped his pencil on the desk.

As he continued to take notes, a small folded piece of paper was slipped to him. This interruption annoyed him slightly. He was never this popular. Cory held the note just out of view under his desk and opened it with his left hand as his right kept writing. It was from the girl asking to borrow his notes. All that annoyance he felt drifted away and was replaced with a giddy feeling. He thought about it for a minute. When the professor's back was turned, he looked back behind him, where the girl sat a few rows up and nodded. He then returned to his work.

However, behind him and up to the right of the classroom, he heard students talking and cutting up. It was that guy and his friends. They were distracting, and they were not going unnoticed by the professor. He placed his pointer stick on the desk and picked up a small black scepter with a wolf's head grasping an enormous diamond in its mouth. He cleared his throat and raised the scepter over his head. However, they continued.

"Excuse me; I am trying to teach you about the biology of our old enemy and now current ally, the Nebulians. So should the day come that they are no longer our allies, you will know how to kill them. They are one of the harder-to-kill races that we know of. Unlike what we covered previously, they aren't as frail as a Vampirian. I will have silence, and you will pay attention." Explained the professor.

The students became quiet momentarily, but as the lecture resumed, they began talking again. This time, the professor said nothing to stop them. He started walking up the side of the classroom toward the students. Everyone else sat perfectly still and silent. Three boys were talking amongst themselves and cracking jokes. He didn't have to deal with all of them; he'd make an example of one, their leader. Two boys quickly grew silent upon coming into view, and fear overcame their faces. The third boy failed to realize that there was danger too late. His eyes barely turned to the side when he was grabbed by the hair, and his head was yanked backward.

The diamond scepter cracked the student across his jaw. "Disrespectful mutt. When I say I want silence, I expect silence!" The professor followed the first strike with repeated strikes to the student's head. He pulled the boy from his seat onto the ground and delivered blow after blow to the student's face. The student struggled to defend himself, but the professor had a firm grip on a handful of hair and easily kept control. "You think you can disrespect me because you are good-looking and popular? Do you think what I have to teach is not important?" Several more skull-cracking blows landed on the boy's head. The sickening heavy thunks of each hit landing filled the room and echoed in the ears of the students. At last, the professor shoved the student back onto the ground. Blood dripped from the diamond. "Take yourself to the nurse and get cleaned up. See if she has anything to cure your disrespect." He turns to face the rest of the class. "Let this be a lesson to all of you! Respect. It is what separates us from the savages."

The professor returned to the front of the classroom and pulled out a handkerchief to wipe down his scepter. He resumed the lecture as though nothing had happened. Cory gulped. He glanced around the room at everyone's reaction. They were all paying attention now. But he focused on a couple in particular. The guy was Justin, Alisandra's boyfriend, and she looked as though she would cry or be sick. Her girlfriends were consoling her quietly. He wanted to comfort her, but a dark part of him wasn't upset that Justin got what he had coming in some regard. That thought made him feel sick. *No. That was a bit much, even for that fracker.* Cory then turned his attention to Leen. She was visibly scared and scribbled notes down as she tried to focus on the professor's words.

Cogeta entered the Dome, trying to sneak quickly into line before the coach spotted him. "Fairway!"

Ah, shi—.

"Hurry and get in line! You're late!" yelled the Coach at the top of his lungs. The man known as "Coach" was a tall man at seven foot eight. He had a very predominant chin, shortcut brown hair that was spiked and brown eyes. From years of lifting and exercising, his body was defined by his large, toned muscles. He usually wore tight workout shirts and shorts, showing off the hard work he put into his body. On rare occasions, one might see him in a suit and tie.

"Late? I'm on time, aren't I?" Cogeta asked, getting in line and pretending to look at a watch that was nowhere on his wrist.

"If you were paying attention and not wasting time, you would have heard me say to be here early yesterday. But no! You were too busy eyeing the female class as they did their post-class stretches."

"Can you honestly blame me, Coach?" Cogeta held out his arms with a toothy smile.

"Shut that trap! Now we will start with our morning workouts. Cogeta, you will double the amount for being late, and then we will start with our Wolf Duels. We will continue to practice until, well, until I say stop!" The Coach blew his whistle, dropped to the ground, and started doing pushups. The students immediately followed suit. With each following whistle after a specific time had passed, they immediately changed to a different exercise, mimicking whatever the Coach did. This went on for nearly twenty minutes before the Coach called for enough. The rest of the class relaxed for another ten minutes while Cogeta finished his punishment. Afterward, twenty-five boys gathered around a mat six feet high, ten feet long, and thirteen and a half feet wide.

"Cogeta, you will be first, and your opponent will be," the Coach paused and glanced around, "Stone, get up there."

Stone stood like a giant among most, standing eight and a half feet tall. Cogeta looked over at him. He had long, spiked golden hair, similar to Cogeta's own. He was wearing a loose red training dogi with a black undershirt. Cogeta smiled as he looked at the big guy. The two were good friends, and he couldn't help but think back. He knew the real reason Stone came to the academy. It was in search of a girl.

He used to work in a lumberyard, but his boss was generous. He saw

Stone's apparent interest in the young lady when her father brought her on his business trip. They arrived in their horse-drawn carriage to place an order. The boss had called Stone into his office after they had left and sat him down. He told him that as a lumber grunt, he would never be worthy enough for the young lady, especially in her father's eyes. He gave Stone a small sack filled to the brim with money, his last payment for all his hard work, and told him to go out and seek a better education. Then afterward, to win the girl's heart and her father's respect. Stone thanked his former boss, who had been like a father figure since his had passed away, and set out to woo his heart's desire.

The two met accidentally in class. She bumped into him, and all Stone could do was stand there dumbfounded and silent as the trees he had cut down. Afterward, he met with Cogeta, whom he had met prior. Cogeta then set up a meeting so that Stone could have the chance to speak to her. Stone and the young girl have been dating for over three months, and things were looking up for them. Because of his size and deep voice, many who do not know him find Stone intimidating. He is a very easy-going and caring guy until you make him angry.

Cogeta and Stone stepped onto the mat, using the steps at the corner. Cogeta extended his hand, and Stone respectively shook it. Their grips tightened, testing each other's strength. "May the best wolf win." Cogeta grinned, looking Stone in the eyes. Stone nodded, and they stepped back a few paces. Neither one broke eye contact with the other.

The Coach glanced back and forth between the two, "Ok, you Mutts, you know the rules. You must fight in wolf form; no shifting out. If you do, it is considered surrendering. If you are knocked out of the ring, you have five seconds to get your furry ass back in there. No going for the eyes or gonads, either. With that all said, SHIFT NOW!" When the word SHIFT left his mouth, they were morphing into wolf forms.

Cogeta turned into a reddish-orange wolf. Stone turned into a dark gray one. The Coach raised his hand and slung it down to signal them to begin. Cogeta and Stone charged forward. Their fangs dug deep into each other's fur. Blood gushed from each as they ripped their flesh. The crimson liquid splattered across the ring. They both released their holds and leaped back from each other. The two circled one another before charging once more.

Cogeta went to chomp down on Stone's neck once more. Stone dashed to the side, successfully dodging Cogeta's jaws. He then rushed forward, ramming his head into Cogeta's ribs. Cogeta skidded across the mat. He straightened up and quickly rolled out of the way as Stone landed with his claws digging into the mat where Cogeta had once laid. They again circled each other before leaping for each other once more.

This time, Cogeta let himself be taken down. While Stone latched onto his throat and chomped, Cogeta rolled under him. He began using his hind legs to tear into Stone's underside. Stone closed his eyes tightly in pain as Cogeta delivered the vicious attack. He bit down even harder into Cogeta's neck. Unable to bear the pain, he yanked him out from under him and threw Cogeta into the air. Cogeta landed back down on his feet, poising himself to strike again but instead watched as Stone turned back into his human form.

He stood up, holding his stomach. "I back down." He said softly, dealing with the pain as his body mended itself slowly.

"Stone, I am surprised. As big and strong as you are, you didn't last long. You BRAIN DEAD, MUTT! Heal your DUMB ASS and get off MY mat!" yelled the Coach.

Cogeta transformed back, putting his hand on Stone's shoulder. "Yo, you did good, man. Coach is just an old fart. In fact, birds have been telling me the big guy hasn't been getting much TLC at home if you know what I mean," he said while rubbing the back of his neck with one hand while motioning toward the Coach.

Stone smiled, nodding his head. He then stood up straight, fully healed from his battle. "Next time, Cogeta," he said as they stepped down, and the next two jumped onto the map and prepared to battle.

"Cogeta! I heard that you little runt, hundred and fifty laps around the campus NOW!" boomed the Coach looking over at him.

"Aww, man" Cogeta closed his eyes, rolled his head, and took off.

Angel walked down the path, making his way to the close combat training grounds. He entered the open door to the sword and fist combat building. People were already sparring in different fighting styles and showing off their techniques. Sensing him enter, the instructor looked over and greeted Angel with a nod.

"Is everyone here now?" he glanced around. "Good. Everyone file in." As everyone filed into a straight line, he continued again, "As you all know, we will have a school tournament soon. It has been nearly a year since the last one, and our University took home the victory. Now we are lucky to have such fine warriors returning this year, such as Mochi, Stone, Tomus, Cogeta, Zach, and Angel, to name a few."

Angel stepped forward, "We should not underestimate our competition, especially when it is MidStar whom Shaw Inc sponsors. They have their own extraordinarily talented fighters. Such as Shaw himself, Sage, Barburata, Atila, Syph, and Jaketon, to name a few, sir."

"Do you doubt your and your team's abilities, Angel?" asked the instructor, feigning shock to hear Angel say such things. "It was you who surprised us all when you beat Shaw. He was known for never losing a match until you came along. He was the pride and soul of MidStar, the Golden Dragon, and you left him unconscious in a pool of his blood. Now I ask you again, do you doubt your capabilities and those of your team?"

"No, sir. I am saying we should not get overconfident. I know that I

74

have beaten Shaw in and out of the ring many times, and each time I face him, he is stronger than before. Each loss only fuels his hatred for me. I know my and my teammates' abilities, but we should underestimate no one. No matter how often we defeat them, we should never go in expecting we already won." Angel replied sternly, staring into his instructor's green eyes.

"Well said. I would expect nothing less from my team's captain," remarked the instructor as he placed his hand on Angel's shoulder and took a severe tone. "He is right. Never, under any circumstances, underestimate your opponent's capabilities. When you let your guard down, that's when you lose. It might not mean much to you now, only fighting in tournaments and for sport. In those, you are bound to get hurt or seriously injured, but if you are called into war, that lesson may very well keep you stay alive. Now go outside and gather around mat five. We are going to spar until we can hardly bear to stand! We must ensure we are in tip-top shape to bring the gold home!" The students did as instructed, rushing out the doors to begin their sparring matches.

Angel stood beside the instructor, watching and studying the fighters' movements. As team captain, he had to know their strengths and weaknesses. He would then use that information to decide who would fight whom at the tournament. The instructor peered over his shoulder as he examined the two fighters' stats on his clipboard.

"They have improved well. Do you think they will be ready for next week?" The instructor asked, curious to know Angel's opinions.

"Yes, I believe so. Zach and Mochi are showing great promise this year. They must have been training all year for this moment." Angel replied, "I may have to watch my back this year if I want to remain captain."

"I just wish all were as unwavering in improving their physical abilities. So many youngsters these days want to sit behind a desk or do easy work, not serve in the army. Makes me desire the olden days when the weak were killed at birth, and the strong were raised to fight first and foremost," the instructor stated.

"All those who attend this academy do so to become the best, sir. We will be fully prepared for the tournament next week and bring back another trophy for our case." Angel looked on with confidence.

"That's what I want to hear, Angel. Personal question, are you going to enjoy beating Shaw again?" The instructor asked with a beaming smile, gently nudging Angel's side with his elbow.

Angel smirked, "Sir, remember that these tournaments are nothing personal. But with that aside, yes, I will."

The instructor broke out in laughter, patting Angel on the back. "Boy, I am glad you are on my team. I can't wait until I see the final match next week. You know Shaw and yourself are the headliners. Ever since you came along and put that rich boy on his ass, you have become famous throughout the school and, I dare say, Utopia."

"Becoming famous was… never my intent, however. I enjoy a good fight." Angel answered truthfully.

"And that's what makes you a great Utopian, your undying urges never to give up and never to surrender. Last year's battle was pure magnificence. You and Shaw were so bloody and torn up. Neither one of you could stand properly near the end. Then you, with that finishing blow. POW! Right to the kisser. You laid him out flatter than Sundo pancakes. Then the referee raised your hand, my captain's hand, in victory. That was a glorious thing to watch, Angel. Truly glorious!" Exclaimed the instructor as he reminisced about last year's events.

Until last year's tournament, Midstar had been victorious for several years, thanks to Shaw. He had crushed all who stepped onto the stage. It was a shock to everyone watching when Angel achieved his victory. A shock that rippled outward to those who could not attend or watch the tournament. Overnight, Angel went from a nobody rogue to a mild celebrity. After that day, people knew his name and face. People would ask for his autograph or to take a photograph with him. Such attention made him feel awkward, but he obliged and was thankful when the hype died down.

"Thank you, sir. That was a fight to remember. Only hope it is as good, if not better, this year," commented Angel as the next set of fighters jumped onto the mat and sparred. "I have one request, though."

"Speak your mind."

"I wish to have Ryker rejoin my team this year for the championship," Angel said.

"Ryker? Do you speak of Cory Ryker?" The instructor looked at him quizzically.

"Yes, sir."

"Whatever for? As I recall, he lost rather sadly against a woman last year. Since the new mandate came down, changing the tournament's participation qualifying requirements, he hasn't fought in any qualifying battles with the competing schools."

Angel snapped his head to look at the instructor. "That was a woman?"

The instructor let loose a hearty laugh. "Yes, Angel, that was a woman. I won't hold that against you. Truth be told, I was flabbergasted to learn the truth as well. She was truly a wonder to behold and a damn good fighter."

"Well, even so. I wish to have him fighting on my side once more. He is actually a very talented fighter, and he doesn't realize it. He took last year's defeat to heart. It was his first time competing. He was eliminated in the first round. I knew he would need time to overcome that. According to the letter you received, this year's tournament was being restructured. It would no longer be one major event with all the schools competing at once, but have us knock out other competing schools over the year until two remained. So, I hadn't asked him to join us. From my scouting reports on the other schools, I calculated we wouldn't have too much of a threat from them. Even if we didn't have a full roster, the letter didn't state we had to, so long as we won the most out of ten fights. I knew I or Cogeta, or anyone of the others, could pick up a fight or two to secure a victory. I just told the other teams we were giving them a handicap. That idea worked on multiple levels. It got under most of their fighters' skin when they heard about it, so they gave a stronger showing than they may have otherwise—it also made many of them start the match unfocused, giving us the mental advantage. Then, when we won, it was just another way for us to brag about our team's capabilities. There was no doubt in my mind that it would not come down to us versus Midstar."

"What about Justin instead? He is a talented fighter as well. I will say better than your friend and some here. If you recall, he was captain before you took that title away from him."

"Justin... is a good fighter. Sure. But he would be a terrible addition to the team. He would bring morale down."

"And Ryker wouldn't?"

"When I first began attending classes here, I saw how Justin treated his teammates. He berated and undermined any evidence of improvement. He tried to treat me just as poorly. But I wouldn't let him, so when open challenges came to take the captain's spot, I saw it as an opportunity to take him down several notches. I only let him stay on the team to see if he could change. He didn't accept his loss and did not use it to grow and improve himself. He remained the same shallow blowhard as before and continued to impede the others on their journey to get better. That's why I kicked him from the team. If I brought him back, he would return to his old antics."

"Fair points. I didn't argue when you made your decision. As captain, that is within your power to choose who competes. I was surprised, but given his last few performances and utter losses, I was willing to see what you were playing at. The result was very satisfying. But what is it that you see in Ryker?" The instructor chuckled, "Is his family bankrolling his participation, perhaps?"

"No. After the last time, I doubt they would want him to compete again. I heard his father was furious over his failure. But how much do you remember from that fight, sir?"

"He lost in the first preliminary round, and it was against a woman."

"That fight lasted nearly as long as mine. Cory had only been training a few months before the match after I asked him to join us. He doesn't train here because he's self-conscious and insecure but trains with Cogeta and me. For someone who doesn't like to fight, he didn't back down or give up after the first knockdown. He didn't give up after the fifth time or the thirtieth time. He never gave up. The match only ended when he could no longer stand up. His opponent struggled to leave on their own. Never giving up, never surrendering. Didn't you say those were the traits of a great Utopian?"

The instructor stared at Angel briefly, thinking about what he had said. He then shrugged. "You are the captain, Angel. If you think he would help the team, then go ahead. I hope he doesn't cost us a championship."

"Given a chance, he could surprise you."

The bell finally sounded, and everyone began filing out of his or her first block class. Cory gathered his things and got his notes together to hand off. He saw Alisandra waiting by the door with a couple of her friends. Gazing down upon her, her beauty on display for his eyes. Her blonde wavy hair flowed around her as she laughed angelically at a joke that her friend told her. She appeared calmed down after Justin's violent ejection from the classroom. Cory took a deep breath and headed over to them.

"Hey. Rather interesting lesson today. I mean, it sucks what happened to Justin."

"It's okay. He messaged me a while ago and said he would be okay. We're going to meet up after school."

"Oh, well, that's good. So yeah, umm, interesting lesson otherwise, right? Nebulians having skin of liquid metal that they can morph into whatever they can come up with. I wish I could do that sometimes. Would never be without a weapon." His tone was different, and his words felt forced into being so that a conversation could be born. *That sounded so stupid!* "Or never without a pen, I guess."

One girl standing beside his focus spoke in a jarring, snotty voice, "How would they produce the ink?"

Cory froze momentarily as his mind processed the obvious flaw in his statement, "I um..don't know. Their blood, perhaps?"

"Weren't you paying attention? Do Nebulians even bleed?" Asked the same girl. This caused the group of girls to snicker. In response, Cory's face turned red from embarrassment. "Aren't you supposed to be super smart? The school's bookworm?"

"I wouldn't go that far. I, umm, just like to read and learn various things."

"What good is that knowledge if you can't apply and use it?"

Finally, Alisandra stepped in, "It's fine, Christy. Cody is very smart. I think he downplays it so he doesn't draw too much attention to himself."

"Umm, m-my name i-is Cory." *Did she really forget my name?*

"Oh gosh! I'm sorry, Cory."

"I-it's fine. So um yeah. Here are my notes. H-hope, you know, find them useful." Cory handed his papers to the girl. His shoulders dropped, and he felt like the world reminded him of his place again. Who was he to think he was of any importance? The girl he felt a strong affinity towards couldn't even remember his name.

"Hopefully, they are legible and not st-st-stuttering or mumbling," said Christy with a snide smile.

"Shush, Christy," giggled Alisandra. "Thank you, Cory. You are the best."

"Heh, yeah, sure. No problem." He stood still and watched Alisandra and her friends walk away, giggling and carrying on. Dropping his head and adjusting his bag over his shoulder, he turned and went in the opposite direction.

Leen had stood back and watched the conversation. She wasn't trying to eavesdrop; they were standing in her way. So as not to be rude, she waited for them to stop talking. That's what she told herself. When Christy started talking, Leen's blood boiled—the nerve of her talking to him like that. Leen glared down the hall at the back of their heads, feeling a shiver of desire for retaliation. She shook it off and immediately caught up with Cory.

"Hey," she said with a smile, "Some class, right? I didn't know Nebulians had skin like liquid metal and form it into tools and weapons just by willing it."

"Yeah," he said somberly, not even bothering to glance at her.

Those girls, Leen quietly growled, *splintered his spirits.*

"So, what did you want to talk to me about?" Cory queried as he walked alongside Leen, shocking her out of her thoughts.

"Oh umm," her smile dimmed a little, "Well, I saw you looking at you know who during class. And did you just let her borrow your notes?"

"Oh, that? It's nothing, just being nice. She asked to copy them because she couldn't keep up with the professor's lecture. Even I have trouble at times. Though, I really wish she and her boyfriend didn't do that public display every day in front of the class. That was distracting, but then... he got roughed up pretty badly by the professor today. But he's healing okay, so she said." Cory tried his best to sound nonchalant. He knew, or he felt as if he was to the point of annoying his friends by constantly talking about the girl. He tried to hide his sadness with a wall of positivity, even if it was paper thin. Cory knew he wasn't hiding anything truly, though his friends could see right through them. Especially Leen, she was the most caring out of all of them; no way she didn't see or sense his agony.

"Yeah? Well, that's good. I know it is rather… disgusting to watch when they kiss like that. I see the pain it's causing you. You know she is only using you to get what she wants." Leen said sympathetically.

"Leen, I don't want to talk about this," He spoke calmly, though he was annoyed, not with her, but with himself.

"What attracts you to her?" She asked, ignoring his statement.

"I don't know. It's just something I cannot explain."

"Come on. She is pretty and smart." Leen attempted to pull the information out of her friend.

"Yeah, that she is." A small smile returned to his lips while he envisioned the girl. "She has a bright, warming smile that pushes the darkness away. When she laughs, it brings an uplifting feeling to me. Is that weird?"

Leen smiled, "Not at all, Cory."

"Well, I know you don't need someone else telling you there are more fish in the sea, but---"

"Yeah, I know there are." Cory interrupted her, "But I'm not interested in them. I'm interested in her. I'm not in love with her. How can I be? I don't even know her... and that's what I would really want to do, get to know her. Perhaps then I could decide whether there is something there. Maybe something there turns me away, and I can't love her, or maybe she's that missing part of my life, and together we'd make each other whole. But it seems the ones I find interest in are always already scooped up or show no interest in me..."

"Both boxes checked on that girl."

Cory lowered his head. "I know. I've tried to stop, Leen. I have, but I can't get her out of my head. I always want to talk to her, to be around her. When I am near her, my troubles melt away. My... spirit feels at peace. It's hard for me to put it into better words. I don't feel that way around everyone. But like I said, I'm attracted to her, but she doesn't show any interest in me, even before Justin was in the picture. I hate that I feel this way. The fact that she is dating someone should stop my attraction toward her, but it doesn't, and it's worse because Justin is a horrible person. How can she be happy with someone like that? Did I do something wrong in the past to make her not even want to get to know me, to give me a chance? Am I not worth being interested in? Am I that boring... am I that worthless?" His voice was breaking.

Leen grabbed her friend by the arms, and with the strength she rarely displayed, she turned him around and pulled him into her arms. "You are not worthless! You are not boring." She rubbed the back of his head and his back. "You are amazing and one of my closest and best friends. Cory, you've been there for me when I needed help on some of my hardest exams. Angel couldn't help me, and certainly not Cogeta. But you made the time to help me and made it easy for me to grasp the subjects I struggled with. You've listened to my troubles and helped me decide what paths I should take."

"Heh... so? I was doing what a friend should do. Of course, I will make time to help you. Anyone literally would. I am not the smartest person in the school. You could've found someone who could have done the same for you and maybe even better."

"Nope. I beg to differ. You were the one I needed. You say you aren't the smartest, but you're pretty high up there." Leen said.

"That's why I also help Alisandra. Because I want to, not because she's making me. To show that... I'm there for her."

"Yeah, but... I don't feel she appreciates it as I do. I think she is just using you, Cory, because she knows she can manipulate you into doing anything she wants. Some girls see a guy willing to be there for them and use it against them."

"No... Alisandra... Alisandra isn't like that. I truly feel there is more to her than what she shows everyone."

"Perhaps you are right. But it would be best if you didn't waste your time on someone who doesn't value your time. Maybe I can help you for a change. I might know someone who could be good for you," Leen proceeded.

"Just who would that be?" He asked, struggling to get his emotions back into check.

"My sister, Arieta. She is pretty, smart, and single. And I know she likes you. Win-win." She smiled.

He smiled and chuckled softly, "I appreciate the thought, but Leen, do you really want me to be dating your sister? You know my faults. Look at me. I'm an emotional mess. In addition, she and I have nothing in common. Not to mention, she is rather young and single because she wants to be." He was trying not to be rude. Cory didn't have those kinds of feelings for Arieta.

"Oh please, she is almost finished with her junior education. She's not even two years younger than you. Yes, I know you have faults, but everyone has some. I also know you have a lot more good points going for you. Even if you are blind to them, I see them, and others see them. So, what if you two have nothing in common? Universal law says opposites attract. Look at Angel and me. Having nothing in common gives a clean foundation to build on. This way, you two can get into something together. She is single because she hasn't found the man she wants yet. Don't waste your life trying to catch a glimpse from someone who doesn't deserve your gaze." Leen was trying to express her concern for him, even if it seemed a little pushy. She wanted him to see things differently.

Cory smiled, straightened up, and stepped away, "Thanks, Leen. But... Okay, I don't want to be rude, but Arieta is kinda..."

"She's what?" Leen raised her right brow.

"Well, umm, she's ... dark, kinda scary and, um... creepy. To name a few, she enjoys her horror and ghoulish stories, leans a little heavily into gory things, and can get competitive. She has a dark sense of humor and pushes to see how far she can go. And when we play and roughhouse with her, it starts in good fun, but I think at some point she switches to really trying to hurt us," Cory looked shamefully at Leen, "It's not that I don't like her as a friend, but as a girlfriend, I don't know. I doubt her, and I would work out. Besides, she has shown no interest in me either. We don't talk a great deal about anything of importance, and I would feel weird asking."

"Please, that dark creepiness with liking horror and gore is just a front. She is a nice girl, Cory."

"I know that. I'm not saying she isn't. It's just...." He pondered what he wanted to say.

She smiled, stepped closer, hugged him, and kissed his cheek. "Cory, you are a dear friend to me, and I want to see you happy. Keep Arieta in mind, please. Who knows, maybe she will be the one." She then went to her next class, leaving Cory to think about what she said.

Later that day, Leen was in the hall with her friends collecting her books for her next class when she saw the girl Cory had a crush on laughing with her friends. Leen stopped talking and listened a little closer.

Christy's loud voice made it easy as she mockingly pretended to be Cory, "I-uh-I-uh um, gosh d-didn't you like the class about a-liens. I mean, wow, so fascinating." She laughed. "For someone who is supposed to be so smart, he is so stupid."

Leen's blood boiled.

"Christy, that's mean. He has trouble speaking. Not everyone can speak properly. Many people stutter and mumble."

"Girl, that isn't the reason he stutters. It's obvious that he is infatuated with you."

"I kinda had that feeling. It's been a few years, and he's always been sweet to me. He's even gotten me gifts and made some outrageous gestures. I once mentioned I was looking for this little statue to go into my collection, and he spent weeks looking for it and then brought it to me after I got off work, even though it was super late. It was a little flattering, but like... who does that... weirdos. But now I'm spoken for. And he isn't my type, anyway." The girl's body shook with a sudden chill. "I mean, he's creepy, in a way. Sometimes I catch him looking my way in class or the halls. Stalker-ish almost, you know."

Leen had heard enough. She stepped forward, but her arm was suddenly grabbed.

"Leen, what are you doing?"

Leen ignored her friend and pulled free. She clenched her fists as she approached the two girls. "You two have no clue how good of a person Cory is. He only has trouble speaking when around you because he doesn't wish to look like a fool in front of you."

"Well, he is failing in that regard," laughed Christy.

"You don't have room to run your mouth, Christy. Everyone knows whom you hang out with after school. He's more of a slob than your previous tryst with the groundskeeper." Leen turned her gaze back to her principal focus. "Cory likes you. Why, I don't know. From what I see, you're a cheap off-brand cutout of an already foregone beauty magazine. He deserves much better and should leave you with your disloyal degenerate boyfriend you have now, whom we've all seen treat his previous girlfriends like a tool to be thrown around and then thrown away."

The two girls stood, shocked for a moment. Never had they seen Leen display such an outburst. Alisandra's face burned red.

"As if you have any room to talk, oh princess. If you haven't noticed, your choice of company has tarnished and crumbled your former radiance. You once had men of all standing throwing themselves at you. You made every girl jealous just by entering the room. I bet you only have girlfriends now, as they hope to snatch up your scraps. The Justin you think you know is not the person I am dating. He's," she hesitated a moment, "changed. A lot. Those girls didn't understand or know how to make him happy. And anyway, at least he isn't some wild and dangerous animal like you've chosen to associate with."

"I chose someone of higher quality rather than settling for a shallow imitation of happiness. Some of those guys were certainly handsome, some even wealthy, but most just wanted me for their selfish desires. Dark treats me as an equal, not as a trophy. You should really open your eyes and see that Justin is just using you for his desires. Once bored with you, he will find someone he thinks is prettier and throw you aside as if you didn't exist, just like he's done to his previous flings. Maybe one day you'll wise up and find someone better."

The girl scoffed, "And you think it will be Ryker? He'll be lucky if anyone ever sees past his queer mannerisms. He's so weird. Talking to himself, mumbling nonsense, constantly hanging back in the shadows alone and watching everyone."

Christy suddenly chimed in, "And he's a coward! He couldn't even beat that Midstar student last tournament. He was destroyed. But even before then, he's been an easy mark for others to kick around. He doesn't even try to fight back. He curls up and waits for them to get bored and leave. Why would anyone date someone so weak? Does he think his books will save him? Justin can snap him in half if he ever found out he was trying to move in on his girl."

"You two are so wrong about him. He's not weird. He's shy and unsure of himself."

The girls looked at each other, then back to Leen, and shrugged, "And who wants that in a possible mate?" The two girls then turned and walked away, leaving Leen with mixed feelings. She wanted to chase them down and continue fighting for her friend, but it felt futile, which left her feeling defeated.

After they had left, Leen's friend stepped forward. She'd been watching the whole confrontation with mild curiosity.

"So, Leen, what the heck was all that?"

"Pardon? I was trying to defend Cory."

"Oh, no, I got that. But the Leen I knew would never have attacked a person's looks or dating partner. Heck, you looked ready to throw a punch at times."

"There were a few times I wanted to smack them. I mean, how could they be so thoughtless towards his feelings?"

"I'm more concerned about you."

"What? Why? I'm fine." Leen liked at her friend curiously.

"The Leen I used to know would never have talked to someone like that, openly talking about her boyfriend's abusive past or admitting to wanting to strike someone. These are all things I'd expect from, say, Dark. Not you."

Leen paused for a moment and thought about what her friend had said. Had she changed and not seen it? She may have been a bit harsh, but it was in defense of her friend. "I don't know if I've changed that much. I mean, I'd say Dark has been the one to make the most changes."

"Oh, he certainly has changed. But where he's become more friendly and approachable, you've become more forward. I've heard you curse and would never do that before."

"Do you think we've both taken on some traits of each other?"

"In a manner of speaking, yes."

Leen smiled, "I can live with that."

Becky sighed as she entered her next classroom. The classroom was large and shared; the front half was set up like an average class, with desks facing the front of the room where a large whiteboard ran the length of the wall and the instructor's desk. The back half of the classroom was a range that had walls that could retract, opening the practice range further. This is where the students would practice various magic skills and primitive ranged weapons. Becky wasn't feeling in the mood to practice magic incantations. It was a skill she found she had little talent for. However, when it came to spears and archery, she was a master. Upon entering, Becky was immediately taken aback by a wave of intense heat and bright light she wasn't prepared for. She shielded her eyes and saw who was causing the commotion. Other students were huddled by the desks while one lone woman stood at the range, her long lavender hair blowing furiously in the wind while she stood legs apart and her arms outstretched. A white sigil was in front of her. The outer rings pulsated with a blue hue. From the center of the circular magic symbol, white and blue flame blew forth in a massive stream. Becky quickly glanced around and didn't see the instructor, and the other students were too afraid to approach the girl. Becky shook her head and strolled up to her.

"Leen, sweetie, what's wrong?" She asked her dear friend sweetly.

Leen growled, "That girl… she just aargh!" Leen roared again, and a large flame erupted from the magic sigil.

"Okay, which girl are we exactly mad at? I want to know so I too can be mad at her, and her… ugly face?"

"Cory's crush. She just, she just…."

"Okay, okay. Let's dispel the flames and talk about it before Mrs.

90

Sanmere gets here and flips her wig." Becky reached out and gently rested her hand on her friend's shoulder.

"It's fine, Becky. Did you not see the board? Free study day."

Becky looked back at the board. A message had been written in purple scribble, letting the students know they could study whatever they wished and that she would return later.

"Awesome. In that case, we will train together over there with bows."

Leen took a deep breath, and the sigil broke apart and dissolved into the air. The flames died with it. She looked around but said nothing as she was pulled over to the other side of the room, where racks of bows and arrows were stored.

"All right, so let's have it." Becky smiled, feeling a sense of some accomplishment.

"She had asked for Cory's notes—"

"Which, Cory being Cory, gave them to her with no questions asked," Becky said with a sigh.

"Yep. Then he tried to talk to her, and he was bashful and struggled. Then that bat-face Christy butted her face into the conversation, that gragfriggin katoosh—"

"Woah, woah, sweetie. Language. Where did you learn that kind of talk? Did Angel teach you that?" Becky stifled a laugh.

Leen blushed. "No, my father says it sometimes."

"That makes sense. I could definitely see that. So, then what happened?"

"She tried to act like she was defending Cory to her, but she called him by the wrong name. She thanked Cory for the notes, then left with her goop squad." Becky again tried not to laugh at her friend's choice of insults while she continued. "I tried to talk to him afterward, but he just wasn't there, emotionally. He came off as an empty shell when he was… being himself moments ago. That witch had sucked his spirit dry. Then I saw them making fun of him."

Becky's expression and tone immediately shifted to that of seriousness. "They were doing what?"

"Mocking him, making fun of his shyness and everything. Christy was pretending to be him, and they were laughing. Alisandra was laughing. So, I decided to confront them."

"Did you stuff them into the storage closet? Smash their face against the walls? Boot-stomp them into the tiles?" Becky asked, getting excited that she was about to hear something amazing.

"What? N-no. Gosh no. I just walked over and had a conversation with them." Leen said quickly, a little taken aback by her friend's suggested ideas.

"Oh…" Becky said, visibly less than enthusiastic by her response.

"… I brought up Christy's time with the groundskeeper and Justin's abusive behavior." Leen rolled her eyes. "She claims he's changed. But we know he hasn't. He still bullies people. And it's known that he beat his ex-girlfriend. It just infuriated me to see them acting like that."

Becky smiled and hugged her friend around her shoulders. "It'll be okay. Maybe one day, the scales will be removed from her eyes, and she'll see what a terrible person he truly is. Or she will stop pretending she doesn't see him for what he is. Come on, shoot with me. It's less destructive than burning the campus down."

Becky grabbed two bows off the rack and handed one to Leen. Then reached over and grabbed three arrows. Leen watched as her friend notched the first arrow and drew back the bowstring. Laying eyes on her target, Becky let loose her arrow, and with lightning speed and skill, she fired off the next two before the first had reached its intended mark. In seconds there were three thuds from the arrows hitting the wooden mannequin. Two were stuck in the head, and one square in the chest.

"It's amazing how you can do that but struggle with magic," teased Leen.

"Wish I knew why, but I just can't seem to get the hang of that. This," Becky fired off six shots in rapid succession, each one hitting the mannequin's chest, "has come so much more naturally to me. It took practice, but it paid off. However, magic still eludes me. Perhaps I wasn't born with an affinity for it. Fire is certainly my element, but unlike Cogeta, I wasn't born with the power to manifest it. Perhaps that's why he and I get along so merrily." She chuckled.

"Well, magic is more about remembering the words of power to draw out the energy in the world. I mean, there are various forms of magic. Some use incantations, and others use sigils and catalysts. But with practice, you can get skilled enough to recite the incantation in your mind and summon the power. I can with a few spells, mainly holy magic, pertaining to healing and protection. I use them so often when assisting at the cathedral and clinics. They are second nature to me, almost."

"Some of us just can't master it. Some of us can call forth the elements readily, like Cogeta with fire and Cory with lightning. We also had a few students like that back at my old school. One could form rocks, and another could also generate flames. Gifts from Odin and the Gods, I suppose. Not everyone is born with those abilities. Not that we aren't gifted enough as it is when compared to other races out there."

"That's true. Many can't fly using their spiritual energy or form that energy into beams of power. Can't read or" *Talk telepathically*. Leen smirked. "It's said in the scriptures that Odin designed us to be a race of warriors, that we would have no equal in combat. He made us with all the tools to achieve that goal." Leen watched as her close friend fired the bow once more and watched as the arrows sunk into the head of the mannequin's head. "Why didn't you sign up to be in the military? You would've been able to learn and train with the advanced weapons in the lower levels."

Becky shrugged. "I don't like being given orders. I'd rather focus on what I want to do and be what I want to be. As a woman, they gave us a choice. That was my choice. I can be a skilled warrior without becoming a soldier. You didn't sign up either."

"No. I feel my calling is to help people. I thought about joining as a medic but found I could do more by possibly joining the church or becoming a nurse. However, like you," Leen raised her bow for the first time since being handed the tool. She drew three arrows from a quiver and gracefully shot them in quick succession. Two arrows lodged in her mannequin's head, and the third went into the groin section. "I want to learn the skills needed to defend myself should the need arise."

Becky looked at where her friend's arrows had landed. "I would say you have that well covered." Leen smiles appreciatively at her best friend.

The day chugged on like a slow train, but at long last, it was over. The friends met up at the entrance as the last bell of the day died out. Cogeta had Becky in his arms, and Angel stood side-by-side with Leen. Cogeta was talking about his day, bragging that he was the greatest this school had ever had, to be graced with his presence as he came and went. His great boasting and over-enthusiastic self-indulging speeches were nothing new. Whether he genuinely believed the full extent of his hype wasn't always straightforward. Cogeta loved being in the limelight, always a showman. His boasting could be humorous, such as when he was mistaken for a male model.

He was new to the school and had just finished showering, but he somehow wandered from the locker room with only a towel around his waist and made his way across campus and into an art studies class where the teacher thought he was there to be the model. Not wanting to look a fool at the new school, he played along and dropped the towel. When the actual model arrived, he was sent away as he was no longer needed. Other times, it got him into trouble.

"I'm the best at sports, fighting, and women, ain't that right, baby?" He looked at Becky before whispering into her ear, then nibbling on her earlobe after the ending statement made her giggle. Following the playful nibbling, he placed a light kiss on her lips, it quickly turning passionate.

Leen smiled at the two lovers as she held onto Angel's arm.

Cogeta stopped kissing so that he could continue talking. "Anyway, I'm heading home. Got to train for next week. What about you three?"

"Well, I am going to the old man's shop and get to work, afterward probably train a bit myself," Angel replied while he rubbed Leen's hand.

"I am going with him to ensure he gets something to eat between the two. Otherwise, he won't be awake during his classes tomorrow," Leen smiled at Angel.

Cogeta laughed, "And what about you, Cory?"

"I'm going home, do tomorrow's homework, then perhaps read or write."

"What do you mean tomorrow's homework? What happened to tonight's?" asked Becky.

"I got most of tonight's finished during lunch, and what was left over, I did in the last class." He explained, "I try to keep a day ahead so I don't fall behind."

Cogeta looked at him with a raised eyebrow. "Dude, why the rush? I mean, all we have to do is live and die. So why push yourself to do today that can wait until tomorrow? You need to have fun! Tell you what, come over to my place and spar with me. Have to make sure you aren't slacking on your martial arts studies. After all, isn't that why your parents sent you to Utopia University to learn to defend yourself?" Cogeta smiled, putting up his fists and moving from side to side.

"That reminds me. Thanks, Cogeta. Cory, are you interested in participating this year?" asked Angel.

"Me, participate in the tournament between the two strongest schools of all Utopia? I don't know. I tried that before. I don't think I did so well last year. I tried my best, but I was beaten pretty badly." Cory lowered his head, feeling shame creep up on him.

"Whoa, whoa, whoa, back it up. As I recall, you made it to the top five of the list from this school. You gave everyone a hell of a match. You never gave up. The match ended because you were unconscious. The guy that beat you was a behemoth of a man, and he didn't leave unscathed. They were bleeding and limping." Cogeta stated with little exaggeration.

Cory cleared his throat just a bit, took a deep breath looking down at the ground, "That behemoth was a girl."

Cogeta's eyes just about popped out, "NO WAY! It had no…." His hands came to his chest, "You know! No, that couldn't have been a female. It looked more like a... Well, I will not say since there are ladies present. The point is, it didn't look female. I'd say it belonged on the Forgotten Isles."

The group laughed at Cogeta's exaggerations and gestures. When he stopped laughing, Angel spoke again, "Cory, you are a good fighter, one of this school's best. Trust me. Everyone was cheering for you when you took part last year. For the record, I've been re-watching the fights, and your bout lasted nearly as long as mine. It was close to thirty-five minutes. Should they allow weapons this year, we could use a good lancer on the team."

"I don't know, Angel. Hurting someone for sport isn't really my thing. I wouldn't want to let you down, "Cory said.

"Cory, you could only let me down if you didn't follow your heart. I respect the fact that you don't want to fight for the sake of entertainment, but if you never use the skills you've learned, they may leave you. You never know when you will need them, so it is best to keep them sharp and prepared. That is the point of these school competitions, after all." Angel spoke sincerely.

"What if I fall in the first match? Would that not disappoint you?" Cory questioned, looking solely at Angel.

Angel smirked, "Cory, I know if you fell in the first round, then you fell while giving it your all. That my friend wouldn't disappoint me, not in the least. I know you. You have the potential to do great things. I believe in you and want to help you see the strength within. We only hold these games to get the taste of battle because we never know when the need will arise. They help build confidence and awareness of ourselves."

"What about the instructor? What does he say?"

"He told me the choice was mine to make. I am the Captain. Therefore, I make the choices, and Cory, I want you on my team. What's the point of calling ourselves the Wolf Pack if we aren't seen fighting together?"

Cory smiled weakly, "All right, I am in. I don't know if I'll tell my folks, however. Sure, they sent me here to learn to defend myself, but I mainly came here for the library and other classes. It disappointed him that after all this time, I couldn't win the first fight he saw me in. Mom was worried about me too. She got distraught when she saw how badly I got hurt."

Angel nodded, "I understand. So don't tell them. That way, you don't make them worry either way. This is about you bettering yourself. They can't be out there helping you. This is your life, your journey. Besides, you got us beside you." Angel smiled. "We're family too."

Cory smiled and nodded.

"Great! With that, all settled. Welcome to the team, buddy." Cogeta broke in with a smile.

Angel patted Cory on his back. "Glad you agreed. This year I give you the honor of fighting Shaw. So train hard. You have one week."

"What? You got to be joking. Angel, that's... No way! No! I mean, it can't be me! That would be borderline suicide." Cory shouted, spinning around to face Angel.

Angel looked at him straight-faced momentarily before cracking a smile and then laughed, "I am only joking." There was a great sigh of relief from Cory as the others joined Angel in laughing while Cogeta continued patting Cory on his back.

"Buddy, we got a long way to go to work on your confidence." Cogeta smiled.

CHAPTER 5

FISTS AND IRON

Cory followed Becky and Cogeta into their home. It was a decent size home constructed out of hardwood. The inside was a maze of sliding paper doors with several hidden rooms. Cogeta's in-home dojo was furthest to the right, where he had led Cory. Around the room were racks of various weapons, weightlifting equipment, a hanging punching bag, and various practice dummies. Cogeta handed him an orange sparring outfit so they would move more freely and not ruin their school uniforms. After changing, Cogeta walked to a rack lined with different practice weapons.

"Angel said you would be the lancer, so we can start there. I know this isn't like the one you will use, but all well. Catch." Cogeta spoke as he pulled out two wooden staffs with a rubbery blade tip at one end and tossed one to Cory, who caught it in his hands.

With no warning, Cogeta swung the practice weapon down from over his head, but Cory brought his staff up in both hands to block. Pushing one end of the pole, Cory spun it around, smacking Cogeta on the back. He struck Cogeta three times before he could get to a safe distance.

"Why do you not enjoy fighting, Cory? You aren't bad at all."

Cory shrugged. "I guess it was my mom's doing. I don't like hurting people. My folks sent me to the University to have the best education, not just academically, … they wanted me to learn to defend myself. So, of course, I've studied and learned, but I wouldn't say I like fighting. As I said, I don't like hurting people."

"Ah, I see," Cogeta said while nodding his head. "But really, you don't have to like hurting others to be an accomplished warrior."

"I'm well aware. But that doesn't justify my participating in tournaments, showing off my abilities for fame and fortune. I am not that great, honestly. I'm constantly thinking about and reminded that I lost so quickly to a woman no less last year."

Cogeta reached out and placed his hand on his best friend's shoulder. "Don't let that bother you or hold you back. She was powerful, and you gave it your all. After the fight, she couldn't fight anymore either, she may have won, but she was still eliminated from the competition. That's still something. Your lack of faith in yourself is your biggest enemy. You say you aren't talented, but I see it, man."

"You and Angel can still beat me easily."

"Dude, you focus on your brain. We focus more on our muscles. And some people can still beat us. There is always going to be someone stronger. That's just the law of the universe. No matter what, there will always be someone stronger, faster, smarter, and hungrier than you are. That's part of the thrill of pursuing the warrior's path, to push yourself, to exceed your limits, and to go past them, to reach a level even beyond."

Cogeta's words warmed Cory's spirit. His conviction and passion were sincere, and they moved him. However, his spirit didn't burn with the same desire. "I don't think the warrior's path is the path set for me."

Cogeta laughed. "Less competition for me."

Cogeta leaped into the air, coming back down, jabbing his lance rapidly. Cory stood his ground, deflecting each attack with one end of the staff. When Cogeta landed, Cory quickly brought the bottom end of his weapon up, smacking Cogeta's chin.

"Agh! Dang it!" Cogeta stepped backward, rubbing his chin sorely,

"That hurt!" He started to laugh. Cogeta took his lance into both hands. Holding it out, he snapped it over his knee. Spinning the two halves around his hands, "All right, man, let's go!" He smirked before charging Cory once more. Cory took a defensive stance and blocked Cogeta's barrage of attacks.

"You are a defensive player, perhaps too defensive," Cogeta said.

"The best offense is a good defense." Cory retorted with a grin.

"I think you have that backward."

"Nope!" Cory said excitedly as he brought the pole up, blocking each attack, then slid inward, entrapping Cogeta's arms as he spun behind him, quickly flipping Cogeta over onto the back of his head.

"You are all offense. It allows me to see what move you will make so I can counter it." Cory stated.

"Counter this!" Cogeta somersaulted up onto his feet. He leaped into the air and came down, spinning with his feet together at an angle toward the floor. Sliding along the floorboards, he launched himself upward, using his hands, towards Cory's chest.

It all happened so quickly that Cory could barely move his staff into a position to protect himself. However, Cogeta's feet snapped the pole in half as they found their intended target. The force of the blow caused Cory to gasp for air as he was thrown back against the wall. Cogeta landed on his feet and moved about in a dancing manner as Cory returned to a defensive stance.

"And that, my friend, is how you play the "Tootsie Roll,"" Cogeta sang before swinging his leg around, attempting to kick Cory in the face, but Cory's arm blocked it.

Cory spat out some blood from the blow to his chest. "Nice move. Not sure about the name, though." He quickly rolled out of the way as a wave of fire shot by him.

"Who are you, my creative agent? You need to give your big moves names. Everyone does it. It adds to the excitement, call out whatever feels natural. Now less talk, more fighting," smirked Cogeta. "Come on, man. We need to get you ready for battle. I know you got what it takes now; SHOW ME! HELL'S GUARDIAN!" Cogeta's body was engulfed in flames as he approached Cory at top speed. Cory quickly formed an energy barrier around him before Cogeta could get a hit.

"Cory, stop being defensive and come at me offensively. Be like a rabid wolf in these fights. Your opponents will not be as kind. MidStar trains their students to be as ruthless as possible, so you need to be just as hungry," yelled Cogeta, not letting up his attacks, each pushing Cory further and further toward the wall.

"So, you want me to be offensive, huh? How is this, then? Thunder Slasher!" While maintaining the shield, he raised his arms to his head in an "X" and slashed the air downward. As he did so, two arcs of electricity shot forth in the same "X" pattern his arms had been in. The attack found its mark perfectly, shredding Cogeta's shirt and searing the skin beneath as he was thrown back.

"Now that is more like it!" Cogeta shouted, standing up, but was slammed against the wall by Cory's elbow as it bore into his chest with electrical sparks coursing around it. Cogeta could not hold back the blood as he coughed for air. Cory jumped back to give him some room. Cogeta wiped the remaining blood from his chin.

"Much better. See, I knew there was a fighter in you." Cogeta laughed as he pushed off the wall and charged Cory. Cory did the same, sparks of electricity arcing around his body. Blow after heavy blow found its mark on both fighters.

Cory was doing precisely as Cogeta had asked, staying aggressive. His fighting style had changed entirely from his passive nature to the animal, the wolf that he had wanted him to become. Staying close, he kept Cogeta from using many of his flashier moves, each strike sharp like a fang, with bursts and arcs of electricity passing from his fists into Cogeta as an added effect.

That's it, Cory! Let me see that look in your eyes. Yes, there it is. That hunger, that desire, that's what I wanted to see. Let the animal out, and show everyone you are not one to glance over. Become the hunter, not someone's prey. You must have that fire when you enter the ring, or you will lose. Some call it the killer intent when the fighter focuses on nothing but winning. Shaw has undoubtedly enforced it into his fighter's minds that they must go all the way to win. We saw that last year and it stands to reason that we'll see the same ferocity from his warriors again this year. We need to be ready.

Cogeta took hit after hit, watching Cory's movements and observing his breathing. All the training he had gone through since childhood showed through to Cogeta. He couldn't help being impressed. He knew as Angel did that an animal lay dormant, but to see it in action. It made him proud. All that time, training, and sparring for fun like this before had indeed paid off. He holds it all in well, especially dealing with those pricks at school.

"AHA! Opening!" Cogeta shouted as Cory came in with a right.

Cory lost focus for a split moment as he glanced down. Cogeta's knee collided with the bottom of his chin, snapping his bottom jaw and lifting him from his feet. In one moment, Cory was going up; the next, he was flying back and crashed against the wall with a crushing pain in his chest. Replaying the scene in his mind, his friend lifted his knee to hit his chin to send him airward but then kicked out with his foot to send him flying back. Cory got back to his feet. However, as he regained his balance, the back of his head was suddenly grabbed and driven downward. He watched in disbelief as he saw Cogeta's knee racing upward to meet him.

Again and again, his hard knee was smashed against Cory's face. After six blows in rapid succession, Cogeta spun Cory's wobbling body around him. As Cory stumbled to stay on his feet, a sharp pain shot through him as Cogeta whipped his elbow around and connected it with the back of Cory's neck. Again, Cogeta attacked rapidly, landing multiple blows in the same spot before Cory could get out of his range. He at last did, but not on his own. Cogeta had spun around and delivered a crushing kick to his back that sent him flying forward.

Cory landed face-first onto the mat. His body racked with pain. He could hear Cogeta coming closer. *To finish me off? No. I'm not finished yet. I have to show him I can win this year. I won't let my friends down again!*

Cogeta was about to ask if Cory was all right since he hadn't seen his friend move, but suddenly Cory raised his hands. In the next moment, Cogeta saw him disappear from the mat and spin through the air toward him. His body was wrapped in crackling electricity. Like a spear, he flew effortlessly through the air and found his target, sending Cogeta back. As soon as his feet touched the ground, Cory dashed forward, his elbow raised. Cogeta hadn't even touched the ground when he found himself hunched over Cory's shoulder as his elbow drove into his stomach. Then his fist snapped up, forcing Cogeta to straighten up, only to be struck again, this time by both Cory's fists as they flew outward after being drawn in briefly.

Cogeta crashed against the wall in the same spot he had sent his friend moments earlier. He was having trouble getting his breath from the hits his lungs had endured. As he looked up, he saw Cory breathing heavily, hunched over with his hands on his knees. Cogeta held out his hand for help. Cory grasped it and helped heave his friend to his feet, nearly falling himself, but Cogeta caught him.

"Now, of course, you shouldn't be so willing to help your opponent in the tournament. They will—"

"Take advantage. I know. I hoped that you would not be a jerk and try something."

"Nah, I'm not that mean. You did a great job. Now I hope to see this in the tournament."

"I'm going to do my best, I promise."

"I know you will." Cogeta put his arm around Cory's shoulder to hold himself up. Cory did the same in return. "Sorry if I went too far."

"It's all right. You didn't seem to hold back, which is what I needed. It still hurts like hell, though."

"Yeah, the same goes for you. I'm looking forward to seeing you fight in the ring again. I mean that."

"I just hope it is not against that woman again."

Cogeta started laughing. Cory narrowed his gaze and pushed Cogeta away. He kept laughing, holding his sides as he hit the floor.

"Oh man, it hurts, but I needed that," he continued laughing. "How about," he took a deep breath to calm himself, "one more round?"

Cory nodded and helped his friend to his feet once more. The two took a few steps away from each other and got set. Suddenly, fiery, crackling auras swarmed around them. This was known by many names; spirit energy, fighting presence. Some even called it one's inner life force. Each person's power was unique, and with training, one could learn to sense, track, and even hide from others. Everyone was born with spirit energy, but it rarely grew or became stronger without training. At that exact moment, the two charged each other. They had their fists in the air like vipers preparing to strike. Their eyes were burning for the fight. Their fiery blood surging through their veins. At that moment, their minds were clear.

"STOP!"

Both men stopped midair and looked at the open doorway, where Becky stood with her arms crossed.

"I have dinner ready," she said.

"Ah, sweet. Thanks, honey. Has it been that long already? Dang, time sure flies." Cogeta put his feet on the ground and dashed over to her, lifting and spinning her around several times before kissing her.

"Yeah, it sure does." She laughed. "Now down, boy. Come on. It's on the table. Cory, I already sent word to your family that you were eating here," stated Becky before Cory could refuse the dinner invitation.

"Do I even have a choice?" He smiled as he looked at Becky.

"Not anymore, you don't." She smiled back, sticking her tongue out.

"Hey, hey, that's mine, not his." Cogeta whimpered before kissing her once more.

Becky stepped back and pummeled his head. "Stop it! Cogeta, you goof." She turned on her heel and walked back towards the kitchen, leaving Cogeta and Cory laughing.

"Man, I love that woman. With every bit of my heart, mind, and soul, those three things will ensure a great relationship. If the two of you share those, man, nothing will come between you. Let all Hela's and Loki's armies try. Now getting back to the matter at hand," Cogeta disappeared and reappeared beside Cory, grabbing his arm and sweeping his feet out from under him, sending Cory to the ground. "We have to be even before we leave this room." He came down with his fist, but Cory grabbed it before it hit him. Holding on to his arm, Cory rolled over, taking Cogeta with him. The two rolled around, neither getting the upper hand until they finally broke apart.

"All right, I guess you are ready. Let's go before we anger her. She is scary when she is angry. Not even the mighty Thor would tangle with her when she's fired up. I got the scars to prove it." Cogeta laughed as he put his arm around Cory's shoulder. As they walked out of the sparring room, he bopped Cory on the back of the head. "Now we are even." He smiled as he gave Cory a noogie before walking to the kitchen.

The clanging of metal upon metal grew ever closer with each step Angel took as he neared Leen's father's shop. The smell of melting metal, smoke, coal, and sweat filled his lungs as it filled the air around the place. It was a good size shop made of stone, as most businesses along the market square were prone to be. The front had two large doors that were left open during the day. It was built alongside a grassy hill, where a small array of flowers grew. Thick wooden beams held the red clay roof up.

"Have a good day at work, dear," Leen said, kissing him on his cheek.

"Oh, is your dad taking a day off?" Angel smiled as they walked towards the entrance of the shop.

"No," Leen replied, looking at him curiously.

"Then what will be so good about it?" Angel asked. Leen's facial expression showed he had crossed the line. "I am only kidding," he said, gently hugging her while trying to sound convincing.

"You are late, Everlast!" Her father's voice boomed from inside the shop, "Release my daughter and get in here, change, and then get to work. These orders will not make themselves."

"See, I told you, he hates me." Angel grinned, looking down at Leen. She shook her head.

"I'll be back later to bring your lunch. I have to go to the monastery. I promised the priestess I would come and help today." Leen said as she felt that he might have forgotten.

"I remember. Have a good day, sweetheart." He kissed her once more before walking into the smoldering hot shop. Feeling the heat from the glowing furnace, Angel sighed and stepped through the entryway, removing his top shirt and putting on the smock with a few tools in loops.

"Must you kiss her in front of me? You know I don't like seeing that. My lovely daughter kissing your scuzzy lips." grumbled her father, looking up at Angel shortly.

"Then look away," retorted Angel.

"If I did, your hands might wander someplace they should not be."

"I am not like that," Angel replied. After reviewing a work order, he grabbed a piece of iron, shoved it into the furnace, and slowly turned it.

"Most men your age are. We must make fifteen swords, twelve axes, thirty shields, and ten lances. So don't slow down," His eyes returned to the job.

"Yes, sir," Angel answered with respect.

Angel was a hard worker. Leen's father knew this, but he was also aware of the rumors surrounding him. He was protective of his daughters since he felt that was all he had left in the world to live for. Seeing Leen fall for such a man troubled him, yet he knew his daughter to be an expert judge of character. She had repeatedly argued his virtues and denounced the rumors. However, the rumors persisted and grew, so he didn't ignore them. As any good father wouldn't, he told himself that there might be a grain of truth to each story.

Soon the shop was alive with the sounds of their hammers clanging in unison as they worked. Large billows of black smoke puffed through the chimney as they stoked the fires with the metal, constantly filling it with coal so the fires remained hot.

As the day lagged, customers came asking for their orders. Leen's father would greet them and ask them to wait a moment. He would then walk into the back room, which led to a long underground tunnel where he stored all orders and randomly created works. The tunnel went all the way to the basement of his house. He had dug this tunnel to get to and from work faster. For security reasons, traps became set once the store's entrance and the door in Angel's room were locked.

Throughout the day, couriers also arrived and dropped off stockpiles of materials that the old man had purchased that morning. Large bins separated each material by name. Everything had its place, and it was rare that they ever got empty. When a new customer would come in asking for an order, Vox graciously took it down and asked them to return in a week, a month, or longer, depending on what was requested. He would then return to his work. He rarely let Angel handle the customers unless it was delivering an order.

For the most part, Vox liked to do things himself. From start to finish, he would tend to custom orders; rarely letting anyone assist. This way, he could, without a doubt, guarantee his work. However, as word spread of his talent and quality of work, he was getting overwhelmed by the sheer number of orders. Therefore, when Leen brought Angel home for the first time and tried to convince him he was a good man, contrary to the stories he had heard, a light flickered on in his head. If the boy agreed to straighten himself up and work for him, he could keep an eye on him and get extra help in the shop. It was sheer brilliance to him, killing multiple pigeontails with one shot. Of course, he didn't expect the boy to learn so rapidly. For someone with no prior learning, he mastered the art well. In a few more years, he could rival me. Bringing him on as an apprentice was one of the best ideas I have ever had. He patted himself on the back.

Angel was focused on his task that he didn't even notice when Arieta walked into the shop. He only looked up when he heard the old man call her name.

"What brings you here, sweetie?"

"Hey, Dad. Just on my way home. You got many orders to fill?"

"Quite a few, but I can make time. What do you need, dear?"

"I, um... could I borrow, Angel?" She asked shyly, nervously biting her lower lip.

Her father looked over his shoulder at Angel, who quickly looked back down at his work.

Why the hell does she want me? He thought to himself.

"Angel! Come over here."

With a heavy sigh, Angel prepared himself. He quenched the blade he was working on in a bucket of water beside him and set his hammer into his apron. He then walked over.

"Yes, sir?"

"Arieta would like to see you." The older man said.

"Privately, if that's okay," she softly spoke up.

"Privately?" Her father looked over at her.

She nodded, "But I won't keep him long."

"... Fine. Make it quick. I can't have him skipping out on work. He has orders to fulfill."

Angel followed Arieta out of the shop and around the corner. They stood between a leather smith and a jeweler, a few shops from her father's. She looked upset about something. He surmised it was probably the confrontation earlier.

"Arieta, look if this is about earlier—"

"Shut up!... And listen." She snapped.

Taken back by her outburst, Angel nodded and leaned against the side of the building, ready to listen to what she had to say.

"About earlier today. I don't want you telling Leen about it. I don't want you telling anyone about it."

"Why not? How often has that happened to you?"

"This was the first time. But I've gotten notes on behalf of others to get them on my sister's good side. To leave you for them. I always threw them away. I mean, it is cowardly to go through me to get to her."

"Yeah, but some are too shy and insecure to approach her."

"Yeah, well, I don't see her dating any of them. Most are like the one you met today, jerks. But I don't want her to know because I don't need you or anyone else babysitting me. Treating me like, I can't take care of myself! What you did today, do you have any idea how that makes me feel?"

"I just stepped in 'cause they were about to hurt you. I would've done the same no matter who it was. Sorry, you were in that situation" Angel felt her push him, and her fist smacked down on his shoulder. He stood there, stunned by her actions.

"I don't want you to feel sorry for me! I don't want you to protect me. I don't... I... I froze up." Arieta's words were hard to get out. Her eyes burned as they filled with tears. She hadn't cried since her mother died. She tried so hard never to cry again, and now, all those times, seemed to be ganging up on her. "All the training I've gone through at school, all the classes I've taken, and I freeze up when it matters. I hit the guy, and it was as if he didn't even feel it. I remember playing with Cory and Cogeta; when I got rough, they seemed hurt. I enjoyed feeling strong. Now I realize they were playing along and acting."

Angel slid down the wall and got eye level with her. He put his hands on her shoulders, relieved she didn't fight his touch.

"I don't like being weak, Angel. I want to be strong enough to care for myself and protect my sister. She is the closest thing to a mother I have now, and I will not let you or anyone else take her from me."

"Stop, Arieta. I will not take Leen away from you. She loves you just as much as she ever has. That's never going to change. Not by anyone's hand, especially not by mine. I love your sister. I love her very much and will keep her safe as long as I breathe. Again, I will not take her from you. I won't impede your bond with her. As for what happened today, every fighter, every warrior in history, has that moment where they freeze up."

"Even you?"

"I've had it happen before, yeah. I've not won every battle I've been in. But every loss I suffered added fuel to my desire to get stronger. It is pushing me to train as hard as I do. It isn't easy, Arieta. Not easy at all."

"But you make it look easy."

Angel smiled, a little flattered. "I've been fighting for most of my life. To survive in the wild, I had to. I had no direction until I met your sister and fell for her. I've only gotten stronger cause of her. She is the reason I want to get stronger. Part of it, at least. The other half is that I want to improve myself. The stronger I am, the more I can do. The stronger I am, the more intimidating I am, then I'll be able to win more fights without fighting. In that respect, you and I are alike. But there is something you need to realize now. When you win, it doesn't get any easier. It gets harder. As soon as you defeat an opponent, you are then the target. Not only are you fighting your demons, the people you wish to beat, but now everyone who wanted to defeat that guy that you just did wants to defeat you, to prove themselves. It's an endless cycle and not an easy one. There is always going to be someone stronger."

"Do you think I could get stronger and one day be able to protect Leen?"

"Oh yeah. Without a doubt. If you want, I could start training you personally if you—"

"No! I mean, no, thank you. I don't want you to do that."

"Umm okay, well perhaps Cogeta—"

"No." Arieta shook her head.

"Well, I'm sure Cory would make an excellent teacher—"

"Ummm, no, that's okay." She wrinkled her nose and furrowed her brow as she shook her head. "I'll learn on my own. My own path."

"Very well. Don't worry; I won't tell your sister about today." Angel said.

"Nor of this conversation. No one." Arieta insisted.

"All right." Angel agreed.

"Promise?"

"I promise. You have my word." Angel nodded reassuringly.

"Thank you. You really aren't so bad, are you?"

"Only to those who deserve it."

Arieta smirked. She felt his thumbs against her cheeks and wiped her tears away. Her heart was filled with multiple emotions from the day that his thoughtful gesture made her feel something more for him. At that instant, she thought she saw what her sister did. Swept up in her emotions, she fell deeper into them and, in reality, let herself fall toward him. Her eyes were half closed, her lips slightly puckered. Just when she thought she was about to give him her first kiss, she felt his finger holding her lips back. She opened up her eyes and saw him smiling warmly at her.

"Save this for someone dearer to you," he whispered.

She returned his smile, moved around his finger, and kissed him on his cheek.

"You passed," she whispered.

"I passed?"

"Mmhmm. A real sleaze would've taken his chance to kiss both the Puraday sisters. Do you find me as attractive as my sister?" She asked while slipping her arms around his neck.

"Yes, you are," Angel replied, holding her by her waist. He was sitting with his knees up, and her sitting partly in his lap.

For a while, they sat that way. Angel knew that today had been a trying day for her and that she needed this quiet moment to relax and put things in order so he didn't rush her. When she moved closer to rest her head on his shoulder, he put his arms around her, rubbed her back, and caressed the back of her head. After a few more minutes, she stretched her arms and nuzzled into his neck as a small kitten would.

"My sister chose wisely. She's lucky."

"You will find your prince in time."

"Yeah, but I like you. You are good to her."

"Thank you. I am glad to get some approval."

She sat up and used his knees for support to stand up. Spinning around, she reached out and helped him up.

"Thank you for putting up with my emotional self." She smiled, returning to her usual demeanor.

"Anytime, I'm more than happy to help you, Arieta, with these matters or otherwise."

She threw her bag over her back. "Well, thank you. I am going to head home and get started on my homework. Tell Dad I said I love him, and, Angel, for now, I leave protecting my sister in your hands until I'm strong enough to do it myself."

Angel smirked. "Very well. Until that day, I will do my best. Will you also protect me?"

"Pfft, you are on your own." She stuck out her tongue, smiled, and ran out of the alley to the right.

Angel laughed to himself. He found that her father had finished the blade he had left behind upon his return. When he asked what took so long, Angel told him she needed help with some friend of hers. When he asked why she didn't just come to him, Angel shrugged and suggested that perhaps her friend needed a younger point of view than he could offer. Vox then told Angel to shut up and get back to work.

Hours passed without the two men noticing, as they had been hard at work. The sound of constant pounding hammers on steel filled the street in front of the shop. With all the heat, waves of sweat poured down their faces. After hardening the blade, Angel let it cool down, then put a tag on the tang and set it with the others he had finished to start anew.

"Wow! Don't you two look sexy? Two hard-working men, soaked in sweat." From the doorway came the gentle voice of Leen, smiling and holding a basket in front of her.

"Thank you, darling, and here I thought time had stolen my good looks."

"You weren't wrong," Angel smirked.

"Didn't ask for your opinion. Continue working." Leen's father growled before turning his attention back to his daughter, his voice becoming softer and kinder once more, "Is that our lunch?" her dad grinned as he set the axe blade he was working on into the water to cool, ignoring Angel as he made expressions on his face as he worked on.

"Yes. It isn't anything special, just a couple of sandwiches for each of you and a bottle of your preferred beverage." Leen proudly said, refraining from speaking about the two fighting. She had taken the time to make them their favorite sandwiches, which were very simple. They consisted of the unique grain bread her mother taught her to make, a variety of meats, and a few added condiments for added flavor.

"Anything prepared by you is special, love," Angel said, smiling at her.

"I was going to say that, just instead of love, it would have been daughter," grumbled the old man. Angel laughed softly, having been able to get his line in before her dad could.

Leen walked over to her dad, who was wiping his hands and head on a wet rag and handed him his lunch, prepared in a small bag with his drink.

"Thank you, dear. How is your sister?" Her father asked while opening his lunch sack.

"She is all right, at home doing her homework. She is looking forward to next week's big day." Leen answered her father. Smiling, she kissed her father on the cheek.

"Oh yes, the tournament. Angel, are you competing again this year?" Leen's father asked as he sat down to eat and make light conversation with Angel, for nothing else but to please his daughter.

"Yes, sir, I am. I am the captain of the school's team," Angel replied, "And I have seen much improvement in them since last year. I believe we have a good chance at the title this year, sir."

Leen walked over, dabbed Angel's rag into the water, and wiped his brow and around his neck before handing him his lunch. Leen beamed with pride as she listened to her two favorite men talk. She could see how they were a lot alike, though they would never see it her way.

"I have yet to find any genuine enjoyment in watching the tournaments. It is just two people pounding the crap out of each other until someone surrenders or cannot continue. Granted, we get stronger after every battle, but must we fight amongst ourselves?" The father went on as he ate, "When you first beat Shaw, did you ever stop and think about how many people you were going to piss off by winning? You were a nobody and still are by my standards." His comments stung Angel like burning needles.

Leen could see Angel's anger building as her father continued to put him down. She slowly wiped more sweat from his face. As she did so, she turned his head towards her. She smiled at him, and Angel could not help but smile back. Instantly, the blood inside him that had begun to boil cooled as rapidly as the hot steel he plunged into the bucket of water, and his body relaxed as he gazed into her eyes.

"Sir, I don't care if they hate me. I only need one fan, and that is your daughter. Frankly, I do not give a flip if you like me or not. The point is that I am not going anywhere. So get used to it." Angel took a swig from the bottle of cold water before pulling another iron rod out of the furnace and began clanging away again. Leen walked over to her dad with a sad expression. Her dad only looked at her and gave her a reassuring smile. She quickly caught on and smiled back.

"All right, boys, I hope you enjoyed your lunch. I am headed home. Dad, don't overwork him tonight. He needs to prepare for the tournament." Leen said as she got ready to leave the shop.

"Leen, tournaments aren't everything. One cannot live from fight to fight. He must have a skill. I am doing him a favor, taking him under my wing, sort of speaking. I want him to know a skill that he can fall back on and support himself and others if need be."

"He is right, Leen. Don't worry; I will find time to train." Angel smiled and waved goodbye to her. She knew her father was right in what he said, but he wasn't about to say that out loud and give the old man room to gloat.

After Leen had left, Angel glanced over at her father, and for a moment, they made eye contact, which seemed to be as though they were locked in time as the tension grew. Then, without a word between them, they returned to work. Angel took great care in his work, being sure not to make a mistake because of his emotions, as he had learned long ago that one mistake of the slightest, and you would have to start completely over.

At last, the old man was stopping for the day. He ordered Angel to close the shop as he walked out with a wet towel draped over his head. After putting out the furnace fires, he checked each newly created item with the customer's name to ensure they matched the order. He then covered them up and locked them away nearby, where the tools were stored inside the tunnel. After all that, he could finally close and lock the large doors. First were the metal locks, and then he lifted a massive heavy beam that he set across the door. He took one last look around before he headed home through the tunnel as Vox had done.

The tunnel served as a quick means from the house to the shop and a fantastic showcase of old and new weapons stacked along the walls. Leen's dad did terrific work. He had gotten into blacksmithing after serving his time in the military. He had been doing it for ages now; hard to count how many years they all seemed to blend into one another, especially since his wife passed away. Angel couldn't help but marvel at all the weapons that hung and lay along the stone walls. Each one was more beautiful than the last, as if each had a story behind it. Angel, at last, came to a small rickety door, which would take him to his poor living quarters.

He walked in, throwing off the sweaty shirt he had put back on as he closed the shop before shutting and locking the door. He couldn't see the security system Leen's dad had in the tunnel, but he could hear it click a moment after the door was locked. Leaping to one of the large beams running along the ceiling, he began doing pull-ups, first with both arms, then periodically with one arm at a time. He needed to be in perfect condition if he was going to face Shaw. Last year, Shaw almost had him beat. If Angel had been a millisecond slower, Shaw would have won.

Since that first upset, Angel had had a target on his head. Grown men and kids would walk up to him and ask him for the right to challenge to test their skills. The polite ones would, at least. A few came close to matching Shaw's skill, but none made Angel feel as he had when he and Shaw had fought. Not even when Cogeta and Angel had fought for the first time made him feel the same way. That was back when Angel was still the new kid on campus and scoffed when he overheard Cogeta proclaim himself, as he still does, "The Greatest." Thinking back on that moment and realizing that was how the two became friends, Angel laughed. That fight got him onto the tournament team.

The instructor had seen the fight. He was so impressed that he had offered him a spot on the school's battle team. Angel took it. He then met Cory and helped him out of his jam. The three somehow became friends. He didn't know how it happened. *Probably Cogeta's fault.* Angel laughed to himself. *It was definitely his fault. He wouldn't stop pestering me after I beat him. Cory, I became like a guardian of or something. He started following Cogeta and me around. People got the impression that we were a group, and it just happened, I suppose. Then Cogeta met Becky, and she joined us. Funny how things happen. I went from being a loner to having real friends by my side. Literally by my side. I can still remember the day I picked a fight with a group of guys who were acting tough, and just before I jumped in to take them all, there was Cogeta on my right and Cory on my left. That was the day I learned Cory knew how to fight. He doesn't like to. He only stepped in because Cogeta talked him into it. The Wolf Pack was really born then. After teaching the punks who were actually tough, and I admitted that I may have had a hand in starting it, they were upset at first, but then we just started laughing.*

Not long after, he finally gave in to Leen's perseverance. He and Leen kept their courtship secret, except Cory, Cogeta, and Becky knew. It wasn't till years later that word got out that they were dating. Time seemed to fly by when he was with her and his new friends. Her father, who wasn't entirely pleased to hear the news, had to tell everyone who came calling for her, and that's when Shaw learned of Angel. That spark started their rivalry, and then came the day of Angel's first tournament. He shocked everyone by winning it, taking the longest-running champion, Shaw, off his high horse. That's when the fire turned into an inferno.

Angel was working out strenuously and so focused that he never heard Leen come down the stairs to check on him. She watched intently as she sat on the stairs watching him, now fighting imaginary opponents with great speed and agility. Angel's muscles were powerful, and one could see them tense with each movement. She couldn't help but smirk as she thought to herself how much she enjoyed just tracing the lines of his muscles with her fingers.

"Look out behind you," she yelled, pointing. Angel glanced up at her, smiling as he ducked down and swung around as though to trip up the imaginary attacker.

"To your right, look out," she yelled again as Angel once more dodged the impending attack and countered.

"Oh no, Angel, the entire coliseum is getting into it, and they all want to claim the prize for themselves." Leen smiled as she watched Angel move in a blur of movement. Sweat flew off his fists as he blocked, then countered each imaginary foe.

"Oooo, and Shaw gets in a low blow," she teased, then began giggling as Angel pretended to have been brutally hit in his groin, slowly fell to his knees, and then toppled over. Leen ran to his side and pulled his head into her lap.

"Oh no, Angel, please don't go, please. Don't die, my love. It's only a flesh wound," she said, pretending to cry.

"Leen, before I go, there is something I want to tell you…." Angel said, acting as though it was hard to speak.

"Yes, my love, I am here. Tell me." Leen whispered.

"It's your dad…" Angel said in his regular voice, looking upward towards the stairs.

"What do you mean, my dad? What about him? Why are you thinking of him in your final moments?" She looked up the stairs as Angel was doing to understand what he meant, and there, at the top, looking down at them, was none other than her father. His arms crossed his chest, and he slowly tapped his foot. "Oooh. Hi, Dad."

"It's bedtime… now." He said in his rough voice.

Angel smiled and sat up, "Good night, dear, thank you for your help," he said before kissing Leen on the cheek. She smiled and nodded before putting her head down and walking up the stairs.

"Night, old man," Angel yelled before the door slammed shut. Angel softly laughed while shaking his head. He grabbed a towel and a pair of black sweats, went upstairs to shower, and changed into his sleeping attire. Once he finished, he grabbed a tray marked as his dinner from the fridge. He smirked at the little hearts she had put on either side of his name. After finishing everything, he put the tray into the sink, returned to his dusty room, and got into bed. Exhausted, sleep came quickly.

During the night, someone crawling into bed next to him awoke him. He gently placed his arm around the warm form and whispered, "Your dad is going to kill me. You know that." The reply was a little giggle, then Leen rolled over and kissed him gently.

"No, he won't," she smiled. "I wouldn't let him take you away."

"Is Arieta going to be joining us again tonight?" Angel whispered.

"No, I have already sung her to sleep. She seemed upset about something, but she wouldn't tell me," Leen said while snuggling up to Angel.

"Ah, okay. Well, I'm sure she will when she feels ready."

"Dad told me she came to the shop a few hours before I had and asked to speak to you. He said the conversation lasted for over twenty minutes by his count."

"Well, I am as pleased as you are that your father can still count and tell time."

"Angel. Did she speak with you?" Leen's tone was more severe than before, but he could hear the concern in her words.

"Yes, she did. But she asked that I keep it between us. I am positive she will tell you when she feels ready, but I will not betray her trust."

"So you two are... bonding?"

"Yeah, you could call it that."

"So, you two are bonding by keeping secrets from Dad and me?"

"Got to start somewhere."

She playfully smacked his chest. "Stop being mean. I wish you two wouldn't keep secrets. At least from me. Should I be worried? Can you tell me that much?"

"You have nothing to worry about, and I think it is safe to say that she loves you very much. Good night Leen," He gently gave her lips a small peck, followed by a passionate kiss of lovers with arms entwined.

"Mmm... Good night, Angel." She murmured as she snuggled closer to him, and soon they were both off to the land of dreams.

CHAPTER 6

ABSORB THE SOUNDS OF THE COLISEUM

The rest of the week passed quickly, and all the contestants had been preparing hard for the upcoming tournament. The Wolf Pack had been training extra hard. They would leave their homes early in the morning, before the sun broke the horizon, and meet in a wide-open field. There they exercised to wake up and prepare their bodies before they sparred with each other like rabid wolves. As the day drew closer, it became common to see the three walking into school with cuts and bruises, heading to the locker rooms to clean up before class. At last, the day they had come. The day that all eyes would be watching. It was the day when the title of "Intercontinental Martial Academics Champion" would be awarded to the victor. The day that would see if last year was a fluke or if the underwolf could once again topple the prince of gold.

Shops, schools, and many other businesses were closed for this event. People crowded the streets. They came from all over the world and tried to get in quickly and get a good seat inside the coliseum. They paid thirty silver coins or lunars at the entrance. The currency system was simple. So many of one type of coin equaled another. Copper lunars would equal a one-hundred-dollar value on Earth, one silver lunar would equal a thousand lunars, and gold lunars were worth a thousand silver, but the white lunar was the hardest to earn. They would equal a thousand gold lunars. So popular was the tournament of schools that people would save up several wages to enjoy the event in person.

The Utopian ancestors carved the coliseum from the giant mountain centuries ago and named it "Spartaliseum." The coliseum had a long oval shape. Hanging from its ceiling were dozens of big screens pointed so that everyone could see the action in the ring. It could sit three hundred thousand people inside without strain. Seating areas were carved out as half-circled booths with a table in the center. The booths could sit ten comfortably with plenty of elbow room. Waiters and waitresses were constantly going through aisle ways serving meals and making sure glasses were not empty. There were four massive restrooms for each gender in either direction. People entered from the south, and as they entered the mouth of the mountain, they were flanked on either side by offices that had also been carved directly out of the mountain for paying and placing bets on the tournament's fighters, as well as shops for souvenirs.

The group of friends slowly made their way into view of the coliseum, and all around them were people dressed in their best. Tuxedoes and dresses of different colors and designs were everywhere. Dressing up was optional, but tournaments gave one other reason for Utopians to look their best. Some might think of it as one way of showing they were no longer the savages they had been many years ago, back when their race was still young—the dark ages, as they were now referred to. However, too many, it was simply enjoyable to do from time to time.

"This place never stops to amaze me," whispered Leen as she and the rest of the group entered the shadow of the Coliseum. Its grand entryway had massive statues of heroes and gods that loomed over the crowd while welcoming them into the hallowed halls.

On this day, Leen wore another of her saterous dresses. It was white with spaghetti straps tied around her neck and flowing down her ankles. A snowflake pattern ran along the hemline. On her feet, she wore white high heels with a single gold snowflake decorating the toe. She had tiny beads in her hair and a few bangs braided. The earrings she wore had three small black and white feathers hanging down. Around her neck, she wore a multi-tiered crystal necklace, an heirloom from her great-grandmother. Her wrists were adorned with ornate gold bracelets with a string of white pearls attached running down and around her forefinger and back up. She even had her nails done specially for today.

"I agree. It's truly a wonder to behold. That it was completed in ten years is amazing." Cory added as he stared up at the massive statues. The incredible attention to detail taken by the artisans was awe-inspiring. He could never tire of admiring them, even if he felt out of place standing before them.

He had come dressed in a simple light blue collared t-shirt, black jeans, and his favorite black leather boots. Over his shoulder hung a red locker bag that contained his fighting attire that he would change into later.

"I could have done it in five," Cogeta jokingly boasted. "Come on, man, this way. We, participants, have a special entrance, remember? It beats fighting the crowd who want autographs and taking pictures of the greatest fighter since… oh wait. There has been none greater than me. Wish me luck, honey." He smiled over at Becky.

Cogeta wore the least of everyone. He came pre-dressed in his fighting gear, a pair of orange silk shorts, with the words "The Greatest" printed in big blue letters along the waistband. His hands and feet were wrapped in white cloth that went halfway up his arms and calves. Around his head, he wore a small blue bandana, a good luck charm that Becky had given him at the start of the season. Inside his duffle bag was a change of clothes for after the tournament.

Though less finely dressed than Leen had come, Becky's attire was more of a casual style. A silky yellow dress folded around her body and then buttoned up at an angle along the edge with small yellow loops of lace that lassoed around little metal pins shaped like hummingbirds whose bodies were dark green, bright red heads, and their wings were white with black tips. A dark green vine print that sprouted pink roses and had the same-colored hummingbirds as the pins enhanced the dress. She had on laced sandals. Their soles were white with yellow ribbons crisscrossing around her calves, while a toe ring on either sole helped hold them in place. On her wrists, she wore thick opal bracelets and round, oval-shaped opal earrings with a golden edge to match that hung down just a little.

"Good luck, my mighty lyzon. Don't let your "greatness" blind you from victory." Becky smiled back before kissing him.

He gave her a warm embrace. "I would never." He smiled. "Just keeping my spirits high and Cory's morale up."

"My morale is fine."

"Of course, it is because you are standing beside me and all my optimistic glory! HA! HA!" He released Becky and jumped over to Cory, and embraced him. "My greatness is limitless in its power! Feel it empower you!"

"Get off me." Cory struggled to push Cogeta away as he started laughing.

Cogeta clung on for a second more before letting himself be pushed away with a big smile. "There, I have transferred some of my raw greatness into you. Everyone will think you are a clone of me... wait, no. I can't have that. All my female fans will be so confused. Cory, quick give my greatness back. We cannot confuse the fangirls!"

"Cogeta, that's enough goofing around," Becky said, putting her hand on his shoulder.

Cogeta stopped from going to give Cory another hug and looked over his shoulder at Becky with a warm smile. "Yes, my love. All right, Cory, time to put our game faces on and get serious."

"Be careful, okay, Angel? I don't want to nurse your wounds when this is over," said Leen softly, slowly brushing the hair from his eyes.

Angel had come wearing a simple black dogi, which he planned to fight in. He had black makeshift bracers on his arms, made from scrap metal out of the blacksmith shop, with the head of a snarling red wolf painted on them. The black belt he had on was wrapped around his waist several times, leaving no loose ends hanging. His black pants were loose around the legs for more mobility. Upon his feet, he wore black padding with similar wolf head patterns stitched onto the front. A small gift Leen made for Angel when she saw his finished bracers.

Angel's hand took Leen's and brought it to his lips, kissing the knuckle softly, "Don't worry, I will be careful."

"You know, Leen, you would look hot in a nurse's outfit." SLAP! Cogeta's face suddenly stung, and he lay face down on the stone. Shaking off the sudden pain, he looked back at the one who had hit him. "Honey, you would too." With a face so red, Becky glared at him.

"Just for that remark, I take back my good luck and give it to someone who DESERVES it." She walked over to Cory and gave him a quick kiss. "Good luck Cory."

"Aww, honey, you know that was his first kiss. You've gone and ruined all his chances for having his first kiss with his first girlfriend." Cogeta laughed.

"Oh, I did? I'm sorry, Cory. If it makes you feel any better, you were much better than the "Greatest" over there." Becky smiled as Cory blushed.

"Oh, hell no! That's low!" Cogeta hollered, unable to control his laughter, playfully striking an aggressive pose and shaking his fist.

After the laughter had stopped, Angel looked around. "You know we still have time. Before we go in, why don't we get the girls to their seats? That way, we can get them their discounts."

"Good point. I'd forgotten about that. Plus, it'll be more time for me to show off my beautiful flower." Cogeta smiled over at Becky.

"Nice try, but no. I am still mad at you," she teased, pretending to pout and crossing her arms.

"Sure," Cory shrugged. He was the only one who was without someone. He didn't think his parents would be there to watch. They were among those who didn't see the enjoyment in the games, and after last year, he didn't bother to tell them he was competing.

The group proceeded into the coliseum. Cogeta led the way as they joined the growing crowd. He paid for Becky's fee with some money from his duffle bag. Those who came with a tournament contender, be it family or guest, had their entrance fee halved. Of course, some tried to take advantage of it, saying they were with so and so, but the discount wasn't given unless that person was standing with them as proof. Angel paid for Leen. They were escorted to a perfect booth. The girls could see the events unfolding within the sandy arena without resorting to the screens.

The guys stuck around and talked with them. Becky returned to her usual cheerful self and stopped teasing Cogeta with her angry act. Whenever people came and took a seat, Angel and Cogeta would glance over to see who they were. Of course, they didn't recognize them, but when the people saw them looking their way, they greeted them and introduced themselves. Cogeta and Angel would then politely greet them back. Becky couldn't help but laugh to herself at the spectacle the boys gave. She knew that their only reason for taking the time to escort them to their booth and for acting nicely to the strangers was so that they could see who would sit with them in the   booth. *Men and their cute desires to protect.* She glanced over at Cory. *Even Cory's checking out who's sitting with us. They are so cute. I wonder if Leen is aware of what they are doing.* She glanced over, but Leen was either oblivious to their actions or didn't mind. She was used to it, in any case. Even though Becky could easily best many of the men and women here, and even though Cogeta knew that, he still wished to ensure she was safe.

Becky reached her foot out and gently brushed the bare skin of Cogeta's leg to get his attention. *Well, my noble guardian, the booth is full. Do you believe me to be safe here?*

Her words never left her lips, but they entered Cogeta's mind as if placed there. He looked up and saw her smiling at him. She gave him a wink.

Yes, my dove, I can leave you here in good conscience. I'm not getting any creepy vibes from these people. Nor is Angel or Cory, so I think you and Leen are safe.

Mmmm, I'm pleased to hear that. She said mentally.

The two shared a smile, their mental conversation going unnoticed by the others. Just then, they could hear a loud gong echoing throughout the coliseum. Even those three miles away could hear its low tone.

"All right, that's our last-minute bell. Let's get going, guys," Angel leaned over and hugged Leen one last time. "Will you root for me?" he asked her softly.

She giggled, "Of course, I will. Do your best." The two shared a gentle kiss. "I will watch you from here," she let go of him. She smiled and waved over to Cory. He stepped past Angel and leaned over to her. She smiled, whispered, "Good luck," and kissed his cheek. He slowly turned a deeper shade of red while Cogeta stood there with his jaw open.

"Angel, Cory's luck has been doubled. He got luck from both of our girls. I say when we get around the corner there, we jump him. He's gotten too much good luck, and on top of that, he has some of my greatness in him. It's too much for one person to handle. He may explode."

Angel just smiled and shook his head as he laughed softly. The three of them waved goodbye and went back outside. Then they went around the mountain's edge, joining many other fighters from their school and those from MidStar. The warriors entered through a sliding rock door on the mountain's west side and walked down a ramp into a large locker room. It was outfitted with a small bar and a giant screen where they could watch the fights themselves. Down the hall was a bathroom, and further down was the kitchen where the food was prepared for those above them sitting in the stands. Halfway between the bathroom and the kitchen was a ramp leading down to an infirmary with doctors on standby for the violence that was about to occur.

"Well, well, well, look who it is. None other than the champion of the last year's tournament," a cold, sinister voice remarked from behind the group.

Angel took a deep breath and slowly said, "Hello, Shaw. What a shame we must be stuck in this room together. I heard the room where your team stayed last year is still being remodeled after someone lost their temper." Angel turned around and looked at him.

Shaw had worn his gold silk fighting uniform. The top was long, folded across itself, and went under his black belt, creating overhangs. It also had images of black dragon heads falling over his shoulders and a black flame rising from the hem below the belt. His pants matched the top in color and were loose like Angel's. Over his hands and covering his feet were gold pads for protection. Black hook and loop fasteners strapped them on.

Within moments, the room was split. Angel's team stood behind him, as those on Shaw's team stood behind him. Both sides were ready to clash within the small space.

Shaw smiled as Angel smirked as they glared at each other.

The TV popped to life as a man in bright yellow, with red flashing lights on his shoulders, stepped onto a floating yellow podium in the center of the ring. With a large microphone in hand, he began welcoming all the guests.

"Let's play it cool. We fight out there, not in here," suggested Angel, holding out his hand. Shaw glanced at it, then at Angel, back to his men, and then nodded, grasping Angel's hand. He tried to pull Angel forward, but he did not budge. He tried tightening his grip, but the tighter he squeezed, so did Angel.

Shaw smiled, "Deal. We'll sit separately, though."

"Yeah, whatever. Everyone, sit down and relax. As usual, he will read off who is sponsoring this event and some of its history. Remind people of major fights here and then introduce our two teams, today's events, and how they will play out. I swear he makes the same speech at every tournament," Angel remarked as he took a back-row seat, with Cory taking the chair to his right and Cogeta to his left. "Probably mention the changes the letter told all the schools about."

"Yeah, but he does it with such fire, such excitement," Cogeta stated, always enjoying the announcer's build-up.

"He's also annoying, like you, Fairway," retorted Shaw.

Cogeta chuckled and shook his head. "Oh, hey, I wonder if he will remind everyone how you got introduced to complete annihilation."

"This year is going to be diff—"

"Complete annihilation," Cogeta repeated.

"Shove it, Fairway."

"Complete and utter annihilation."

Shaw glared in Cogeta's direction but said no more. As Shaw had stated, the two teams sat so that one column of seats was empty, dividing them apart. Everyone watched the screen as the announcer did his thing to get the fans ready and riled up. Angel peered over toward the other team. *I see some returning contenders. Let me see if I can remember everyone; Barburata, Atila, Syph, Casey, and I think his name was Jaketon. He's new, but his duffle bag has Alex stitched onto it. That's nice. Wonder if his mom did that for him. Ah, there are Sage and Wayne, and it looks like Kang and Marty. Dang, Marty is a big fellow.*

As Angel scoped out his opponent's team, Shaw was doing the same. *All right, he brought Cogeta and Cory. No surprises there. I should've brought Moria back so she could crush Ryker again. That would've given me some entertainment, at least. Shame she had to miss this. Stone, the big dumb fool. Logan and Wes, the wonder twins. Zach, Tomus, and Mochi are regulars; I see he brought Jet and Peter. What was it they called him... Zoom? Grawfriggin morus. The only ones that pose any real threat are Cogeta, Stone, the wonder twins, and perhaps Zach and Mochi. We had better win this year.*

CHAPTER 7

LET THE TOURNAMENT BEGIN

"Welcome to this year's annual tournament! To test the strength of two great universities! This is the ultimate test between the schools; to the victor goes the spoils. The school would not only receive a trophy to display its greatness, but it shall also be able to request the loser to do one thing! Those lesser should always serve the superiors after all. I heard our last year's winner had a grand dance, complete with a gracious supply of food and drink, all at the expense of the losing school. Now, wasn't that nice of them?"

The announcer was met with overwhelming cheers and screams that drowned out those who showed their displeasure.

"The losing team does not go home empty-handed, oh no! We here at the Spartaliseum are a caring bunch. The losers shall leave here with disgrace, bruises, broken bones, and tails between their legs! In this game, there can be no second place. It is, be the BEST or nothing!" The announcer shouted with charisma and excitement into his microphone before continuing in the same outrageous manner. "We here at the Spartaliseum would like to thank those who help us hold this fantastic event every year, first and foremost, our GREAT AND GRAND EMPEROR! May his reign be long and have Odin's blessing in all that he does. Secondly, Shaw Inc. is your everyday supplier for all your daily needs. If it is not made with quality, it's probably imported. Lastly, we want to thank all of YOU! Yes, you, too, make this possible! Your cheers and hollers fuel these boys to bring you the finest entertainment their bodies can provide. Now for those of you who are new. Yes, I see you up there with handfuls of souvenirs; I shall review how the fights will go.

Each MidStar and Utopia University captain has hand-selected ten of their best fighters. In the first round, two from either team will go at it. The victor's captain then gets the privilege of choosing who of the other team has to fight, AND then the captain OR either one of his men can choose to select a challenge for that fighter to accomplish.

Challenges vary from animal battles, breaking a certain amount of any object, to even collecting items from the crowd. If the fighter cannot complete the challenge or loses the fight, the captain, the selector, gets to go again. This continues until his challenge is completed.

I know what some of you are thinking, and yes, this differs from last year's fifty-man tournament. Changes were made by the committee and voted upon by the Intercontinental Martial Academics Championship sponsors to get to the main event faster. After last year, who can wait to see those two go at it again? So starting this year and henceforth, there will be smaller events as schools fight amongst themselves on each continent until only one school remains on each. Then they will compete against each other on this day at the grandest stadium of them all. The Spartaliseum! As enjoyable as the fifty-man battle royal was, now we can focus on the highest tier of talent that our schools have to show. Everyone will have a chance to shine! Only the best schools will make it to this glorious stage! So do your best, kids. The world is watching!" The announcer leans close to the microphone with a devilish grin and says softly, "No pressure."

Shaw and Angel exchanged looks.

"Now then!" continued the announcer back to his boisterous and over-the-top performance, "Once every team member has fought and cannot compete anymore, it is time for the captains to step up to the plate for our FINAL ROUND! That's right, folks! No more waiting for forty-eight other people to be eliminated until it comes down to the top two fighters! The final round is the battle of the captains! However, to be victorious, you must meet two stipulations. That's right; I said TWO! First, your team must have more points than the other! Secondly, the captain of the school must prevail over the other.

Points? What points? Where do these points come from? I hear you asking yourselves. Hang on, folks. I'm about to explain, so listen close. Each type of fight has its number of points to be received. Four-person battles are eight points, one-on-one battles two points, three on three battles six points. Challenges vary with each one, depending on the difficulty, ranging from one to TWO HUNDRED POINTS! If the person challenged loses his trial, the points go to the challenge issuer. For example, say I were to challenge cameraman Billy down there, wave Billy, yeah there he is, to run around the ring, with flaming obstacles WHILE being chased by a Triranadon, without being burnt or falling, or being horribly maimed, the judges would measure the difficulty level and if Billy succeeds his team gets the points. However, if he grawfriggins it up, my team gets the points. Now I can hear you thinking, what if the victorious captain has fewer points than the loser? I will tell you. The captain who got his ass beat has to deal with a very irate team. To have put so much effort into it and then to have your captain LOSE; what SHAME, what DISHONOR! But take heart! The final match between the two captains is worth a whopping HUNDRED and FIFTY POINTS!

Now, in case of a tie, we will go to sudden death. Granted, we are not allowed to have any actual deaths. It is sad but true," the announcer made a sad face for the crowd, "However, we will have every member of the two teams come out and have one giant slugfest! A good old fashion BEAT DOWN! Whichever school the last man standing belongs to is the WINNER! Now, would the captains please choose their first two fighters from each school to come on out and SHOW US WHAT THEY GOT! WOOOOOOO!" The announcer screamed into his microphone, jumping up and down crazily.

Angel and Shaw began scouting their team for the best two to start things off. After selecting their two fighters, the four entered another room adjacent to where the teams sat and rode up on a platform into the center of the ring. Angel picked the two who fought best when together. He had complete confidence in his choice even when Shaw's two picks stepped forward. They both appeared well-trained, though it was uncertain how well they worked together. Everyone's eyes turned to the screen. With the announcer clear of the battlefield, the mighty gong was sounded, and the fight was underway. Angel and the others watched the fight vividly and cheered when their team scored a good hit on the other.

"I see you brought the young Mr. Ryker along. Is that because you pity him, you didn't want him to feel left out? As I recall, he was so useless that the pup lost to a woman," Shaw laughed while glancing at Angel's team.

"He is here on his own accord. Besides, speaking of which, how is that ape mother of yours?" Angel replied with a sly smirk.

Angel's teammates laughed as Shaw slowly grew hot under the collar. "That was not my mother, you bastard of a sow."

"Guys, guys," Cogeta said, "repeat with me. Love and peace, love and peace, Shaw still suckles on his mother's…."

Just then, the crowd's cheers hit a high note at what was happening in the ring, blocking out what Cogeta said. However, that did not stop Shaw from trying to get over the chairs to Cogeta, who stood back waving his hands, telling him to bring on his best shot. It took all of MidStar's strength to hold their infuriated captain back.

"And the winner is MidStar," announced the commentators. "That was a real close one."

There were sudden cheers in the locker room from Shaw's side, and Shaw was grinning maliciously. A man walked in carrying a controller-like device. On it were the names of each team member and a small assortment of buttons, and a keypad beneath. Every selection would then be transmitted to the large televisions in the coliseum so the audience knew what was coming.

"Well, I guess I get to go first. You know what that means, Angel. I choose Cory Ryker to be the next fighter from your side, and his challenge will be," Shaw pressed the button labeled challenges.

The screen brought up several categories and briefly described what each entailed. Man Versus Wild, as it suggested, is when the fighter would have to fight whatever animal or animals the opposing team chose. Power Breaking was where he had to break a set amount of objects. There was even the option for a handicap match where, just as it suggests, the fighter selected would have to take on two or more of the other team's fighters. Lastly, there was the Scavenger, where the challenger would have to rely on the audience's mercy to collect several items before a specific time limit.

Shaw smiled at his choices. "Handicap match against…."

Shaw looked over at his men, many of whom were smiling or cracking their knuckles, hoping to be the ones chosen. At last, Shaw's eyes rested on two men.

The first of the two men Shaw chose to battle stood eight feet tall with spiky dark orange hair. Around his neck was a chain with a silver ring dangling from it. He wore an average blue T-shirt, a gold belt that fastened on the backside with a chain hanging in the front, a pair of white baggy martial arts pants, and a pair of brown boots.

The other man was six feet with spiky black hair that ran down his neck. A few blue streaks blended in. He wore a black closed vest with two symbols on either side. On his left was a circle with a dagger with a handle that ended at a 90-degree angle, and on his right side was the letter "N" for one of his favorite bands. Around his waist was a blue sash. His pants and bracers matched in color and design; both were primarily black with a bold red design across the middle. On his feet, he wore what resembled cowboy boots. Similar to his pants and bracers, they were red and black, but the difference was that the red ran along the side, rising like fire.

This man also openly showed his tail. Something very few, and typically either the gutsy or amateur Utopian, would do in a time of battle. The tail of the Utopians is extremely sensitive to the touch. Many keep them hidden around their waist, or if they can afford it, they would get a tail guard specially made for them.

"Barburata and Atila, you two will be his opponents. Oh, and Atila, take your "Moon-Smasher" with you." Shaw grinned, glancing at the obvious worry covering Cory's face.

Atila's weapon, "Moon-Smasher," was wise to be wary of and avoid at all costs. It was unique, as it was the only one ever made. Atila had fashioned two large lumpy boulders with a mythril rod decorated with matching designs along the shaft, as were on his pants. However, one end was nastier than the other. Fore at one end, blades were attached to the stone. The other end was not as gruesome because Atila ran low on funds and could not afford to have them put in. Each boulder weighed upwards of two tons. He had become accustomed to its size and speed after many years of practicing and injuries. So powerful was the weapon that, with one swing, it would snap the trunk of an oak. Shaw walked over and lifted the bulky weapon with both hands and flung it to Atila, who, with one hand, caught it, twirled it, and passed it to his other hand as if it weighed no more than a feather.

Cory gazed on, his palms becoming sweaty as a cold sweat began to run down his face. Cory was so nervous that he jumped slightly when Angel touched his shoulder. Angel felt the sudden response to his touch, so he tightened his grip to comfort his friend.

"You can take these two. Believe in yourself. If you must become as vicious as a rabid wolf as we did in training, do it. Don't hold yourself back. Here." Angel handed him an iron staff since Cory could not bring his weapon.

"Oh no, he isn't allowed weapons," Shaw intervened smugly.

"Fine. He doesn't need it to kick their asses," said Cogeta confidently, taking the staff away from Cory's clammy hands. Taking on an old master-like tone, he turned back to Cory, "Be like water. Water can flow, and it can crash. Be like water, Cory-San." Cogeta smiled, patting his shoulder, and nodded with his eyes closed.

"You stole that from a movie, didn't you?" Angel asked.

"Shut up. There was a martial arts movie marathon the other night. Helped get me ready for today," Cogeta laughed, scratching the back of his head even though it didn't itch.

"All right, do I have a moment to change, Shaw? I don't fight in my street clothes," asked Cory, still nervous but at the same time refusing to let his friends down without a fight.

Shaw rolled his eyes. "Make it quick. It would have been best if you came dressed to fight or had already gotten ready. I don't see why you brought him. Is Utopia University drawing from the bottom of the barrel now? I wouldn't even give him a spot on the team as a towel boy if he went to Midstar."

Cory picked up his duffle bag and quietly walked to the restroom to change. On his way, he overheard Angel.

"Shaw, you are going to eat those words. I assure you of that. There is much power waiting to burst out from within him. Cory may not be the strongest here, but he's more than earned his spot on this team."

Cory closed the door. *Why? How can he say such a thing? I don't feel like I have some untapped power within me. For crying out loud, I lost last year. That's all everyone remembers. That's what I'm known for. I'm a loser... I... don't belong here. I'm not like them. I wish I were. I want their confidence, their strength. But it's just not me. I'm the loser who can't even get a girl to take notice of me. No. They are counting on me. They believe in me. I can't let them down now. What would that training have been for if I ran away now? What kind of friend would I be? I won't let them down. I'm going to give them everything I have.*

"Simpleton, everyone here knows that the boy is only here because he is your friend."

"Yeah, you are right. Cory is my friend." Angel motioned his head to the side, "Mochi, there, is my friend. Wes and Logan are my friends," again he gestured over his shoulder to a pair of men who were sitting behind him, the same duo who had fought in the very first round, "We've worked hard, and trained hard together. There is a bond between us. You can easily call it friendship. Can you say your team shares that? Where are your friends?"

"Silly ideology. My men are here because they earned it by being the strongest of the strong, not cause of being friends of mine. I had friends who wished to join us here, but I turned them down because they were weak, and I told them as much. I am here to win, not have fun."

"Then you miss the point of these games, and if you think I chose these men, many of whom I've chosen before, simply because they were friends. You are sorely mistaken."

"Fool, the point of these tournaments is to test our strength and prepare us for the harshness of life. It's to see whose school is the best. Our schools have defeated the competition, as we repeatedly have over the past few years. However, that is no impressive feat when looking at the muck you must compete with. They probably barely put up a struggle. The other thing these tournaments prepare us for is war and the hardships and pain of battle."

"What does that say about you when I have beaten you? How many is it so far? I honestly don't even bother keeping count."

Angel watched as his remark made Shaw turn red from his neck to the edge of his blond hair. His eyes glared at Angel. He knew all too well how many times he tasted defeat by Angel's hand, and for him to say that, he didn't even bother keeping count. His blood boiled within his veins, his muscles tightened, and his fist and teeth clenched tightly.

"Very soon, Everlast, I will smash your teeth down your throat."

"And so, the wounded beast continues to whine."

"AAARGH!" Shaw spun around and punched the wall behind him.

The audience up above heard a muffled explosion accompanied by a tremor. People looked around with concern, unsure of what had happened. The announcer flew out to the center of the ring and tried to help relax everyone.

"Whoa! It looks like someone down there is getting antsy!" He chimed into his microphone with a laugh.

However, Leen didn't find the quip all that amusing. She was concerned that something had happened to Angel. Becky reached over and took her hand, giving it a comforting squeeze. Coming out of her daze, Leen looked over and saw Becky smiling at her.

"Everything is going to be okay. Don't worry. Shaw wouldn't attack Angel outside of the ring, not here. He wants to win and can't do that if he is disqualified."

Leen smiled back and nodded. Her concern was eased slightly, ever so slightly.

In the locker room, a camera crew and security inspected the commotion. The cameraman looked around through his lens, his feed shown on the monitors above. The room was filled with a cloud of grey dust, and that was all he saw for a moment. But when it settled and dissipated, the fuzzy image focused on Shaw's figure, standing motionless as a statue. His fist rested in the center of a crater in the thick stone wall. A pile of rubble lay at his feet. *That crater must be at least two meters across and several inches deep. I would hate to be on the other end of this guy's fist.* The cameraman thought.

A moment later, Cory walked out of the restroom, looking down as he straightened his black belt around his waist and tightened it up. He was wearing a red dogi with a black undershirt. Standing there barefoot, he looked up at everyone.

"The floor is kind of cold," he half-heartedly smiled. He then joined the others in looking over at Shaw. *Yep, I thought that's what the racket was. Glad I am not fighting him.* As Shaw apologized to the cleanup crew as they swept and removed the debris from the floor, Midstar's two fighters laughed and smiled, getting onto the platform. Angel's team relaxed and again wished Cory good luck as he joined the other two men. Everyone's attention left the crater in the wall and turned to the television, anticipating the coming battle.

The ride-up was tense. Cory stood between the two men, half expecting them not to wait for the match to begin officially and jumping him at that moment. Looking back and forth between the two, he saw them towering over him. Both men smirked, scoffed, growled, and cracked their knuckles while looking at Cory as they tried to intimidate him. It was working. He clenched his hands into fists to keep them from shaking. The lift ride seemed to take forever as the pressure in his chest grew. To his surprise, neither moved before the doors opened overhead, and the lift brought the fighters into the center of the coliseum for all to see.

The crowd greeted the three warriors with echoing hollers and cheers from all sides. Cory looked around in astonishment. The feeling of being center stage to so many people was overwhelming. *I hate to admit it, but this feels good.* He thought to himself as he took a deep breath, closed his eyes, and took in the sounds and smells. *So many elite warriors have fought and shed their blood in this ring. To be among such stars, man, what a feeling.* He slowly opened his eyes. *Show time.* The fear creeping up on him was suddenly whisked away as he steeled himself for what was about to come.

"Ladies and gentlemen! Lords and ladies! Here before you, in our next match of the night, we have two skilled warriors from Midstar. Barburata and Atila! And Atila has come ready to fight, bringing his nasty weapon, the "Moon-Smasher"! And who is to take them on? None other than the young Cory Ryker! Be sure to show these brave boys some love, and let's start this party!" After the announcer finished, the gong sounded.

Immediately, Cory flew upward to avoid Barburata's rush. Seconds later, he was ducking and shifting side to side as he narrowly dodged Atila's attacks. From below, Barburata charged up an energy blast and sent it soaring at Cory. Catching the green aura out of the corner of his eye, Cory phased to the side of Atila. Grabbing hold of the middle section of Atila's weapon, he tried with all his might to turn Atila towards the attack. As Atila wouldn't budge, the plan backfired, and Cory was quickly swung into the blast back first. In the locker room below, cheers and screams came from Shaw's side as Angel and Cogeta sat clenching their teeth.

Cory had just landed on his feet when Barburata jumped toward him, and the two began exchanging blows back and forth. Grabbing one fist and then the other, Cory held Barburata at bay. However, not to be outdone, Baraburata opened his hands and grabbed onto Cory's, and started squeezing with all his might. Cory hollered out as he tried to fight the pain, his knees growing weak.

"Come on, Cory! You can do it!"

A voice erupted from the crowd. Glancing over, Cory saw Becky and Leen standing, waving their arms and calling his name. He looked back at his opponent with a surge of confidence, and before he dropped to one knee, he found the strength to push his body back up. Now the two were in a struggle of strength, and neither one was budging. In the form of crackling lightning, arcs of power jumped around them. Their battle auras burst into full view. Barburata's was deep amber, while Cory's was light blue, nearly white. The crowd loved the classic struggle to see whom the Gods would favor. Suddenly, Atila attacked Cory at his side, jabbing the un-bladed end of his weapon into his ribs. Cory's aura instantly vanished as he felt four ribs crack and shatter from the assault. The cameras replayed this highlight in slow motion so people could see the hit. Cory was sent flying into the far wall. Before he could recover, Barburata was driving his hard knee into Cory's already damaged rib cage.

He was gritting his teeth so that the blood would not escape. The strong metallic taste filled his mouth. Cory grabbed hold of Barburata's sides. His hands lit up with electricity, sending wave after wave into him. Barburata flung his head back and screamed as people could see his body lighting up. Out of desperation, Atila smacked his partner out of Cory's grasp at a safe distance with his prized weapon. Nevertheless, as Atila was off balance, Cory charged at him in wolf form.

The fans watched as a light blue wolf with white streaks jumped onto Atila's back. Cory then latched onto the base of Atila's neck while digging his claws into his flesh. Ripping and shredding muscle and tissue, the wolf tried to inflict immense damage. Blood flowed down his back and splattered onto the sand. Swinging around, Atila shook the wolf off him while clipping Cory's hind right hip with his massive weapon, filling the coliseum with an echoing whimper.

Getting up to his feet, Cory was now nursing a bad leg. Then out of nowhere, Barburata wrapped his arms around Cory's shoulders and locked them behind his neck, hoisting him off the ground. Atila took the chance and jabbed the bladed end of his weapon repeatedly into Cory's torso. Atila viciously laughed as he twirled his weapon over his head, then swung downward, bashing Cory's left shoulder and the side of his face with the un-bladed end.

After that devastating blow, Cory hung limp in Barburata's arms. Confident that they had beaten him, Barburata dropped Cory's body. While falling, Barburata kicked Cory's lifeless body across the field. He and Atila both raised their arms with thoughts of victory.

"Come on, Cory! Get up!"

"You can do it! You can beat these guys! Just stand up!"

Becky? Leen? Everyone. I can't let them down. I can't. Grruugh, but it hurts so much. Four, no, seven ribs are broken. Left shoulder is dislocated. Oh god, my jaw feels like it is about to fall off. I don't think I can go on. I got to. I can't let them down. Not like last year. Not this time! I won't let my friends down!

Cory thought as he forced himself to stand. Quickly popping his shoulder back into its socket, he then placed his arms out before him, fists together, and began charging his attack. His eyes were blank, and he appeared lost in a trance. Arcs of lightning sparked around his fists.

"THUNDER CANNON!" Cory yelled, releasing a blast so large that it covered all that lay before him. The force from the attack caused him to slide back in the sand.

Atila turned around the fastest to see what was coming. His eyes widened in fear. Arcs of electricity danced over their bodies, searing and charring their flesh. The attack lasted only a few seconds, but the power that it carried seemed to make it last longer. Its brightness temporarily blinded the entire coliseum, and everyone sat silently, waiting to find out what lay in the ring. Even the teams down below were on the edge of their seats, staring at the whiteout screen. Angel and Cogeta smiled as they glanced at each other, then back to the screen. Shaw found it hard to believe the boy had lasted this long against his two fighters.

When all the flashing and dust had subsided at last, enough for the cameras to refocus and become clear, Atila lay unconscious. His weapon lay yards away, carried off by the wave of force. Barburata, however, still stood like a lone tower. He had not turned around like Atila. His back was black. Patches of skin were gone. Still, he stood. Smoke rose from his charred back, off his baked skin and muscle. He slowly turned to face Cory, who was dumbfounded that his attack had not knocked him down.

Cory gathered the last of his energy in complete desperation and charged forth!

"Rin-!" Cory shouted as he sunk his left elbow while pushing it further with the palm of his right hand against his fist into his towering opponent's open gut. "Ken-" His fist snapped up and slammed into the chest of Barburata. Cory then pulled back into a wide crouching stance, cupping his open hands near his right side. A globe of blue energy, with arcing waves of electricity, formed in the center of his palms. "SO-AH!"

He shouted, thrusting his open palms forward directly at Barburata. He didn't even try to move as he was struck by another powerful wave of energy straight to his chest. Unlike Cory's last blast, this one was more concentrated. Its body was more streamlined, more precise. Upon impact, the explosion seared away his flesh, exposing the muscle underneath. Still, Barburata didn't move.

Cory hunched over and tried to catch his breath, his eyes never leaving his opponent. *Why is he still standing? How? I... don't... know... if... I can beat him.* Cory thought as he paused in between to breathe deeply. The crowd was not as silent as the ring. The coliseum was alive with the roars of fans from all around. Cries of "What are you waiting for?" and "Finish him, you fool!" rang out amongst the cheering and jeering. Then suddenly, he thought he heard distinct voices in amongst the crowd. Focusing his hearing, he shut out all others and concentrated on the voices.

"Cory! Cory! Cory! You can do it! WOO! You can win this! Believe in yourself!"

"You got him beat, Cory! He just doesn't know it! Just a little more, Cory, you can do it!"

Again his friends, Leen and Becky, pulled him back from the brink of despair, of defeat. Their voices filled him with strength. Their encouragement, their faith, filled him with power. Standing up straight once more, his eyes burned with confidence. Dashing in, he immediately landed a powerful right hook into Barburata's side. Through his fist, Cory felt two of his ribs break from the impact. Feeling empowered, he followed through with a left to his other side. More ribs were broken. Cory built his momentum and unleashed a flurry of punches to his opponent's upper body. Feeding off his friend's encouragement, his attacks only seemed to get stronger. He moved faster and added more weight behind each blow. Fans of Utopia University were eating it all up, cheering his name, screaming their praises, and shouting for more. Down in the locker room, his teammates were ecstatic and cheered as loud as they could for their comrade.

However, as quickly as that second wind got him going again, it began to fade. For several minutes, Cory had made Barburata his punching bag, and not once had the large man moved to defend himself nor fall. Cory didn't know what was keeping him standing. Nor did he know if he would last much longer. Hoping to finish him in a final sounding blow, he quickly crouched down and, with all the might in his legs, he lunged himself upward. With the rising uppercut, his fist was alive with bolts of electricity surrounding it down his arm and leaving a trail in its wake. His fist contacted Barburata's chin, which sent his head flying back. Cory thought for sure that was it, but still, he stood.

Is he…unconscious on his feet? Cory thought as he took a few steps back after landing on his feet. However, Barburata started to laugh. *He's laughing? Why is he laughing? …All my attacks packed a lot of power and force behind them. Why is he laughing?* Barburata continued to laugh as he rolled his neck back around. *I have to stay calm. But how can I when he is laughing at me? I have to finish this now!*

Cory rushed and jumped forward, soaring through the air and ramming his knee into Barburata's face. Blood shot out from his broken nose, but Barburata stood motionless and laughed. Once again shocked and growing frustrated, Cory grabbed Barburata by the head and repeatedly rammed his knee into his face. *Fall down! Fall Down! FALL DOWN!!* The crowd was so into it that they counted every hit and cheered as more blood ran down his opponent's face. The flowing streams and blood splattering painted his skin like war paint.

After ten powerful knee shots, Cory pushed off and flipped through the air, landing on his feet. He quickly stepped back into a defensive stance. Momentarily trying to catch his breath and think of a new strategy. Barburata licked some of the blood from his lips and whispered,

"Never give up. Break them all." He muttered.

In a sudden burst of speed, Cory found himself hunched over Barburata's hulking forearm. A fist buried deep in his stomach. His face twitched with shock and pain. He violently coughed. Dark red flakes from the blood that had dried early flew out of his mouth, along with a sprinkling of fresh blood. Barburata lifted him on his arm and tossed Cory over his shoulder. Cory landed a few feet away on his back, twitching and blood leaking from his mouth. However, Barburata wasn't through yet.

He menacingly walked over. A predator focused on its prey. He got on top of Cory's defenseless body. Looking down with a sadistic grin, he began to beat and pound and smash his fists and elbows into the skull of his fallen opponent. Such violence only excited the Midstar spectators more since the tables had turned, and now their fighter was pummeling the weak Utopia University contender. His friends could only watch as Cory was mercilessly beaten into the arena's sand.

"You thought you could beat me! You weak puppy! Moira was right. No wonder she beat you so easily. Pathetic! Useless! I will show you power!" He dug his thumbs into the eye sockets as his hands tightened around Cory's skull. "I will honor these grounds by ensuring you never enter this arena again!"

Cory cried out in anguish. Desperately, he clawed at the forearms of Barburata, futilely trying to break the grasp. With the last of his strength, he grasped Barbaruta's forearms and mustered enough energy to release arcs of electricity up his arms and whipped across his face. It was all he could do. Barburata roared as the volts surged through him. He released Cory's skull and returned to punching. After a few brutal strikes, Cory's arms fell to his sides.

The once glimmer of victory that shined before Cory's eyes was suddenly ripped from his grasp. Medics were coming out of the ground with stretchers within moments as the announcer proclaimed MidStar, the winner. They pulled Barburata off Cory. He got more cheap shots before allowing them to carry him out on a stretcher. As they carried Cory away, Barburata played to the crowd, raising his arms in victory.

MidStar celebrated as the Utopia University fighters fumed. Angel and Cogeta got up and followed their friend into the infirmary before being pushed back out by doctors.

"Well, strike another loss to his record. He didn't have what it took to go all the way. He's a failure now and forever."

"Shaw…" Cogeta growled through clenched teeth. He could not find the words to express his feelings, so he chose the next best way to do it. He lunged at Shaw over the chairs; his hands outstretched, his nails protruding into claws. Before he could get close to his target, however, Angel grabbed hold of him and pulled him back. Snapping his head around, Cogeta glared at him with confusion, but Angel stared back with a stern calmness.

"Save it for the ring, Cogeta."

"Aww, did I break someone's cool? Go cry to your mother… oh wait, she's dead," said Shaw, sitting in a chair.

"Funny, so is your cowardly dad," replied Cogeta with great malice.

Shaw kicked the chair in front of him into the wall as he jumped up and turned to face Cogeta. "He was NOT a coward!"

"Not what I heard. They say he was such an incompetent soldier that he could only save his honor by becoming a businessman. Then he turned around and paid off all those who would have exposed his cowardice," Cogeta carried on.

"You will eat those words," muttered Shaw, sitting back down.

Just then, a nurse came out of the infirmary. "Atila and Cory are stable. Their wounds are healing without complications. They are, however, out of commission for the rest of the tournament and will need plenty of rest for their bodies to mend." She then went back inside the infirmary. Angel gave out a quiet sigh of relief and took his seat. Meanwhile, Shaw was busy thinking of his next challenge for his rival's team.

"Well, let's see. Ah, I got it. Cogeta, this is for you. Your challenge is to collect twenty-five pairs of underwear from the audience within one; no, I better make it six minutes. Some may take their time." Shaw typed the stipulations into the remote as he spoke.

"Piece of cake," Cogeta laughed, calming himself down.

"Glad you finally admit your true self."

"Pardon me?"

"The undergarments you must collect are from the male audience."

Shaw's tone was serious, but he spoke them in such a way as to taunt Cogeta. Shaw's team began laughing, and even some of Angel's team snickered before quickly stopping it from a sharp glance from Angel.

"Angel, tell me that is not possible. Tell me there are rules about making up ridiculous challenges like this."

"Oh, there is no rule about this at all. It is perfectly legal. Of course, you can always decline, but that would be the same as forfeiting, and I get to select the fate of another member of your team." Shaw grinned wickedly.

"Damnit…" Cogeta muttered under his breath.

"That's only part of the challenge," Shaw smirked. "The other part is that you must defeat Jaketon here within the remaining time."

Cogeta looked at the guy who stepped forward upon his name being called. He had long, spiky, purple hair and wore a blue shirt over the top, a green shirt with black shoulder pads strapped on, blue pants, and black boots. The shoulder pads had several spikes sticking up from them. A yellow scabbard hung from a sagging green belt. *I've seen this guy before. He's not too bad of a fighter, but… with that stupid time limit. I cannot afford to take any chances.* Cogeta growled to himself.

"Angel, if I pull this off, you better get him back good for this."

Angel nodded, and Cogeta entered the platform room, preparing himself to move as fast as possible. He was staring at the doors as the platform rose when an idea suddenly popped into his head. *It's crazy, but it may just work. Ooooh, this is going to be good.*

When the doors slid open, Cogeta immediately flew out to the audience, not waiting for the long entrance and passing up the chance to show off. The cameras watched him as he flew about, asking the men in the stands if they would be so kind as to remove their underwear. To everyone's surprise, one after another, men were getting up and going into the restrooms to comply. After only three minutes, he had collected the set number.

Upon landing in the ring, he placed the garments in a pile. Turning around, he quickly let himself fall backward as Jaketon's sword swung around and cut through the air where he had been. He then ducked forward as Jaketon swung his blade back around, trying to catch Cogeta when he came back up. After the second swing, Cogeta stood up straight and shot his leg out to the side, sending Jaketon sliding back on his toes. Cogeta walked after him. Glancing up at the large monitor that displayed his remaining time, his mind quickly filtered through his repertoire of techniques. *Have to make this quick. Can't be too fancy. Two minutes remaining. Here we go!*

Cogeta sprinted forward, his full attention on Jaketon. When he saw the flashing steel of his sword moving around to slice him through from the corner of his eye, he leaped into the air without pause and maneuvered his body around the blade in a sideways flip. As soon as his feet touched down on the sand again, on the other side of the blade, his left foot spun and whipped through the air at blinding speed, connecting soundly with Jaketon's temple. Not missing a beat, Cogeta leaped off his right foot as the left one came back around and nailed his opponent in the chest with the full force of another kick. Jaketon once again slid back on his feet, but not as far as before.

The people sitting at Becky and Leen's booth were suddenly startled as Becky stood up, stomped her foot down onto the table, and made a crude gesture with her arms in the air as she shouted out above the crowd. Even Leen looked up in surprise at her close friend but then stifled a laugh.

"That's my Cogeta! Kick that man's ass into a bloody pulp! Then beat him some more! Show him like the rest. What happens when you fruck with the WOLF PACK!"

Seeing how he was still within striking range, Jaketon quickly swung his sword downward to slash Cogeta. However, just as he began his downward stroke, the bottom of his hand and the pummel of his sword were met by the top of Cogeta's foot. The impact force sent his sword flying out of his hand, over his head, to land a few feet away. When Jaketon looked back from watching his sword fly, he was greeted with a powerful right hook to his jaw. As Jaketon hunched over from the blow, Cogeta saw his opening instantly. In a whirlwind of punches, he unleashed strike after strike upon Jaketon. Rights and lefts pummeled his face as he could not block or escape the onslaught. Then suddenly, Cogeta pulled back, his right foot making a large semicircle in the sand as he crouched down. For an instant, Jaketon thought he had a chance, but just for a moment. For then he heard,

"BURN OUT!"

Before his eyes and the eyes of the audience watching, a ring of fire surrounded Cogeta. Shortly after that, Cogeta's right foot swept around, a fire trail following in its wake, and slammed into the gut of his opponent. Jaketon's body lurched and hunched forward, the blow sending waves of pain racing through his body. Cogeta's leg followed through, and Jaketon found himself suddenly flying back through the air moments before hitting the hard, rough sand, creating a body-size trench as he slid along to a stop. His body was racked with so much pain. He found the only thing he could do with slight ease was close his eyes as the announcer called the match in Cogeta's favor.

"YES! That's my man!"

Becky screamed with all her might as the crowd cheered at his impressive victory. Cogeta raised his fist to the heavens as he returned to the undergarments he had collected from the kind people. While gathering them up, he waved a cameraman over, asking him to follow him. They both traveled down the platform and into the locker room. When Cogeta was out of sight, Becky sat with an enormous smile. Looking at Leen, she beamed proudly, playfully celebrated with a hug, and kissed her cheek. She turned to the others at their booth and smiled proudly.

"That's my man. Isn't he amazing?"

"Y-yes, ma'am, h-he certainly is."

The man next to her said as the others nodded in agreement. Moments before, this kind woman was speaking with them in a friendly conversation after the defeat of her poor friend, and then suddenly, she turned into a boisterous and fierce woman. *Damn, this chick is scary.* He thought to himself as Becky went back to talking to Leen and looking out to the monitors, the occasional joyful squeal escaping her as she immersed herself in the afterglow of her man's triumphant victory.

"Well, I did it," Cogeta said confidently as he walked into the locker room with his arms full. His body was covered in sweat from the exertion.

"I am surprised you could complete it. Tell me, did you bribe them?" Shaw questioned with a snide grin.

Cogeta smiled, "Nah, didn't have to. All I did was tell them that if they gave me their underwear, I would," he then chucked all the underwear into Shaw's smug face, "throw them into the face of Midstar." Cogeta laughed. "Would have taken me less time, but one man up there wanted to really work something up good for ya. It is rank. I'm sure you will agree. Think he had the chili. You seem to have a lot of enemies, or people don't like you."

Shaw stood up from his seat, redder than ever, letting the foul garments fall to the floor and ready to kill Cogeta.

"Sit down, Shaw. Everyone knows you sent Cogeta on that ridiculous challenge because you were too embarrassed to collect them yourself," Angel stepped in.

Shaw's anger now turned towards Angel. "Make your blasted challenge so you and I can get in the ring faster. Then we'll see who's laughing."

"Uh oh, Angel, I think he is after your shorts too," Cogeta laughed.

"Shut up, you loudmouth buffoon. May you never find glory in this life or any after," snapped Shaw with a growl in his throat.

"Yeah, yeah, whatever. We are the ones who are ahead in points, one hundred to fifty-eight." Cogeta brushed him off, sitting down.

Angel looked through MidStar's ranks. "He will do," pointing to one of Shaw's larger fighters, "and your challenge is to break one solid bar of mythril."

Shaw's jaw dropped. "You can't do that. It is an impossible task. Mythril is indestructible. Even YOU know that!"

"You made Cogeta collect men's underwear for you. I want him to break a bar of mythril. He can always refuse," Angel retorted back with an evil smirk. "Look at the bright side. If he manages to do it, that's two hundred points in the bank, and you take the lead. Plus, think of the bragging rights Midstar will have if one of their own can break a bar of mythril."

Shaw closed his mouth as the man stood and quietly walked to the platform. The cameraman hitched a ride with him, filming his slow ascend to the ring.

"Wow, folks! No love between our two teams this year, that's for sure. WHEW! Is it hot in here, or is it just me? I don't know about you, but I can't wait for those two to throw down in the center of the ring. Wouldn't want to miss it!" The announcer shouted out in his typical energetic manner as he floated around on his yellow podium.

Back in the ring, coliseum hands had already placed two cinder blocks down with one bar of mythril centered on top. The man from Midstar took his position and readied himself. Then, with all his might, he brought his hand straight down onto the slab of metal. A noise like thunder echoed throughout the building. The whole Spartliseum was silent as many held their breath. Would today be the day history was made? A cloud of dust hid the area where the bar had rested.

Judges ran over to see if there was any visible difference in the bar. One stood up, shaking his head and waving his arms. There was no difference. The cinder blocks laid in pieces, and a small crater formed around the area, but not even a dent on the bar of mythril. The cameras replayed the stunt for all to see as the defeated warrior solemnly stepped back onto the platform. He had remained quiet the whole time. However, upon entering the locker room, he dropped to his knees and grasped his twitching red hand. Tears of overwhelming pain ran down his face. He just kneeled there in utter agony, screaming at the top of his lungs, until one of his friends helped him to the infirmary.

"Guess you were right. It is indestructible," Angel smirked toward Shaw's venomous gaze. His words came calmly, almost coldly. "Don't worry. I'd say his hand should heal in a little while, maybe in a few hours. He could still fight if he used his other hand."

Just then, the announcer came onto the screen of all the monitors. "The judges have decided not to award the two hundred points to Utopia University for the last challenge, as they deemed it unreasonable. Henceforth, this particular challenge is banned from the tournaments. Thank you."

Both teams were on edge. A tiny spark and the entire room would no doubt explode from the tension built up like a tinderbox. Angel sat back in his chair and pondered his next move.

CHAPTER 8

CLASH OF THE CAPTAINS

The remote passed between the captains several more times until all their men had fought or completed a challenge. The final score going into the last match was MidStar 345, Utopia University 196. Fans anxiously awaited the fighters they came to see enter the ring. They had seen it all, from man-eating Tirexidons and then a pack of ferocious Lavasaurs. They flooded the ring for a swimming race with proximity mines and ugly shark-like terrors built for speed and jaws strong enough to tear through chainmail. A vicious four-on-one battle where much blood and sweat was spilled. They set traps for a dangerous obstacle course that had to be run in wolf form only, and the challenge was that a team had to stop a runner. Through it all, the spectators witnessed the fighters' skills on display. The blood and sweat left in the ring were a testament to that. In the next bout, the winning team would be determined. It all came down to these last two men.

"These two men are no strangers, nor are they, friends. They are bitter rivals and even worse enemies. Our gracious Emperor, gentlemen and ladies LET'S PREPARE FOR THE FINAL COU- ha-ha I'm sorry, SHOWDOWN!" hollered the announcer with all his might into his little microphone, rallying the crowd once more for the last battle.

Thunderous music began playing throughout the building. It echoed off the stone walls. It was a strong beat. One that got the heart pounding and the blood surging with adrenaline. One that told the onlookers they were about to see a fight of a lifetime.

Meanwhile, just below the arena floor, the two men stood silently, waiting. On the left was Shaw, captain of the MidStar team from across the ocean. Boy born into money and maker of so much more. To his right stood

Dark Everlast, a boy who came from nowhere and has henceforth been a significant thorn in Shaw's side. First, taking the one he most desired. Then defeating him repeatedly, making him a mockery of what he once stood for.

"May the best man win." Shaw extended his hand to Angel. Angel nodded silently, taking Shaw's hand and shaking it. Their hands were tightening on the other. Both were vying to outdo the other. "Just so we are clear, that will be ME!" Shaw suddenly pulled Angel in close, ramming his knee into his stomach. He then began swinging Angel by his arm up against the walls of the confined dark room. Fans above could hear the banging and feel the slight tremors as each thunderous blow hit.

The team members in the infirmary heard and felt the battle the loudest. They watched as the walls buckled under the impact of whatever was hitting them on the other side. While still holding onto the arm and shoulder of Angel, Shaw whipped him around off balance and then threw him upward. Before he could regain control, Shaw flew into the air after him, like a shark chasing its prey. With his fists aimed upward, he slammed into Angel's ribs. Angel's body folded over as the air was knocked out of him. Shaw continued his ascent with Angel toward the sliding door that led to the arena and the anxiously awaiting fans. The sliding door, however, had not been activated. Using Angel like a battering ram, Shaw broke through the reinforced steel doors. Shaw then sent his opponent skidding across the rough, sandy arena floor. The fans were awestruck by the sheer brutality but soon found their voices and began cheering again.

Leen watched in agony as they replayed the scene repeatedly on the many gigantic screens. It showed how Angel's body was used to open the arena door and now was merely a punching bag for Shaw's enjoyment. She could feel all the hatred in Shaw's heart and the hint of joy that hurting Angel was giving him. Becky put her arm around her shoulder to comfort her. She knew all too well what seeing this was like. Cogeta was known for jumping into reckless brawls in unofficial street fights or sanctioned tournaments. Being his biggest fan also meant she had to suffer with him with every punch or kick, just as Leen did now.

She hugged her shoulder. "He's going to be okay, Leen. Just wait and see."

Leen forced a smile and nodded.

Back in the arena, Angel still had not been given a chance to fight back as Shaw kept him pinned against the wall as his fists burrowed into Angel with great malice.

"THIS IS FOR YOU, LEEN!"

Shaw's right fist plowed into Angel's jaw. Time seemed to slow as everyone watched on the screen as Angel's head snapped to one side. His blood shot out of his mouth, along with what appeared to be a tooth— Time quickly returned to normal as Shaw continued his onslaught.

Enough is enough!

With a loud barbaric battle cry, Angel sent out a surge of energy that shoved Shaw away. It gave him that dire moment needed to get his wits about him and get into the fight. When Shaw came back with a left hook, Angel blocked it—then responded by bashing his head into Shaw's nose, shattering the bone, and causing him to stumble back. Within those few seconds, the tide of the battle had shifted in Angel's favor. He was now the aggressor, and Shaw became the defender.

The fighting only got more and more intense as it ran on. The pace never slowed. Their punches were not showing any signs of weakening. The two zipped around the arena at super speeds. They exchanged explosive energy blasts as they flew about that collided in mid-flight with great eruptions of power. When that tactic proved futile, they again clashed in hand-to-hand exchanges—giving the onlookers a brutal slugfest several feet above the ring to digest. Both refused to back down.

In the heat of it, Angel saw an opening. He quickly brought his knee up into Shaw's side. Shaw was surprised by the instant pressure and the sudden rush of pain as his ribs cracked, then shattered under the sudden trauma. Angel sent him flying to the ground with a powerful right-overhand punch.

Shaw slammed into the ground in an explosion of sand. He only had an instant to glare upward before quickly jumping out of the way as Angel crashed into the ground where he had once been. Angel did not hesitate and kicked off from the ground, charging his target. Shaw put up a barrier to block him. Angel ran into the invisible shield and stumbled backward, giving Shaw the opening he desperately needed to get the fight back under his control.

With each thundering blow, the arena's foundation trembled. Leen sat helplessly in the stands. Every hit to Angel was like a blow to her heart. No matter how much Becky reassured her he would be okay, it was still hard to swallow when she could see clearly that he was not. Meanwhile, all around, she could hear the roars and cheers of the crowd. It was deafening. Even as she and Becky tried to cheer Angel on, those around them drowned them out. Down below, the two teams sat silently cheering for their captains, but none daring to speak. They knew their captains were going all out and did not want to miss the sound of every bone-crunching blow hitting its mark.

In the infirmary, Cogeta sat next to Cory. He had regained consciousness while Shaw was assaulting Angel in the elevator. His body was still recovering from his battle. He was hooked up to monitors and a breathing apparatus. They had plugged tubes into his arms, feeding his veins with small doses of medicinal concoctions to improve his natural regenerative powers. Hardened, charred chunks of flesh remained on some parts of his body but were slowly falling off with newly formed skin underneath. Cogeta sat clasping his friend's hand while they transfixed their attention on the screen, watching the fight with the others in the room.

Both fierce warriors in the arena looked like they had jumped in a pool of blood. They both wore deep cuts and bruises from their attacker and the unforgiving arena, scorch marks from their blasts of energy that they traded throughout the battle, and bite and claw marks from their transforming into wolves to claim the prize. The audience saw Angel in his black wolf form battling with Shaw as a golden wolf with black highlights. The two fighters could sense that the end was nearing rapidly. They had given it their all, and now the wear and tear were there for all to see. Shaw, driving his body to continue, charged at Angel once more. Angel shot into the air as Shaw was about to hit his mark. Shaw forced his body to stop. His sudden halt caused his already sore muscles to scream even more. Spinning around quickly, Angel looked down and saw Shaw correcting his error. He'd turned around and was flying up to continue the fight. Angel stretched out his arms and legs, leaving himself completely open.

Is he taunting me?! I'll devour his heart!

Shaw's eyes burned with rage as a golden aura exploded around his body, summoning all his energy into one final attack.

Angel was summoning his power for his ultimate attack. His body took on a bluish glow as his power surged and peaked. Angel smirked, sensing his readiness, then with all his remaining might,

"MEGA-BLAST!"

In an instant, a tremendous burst of blue energy shot forth from his body. It stopped Shaw in his tracks. His fingertips were mere inches away from Angel. He tried to fight the current within the blast with all the strength he could muster. Shaw screamed in utter rage as he clawed and struggled to get at Angel as the blast of energy burned and seared his flesh off. His attempt was in vain as his body convulsed and fell to the ground. As the wave washed over him, he screamed out in pain. The blast created a deep crater in the ground for Shaw to writhe in agony once the blast subsided. Angel slowly floated downward, wholly exhausted. Setting his feet on the ground again, he immediately dropped to one knee as paramedics rushed to the scene. The fight was finally over, and the team of

Utopia University had once again prevailed for the second year in a row. Paramedics rushed to Angel as another group carried an unconscious Shaw out of the hole.

"Is he going to be all right?" Angel asked. He could barely open his eyes from the blood pouring down his face.

"Yeah, he will be fine. Hell of an attack you hit him with," replied the paramedic, strapping Angel to the stretcher.

"It just came to me," whispered Angel softly as he closed his eyes as the last of his strength seemed to leave him, and his exhaustion took over. The last things he heard were the roars and cheers of the crowd as the announcer announced his victory repeatedly.

"Utopia University is victorious! Final score! Midstar, 345! Utopia University, 346! It doesn't get much closer than that, folks! It looks like last year was not a trick of our eyes! It was no mere fluke! Dark Everlast attains his second victory over Midstar's former dominating champion, Shaw! There is a new Alpha prowling these hallowed halls! And he's accepting all challengers and taking no prisoners! Dark Everlast! Remember that name, folks! Dark Everlast, the everlasting! Thank you for coming, and goodnight! Be safe, and be sure to buy souvenirs on your way out to remember this historic event! For the second year in a row, Utopia University takes home the gold!"

Within a relatively short time, the coliseum was more or less emptied, and the staff got to work on cleaning and making repairs. Leen and Becky met with the guys as they slowly walked and limped out of the exit, following the other bruised and roughed-up fighters. Angel came out wearing a black long-sleeve jacket, a plain white T-shirt underneath, black jeans, and boots. Cory was once again wearing what he had when they arrived. Underneath his clothes, he had some leftover bandages still wrapped around areas that had almost finished healing. Cogeta had brought no extra clothes and came out wearing precisely what he had arrived wearing. His wrappings were torn and shredded, dangling loosely on his arms and legs, but he still walked proudly. After all, he was one of the champions today. While the others winced and made faces in pain as they changed, he got to sit back and laugh at their discomfort.

"Are you three okay?" Leen looked at the three of them with worry on her face.

"Leen, it will take more than four fighters to beat me. Remember, I won that round," Cogeta smiled. "That's 'cause I am THE GREATEST!" He threw his arm into the air, then suddenly froze, his face pale.

Becky shook her head and smiled. "The Greatest is still healing from his injuries from that round and shouldn't be raising his arms so high. In fact, he probably shouldn't try doing anything aside from breathing."

Cogeta tried to laugh, but it hurt him even more. Becky put one of his arms around her shoulders as she helped him walk. He kissed her on the side of her head and whispered that he loved her in her ear. Leen busied herself looking Angel over for any severe injuries from his battle with Shaw. For the most part, however, she saw the cuts and abrasions she had seen him sustain had already healed over. Even the teeth that Shaw had knocked out were replaced. She did see the bruising, and he was sensitive to touch, so she knew he was still in great pain as his body tasked itself with healing his more profound injuries that her eyes couldn't see.

Cory stood back and smiled as the girls treated his friends individually. Like the nurses who tended to him while he was unconscious, they checked for any remaining open wounds. Then to his utter surprise, Leen stepped over to him and checked him as well.

"Uh, I-I'm fine, Leen."

"Shush, you did extremely well. Are you still sore as well?"

He stared into her smiling face for a moment. Her fingers lightly checked his head and around his side, and just her closeness set him at ease but made him nervous.

"Cory?"

"Huh?" Her soft, dulcet words finally registered in his head.

"Are you all right? Have you healed completely? Are you still rather sore?"

"Oh! Y-yeah. I mean, my outer wounds have all healed, mostly. My body is still healing, and I have some bandages around my body. I'm still really sore, in any case. But I will be fine... really. Shouldn't you be focusing on Angel?"

He glanced at Angel, worried her attention toward him may upset his friend. When he looked over, he saw Angel smiling at him, no malice in his eyes or apparent anywhere. So often, when girls paid attention to him, he had to be wary of their significant other. Sometimes he forgot that there was no cause for such fears among his friends.

Leen smiled, "You are my friend. I worry about you, too. You gave it your all today. I'm proud of you." She placed a soft kiss on his cheek.

His cheeks burned with embarrassment. Receiving this type of attention from Leen and Becky made him uncomfortable but in a good way. He wasn't used to being given such attention by girls. Due to his shyness, Cory didn't interact with girls like this. Be it his shyness or lack of confidence, he looked upon Cogeta and Angel with admiration and perhaps a tinge of envy at how confident they were. At times he couldn't help himself feeling out of place even amongst them, as he was so different from them. His friends were no fools; they sensed these feelings from their young friend and wished to see him come out of his shell and become the man they saw within him.

"Thank you…" Cory whispered as he looked down at the ground.

His close friends lightly patted his shoulders. The group walked to the front entrance, where a large crowd was still leaving. Spotting Stone and his girlfriend, the party waved goodbye as the two headed off. They hung out there with other teammates who stuck around and signed autographs for fans. Out of nowhere, Angel received a mighty slap on his bruised shoulder. He spun around, ready to throttle the person with the nerve to do such a thing. However, he quickly quelled his anger when he saw Leen's father standing before him.

"Well done, boy. Good fight. Could you have gotten your ass kicked any worse? You know, you are still working when you get home. I won't excuse you, just 'cause you wanted to come up here and roll around in the dirt." Vox then walked past him, heading toward town.

"Sure, he walks away before I ask him why he was even here when he told me he hated these things." Angel glared at the back of the old man's head.

"He came here to cheer for you. Do not let him kid you; he does like you. He told me so." Leen reassured Angel, kissing his cheek. "Where is Shaw, by the way? Is he okay? I didn't see him come out with the others. That attack was... intense, to say the least."

"He will be okay," Angel said quietly. He wasn't surprised by Leen's concern for Shaw. He had always treated her kindly in his attempts to woo her. She didn't wish him harm even if she was not interested in his affections. Angel admired and loved her for her kindness toward everyone, even though some of those people wanted to see him out of the picture. He couldn't fault them for that, either. Leen was the most caring, generous, and loving person he had ever known. Angel did not need belief in divine beings. However, Leen gave him pause. She was the closest thing to a goddess in character and personality, which sometimes made him question if she wasn't a reincarnation of such a being.

"Oh yeah, he is fine," answered Cogeta. "As soon as he was in the infirmary, his boys in black came in and took him away to heal in his own home. Didn't want to deal with the shame of walking out of here a loser, But, man, she is right, Angel. That blast of yours was a sight to behold. And Cory, damn, you did great this year."

"I lost my first match and couldn't continue because I was unconscious for most of the tournament. I failed you all again, just like last year," Cory muttered, lowering his head. *Like last year, I couldn't even get past my first round.* He tightened his fists in frustration. An act that didn't go unnoticed by Angel's sharp gaze.

"Winning isn't everything, Cory. You went out there even though you faced two opponents and gave it your all," Angel spoke assuredly, trying to encourage his friend.

"Cogeta took on four at a time and won."

"Mine were unarmed also; neither of mine went into a berserker rage. Besides, the point is that you tried. That's what winners do. They give it all they got, which is what you did. You pushed yourself to your breaking point. Your body literally short-circuited itself from all the power you exerted in that last blast of lightning you gave out. And for the record, those two guys you faced couldn't compete in any other round, either. Think about that. Shaw thought he was going to humiliate you by having two of his people beat up on you, but instead... you took two of his people out of commission for the rest of the fight." said Cogeta smiling and messing up Cory's hair.

Cory thought about his friend's words. *From that perspective... yeah... that sounds pretty good. But...* "I feel you can say that because we won. It was close. What if we had lost?"

Angel thought for a moment and then shrugged. "If we had lost, I would have had to put up with Shaw's bragging for a year. I wouldn't have blamed you at all for it. So stop thinking I would." Angel slapped his hand down onto Cory's shoulder. Cory uttered a silent scream as it was the same shoulder Atila had bashed real good during their fight. "See? Had you done nothing, this wouldn't have hurt so much. You truly gave it everything you had. You went full-on wolf and tore into that guy's back. I know I said if you had to go rabid as a wolf, then do it. I didn't think you would go so literal."

Angel, Cogeta, and Becky laughed while Leen stifled her laughter before speaking softly.

"I was really surprised by that. Cory, you are a great fighter. You have the skill. You need to work on your confidence some."

"Exactly," Becky agreed. She then reached out and gave him a gentle hug. "You have got to start believing in yourself. You are so much more capable than you know."

"Honestly, if it weren't for you and Becky cheering for me, I wouldn't have gotten as far as I did. I owe as long as I lasted to you two. There were moments where I just didn't have it in me to continue, and then... I heard your voices cheering me on and... I didn't want to let you, or the team, down. Your cheers filled me with the strength I needed each time to continue. Thank you." Cory's eyes watered as he spoke. He meant every word and bowed down to them in gratitude when he finished.

His words shocked the two girls and warmed their hearts. Angel looked at Leen and smiled as they shared a glance. He knew all too well what Cory spoke of, as did Cogeta. Their loved ones gave them the strength to conquer all. That they shared that power and gift with Cory made him proud. Cogeta looked over, and the two smiled and nodded in silent agreement. They walked around on either side of Cory, pulled him back up straight, and put their arms around him. Leen and Becky smiled as the three boys started laughing. They joined arms with their respective man.

As they relaxed, Cogeta looked down the row.

"So, what are we going to do now?"

Angel smiled and looked over at Leen, then back to Cogeta, "Well, I plan to take this angel shopping before I go to her dad's shop."

Leen smiled from ear to ear and hugged Angel, shortly forgetting the pain he was in already. He softly whimpered, and she quickly released him, apologizing repeatedly.

Cogeta nodded. "Sure, make me look bad. I was going to go home and work this soreness out of my body by starting on a new training regime."

Becky shrugged and smiled. "As long as I get to watch, I'm fine with that plan."

It was now Cogeta's turn to grin ear to ear. "Oh, baby, you can watch me any time. I'll even let you pick the mood music. What about you, Cory? Any dates or plans now that we are champions?"

Cory thought for a moment. "I think I will head to the park, find an enormous tree to lie under and rest. Listen to nature's voice while I heal up a bit. I don't know if my folks would be too happy to know I fought in today's tournament. I didn't tell them I was competing."

"Did you not tell them in case you lost again?" Angel asked Cory.

"Yeah... looks like I made a good call there. But I didn't want to worry them. I know they don't want me fighting like this. They only sent me to the university because they wanted me to learn to defend myself, to man up, and not actually go out looking for fights."

"Nothing wrong with not wanting to worry your folks. I think they'd be proud of you, in any case. I can't say it enough, man. You did an amazing job. It was a hell of a fight to watch. What others think, what they will, but if I were facing down Hel and her army of the damned, I'd have more confidence knowing you were by my side."

Cogeta whined, "Aww, and what about me, my captain, my captain?"

"Of course, I'd want you there too. We are the Wolf Pack. Apart, we are strong..."

The others joined in, saying, "Together, we are unbeatable."

"Well, Cory, the park sounds like a good idea. But promise me one thing, man. No moping, okay? Don't forget, recently you took me down," Cogeta laughed.

"He did?" Angel looked back and forth at the two.

Cogeta pretended to be sore about it. "Yeah, he got lucky and beat me in my dojo."

"Stop complaining. You got me back before we ate dinner, you jerk," Cory shot back.

Cogeta only laughed but stopped abruptly to hold his ribs. Saying their goodbyes, they went their separate ways.

CHAPTER 9

DARKENED DAYS

Cogeta and Becky returned home. He changed out of his battle-torn shorts into a pair of loose-fitting orange sweatpants and then went into his dojo, where he began working out with his sword. He moved in slow, methodical movements and occasionally burst into flashy swordplay before slipping back into the slower motions. No matter how sore he was, he would work through the pain. Sometime later, Becky, after changing into more casual clothes and putting her dress away, stood in the doorway smiling while she watched. She chose this man to spend her life with. He was kind, sweet, funny- at times anyway. He always knew how to make her smile, cared for his friends, and was willing to sacrifice for her and those he cared about.

He can be a clueless fool and a horn dog, but I don't care. I kind of like even those traits about him. He makes me feel good about myself, and when he smiles at me with that boyish, innocent grin, I know everything will be all right.

Cogeta suddenly noticed her standing there with a bottle of water for him. Smiling, he walked over, took the bottle from her offering hand, took a drink, and poured some onto himself. He had gotten hot due to the dojo always being warm, combining that with the fact he had fought hard only hours before and still was sore from it. She couldn't help but giggle at him when he did this silly childish thing. She also could not help her eyes from roaming as the water washed over his nicely toned pecks. The combination of water, sweat, and glow from the sun's rays passing through the window only made his muscular figure stand out even more. Her eyes returned to catch him looking back at her and grinning.

Quickly taking his right foot, he swept at her feet, but she grabbed his shoulders and gracefully flipped over him. Landing on her feet, she turned around and smirked at him. He stood there admiring her, with a fire burning within him. He turned around fully and stood before her nodding and flipping his sword. Becky kept her eyes on him, smiling sexily as she slowly backed up to the weapon stand along the far wall.

She reached out and wrapped her fingers around her prized weapon of choice, a glaive type of weapon called "Dragon's Fire". The pole was made of mythril with a wood finish, with a jade-colored grip. A gold dragon head with ruby eyes attached a broad curved blade at one end. The blade came out of its mouth like fire spewing forth, hence its name. At the other end was an ornate, golden decorative cap. The back of the blade was serrated, much as Cogeta's sword was.

Cogeta's sword, called "Great One", had a broad curved blade with serrations along the back. It wasn't fashioned from mythril but forged by mixing two strong types of steel. The pommel was gold and shaped to look like a raging fire was ascending the blade. The grip was dark blue leather with the end capped off with a golden head of a wolf. He watched her closely, his eyes burning with anticipation as hers were. At the exact moment, they charged each other. Their weapons clashed overhead, then separated as sparks flew, and the two spun around the other and backed away slowly, smiling at each other.

Cogeta's toes inched forward on the beige mat. His eyes looked over his beautiful opponent. She wore a short yellow tank top and a pair of black sweats. Her posture was confident, and her defense was strong. *Damn, what a woman,* he growled to himself in admiration. In a split instant, she was gone from his sight. *Shit! Where is she? AH HA!*

He raised his sword over his head just in time to block her strike. He heard her giggling behind him, then felt her step between his legs. She was moving to knock him over, but he wouldn't have that. Releasing the blade of his weapon with his left hand, he reached up, grabbed the pole of hers, and leaned forward, pulling her weapon with him. With a scream of surprise, Becky came flipping over him, still holding onto her weapon and smacking her onto the mat. She lay there, catching her breath as he smiled down at her, panting as she was.

"I win."

"You think? I can still hurt you." She said with a sultry smile.

"Oh?"

She winked, pushed her weapon forward, and poked him with the weapon's point. His eyes grew large as he took notice. She suddenly reached up with her legs, wrapped them around his head, and pulled him down. Quickly, Cogeta jumped with his legs to avoid her blade as she flipped him over her and onto the mat.

"Goodness, girl, you could have really hurt me," he laughed.

She rolled onto her feet, walked over, and stood above him.

"I would never hurt you, baby, not much." She winked teasingly.

"Oh, I see. Well then, in that case."

He reached up with his legs, locking them around her waist. With a squeak, she fell back onto the padded cushion. Cogeta quickly released his sword and moved up her body, pushing her legs to either side of him, pushing her weapon out of reach of her fingers. He was then hovering over her, staring into the depths of her eyes. They were both breathing heavily, their bodies both perspiring. Becky giggled and smiled.

"I guess you win this round." She giggled more as he nuzzled his face into her neck and against her cheek.

"Yep, suppose I did. What is my prize?"

"Guess I am cooking dinner tonight."

"Mmmmm, fantastic."

He kissed and gently nibbled her neck.

"Mmmm, if you want me to get dinner started, you best let me up, silly." She giggled as his lips tickled her.

"I suppose you are right. All right then."

With a groan, he stood up and took her hand to help her get up. Once on her feet, she kissed him and turned to leave when her feet were swept out from under her. She fell back into his arms and was guided down to the beige mat, where he quickly rolled on top of her and grasped her wrists, pinning her down. She gently smiled up at Cogeta, letting her eyes swim within his.

"Dinner can wait. I am hungry for you."

His words came softly as he brought his lips to hers. There was something about their softness, the way they were shaped, and their sweet taste that drew him closer. She didn't resist. Their ritual dance was commonplace. She wanted his lips just as much as he wanted hers. Their lips touched, and before long, as their arms wrapped around one another, they were oblivious to their surroundings as their love overcame them.

Meanwhile, Cory walked through the golden arches that gave entry into an extensive park. He knew where a bench was where all the thick, lush trees surrounding the area had golden leaves. It was like a page straight out of a fairy tale. It was his favorite place and the perfect spot to relax his sore body and mind. Walking along the stone pathway, he smiled, seeing children playing with their parents, couples having picnics, and other people sitting beneath trees reading or sleeping. Getting off the path, he took a shortcut he figured out, cutting through the trees. The best part of his destination was that it was secluded and rarely disturbed. He had spent many hours there alone in his thoughts, lost in a book or napping.

When Cory had the place in sight, he spotted someone standing in front of the bench. It was a girl. As he focused his eyes on her, he realized who it was. It wasn't just any girl; it was her, Alisandra. He closed his eyes as his mind immediately worked to resolve why she was there, and the more he thought about it, the more his mind wandered.

Why is she here? Wouldn't think she knew of this place. Maybe she knew I would come here, so she came to see me. Perhaps she saw me fight today and wanted to know if I was okay. This could be the chance that I've been waiting for. My chance to talk to her, explore who she is, and show her who I am. Perhaps tell her how I feel...

Though the thoughts gave him goosebumps, he built up the courage to talk to her. He walked out from behind the tree where he was standing and up the hill to where she stood waiting. When she noticed him, she smiled, which instantly made him smile. A feeling of almost overwhelming joy swelled within him, and with it, a sense of nervousness gnawed at him.

"I was waiting for you to show up. I overheard you say you were coming, so I wanted to meet you here," she said.

He just nodded. This always happened when he was around her. He could never get words to come out of his mouth. It was as if the vast dictionary of words he had gained was suddenly reduced to the most elementary forms. He could recite epic legends at any other time, yet when around her, they faded into a muddled mess. His brain would ask questions and then try to solve them, coming up with plans and solutions. His inner voice would constantly talk, carrying on inner monologues about anything and everything. However, when he was in her presence, that inner voice in his head became silent. His mind was at ease, content, at peace. It was relaxing. It was comforting. Suddenly, he realized she was staring at him, waiting for him to respond.

"I-I uh- I c-come here to read, n-normally." He finally stuttered. *Stupid. Stupid.*

She giggled. "I came to think," she commented, looking up at the treetops.

"To, um… to think about what?" Cory worried he would sound nosey, but he had to ask.

"Oh, I think about different things while I am here. Things from my past to tomorrow's tests to even what the future has in store for me. Today it's about my choice of companion."

Cory's mouth dropped as he was shocked. *Did she really say that? Is she finally going to give me a chance?* His head was flooded with many emotions and feelings that his brain couldn't keep up.

"I saw your fight today. Are you all right? You took such a beating from those creeps. You were awesome, in any case. Justin sat in the booth laughing as you got hurt, but I know he couldn't have lasted as long as you did. He would have gone down with one shot from that massive weapon."

"Oh, um, I am fine. A bit sore, but I've healed up mostly. What doesn't kill me makes me stronger, after all," he smiled and laughed nervously, rubbing the back of his head.

"He can be such a jerk sometimes. He can even be cruel. I mean, like laughing at you and calling you different names. On the other hand, I've never really seen you hurt or go after anyone. It surprised me that you took part in the tournament. Doesn't seem like you at all."

"Angel and Cogeta asked me to compete. I did it for them. Just wish I hadn't lost."

"We can't win every battle we enter. We can only grow and learn from our losses and continue forward. Look at me; for example, I learned something from your fight."

Cory squinted and turned his head to the side. "You did? What? Don't take on two opponents who dwarf you in body mass?"

Alisandra laughed. "No, silly. I learned that beneath your gentle exterior; you have the power and strength to protect me. Justin could never do that."

She smiled and shyly leaned in close, kissing his lips. Surprised at first, Cory tensed up as though volts of electricity passed from her lips and shot through his body. He could control and harness his power into electrical blasts, and yet she caused him to seize up as though hit by a stun gun. The humor within that irony didn't escape him. He quickly calmed down and let his instincts take over, wrapping his arms around her, then gently pulling her closer. He returned the kiss, closing his eyes and sinking into his pleasure.

When he opened his eyes, he was back behind the tree, looking in her direction. *If only that had been real. Well, it's now, or never,* he thought as he walked toward her. On his way up the hill, though, something caught his attention out of the corner of his eye, causing him to pause in his tracks to see what it was. A man had walked up, hiding something behind his back. Cory was about to dash over there, thinking the worst, but before he could get far, he realized the man was Justin and surprised the girl with a bouquet.

Cory watched as the girl swung her arms around him and embraced him with a kiss. Cory turned to walk away as the wind blew through the park. *What is wrong with me? I should know better. Of course, she wouldn't be here for me. She doesn't even know me. She only talks to me when she needs something.*

Why am I drawn to her, to begin with? I try to stop my feelings, but there is just something about her that draws me in. I just want her to be happy… but not with that jerk. Am I a bad person for wishing it was me? He let an exasperated sigh escape his lips. *Guess I'll need to search out another place where I can be alone,* he thought as he headed out of the once beautiful fairytale park. Its mental visage forever changed in his mind.

Angel and Leen were walking through the crowded streets of the marketplace, her arms snugly wrapped around his right arm. People were lined up as far as the eyes could see on either side of the street. Now that the tournament was over, the stores were open again for business. Stores and open-air shops owned the street for many blocks before ending in a grand circle. It wasn't uncommon to see street performers putting on an act around the enormous multilayered fountain in the center.

Angel had come here with Leen for one reason and one reason only, to view the instruments in a little shop owned by a kind old gentleman. Leen has been very fond of music ever since she was young. Her mother had gotten her into it by singing to her as a child and playing for her and her father. Leen had mastered many instruments since to be just like her. Her favorites to play were the piano, flute, and koto, and she enjoyed singing with her angelic voice. She got Angel into the art of music after constantly asking him to try it, and he quickly excelled in it, if only to please her. His favorite instrument was the violin, but he was also good at the guitar. They practiced together often when alone and could manage the time. They even created a compact disc together. It comprised a mix of her songs and his, with a few duets. A soft bell chimed as he escorted her in through the little wooden door.

"Welcome, welcome. How might I help you two kids today?" The pleasant old man bowed from behind the glass display cases that housed several small instruments.

"Just looking around, thank you." Angel nodded.

"Aww, the harp in the window is gone." Leen frowned.

"Really? Dang, it was a nice one, too. Sorry, sweetie. Go ahead and look around and see if there is anything else you may like. I'm going to check out a few things over here." Angel watched as she disappointedly walked over to look at the racks of sheet music.

He walked over and started looking at different guitars, slowly making his way over to the counter, where inside the glass case was music memorabilia. The old man watched him, and when Leen was out of sight, he tapped the glass. Angel glanced over his shoulder and saw that Leen was out of view for himself. He then moved down to where the old seller stood.

"Is it ready?" Angel asked.

"Indeed, it is. She is a beauty. I added some sheet music for you as well. I think you will like it."

"What do you think he will like? Hum?" Leen's fingers tiptoed up Angel's shoulder.

"Ha-ha, I guess I am caught." He took the package the man had placed on the counter and slid it over to her.

Leen had a quizzical look as she opened the package, throwing the wrapping away into a wastebasket that the merchant provided. Inside was a medium size case made of cherry wood with gold angel wing clasps. Snapping them open, she slowly opened the case. Within, she saw the harp that was missing from the window.

The harp was made of silver with the shape of a Dis, or Valkyrie, at the end of the neck. The cords were fashioned out of the finest steel thread to guarantee the purest of sounds produced. Leen had been eyeing it ever since the shopkeeper had gotten it in. She found the sheet music packed into a pocket in the case's roof. As she looked through them, she also found blank ones among them. This was so she could write her own. With a smile and tears in her eyes, she thanked the old gentleman as Angel paid him. She leaped onto him when they exited the shop, flinging her arms around his neck. She squealed as tears of joy filled and flowed from her eyes.

"Thankyouthankyouthankyou, THANK YOU!"

Angel hugged Leen close, smiling as she buried her head into his broad shoulder and kissed his cheek repeatedly. "You're welcome, sweetheart. Of course, you realize you have to play it for me tonight. Then possibly you could even teach me how to use it later."

She smiled as he reached up and wiped away her tears with his thumb, "I would be more than happy to," she then leaned up and kissed him on his lips.

While they were kissing, a gigantic shadow passed over them, followed by another shadow and then another. Angel and Leen joined the many others looking to the sky with interest. Above them were massive black aircraft cruising at low altitudes.

"What's going on? Maneuvers, you think?"

"I didn't know they had any scheduled for today, and the tournament is over, so it cannot be related to that. They are like no ships I've ever seen." Angel watched in awe.

Doors slowly slid open on the hull with a hiss, and smaller ships dropped out of the giant cruisers. Zooming over the marketplace, they suddenly started shooting green bolts of energy into the buildings and along the streets. As the small fighters began their run, another group of large ships opened their pod bay doors, allowing soldiers to jump into the streets, where they started attacking the unarmed people. Angel pushed

Leen behind him as soldiers ran toward them. Taking them down with a flurry of punches and kicks, Angel looked back at her.

"Are you okay?"

"Yes, but who are they?" Her voice was stricken with worry.

Angel looked down at his attackers. They wore black skintight armor with different colored metal shields over their chest and a black helmet with a shaded visor covering their face. Angel knelt beside one of the fallen enemies and removed his helmet. He only glanced at the face, for when the light touched the skin, it burst into flames and disintegrated. *Pale skin, long and pointed canines, severe allergy to sunlight. Could they really be?* The realization of what was happening sunk in, sending a chill up his spine. He growled and shouted back to Leen over his shoulder as another bunch of black armored soldiers ran at them.

"Vampirians! Stay close, Leen!"

"Angel, are you capable of fighting them?" She was concerned about his physical condition.

"Never mind that now!" Angel parried the first Vampirian's sword, then broke his visor with a right punch. "Just stay back!"

He threw the defeated Vampirian to the ground and ducked as a sword slash nearly took his head. Angel capitalized and returned with an uppercut, knocking the helmet off the Vampirian's head. As the attacker screamed from his face catching ablaze, Angel side-kicked him away into a charging group of his comrades.

Cogeta got to his feet, then helped Becky to hers. They hugged each other and prepared to start dinner when suddenly, a thunderous explosion shook the house down to its foundation. Pictures fell off the walls. Dishes fell from the tables and cabinets, shattering on the floor. The beams overhead snapped under the sudden pressure and came crashing down on them. Pushing Becky under him, he covered her with his body as a shield as the first thick beam hit, followed by the others. Cogeta slowly opened his eyes.

"Now I could have sworn we lived in a high ceiling home… did you forget to pay the roofing company?" Cogeta jested with some strain, supporting the weight on his back.

"Oh, shut up and get these things off us. Now isn't the time for jokes. What in Hel's name is going on?"

Getting serious, he slowly pushed himself up, forcing the debris off himself. Once free, he helped Becky back to her feet once again.

"Are you okay?" He looked her over for injuries and brushed splinters and debris off her.

"Yes, but what was that?"

Cogeta looked around. He could hear shouting and fighting going on outside his home. "I am not so sure. But it sounds like someone started a riot without telling me about it," he looked around, confused. That's when he noticed that there was now a hole in his wall with a black smoking ring around it. Cogeta recognized the signs and knew it had come from a laser bolt. They had been lucky that part of the ceiling had knocked them out of its path. He made his way over the hole in the wall and cautiously peered out. He saw unknown soldiers in black battle suits fighting amongst the citizens, slaughtering people left and right. "Shit, someone is attacking us!"

"What? Who is?"

"Hell if I know, but—"

As he looked back out the hole again, a blade shot through. Cogeta pulled his head away quickly, bending over backward, but the edge still made a small gash on his cheek.

"OUCH! Bastard, you want to play rough? Fine! Let's play rough!"

He moved aside the hole, placing his hands against the wall. He pushed with all his might. The wall gave and fell back onto the attacker with a loud crash. His home having already been partly destroyed, Cogeta didn't think a little more would do it all that much.

"Cogeta, are you okay?"

Becky feared what that strain may have done to his already bruised body.

He turned and looked at her, panting but still smiling.

"Fine… He's not," he pointed over his shoulder, back to the wall. He then felt his cheek as it healed over. "Looks like whomever these idiots are, they mean business. Come on…" He smiled at her. "I don't want to miss this." He jumped onto the wall he had just pushed over, seemingly enjoying the idea of fighting these unknown invaders.

"Here, catch!" Becky tossed him his sword. "We should at least level the playing field."

"Honey, they made the playing field uneven when they attacked us just as we were about to have a nice hot dinner and then wrecked our home. I will show them no mercy." His eyes started to burn with adrenaline as he flipped his sword around.

"Let's not keep them waiting, my love." Becky stepped forward with her bladed staff. Cogeta smiled at her and kissed her cheek.

"I got your back if you got mine."

"Always, my love. Now, stop talking. Our friends need us, and I'm," Her eyes showed the same fire as his, "itching to work off some stress because now I have to clean this shit up!"

Becky leaped high into the air and came down, slashing her blade across the chest of an unsuspecting soldier. She twirled and spun her deadly weapon around, cutting down all who came within her range with lethal accuracy.

Damn, what a woman! Not to be outdone, Cogeta rushed in. Not even bothering to use his sword at first, he punched the first enemy that crossed his path. When his fist connected with the soldier's helmet, the impact caused the protective gear to split. From Cogeta's fist, a burst of flame erupted, shooting forth and enveloping the soldier's head and swallowing up three of his comrades behind him. Cogeta flipped his sword in his hand, catching an enemy to the side just under his chin. Cogeta looked over and smiled, holding the man at bay for a moment before; with lightning speed, he slashed the blade around and cleaved the man's head off.

Side-by-side, they danced through the hordes of attacking soldiers, moving and slashing as if they had rehearsed this battle for months. The steel of their blades flashed with the sun's rays with each stroke. Cogeta occasionally lit up a few with another fire attack while Becky sent others to their grave with an energy blast. The two working together made a wall between the invading party and the citizens, trying to protect their families before engaging the enemy.

Becky cut down four more Vampirians when she heard Cogeta let out a yelp. She quickly turned and saw that a Vampirian had him down on one knee, his sword on the ground, and blood running down his arm. The Vampirian drew back to make a fatal strike. She sensed danger and quickly deflected an attacker's strike. She skewered the Vampirian with her bladed staff. "Be a dear and hold this."

Becky then turned and sprinted toward Cogeta. She let out a roaring howl as she stepped onto Cogeta's shoulder and lunged at his attacker. While in midair, she transformed into a golden-yellow wolf with white streaks through her coat. She latched her jaws around his attacker's helmet and drove him back onto the ground. She crushed the helmet on the Vampirian's skull with her mighty jaw muscles and ripped his head from his shoulders. She tossed it aside as she stood up, reverting to her regular form.

"Do try to be careful, my love." She reached out to help him to his feet.

"Yes, my dear. It was a lucky shot, but I'm all good now." He shows her his arm where the wound he had sustained had mended.

"You do not have my permission to die this day." She smirked.

"Nor are you allowed to. I want to grow old with you and have you bear my thousands of children."

"Thousands? We should probably talk about one or two before forming our own village. Now, if you get into trouble, just whistle. You know how to whistle, don't you?"

"Hubba hubba," Cogeta smiled.

"That is not whistling!"

"It's the sound that comes from my lips whenever I see you. It's uncontrollable!" Cogeta yelled.

"I need you to get serious. These limp-fanged necrobreeders are not here to play." The Vampirian she had stabbed stumbled toward her and prepared to strike at her. Becky smirked, "Aww, thank you for holding my dear "Dragon's Fire" for me." She grabbed the shaft and ripped the weapon upward, cleaving the soldier in two.

"I'm always serious regarding matters of life and death. You don't see it because my dashing smile and amazing battlefield prowess distract you." He picks up his sword and steps aside from an attacking soldier. Cogeta strikes him down from behind.

"I just saved your life!" She squinted her eyes and pursed her lips, playfully scorning him.

"Nonsense, you've had my life long before these vermin appeared."

Becky smiled. "And I intend to keep it from them."

He grasps her arm and pulls her in close, kissing her passionately. "Then let us show them they crossed the wrong pair of Utopians."

The two switched sides, protecting the other's back. They fought with renewed passion. Their bond shined on the battlefield like a blazing pillar of fire. Soon, others were joining them in their fight.

Cory had left the park, flown to another nearby wooded area, and was about to lie down when a large shadow passed overhead. He looked up at the sky and saw a group of ships. *I wonder where they are going. They don't look like ours.* He thought to himself. They were obsidian in color and looked to be made of twisting and winding organic metal. Then he saw the first craft open fire and start bombarding the city with blue and purple plasma cannon fire. The others then joined it. *Are we being attacked?! But who would do that? We are at peace with everyone now, so I thought. I hope everyone is ok. ...Alisandra!* He focused his senses to sense her location. She wasn't in the park anymore. She was further away. In the city. *Feels like she is with others.*

Safe? Maybe... I'll go check. Just to be sure. Gotta hurry. It is too dangerous to fly. I have to stay on the ground. He took off as fast as his legs would take him, ignoring the pain from his sore body.

Cory dashed through a stream, ignoring the small bridge merely a few feet out of the way and then down the dirt path leading to the city. He began picking up speed as he rushed down the rolling hill. As he was running, he heard a humming noise from behind him. Looking over his shoulder, Cory saw four hoverbikes with mounted guns on his tail.

"Oh shit," were the only words he managed to say before they began firing missile-like projectiles at him.

He could stay one step ahead of them with his heightened senses, weaving side to side to avoid their explosions. *I cannot keep this up forever. Think Cory, think!* He glanced around frantically for an answer. To his right was more open ground. To his left, he saw woods. *The woods! Perfect! They can give me the cover I need.* Kicking up a short wall of sand as he made a sharp left, Cory headed toward the trees. The enemy was still hot on his heels. They just barely made the sudden turn to keep their target in sight. Aiming again, they kept the heat on Cory with their mounted guns until he reached the tree line. Cory ducked behind the first thick tree as the rounds from the mini-guns splintered the sides of the trunk. Cory crouched into a ball, with his hands over his head and knees tucked in, as the bark from the other side exploded off the tree. He sat terrified, waiting for the right moment that he'd be able to strike back and be free of this nightmare.

The mini-guns winded down as their shooters took a moment for the dust to clear so that they could see if they had decimated their target. Cory seized the chance and leaped out from behind his shield. A blast of lightning shot out from his fingertips, striking one bike and causing it to burst into flames. Unable to control his machine, the soldier could not stop it from falling into the guy beside him. As the two front bikers fell in a ball of fire, the second two were distracted enough that they did not see Cory coming.

Jumping over the raging fire onto the bike on the right, Cory knocked the guy to the ground and quickly whirled the hovercraft around to open fire on the other guy. The soldier could only stare in terror as twenty rounds from his partner's bike shot into his ride and up into his body. Black blood spurted from his battle suit as each long shell pierced his armor straight through and out his back. Cory jumped onto the guy he had knocked off a second earlier as he tried scrambling away. The bike zoomed into the other before they both fell and exploded into a pile of flaming wreckage. Cory held the man off the ground by his neck. He stared deathly into his reflection on the black visor, his anger, and concern overpowering all his other emotions of fear and guilt in what he had just committed, his adrenaline fueling him to no end.

"Why are you here?!" Cory shouted but got no response. *That tech is not ours. His comrade's blood was black. Not Utopian. Doesn't speak our language. Try Ustand...* "Why are you here?!" He shouted again, using the most commonly shared language known throughout the universe.

"To exterminate your species, mutt!" The soldier shot back with great malice in his voice.

"Who are you? And why are you here?"

"I am the superior race. Here to bring you under the heel of the Vampirian."

"No one is superior to the---" Cory breathed in sharply as his body suddenly was struck with intense pain. As he was speaking, the assailant drove a knife into him. Cory hadn't noticed as he slipped it out of a pocket on the back of his belt before jabbing the blade into Cory's side. Cory punched the helmet in a rage, shattering the rigid shield, then hit the enemy several more times before tossing his unconscious body to the ground. He was momentarily surprised when the face ignited. *That's a strange suicide mechanism... wait, no.* He raised his fist to his nose and took a few sniffs of the blood that was on his knuckles. *This scent... it's familiar... from one of our studies. Vampirian... explains the instant combustion, but why would they attack us... questions for later.* He pulled the knife from between his ribs and waited for a second as it healed over, staring down at the bloody, serrated edges of the blade before throwing it down. *Better hurry to town.* He thought as he began sprinting toward the rising black smoke.

"The Vampirians want to start a war, is that it?" Angel thought aloud. "Leen, stay close and keep your Holy magic coming."

"Got it!"

She quickly put her hands together and began chanting spells as she followed him. Angel wanted to find her shelter to keep her safe. *It's either the school or her father's shop. His tunnel is like a bomb shelter and the closest, so that would be my best bet. Now, I just need to force my body to make it. Damn it, why did they have to attack today? That battle with Shaw has taken its toll on me.*

He tried to maneuver with her through the chaos-ridden streets. Any Vampirians that came close were quickly dispatched with his fists, a controlled blast, or a blinding bolt of pure essence cast by Leen. Angel couldn't help but admire her during this chaos. She was clearly terrified, but she was staying calm enough to focus on helping him by casting her spells. He knew those spells took a lot out of her and were challenging to master. Few could truly harness the potential of Holy magic, as you had to be of a pure heart to wield it. *I will never be able to use any such skills.* He laughed to himself. Even at a time like this, with his body running on instinct, using all the training he had been so adamant about undertaking to protect her, he could take a moment to think and crack jokes. Running into a mob of soldiers, they both came to a stop. Looking over his shoulder, Leen stood close behind Angel and saw a woman about to be struck down as she tried to protect her child.

"Angel! Straight ahead!"

Looking past the Vampirians before him, he saw what she was speaking of.

"Do you trust me?" Angel asked of Leen.

"Y-yes?"

"Good! Hang on!"

He took hold of her arms with his strong hands and pulled her with him as he jumped up and kicked the nearest soldier. She immediately lost her footing and was clueless at what he had in mind when she felt her body spin. Angel had used the momentum to get her air born, and as soon as his foot touched down, he spun her around and released her into the air. She flew over the mob of confused soldiers. His plan instantly became clear; having a clear view of the Vampirian as she neared the defenseless woman, she aimed and released a volley of energy bursts that knocked the soldier around and away from the family. Leen landed on the cobble street and rolled over to the woman and her child. Immediately afterward, she erected a force field around them. The Vampirian snarled and marched forward with his gruesome-looking sword drawn back over his head to strike down on them when from the sky, Angel dropped, planting his fist into the soldier's helmet and smashing him into the ground. He slowly stood up from the small crater the impact had made, leaving the lifeless body of the soldier's now headless remains on the street.

"Behind you!" Leen shouted.

Angel reached back without looking and grabbed the wrist of another soldier as he posed to strike. Glaring at him, Angel tightened his grip and broke the man's wrist. Angel grabbed the Vampirian's falling sword with his free hand as it fell behind his back. He quickly released the soldier, switched the sword to his right hand, grabbed the soldier again by wrapping his left arm around his shoulders, and plunged his steel through his armor and out his back. Pulling it back, Angel thrust the blade into the helpless soldier several times before pushing him back with the sword still embedded in him to the hilt. As the soldier stumbled back, his hands slowly wrapped around his sword's handle to dislodge it. Angel stood firmly with his right hand outstretched, callously watching the man before ending his life with a burst of energy from his palm. The soldier's body vaporized into nothing in the   blast's wake.

Angel looked over at Leen. "Are you all right?"

"Yes."

"Good." Angel winced as his injuries from his previous battle came back to him.

Leen grimaced as she saw him in pain. Then she remembered the woman and child. Turning to them, "Hurry, take your child and get out of here. Get into a building or get out of the city."

The woman nodded quickly as she hurriedly scooped up her small son. "Thank you. Thank you."

Leen dropped her protective shield after they had left its safety. Keeping it up constantly would've drained her of spiritual power more rapidly, and she rushed to Angel's side. She quickly tried to help him ease the pain with her healing magic, hoping it would be effective, realizing momentarily that they weren't being attacked by the mob that he had thrown her over. She glanced over her shoulder and saw them all lying on the ground. Each one with their helmets shattered and their faces a glow with fire. Then she realized the strain he must have put himself through to work through them quickly to get to her.

"Are you going to be okay, Angel?"

"Yeah, of course, but it isn't over yet. More soldiers are being dropped off. I have to get you to safety. Come on."

Angel took her hand and started to walk away when she pulled away. Shocked by the sudden action, he turned around quickly, quizzically looking at her.

"No! We can't just run Angel. People are fighting and getting hurt. We have to help them!"

"My primary concern is making sure you are safe."

"Well, I will not stand by while innocent people are hurt by these... men, Vampirians, or whatever. I have the power, I've been studying and training to help people in need, and now I will help! These people need us, Angel. We have to help them."

He could hear the pleading in her voice, her eyes watering with tears imploring him. She was always one to help people. How could he think she would stop now? Against his better judgment, he couldn't argue her stance nor deny her, even if it was dangerous.

"Fine! But you stay close to me." He instructed while pointing his finger at the ground.

"Okay." She nodded in agreement.

"No, I mean it! You do not leave my sight, got it?"

Leen smiled. His concern for her safety was endearing. "Yes, I understand."

Together, they headed back toward the market center, where people still tried to escape and fight back. Angel jumped in amongst the other Utopians fighting and started cracking skulls while Leen used her magic to support the Utopian defenders. Her spells kept their wounds minor and increased their defenses through shields. Between helping others, she would cast attack spells. Bolts of magic and waves of energy shot into the crowd, striking down Vampirians as they got too close, while binding spells slowed down others for the defenders to take down with ease. People were ushering noncombatants through little pathways the defenders created in the mob. Leen felt a sense of relief when she saw priestesses arrive and tend to the wounded. Knights of the Holy Order appeared as well. Clad in their white robes and armor, holding back and defending the injured with their radiant tower shields. *That could be Angel one day... She briefly thought, Stay focused, Leen!*

She saw motion out of the corner of her eye. Quickly, turning around, she saw a young boy and girl cowering in the corner of a building as a Vampirian stood before them. Vampirians came from behind the defenders, cutting off the people's retreat. Quickly focusing solely on protecting the children, she sent a protective shield around them. When the Vampirian's sword came down, it bounced off the holy barrier. This gave her enough time to summon a wave of arcane energy and sent him flying away. She rushed to the children's side to check on them. They thanked her and took off into the closest store for protection. As Leen smiled to herself, she was struck on the back of the head by the pummel of a Vampirian sword.

There were some among those who were supplying support that began running away like cowards once they noticed more Vampirians were coming. Those fighting were too busy holding the forces from the front; they hadn't seen that they were being surrounded. The shouts and screams from the remaining healers trying to warn the fighters were drowned out by the sounds of combat.

Angel got a second to breathe from the fight. Taking a moment, he looked around for Leen but didn't see her nearby. His body immediately went cold, as he feared the worst. Looking around more frantically, he saw Leen's body on the sidewalk off to his right and was being converged upon by Vampirian soldiers.

"Leen!"

He turned his back on the fight before him and ran over to her as he saw Vampirians forming behind them. A bitter edge of a sword slashed across his back. Yelling out in pain, he spun around, knocking the sword from the Vampirian's hands. Angel grabbed his head and brought it down onto his knee. He then shoved him back so the sun could touch his unprotected face and back into his comrades. He left the line in the care of the others to rush to Leen's aid.

He plowed into the ranks of Vampirians and started tearing them down, dispatching those closest to Leen first. He then turned his enraged gaze to the others. A towering soldier stepped forward, pushing the smaller ones to the side to challenge Angel. Angel looked up at the covered face of this new foe. In his hands, he carried a large double-bladed axe. The brute rushed forward as he swung mightily. Angel caught the weapon by its shaft with his left hand. Leaping in, his left boot landed along the side of the Vampirian's knee. With a sickening crack, his leg buckled. Angel pushed off and did the same to the other knee with the same vicious result. As the Vampirian yelled out in pain, Angel pulled the brute close by his weapon and smashed his fist into the warrior's helmet. The once mighty warrior slid along the street, and his death cries filled the ears of those nearby as his face burst into flames.

However, even with that attacker down, hundreds more were to come. They soon overpowered Angel without the support of Leen's powers. His fight with Shaw came back to haunt him. He gasped for air as he lay on the stone streets, believing this was his end. He looked up and saw a Vampirian with his sword over his head, preparing to take his life, and for a moment, fear touched Angel.

However, the Vampirian stayed his sword and, with the help of a fellow soldier, hoisted Angel's limp body up to his feet. They drug him and the other surviving fighters and people into the grand circle. He looked around, and it seemed that they had indeed lost. *Where is the gawfrigging army?* Angel raged inside. If only he had the strength to continue fighting. If only he had the power to free himself and Leen. *Leen?!* He frantically looked around for her. He finally saw her held in line with other women.

A commanding voice boomed over the crowd suddenly, and all became silent. The soldiers holding Angel forced him to bow his head as if to bow to whoever was approaching. Angel tried to look around, but his view was limited. He only saw that the other men he had been fighting alongside were being held like him, on their knees, arms held outstretched by two soldiers. They could hear footsteps coming closer down the cobbled street.

When he could look up, Angel saw a tall, muscular Vampirian dressed in a dark purple nobleman's attire with an even darker violet cape. His fingers were richly adorned with rings, each with a shiny jewel center. His pale skin clashed with his odd-colored hair. It was orange-ish brown and spiked upward. The stranger, who appeared to be the leader, looked over to the grand fountain of Odin and the first emperor that decorated the center of the circle. He reached out with his left hand. Dark energy surged up his arm and shot forth. A massive explosion turned the elegant piece into crumbling rubble. Pleased with his actions, he laid his arm to rest by his side. As he displayed his power to the subdued captors, Angel wondered *Why* he wasn't *catching fire like the others?* The Vampirian looked down the line of captured men and then over to the row of girls, his eyes lighting up as he perused his captives. He then looked around at his troops. The large Vampirian finally spoke in a low, calm voice with a noble tone.

"Good work, men. Let the universe know that today the Vampirian race took its first step toward being renowned as the superior race! We've attacked and subdued the savages who have long thought they were at the top of the food chain!"

All around, the Vampiran soldiers cheered. When they quieted down, the leader continued.

"There is no sign of their army. Why is that? It is because they are afraid. After all, these mutts have a much worse bark than their bite. They

will talk big and act big, but when it comes to it, they put their tails, their…
disgusting tails, between their legs and run for cover. These savages are
nothing more than brainless beasts. Today, we have tamed and subjugated
them!"

Looking back down the row of female prisoners as his troops cheered
his last words. His eyes stopped on Leen, who had recovered from the
harsh blow to the back of her head. A sniveling, hunched-over creature
rushed to the man's side—a scroll and quill in his hands. The leader
pointed his pale finger toward her.

"Well, well, well, what a beauty this one is. She, I shall claim for my
own. Take her to my ship. Have her cleaned up and placed into my private
quarters. She will be my prize for this glorious victory. The rest of the
stock load up into the cargo holds. Separate them from the men."

As the Vampirian leader spoke, the little man jotted down every order
and took a tally of the captives.

"Never! Not in any lifetime!" Leen squirmed and fought against her
captors.

"Get away from her, blood-sucker, or I will make you nothing more
than a pile of ash!" Angel struggled to no avail against those holding him.

"My name is Serkuma, not blood-sucker, and I do not fear the sunlight.
As you should see, I am standing in it right now. However, don't blame
yourself. I am sure that with your poor education, you assumed I was
wearing some sun protection. Blocking the evil rays that turn my fellow
companions into, what was it, piles of ash? As you can also see, my little
friend here is also not wearing protection from the ultraviolet rays." He
looked over to Leen. "With such a severe threat, though, one is only left to
assume she is your woman or *was* rather. One can only guess why such a
lovely thing as this would go for a thing such as you. She will make a fine
addition to my family, where she will get the proper attention she deserves.

Serving me on her hands and knees, dressed in something more fitting... perhaps sheer or lace, something not too confining but overly revealing."

He moved in closer to her, placing his hand on her cheek. She tried to pull away, but he held her still, gripping her face tight.

"Oh yes, these lips will be most enjoyable."

Forcing her to pucker, he pressed his cold, grey lips to hers. He savored her struggle as he took what he wanted. He broke the kiss and smiled at her, tears falling down her cheeks that were becoming bruised from his grip.

"You will be mine."

"I will never belong to you." She hissed with hatred.

"If that is truly what you wish, my dear," Serkuma looked her over, then glanced back at Angel, who was gritting his teeth, his fangs clearly showing, and pure malice emblazoned all over his face. Turning back to her, he whispered coolly, "Then so be it, my dear." He then turned his attention toward his troops, speaking louder for them to hear.

"You are absolutely right, my dear. You won't belong to me." A vile thought crossed his mind. He turned around to his men. "Men, she is yours! This fine bitch of Utopia is for your pleasure! Feast! Enjoy! You earned it with today's victory! You may also do what you will with these other women. They, too, are not worth my time!" He announced gloriously to his men, who in return began shouting praises.

Angel, who had been trying to find the strength to break free of his captors' hands, found it with those words. Breaking the grips of the soldiers holding him, he dashed towards Serkuma with his fist drawn back. It glowed with blue energy and connected with Serkuma's face as he turned to see what had happened. The might packed behind the punch forced the big man to take a few steps back while holding his jaw. Angel was just about to attack again when soldiers grabbed him around his shoulders and waist, pulling him back into the row of men. The captured Utopians cheered him on.

"Why, you filthy animal, attacking a man while his back is to you? Hold him up, men. Time to teach this dog a lesson!"

The soldiers complied with the order, hoisting Angel up and holding his arms straight. As Angel held his head down, a smirk appeared on his lips. He slowly spread his legs to match his arms. He listened as Serkuma came closer. When his footsteps stopped, he leisurely raised his head to show Serkuma his grin.

"Why are you smirking? Do you enjoy punishment?"

"Not particularly, but I know something you don't know." Angel mocked.

"And what, pray tell savage, is that?"

"Come closer. I want to be sure you hear it right. Every single word," Angel whispered.

It was now Serkuma's turn to smirk, "Very well, dog, what is it?" Stepping closer to Angel and leaning his ear down to his mouth.

"MEGA---!" Angel screamed into Serkuma's ear as those around him felt a surge of power rise from Angel's feet and throughout his body. A blue aura exploded around him.

Serkuma yelled in anger as Angel's scream echoed through his sensitive eardrum. However, the power change in Angel didn't escape his notice. He quickly swung his tightly clenched fist around and delivered an earth-shattering blow to Angel's diaphragm before Angel could finish charging his attack. It struck Angel with such force that his body reacted by snapping his arms together. The soldiers barely held on to him. Those standing around them could see a shock wave shoot out from Angel's back, visible only by the swirling white winds that formed from its path. Angel's power disappeared in a flash as he coughed out mouthfuls of blood. He felt his knees weaken and his entire body slumped in the soldiers' arms. His consciousness waned. His vision was but a blur.

"No! Angel!" Leen once more struggled with her captor, tears rushing down her cheeks.

Serkuma nodded. "This man is filthy, and so is this woman," taking Leen by the hair and pulling her away from the soldier. She screamed louder as he yanked her around until she stood before him. "This vile creature is not good enough for me. Nor is it good enough even for my troops! She is this man's slut and, therefore, defiled and lower than the dirt upon which we piss. We should not ALLOW ourselves to pollute our bodies with the filth she infested with from head to toe! We must not allow ourselves to partake in inferior quality to be superior. Look at this filthy whore's hair, for example. It is not normal. This face is a mask that hides her true grotesqueness," he shouted, being joined in by other shouts from his men. However, some were visibly disappointed and not in favor of the change in plans. Serkuma then pulled a curved black jagged dagger from his belt and held it to her throat. "Let this one be an example to all you other inbred mongrels. You are livestock to be traded, sold, and then discarded in the trash. Utopians are nothing but savages pretending to be a decent society."

"No! Serkuma! If you hurt her, I will splatter your blood all across the universe. I swear it!" Angel gasped and panted. His red eyes blazed with rage, wanting to pull the dagger from Serkuma's hand and ram it through his neck.

"Your words do not frighten me, boy," Serkuma growled in annoyance as he turned around to face Angel, still holding the dagger to Leen's throat. He laughed, "You won't live long enough to make good of your words.

Look at yourself on your knees, defeated. Do you honestly think I would be frightened by your strong desire to save her? As you ponder that, look at her," he grinned, twisting Leen's long lavender hair in his pale hand, tightening his grip on her.

Angel looked up at her and watched as Leen silently mouthed the words while mentally saying to him, *I love you.* He stared on, unable to move, though Odin knows he tried as Serkuma pressed the dagger hard against her neck.

"This is the Forbidden Black Blade of Nozenroth. It is so powerful that it's said a god becomes mortal from a single scratch from its blade. It sucks their godliness right out of them. Now watch as it sucks the life out of your beloved whore!"

He raked the jagged edge across her soft flesh in one swift motion. As the blood squirted out, Serkuma bore a satisfying smile. Her eyes slowly closed, and Serkuma let her slip from his fingers and hit her knees before pushing her limp body onto the cobbled road with his boot. Angel watched, unable to move, as her blood ran between the stones from her motionless body.

"Look at her die so pathetically. Just like any whore from the streets, she dies on them. Now it is your turn, mutt."

Serkuma began walking closer to Angel, holding the blade downward and allowing the blood to drip off the tip.

Angel stared up at him with an ever-growing hatred boiling in his eyes, growling through his gritted teeth. So tight were they clenched that trickles of blood seeped from his gums.

"My name is Dark Angelus Everlast, and I swear I will kill you."

"Oh, cut the melodrama. It all will be over shortly." Serkuma was only a step away when he heard his men screaming.

"It's the Utopian army! They are here!"

Serkuma growled, "It's too soon... this isn't the proper stage." He knelt and took Angel by the chin. "It appears you have a chance to make true your words. I look forward to seeing if you have what it takes to do so. Do not disappoint me." He then shoved Angel's head into the stone street and stood up. "It's time to take our leave! Spread your wings and FLY!"

"What about the women, sire?" Asked the hunched man.

"The demand for Utopian slaves is null. There is better to be had. I may turn some profit from the lowly beasts, however. Bring as many as we can and cage them. Everyone retreat to the ships."

Serkuma flew up into the air and headed for his ship. Mid-flight, his shape changed into a giant black bat. His soldiers followed suit after killing some captives out of pleasure. Other soldiers took to the air with a captive in tow. The skies were soon filled with Vampirian soldiers flying off, joined by the small fighter jets. The Utopian soldiers opened fire with their laser rifles and energy blasts, taking down many and rescuing a few prisoners. But the majority escaped into their spacecraft whence they came. Shortly after that, the large ships had vanished from the skies. All that was left was the destruction and loss that they had brought.

CHAPTER 10

ANSWERING THE CALL

As most Utopian soldiers chased down the straggling Vampirians, others helped the people. Angel paid no attention to them as he crawled over to Leen's body and cradled her in his arms as hot streams of tears rolled down his face. *This can't be happening. Please, Leen, wake up! That dagger's blade really couldn't have stopped her healing ability… but I can't heal her either. Why isn't she healing! How could this have happened? I couldn't protect her. I couldn't protect her! All that time training to get stronger. All those fights, the scars I endured to keep bastards like Shaw away! The hell I went through before I met her. The one time she truly needed me to save her, and I failed! I couldn't protect the one who gave my life meaning… what do I do now? Leen… What do I do now? How am I supposed to continue without you? What's life without your voice, your laugh, your smile… The soft touch of your hand on my face as you tell me it will be okay. Where were your gods! How could they just stand idly by and let your pureness be snuffed out? Why didn't he kill me? Why you, who had more faith in those unseen judges than I? How is this right!* His eyes were shut tight as tears ran down his face. His teeth were tightly clenched that his gums began to bleed. *They will pay… he… will pay. Serkuma. I will find him… and I will…*

A tall man adorned in ornate armor walked up to the side of Angel and looked down at him. Another much younger man dressed in a white royal garb, bearing a bloody sword in his hand, stood beside him. The second man spoke first. He breathed heavily but tried to talk calmly in his soft voice.

"Don't worry. They will not go unpunished."

"You're damn right! We will make those bastards pay for this insult!"

The second man sheathed his long sword in the scabbard on his side.

"Of course, but first, Sparticus, we will see our dead off to Valhalla, and then we'll regroup and discuss a battle plan." *I cannot believe that something like this could happen.*

Sparticus nodded his head. "Of course, Emperor. However, with respect, I suggest we focus more on the latter. There will be time to mourn afterward, but we must move quickly."

The young Emperor sighed, "I am afraid you are right. Do what you must. We'll leave the tending to the dead to their loved ones and citizens while we prepare for war."

"I will have the horn sounded for all the fresh recruits to gather at the academy's auditorium. The veterans will know what to do, and the generals can handle them while getting preparations ready while we address the cadets."

The Emperor nodded, then looked down at Angel holding Leen's lifeless body. "Angel, my friend, I am truly sorry."

"Where were you? Where was the grafrigging army!"

Sparticus stepped closer as the Emperor stepped back, Angel's tone cutting into him deeply. "The Emperor was with me, observing the men in training. The armies were below ground, as they usually are. We would've gotten here sooner had the Vampirians not trapped us down there. Their ships targeted our bases. The rubble blocked the doors. It took us a while to blast our way through. Once we had, we had to fight our way here. We weren't the only ones hit. Reports were coming in that Midstar was also attacked. Do not blame the Emperor or the soldiers for her death. If you must blame someone, blame the Vampirians!"

Angel just growled, "What makes you think I don't? I was here, and I fought them just like others did, and still… I was here, and I still couldn't…" his tears burned as they freely fell from his face unto Leen's cheeks. The anger, frustration, and pain came out as he screamed toward the sky.

When he stopped, Sparticus said, "Leave her and report to the academy. I will have some men take her to Vox. I know it will pain him to bury his daughter, but it is his burden. You have a duty to your people, so get going."

Angel leaned his head and looked at the tall man before him. "Gragfriggin katoosh."

"Excuse me?" Sparticus asked firmly.

"Sorry. Gragfriggin katoosh, sir." Angel replied, putting a sarcastic emphasis on the last word.

Sparticus stepped forward, readying to strike Angel as he glared at him with anger-filled eyes. The Emperor quickly stepped in and placed his hand in front of his chest to stop him. The young man looked down at his broken friend. It was because of Leen that their paths had crossed so many years ago before the passing of the previous emperor dropped the weight of the world upon his shoulders. Those were simpler times. When they were very young, the three played together. When he was taken away to be trained and groomed to be the next ruler, Angel would sneak into the palace to give him a friend to talk to. Leen would sometimes be with him. Then one day, all that stopped, but their friendship endured. Leen would be able to visit while she was helping the clerics, and she would keep him up to speed on life outside of the palace walls.

Angel took a deep breath to calm himself as best he could. "I will not leave her side. I will tend to her first, then go to the academy to hear your long-winded speeches that will only slow me down from going after the bastard who did this."

Sparticus spouted back, "What makes you think you could defeat him? He was clearly out of your league, boy."

"I gave him my word," Angel laughed lowly.

"You did what?" Sparticus tilted his head and raised an eyebrow in confusion.

"I gave the bastard my word that I would be the one to kill him. I tend to keep that promise. He will pay, even if it kills me."

The Emperor nodded. "Very well, I permit you to tend to Leen, but then you must quickly make your way to the academy with the other recruits. She was also my friend, her loss..." he couldn't find the words as he trailed off. Sheathing his sword, they walked away when Sparticus grabbed the Emperor's arm and whispered something into his ear. Whatever he said, Angel did not know, but it visually startled the Emperor. Sparticus whispered something else to the Emperor, who then turned to look at Angel.

"Are you sure?"

Sparticus nodded. "We will test him first to see if he has what it takes. Send him on a quest worthy of the position."

They nodded in agreement, turned, and walked back to Angel.

Cogeta stood by Becky, back-to-back, as the remaining Vampirians fled. Once they were gone, he ensured Becky was okay, but other than a few superficial wounds, the blood on her was not her own.

"Are you all right, sweetheart?"

Breathing heavily, she smiled. "Yes, and what about you?"

"Still in one piece," he said.

"I wonder why they retreated suddenly."

"Probably, cause of them," Cogeta motioned his head to the side. Looking over his shoulder, she saw soldiers rushing toward them.

"Oh, wow, about time."

"Yeah, but at least we won."

The feeling of victory was cut short when they heard the summoning siren blaring.

"Shit! Where's my uniform?" Cogeta scrambled back to his partially destroyed home to look for it. The Vampirian that was unconscious under the wall that Cogeta had pushed over came to at that moment and was trying to push it off. Cogeta jumped and landed on the wall, knocking the soldier back out. After searching for what seemed like hours to Cogeta, he became increasingly worried with each passing moment. Becky finally called out.

"Here it is!" tossing the bagged suit to him.

Cogeta reached out, grabbed it, and kissed her. "Thank you, sweetie. What would I do without you?"

"I sometimes wonder myself," she smirked.

Cogeta gave her a big dumb grin and began trying to get dressed quickly. He fell over more than once, trying to put his pants on. After they were finally on, he moved even faster. Before long, he was fully dressed in the academy's uniform outside the house. By then, the Vampirian had once again come to. As Cogeta passed overhead, the Vampirian punched his way free.

Cogeta quickly jumped out of the way and looked back. "Wow! Are you still alive?"

"You're dead!" He yelled in his native tongue.

The Vampirian soldier charged Cogeta with his arms raised over his head. Unsheathing his sword, Cogeta spun it around with lightning speed, slicing through flesh and bone. He looked back at Becky as the severed arms and head fell. Sheathing his sword once more, he grinned at her.

"Do you mind cleaning this up, dear?"

She gave him a look that he knew all too well. He wisely took off running down the street. While running away, he slipped his university jacket on and tucked his shirt in.

"Well, I guess I had better clean this place up," Becky sighed. She easily lifted one of the fallen beams and threw it out of the house into the empty street. As she tossed out another beam, she saw Cogeta coming back.

He came bounding in and grabbed Becky's hand. "I forgot something."

"What?!"

Spinning around, she felt agitated at him for forgetting something when he needed to get going. He was now going to be late and slowing down her cleanup. Already upset about having to clean up the rubble alone was bad enough. She wanted to get to it immediately. He threw his arms around her and swung her down into a dip as his lips contacted hers.

"I'd be a major fool if I ran off without giving my girl a goodbye kiss and not telling her I love her. I will let you know what is happening once I get back." He set her back on her feet and dashed off once again.

She stood there for a bit in shock. *That's why I chose him over all the others*, she thought to herself before returning to fixing things up.

As Cory ran towards the city, he was ducking through the woods for cover when he came on stragglers of the Vampirian force. They did not hear the call to retreat from their commander, and, worse; they missed their ride home. When Cory came upon them, they crouched in a circle, trying to figure out their next move. Immediately, they jumped up and stood at the ready when Cory appeared. They stared at each other, seeing who would make the first move.

At last, one charged Cory carelessly, and the battle began. Cory blocked his punch and countered with one of his own to the Vampirian's helmet. His fist smashed through the visor and crushed the middle of his face. The unconscious soldier fell back to the ground before his three comrades. They looked down at their friend, then up to Cory, standing battle ready.

They exchanged looks with each other. The three silently agreed that they would not retreat. It would only get them killed in a far more painful way by Serkuma himself if he found out they ran. They charged Cory with everything they had. The skirmish was over quickly, and the ground was saturated with the black blood of the Vampirian soldiers. Cory bound their unconscious bodies with what he could, securely tying them to the base of a tree. He would let someone of authority know where they were so someone could interrogate them later. Cory then quickly continued on his way down the path to the city. While on his way back, he noticed that the skies were now empty of all enemy craft and could hear the siren blowing from the town.

Crap! Have to move faster. Doubt they will really care if I show up in my uniform or not.

From within his pants pocket, he pulled out a small handheld. The small device was receiving message after message. He saw they were from his mother and father, trying to find out where he was, if he was okay, to come home. But he didn't bother to respond just then. His mind was only on one concern. Cory tapped away at the screen with his thumb. He sent out his message and started to reply to his mother's frantic messages when he heard someone wailing ahead. He found a mother in need of help. Her children had been trapped inside their burning home. There was burning debris blocking the doorway, making the entrance inaccessible. Upon seeing him, she pleaded with him to help her. He put his device back into his pocket to focus on helping her. Cory glanced at her hands and saw that they had been singed badly by her attempts to enter. He looked at the front entrance and could not risk moving it. He had to hurry because the summoning siren was going off, and he knew he needed to get there quickly. Not wasting any more time, he ran around to the backside of the house. He tried the backdoor, but it was bolted shut. With a quick blast from his hand, he gained entry. He rushed inside, covering his face from the flickering orange flames.

He foolishly overlooked the fact that he was running on a weak floor. It did not dawn on him until a loud snapping noise rang in his ears. He barely stepped to safety before he fell through. Deciding to hover over the floor, he continued his search the best he could. He checked all the bedrooms, the kitchen, the living room, and even the hall closet, but still, he couldn't find the children. The searing heat made him sweat profusely as the temperature only increased. It was getting harder to breathe the longer he stayed in here.

Suddenly, something caught his attention, making him stop in his tracks.

He could hear screaming. Finally, he heard something other than the crackling and roaring fire. The cries came from below him. Cory looked around for a door leading down or possibly a trap door along the walls. Finding no door around, he was about to punch his way down. Then, as he looked down, the red rug made him take pause. Going with a hunch, he quickly kicked it aside and, by doing so, found a small door. There was a crack in the wood, from which he could use to look down and see one child. Through the scorching flames, he could make out the child's huddled body near a wall, which the fire had not claimed.

Without wasting another minute, he grabbed the latch on the door and ripped it clean off the hinges. Racing down the wooden steps to the child's aid, he suddenly fell. The second to last step gave way under his foot, causing Cory to fall and smack face-first on the stone floor. The little boy who could not lift the door alone took the chance to escape. He ran right over Cory, scrambled up the stairs, then out the back door to his mother's arms. Cory stood up and rubbed his face. Then his ears picked up another sound through the crackling embers. It was the sound of a baby coughing. He made his way to the origin of the noise and found the baby trapped under burning debris. Cory was terrified. He quickly examined the situation.

Armed with a plan, he lunged toward the trapped baby, but a burning board snapped and landed on his back, pinning him to the floor. As Cory shoved the board off him, another board snapped, followed by an encore of others as the house came down on them both.

A single minute seemed like hours outside the house where the mother and her son sat huddled under a tree, crying, praying, and waiting. All appeared lost as they saw the roof give and fall into what was once their home. It seemed forever to them before a blue ball of energy shot from the rubble. The mother was filled with hope as she saw Cory flying out with his arms, cradling something. He landed underneath the tree and uncovered the baby.

However, the infant was no longer breathing. Its round face was a dark blue shade. Cory quickly laid the child down. Time seemed to crawl as he tried to get the baby to breathe again. Repeatedly, he puffed fresh air into his lungs and then pumped the baby's little chest with care thirty times with two fingers before giving the baby two more puffs of air.

Come on, little guy, breathe. Breathe! Come on. You can do it.

As he tried his hardest to revive the child, he couldn't help but take note of other things wrong. The child was burned rather severely, but the child wasn't healing on its own. Cory was trying to boost the baby's regenerative power with his own. It's a shared ability among the people that aided doctors and nurses when a patient's injuries were too significant for their own body to repair. However, it was not affecting the child, which concerned Cory. Either he was doing something wrong, or this baby's body wasn't responding because there was no life to react to it. Another thing that bothered Cory was the smell. Not only from the burnt flesh but what worried and bothered Cory was that he smelt the charred tissue inside each time he pushed and breathed into the baby's lungs. The embers and smoldering smoke had gotten into the baby's throat and lungs and burned them terribly. With the child so young, his regenerative power was relatively weak and still developing. All this was just too much for the little guy to handle.

With a heavy heart, he sat up on his knees and looked up at the woman. She immediately understood by the look in his eyes, the mournful sorrow on his face. She screamed in pain, dropped to her knees, cradled her child, and willed it to come back to life. Cory was at a loss for words and didn't quite know how to console the woman. Deep down, he knew there was nothing he could do to make this less painful, even as he reached out and gently touched the woman's shoulder in an effort to try. The little boy, in his own way, grasped the meaning of the situation and gave Cory an ugly look.

"Leave my mommy alone, murderer!"

"I am sorry, ma'am, I have to go. The siren is calling, and I have to answer it. I'll send someone to help you. You have my word."

The mother didn't utter a reply. She just held her baby's lifeless body close to her chest and rocked back and forth, crying. Her other son clung to her back.

Cory stood up, bowed respectfully to the family, and took off toward the academy. Tears flowed down the already beaten path on his cheeks made from their predecessors from earlier in the day as he made his way toward the gathering point. Upon reaching the city, he again picked up Justin's aura and followed it. He would ensure the girl was safe before he would answer the summons. He had to know she was safe. *This world... would lose meaning without her. Odin, please let her be safe.*

Cory followed his senses to a small park. The ground was scorched black, and bodies were lying about. He saw Justin and a few of his cronies in the middle of it. They looked exhausted, quickly deducing that they had been fighting for their lives like him. He caught their attention as they approached.

"Well, look who it is. How the hell did you manage to survive?" Justin sneered.

Cory was out of breath from running for so long, but he had finally reached his goal. "W-where is she?" He asked through deep breaths.

"Where's who?"

Cory immediately felt annoyed. "Alisandra! Where is she?!"

The three men looked at each other. Justin stepped forward. "Why should I tell you?"

"Is she safe? I just want to know that she is safe, Justin."

"Why? Wait, did you track me down to find her? She doesn't even like you. She hates you. You give her the friggin creeps. She tells me how she catches you looking at her and feels the need to shower because you're so repulsive. She'd rather go blind and deaf than look at or hear your voice. Shame a Vampirian didn't kill you. At least something good would've come out of this hell. And it would've made her so happy."

His words stung harsher than Cory would've liked. They were probably untrue, but... the fear in the back of his mind made them more believable. "I… I don't care! I just need to know she is safe, damn it!"

The outburst momentarily surprised Justin but quickly came around again. He clenched his fists tightly. "What? Do you think I can't protect her? Do you think you could do better scatstain? You couldn't even win a single bout in the tournament. Every time you were out in the first round. You're a disgrace! You don't deserve her. You're less than nothing!"

"I've fought in two tournaments. How many times did you fight, Shaw?"

Justin punched Cory to the ground. "You piece of shit! You think you're better than me, you friggin loser! You're beneath me!" He held Cory by his hair and punched him into the ground. He then shoved him back and stood up. He took a deep breath, then spat upon him.

Cory lay on the ground, taking deep breaths. He struggled to sit up but managed to do so. Looking up with blood and dirt smeared across his face, "Is she safe?" he whispered.

Justin gritted his teeth. With a violent kick, he sent Cory sliding across the ground. "You stupid scat. Come on, guys. Help me show Ryker, mister know it all, mister goodie two shoes, how he really stacks up in the real world." He walked over and stomped on Cory's chest. He was soon joined by the two other men, who began stomping and kicking at him.

All Cory could do was roll up into a ball. *Don't fight back. She wouldn't like you if you hurt him. Don't hurt him. Endure it. You can't win, anyway. You're going to be okay. You'll get through this. I just want to know that she's okay.* "I just want to know that Alisandra is okay!" Cory at last shouted. His vision was becoming blurry as the sound of the alarm began to fade.

"Justin, dude, this isn't that much fun. He's not even trying. Plus, we gotta get going to the assembly."

"Pft fine." Justin gave Cory one last kick to the back of the head. "You're nothing but a piece of scat, Ryker. No one likes you. No one came to help you. Wolf pack? More like a rat pack. They hiss and snarl but run away when you chase them. Alisandra's fine. I got her to a shelter before we separated and came out to fight. Listen closely, though," he squatted over Cory's battered body, wrapped his hands around his throat, and squeezed. "You mean nothing to her. She's mine. She wants nothing to do with you. She hates you. She never wants to see you again. Leave her alone. Do you hear me? She friggin hates your very existence, you waste of space, you're better off dead! You hear me, Ryker? Kill yourself! Or let a Vampirian do it for you so you can keep some small ration of dignity. But never look at her again. Never speak to her. If I see you even try to talk to her again, I'll kill you."

The last words Cory heard were that the girl he desired to be closer to, whose aura drew him like a moth is drawn to the light of a flame, hated him. All other sounds faded as he passed out. When he came to, he was alone. His head was throbbing. Not just his head, but his whole body ached and hurt as he tried to move. He quickly rolled to the side as his insides lurched and threw out what it could. He stared at the mess a moment. His bearings slowly returned. His heart felt so empty and shattered. As he sat up on his knees, he couldn't stop the outpouring of tears running down his face. He struck the ground as he howled.

"Why! Why am I still so weak? Why won't these confounded feelings be done with me! I don't want them anymore! You hear me, gods, above! Please! Rid me of this pain. I'm sorry! You've made your point... I'm not worthy of her or anyone. She's not for me. I see that now. I'll stay away from her and everyone. I'm not worth falling for. I'm undesirable. Unwanted… a lost cause."

As if from the void, he heard the signal's call again. He looked up at the sky and, with a heavy heart, he forced himself to stand up. *Perhaps... he was right. Better to die on a battlefield than to... won't dishonor my family name. I better get going.* He started walking toward the alarm, where he knew the others were gathering.

CHAPTER 11

A Time to Mourn and a Time for Revenge

Answering the summons, all the cadets gathered inside the university's auditorium. Cory found Angel and Cogeta amongst the crowd, and even though he was relieved they survived the attack, Angel appeared in a way he had never had before. The aura around him had changed. What once was a powerful and intimidating aura was now a mere shadow of its former self. Cogeta wasn't his usual upbeat self, either. He was looking down at his feet and clenching his fists. Cory rushed to them, excusing himself through the people as he went. Cory was wheezing, and his face was a little cleaner, but the evidence of his beating remained from the swelling in his face and bruises. He put on a smile to throw off any concerns his friends may have.

"Hey guys, sorry I'm late..." Cory said with some discomfort. He then started coughing.

"Holy shit, Cory, what happened?" Cogeta asked as he and Angel looked over at their friend.

"Y-yeah, I'm fine." Cory started coughing. "Think... I may have a punctured lung. But I'll be fine in a few hours."

"Who did this to you?" Cogeta asked.

"Vampirians... pretty sure that's what they were."

Cogeta looked his friend over with steely eyes. He could clearly see from the tattering of his clothes, the dirt stains, and the Vampirian blood splatter all pointed to the fact he had encountered the enemy. However, something didn't smell right. There were faint scents of Utopian on him as well. Cogeta quickly glanced around and almost immediately caught sight of the one he sought. A few yards away, he saw Justin sneering in their direction. He turned his gaze back to Cory.

"Cory, be honest with me. Did Vampirians do all this?"

"Yeah..." he coughed again, "Did you not notice we were being invaded? I ran into a group of them up at the park. They got the jump on me." He chuckled, "You think I look bad? You should really see them..." He fought another coughing fit as he looked at his friend and tried to laugh. "You would've been proud." As he tried to laugh to hide his urge to cry. He was relieved in a way when he started coughing once more.

"Cory, I'm always proud of you." Cogeta reached out and put his hand on his friend's shoulder. "Are you sure you're okay?"

"Yeah... like I said, I'll be fine in a few hours."

"Dude, we will probably be shipping out in a few hours!"

"Then hey," Cory smiled, "I guess I'll be the first to test out the med-bay" He laughed only to start coughing again. "So, what happened to you two?"

Cogeta smiled, trying to be positive. "We were attacked too, duh."

"I know we were attacked." Cory sighed as he tilted his head, glancing over at Angel.

They made eye contact briefly before Angel looked away. A look of genuine concern was written on Cory's face. He'd never seen Angel in such a way. Something had to have happened. Suddenly, people were moving around to get in straight lines. In all the commotion, Cogeta and Cory lost sight of Angel. They looked up and down their line but didn't see him nearby. Cory turned to Cogeta once again.

"Cogeta, what's going on? Do we know why the Vampirians attacked or why they suddenly retreated?"

Cogeta leaned over to his friend and whispered in his ear sorrowfully, "Cory…Leen's dead."

Before Cory could speak, the High Councilman was up at the podium, and Cogeta motioned to be quiet. The tension was so high in the room that the silence was deafening to their thoughts. Cory's mind was now a muddled mess of questions and confusion. His mouth hung open, his bottom jar trembling, as fresh tears filled his eyes in disbelief. He opened and closed his fists. Trying to get the feeling back in his body, willing this nightmare to end. He stared blankly ahead at the man at the podium. Any other day and Cory would've given his undivided attention to this man of high regard, but today his mind had finally clicked off.

The Councilman was an advisor to the Emperor. He had held that position since the very first Emperor and was known to possess a great temper. His long hair was pure white. He stood proudly, wearing a long white robe with gold cuffs and trim. Running down the center of the robe were the golden symbols of Odin, similar to a cross but with the ends rounded in a crescent fashion. Over the robe, he had a red shoulder cape with gold trim like his robe, and on top, he had a chain of Utopian crosses linked side-by-side around the middle. His skin showed no sign of aging past the age of forty-five. He spoke with a powerful, attention-grabbing voice.

"The attack today by the Vampirians will not go unpunished. We will get our vengeance for what they did to us today. But first, let us say a prayer to guide our lost ones to the realm of Valhalla, where our Lord Odin awaits the brave and lost souls of our fallen." The Councilman raised his hands and bowed his head. "Oh Lord, mighty Odin, our wise father who watches over us through our entire existence from his glorious kingdom of Asgard. We ask that you send your Disirs and take our worthiest fallen warriors into their arms and carry them to Valhalla, where the brave may live forever. We know that through your teachings, the boys will grow into men, and the men will grow far stronger than they could have among us.

Among our brave men who fell defending their homes, some courageous women stood tall beside their brethren until the very end. Freyja, our battle maiden, take and train them well to serve as your next generation of battle maidens, our guardians, Odin's maidens, as valkyrie. May our fallen women, and those who had not yet reached womanhood, come to you and remain beautiful, and their skin shine like the morning sun. May our holy mother, Frigg, take the mothers and old by the hand and small children into her bosom. Restore the youth and health of the old and guide them through the marshes and up to the holy mountain where they may live the rest of their immortal lives in peace and comfort. May they all serve you, Lord Odin, to their utmost ability as they serve our emperor. They died fighting, protecting their homes and families, and fought in your name, great and wise Lord. They died with honor. So forgive them for all their past mistakes they may have committed, Amen."

When he had finished, the Councilman stepped down, and the Emperor took to the podium. He had been the second man to approach Angel at the scene of Leen's death. He had long brown hair and vibrant green eyes that still looked at the world with innocence. He wore a white long-sleeve jacket with gold stripes at the end, white slacks, and black boots. Around his neck was a golden rope, tying on his long cape. The interior of which was gold, while the exterior was white. He looked out over the faces of just some people he was responsible for. Each one was expressing their feelings. A mixture of sorrow and shock that such an event could happen, but mostly he saw the burning anger in their eyes, and how could he blame them? He felt the same way.

"My people, I know your hatred. I feel your pain. The attack today came unprovoked, without reason and cause. I promise you, we will make the Vampirian menace pay for our losses tenfold, no…" he paused, "Make it ONE HUNDRED-FOLD!" Roars filled the large room from the crowd, echoing off the walls. "No matter how long it takes, we will make them regret this day, the day they showed their cowardice." More claps and roars echoed through the crowd. "For today, we declare WAR on the planet Va Blood!" The Emperor shook his fist as he spoke. "Let the universe know we will not stand idly by and let such an act go unpunished. We have a proud heritage and will honor it by showing the universe that we are still a dominant force to reckon with. That they should think it three times over before they try to pull anything like this ever again! We will show them what happens when you tease a slumbering wolf!" After that, he stepped down, and the room was filled with shouts and cheers, which quickly ceased when Sparticus stepped up.

He stood in great ornate armor with rich detail. The chest was formed to have the image of a demonic being with its mouth open, ready to devour the enemy's soul. Its eyes were an empty black, contrasting with the dark green of the armor. Over his right shoulder was a wolf's head covered with golden dragon scales. On his left shoulder was a long white spike. Down his right arm was a white skeletal claw, and on his left arm was a gold dragon serpent circling downward. His gauntlets were made to look like dragonheads, the snout covering his knuckles, while the other end of the head ended with two horns. A belt had a dragon-scaled wolf's head buckle that seemingly connected to the sash hanging down, creating an image that showed a long-scaled serpent-like beast with a head at either end with a demon in the background. His armored pants had scaly monsters grinning, with one horn matching those on his gauntlets on opposite ends.

He stood there holding his helm, which had three horns along the top, two smaller ones on either side of one large horn in the middle. It was also fashioned to resemble that of a demonic dragon to strike fear on the battlefield. With a height of 7'5", it was easy to strike fear in those around him while adorned in his armor. His hair was dark blue, and his eyes were black as night.

"I have no doubt you are ready to fight," he said firmly. "It has been a while since we have had to go to war, but I can see it in your eyes. YOU WILL defeat and get revenge on the Vampirian scum who murdered our friends and family this day! You will crush them beneath your boots. They will rue the day they set foot on our soil and ruined our lives by taking from us. We will show them our might, the might of Utopia! We will show them we will not be stepped on or pushed around. Without fear, we will confront this enemy as we have with all others, head-on!" This brought a resounding cheer from the crowd. "However, I will not be leading you into this war." He paused as the soldiers stopped cheering and whispered amongst themselves in shock. They became quiet once more when he spoke once again. "I am retiring and will no longer be your Planetary General. I will be here as an advisor to the new general and the Emperor if he so needs it. The man I have chosen has already proven worthy of taking up the mantle. So, without further ado, here is the man who will, without a doubt in my mind, lead you to victory!" The whispers began once again as Sparticus stepped aside from the stand.

While Sparticus was still in his speech, his chosen successor was busy preparing for his address. He paced back and forth in the dressing room, his nerves in knots. So much had happened so quickly. Just a few hours ago, he was celebrating a victory with his beloved. The next, there was screaming, yelling, explosions, and people being slain right before them. They fought valiantly, but there were just too many. He watched, helpless, as their leader took her life just a few feet from him. That's when the planet's army finally arrived, too little too late, and now he found himself here, standing in front of a full-length mirror. Dressed in a uniform, he never gave pause to see himself wear. As he looked at his reflection, a few words came to mind.

"That's a lot of white."

Indeed, the uniform's primary color was white, as white as the hottest fire. It comprised a tall-collared short vest with long sleeves and shoulders that stood out at a point. Red flames decorated these shoulders and gold trim. The sleeves were folded up into cuffs. Underneath, he wore a black saterous shirt that fit snuggly against his flesh but was very resilient. He wore a thick belt with two silver buckles. Each buckle was decorated in its own way. The top had a gold lion's head emblazoned upon its silver plate, while the bottom buckle had the image of a black wolf's head. Along the front of the brown leather straps of the belt were black runes that read from left to right, from top to bottom, "Dir a son, Dir a day, Dir a say, Dir take me away." This was a commonly known prayer amongst the people, particularly warriors, to invoke the protection of a Valkyrie and ensure that they'd be taken to Valhalla upon death. Connected to the bottom belt were evenly spaced rectangular red metal armor plates with gold edges. As Angel looked at them in the mirror, he reached down, grabbed one in either hand and flapped them. They were light and had some flexibility to them. These covered his thighs as an extra layer of protection over a white robe with gold trim that remained open in the front. The robe reached to his white boots and covered most of his white pants.

As he gazed into the mirror, he moved his arms about, stretching them, and then rotated his waist. He then began raising his knees one at a time, getting a feel for the new attire that he would be wearing. As with the rest of the uniform, the pants were made of lightweight cloth, granting him much mobility. The one thing he was not too keen on was the choice of footwear. They were made of white leather and went up to his calves. Granted, they blended well with the rest of his uniform, but he wasn't sure of them. As he continued to stretch and adjust to the uniform, he heard Sparticus' speech ending. From the speakers, he listened to his words,

"I am retiring and will no longer be your Planetary General. I will be here as an advisor to the new general and the Emperor if he so needs it. The man I have chosen has already proven worthy of taking up the mantle. So, without further ado, here is the man who will, without a doubt in my mind, lead you to victory!"

Angel looked up at the speaker. "Guess that is my cue."

He walked over, sat on a bench, and strapped on the last pieces of his uniform around his boots, two golden guards that protected his feet, up his shins and knees. Standing up, he took one last look at himself in the mirror and laughed softly.

"I look like some warrior saint in this getup. Well, Leen, I guess I joined that Knighthood after all. Hahaha!" He paused and took a deep breath. "Well, I shouldn't keep them waiting." With that, he straightened his vest out and walked out the door.

The crowd hushed, and Cogeta and Cory stood in awe as their friend walked to the stand. As he stood at the podium overlooking the large assembly. To his friends, he appeared to be an entirely different person. It was no longer a protective feeling one would have with a big brother. That vibe from before was gone, twisted into something dangerous and malevolent. It was now that of a man who only sought vengeance. Angel stood silent as he looked over the faces of those he had never met and those he knew well. Their shocked expressions made the moment even more surreal for him. He couldn't believe he was standing there at that moment.

He looked over the crowd as they stared back at him. Most were in military uniforms, like the one he had worn at the dance only a week ago. Now he stood in a uniform that he never dreamed of being in. Looking out at what he used to have been, he realized all too clearly what his new uniform stood for, and the weight that donning it carried.

"I am Dark Angelus Everlast, and I accept the position, the honor, and the responsibility as Planetary General. I know some of you I see before me, while I don't know most of you." he paused. He spoke in such a way that his friends knew he was serious, "I was but one of the many who fought the Vampirians when the cowards attacked this afternoon. They took something very dear to me." He took a brief pause as if to focus his thoughts. "When the Vampirians attacked, they wounded me deeply. They attacked and killed our people, burnt our homes, and murdered the love of my life, but what got me the most was that they hurt my Utopian PRIDE!" Cheers climbed higher at his statement from the crowd. Angel balled his right hand into a fist and tightened it as he continued, "They do not believe in honor. They would rather perform a cowardly attack than openly declare war and face us like true warriors! History will show that they were wrong to think they could get away with it. They have awoken a beast that has lain dormant since the Nebulian - Utopian Wars from eons ago. It was then that we established we had the strongest military force, and the Vampirians still dared to attack today! I swear that while a drop of blood is in this body, I will hunt them down! We will rescue all that they took from us. I will not rest until I get the one responsible for our pain and the pain suffered by our lost ones! I ask that you be my sword, the sword of Ragnarok, so that we may envelop them in our flames of righteousness and turn them to ash!" Angel slammed his fist down onto the podium as he finished. The auditorium roared with cheers and applause as he bowed and stepped down.

Sparticus came back to the podium. "All right, you heard your Planetary General, whom you will serve loyally with every breath. Now begin heading outside, where you will rally to the general you will fight under."

Sparticus then stepped back down as the crowd cleared. A red curtain came down, concealing the stage. Behind the curtain, Angel approached Sparticus.

"Pardon me, sir, but was it wise to say I have proven myself? I have yet to be told my task so that I can prove my worthiness for this responsibility." As Angel spoke, the other two speakers joined them in a circle.

"Indeed, we know this, but we had to tell them that to build their confidence. Morale is as important as food and water in an army. It can either make you or break you when on the field. Your task, Angel, begins now. You are to infiltrate Gilgamesh's Temple, find him, and prove your worthiness to him. You have until tomorrow morning to fulfill this."

"And bring back proof!" snapped the High Councilman in a sharp tone.

Angel glared at the High Councilman, then returned to Sparticus and nodded. "Do I get any weapons for this?"

Sparticus shook his head, "No, your only weapons are your mind and body. Those should be good enough."

The Emperor patted Angel on his back. "We have faith in you, my friend. We saw today the strength you possess in the tournament and the strategic thinking of your mind when you chose your opponent's challenges. You will do a great job and lead us to victory. I understand that Sparticus has had his eye on you for a while. Know that we did not make our decision lightly."

"Feels like you've tasked me with something unachievable. No man has ever made it out of Gilgamesh's temple. It would seem only women may enter freely and return."

"Confound it, boy, that's the whole idea. You must prove yourself to an ancient god. Prove to him that you are worthy and, in return, prove it to us. For such a high-ranking position, the quest has to be nigh impossible to complete." Retorted the High Councilman in contempt.

"...I understand that. It just seems---" The High Councilman cut off Angel.

"You are wasting time, boy. You best be on your way."

Angel stifled a growl as he glared at the High Councilman. He wanted to thrash him but knew he had to stay in control. So instead, he bowed to the three men before sneaking out the backdoor so as not to be spotted as he headed off into the wilderness. The three high-ranking officials made their way out down a hallway from the backstage. As the three walked together down the hallway on their way to their tasks, the High Councilman made his thoughts known loudly to the other two. He was shaking his head.

"I cannot believe that, at this time, you draft a boy to do a veteran's job."

"I have a son to take care of, Councilman. He is gravely wounded… and is weak, and I have no other to look after him. The wound he suffered is not mending and needs constant care to keep the infection out. As much as the boy infuriates me with his weakness, he is the only thing I have left that keeps his mother's memory alive. I won't be across the damn universe when I hear of his death. I've been keeping an eye on Dark since he entered the University. I've observed him train diligently in the ways of war and take his military studies seriously. As Planetary General, it is part of my job to keep a watchful eye on the up-and-coming cadets. I've spoken to a few and sparred some days with them. Dark was one of the few who was never afraid to cross blades with me. We have all seen Dark perform in the school championships, which he has won twice now in a row against Shaw. He is a very skilled fighter. Since he's been made captain of his team, he has only improved himself and his comrades' talents. He may not realize it, but many consider him a leader. He is a top-ranking student in all forms of military tactics and warfare. His scores are even higher than Shaw's from MidStar. Now tell me, why do you think I had poor judgment in choosing *my* successor?" Sparticus stopped in the middle of the hallway and looked sternly at the Councilman.

"We have no records of him before he showed his face at that primary school. It is as if that boy came out of the fog on a gloomy morning. He has no parents, no relatives to speak of. I am not even sure he is a Utopian. Growing up, he has been a nuisance and a lawbreaker. If it were not for the fact that he made friends with one of my star pupils and gained her trust, the same one he got killed today might I add, then I would have had him imprisoned and under constant surveillance. We cannot trust him with such a high-priority task. He is a rebellious rogue who will fight this war for the wrong reasons. He won't aim to win it for our people but for his selfishness." The High Councilman angrily answered. "Shaw would've been the more obvious choice. He comes from a well-established family lineage. His scores rival that of the mangy one. Shaw has not yet beaten him in a tournament or a duel, but he is just as tactfully minded. He would fight for the glory of his family and that of all Utopia. If you are concerned with tournament prowess, he's fought in more than the boy and has won far more."

"You speak of the wrong reasons and yet speak of someone whose only motivation would be fame and glory." Sparticus chuckled. "Vengeance is a powerful motivator. It will push him further along in his desire to win. Shaw is competent and a fine candidate as well. When I have sparred with him, Shaw shows promise. He's a hungry little dragon. Shaw has won far more tournaments. However, his competition left a lot to be desired. For the longest, a power gap existed between him and his closest rival by a far margin. Then enters Dark. Suddenly, that power gap is closed and growing in the opposite direction. As you admitted, not only has he lost at the tournaments, he's even challenged Dark outside of the event and has never won. A powerful person must hold the post of Planetary General, not just in body but in spirit and mind, so they may have the fortitude to lead. Let's not forget that I was also a rebellious rogue at his age. Look how many victories I've brought to Utopia."

Just then, the Emperor spoke in his regular soft and calm voice, "I completely understand your concerns. Revenge is indeed a selfish reason to do anything. However, Leen and Angel were both my friends before and after I took the throne. Before I was crowned emperor, I attended that primary school and got to know most of those men now going into battle. I trust Angel, and though we may not have records on him, his blood smells like it should, and he has all the appearances of a Utopian. He has my faith as a Planetary General."

The High Councilman gritted his teeth. "My Emperor, you have a generous heart. Be careful who you open it to. But very well, Sire. I only hope we do not suffer because of this decision later. But for now, I shall keep my opinions to myself."

The Councilman bowed his head to the Emperor, and the three continued to the awaiting troops to lend a hand where needed and instruct the generals with final details before their departure.

CHAPTER 12

LAST NIGHT ON UTOPIA

Cory and Cogeta stood outside, away from everyone. All the cadets and soldiers were forming lines, and at the front, they were being instructed as to which general they'd be reporting to.

"Man, Angel, the Planetary General. Who would have thought," Cogeta said to Cory in astonishment.

"Yeah, tell me about it. Now, Cogeta, will you please tell me what happened? I'm still at a loss. So much has happened in such a brief period. I'm doing all I can to keep it together. What happened to Leen?"

"Relax, I was about to bring you up to speed." He took a deep breath. "When those bastards attacked us, he and Leen were out shopping. Well, they were doing well, but even the best get tired, plus Angel was already worn out from the fight with Shaw. There were just too many of them. Angel and Leen were overpowered. Then, from what I gathered from Angel, the head honcho appeared." He paused a moment, then continued. "He talked a lot of trash in front of Angel and threatened to enslave Leen, and then he just killed her. Angel said it was with some magical forbidden dagger or some crap. He then told me he took Leen and buried her beside her mother with his bare hands. When I met up with him, his hands were still covered with dirt."

Cory stood astonished by all this. "Then what he said up there…"

"Playing to his new position, I guess. He had to say what the crowd needed to hear. You and I know his pride was mainly hurt because he could not protect Leen. Not because so many Utopians lost their lives today. Not that he isn't upset about that. He is fighting to avenge her and her alone. But everyone else doesn't need to know that. Not only that, they took a few people too. I guess, to enslave. Hopefully, we can find and save them as well. I'm sure we will." Cogeta tried to put on a comforting smile. *Smile Cogeta. Your friend needs to see that everything will be okay. Smiling will comfort him and help you get through this. I can't believe she's gone. It must be killing Angel. How can he walk or breathe? How can he go on without her? Damn it, this can't be happening.*

Cory was at a loss for words. There was a lump in his throat. His mind was spinning as he felt the void in his chest grow. *Why? How can this be happening? Leen was the sweetest person, always there for me when I needed to talk.* "…How is Becky? Is she all right?" He finally managed to form words.

"That wild thing? Shoot, no Vampirian could lay a hand on her." Cogeta boasted of his lady. "She was right there by my side. She was amazing, Cory. I wish you had seen her. Becky… man, I couldn't be luckier to have a woman so smart and brave by my side. She bit off a dude's head to protect me, I mean literally. She transformed, bit down on, and ripped his head off his shoulders. It was… to see her go so far to protect me… me of all people…" Cogeta looked at his smiling friend, but he could see that the smile hid his loneliness. He placed his hand on Cory's shoulder. "You'll experience it one day. I know you will." *Confidence. Give him confidence and hope. Keep his mind off the tragedy.*

"Isn't she coming with us? I didn't see her in the auditorium. I thought she had signed up to serve as well."

"No, she didn't sign up for the military. Remember? For girls, serving is not a requirement, just optional." *I'm so relieved that she didn't. She certainly could do it and be amazing… but I don't know what I would do if I lost her. Would I be as strong as Angel? Could I find the strength within to continue?*

"Right. Right."

"For us, though, it's mandatory."

"Unless, of course, you prove yourself to be useless…"

"Saying I'm useless, are ya?" Cogeta cracked a smile, reaching around and locking his arm around Cory's head and rubbing his knuckles over his hair.

"No! No!" Cory pushed Cogeta away and massaged the sore spot. "I am just saying that is one way to get out of the mandatory enlistment. That or having your family pay your way out. However, going that route, you are labeled a coward, and it never goes away unless you sign up and have to die in battle."

"You study too much. Do you know that? Did you memorize the entire handbook too?"

Cory looked down at the ground, which made Cogeta laugh.

"Ah, don't worry about it. I'm sure the info will come in handy at some point. I lost my book a long time ago. All that aside, though, I am glad she didn't choose to sign up. I mean, if she did, I wouldn't be able to focus entirely on the battles at hand. I couldn't stop myself from worrying about her. So nope, she is staying behind. I can't see her before we leave. Heck, we can't even go home to pack. I am going to send her a letter explaining what happened."

"What do you mean we cannot go home tonight?" Cory looked up at his friend with concern. He didn't even know if his family was safe and had wanted to check on them.

"Nope. We ship out with our assigned generals tomorrow. So, I have heard. Tonight is our last night on our soil. So, scoop some up with ya before you go," Cogeta teased, rubbing the top of Cory's head.

Cory smiled weakly, absorbing all the information. His mind was rapidly processing it all. Still, it was hard to accept that this wasn't just some awful dream he wouldn't wake up from. Calming down a bit, he used the skills he was taught and sensed for his parents' unique auras, as he had done to track down Justin. He sighed with relief. *There they are. Sis is with them as well. So glad they are safe. But… I'm about to be shipped out, and I won't even be able to tell them goodbye.* He withdrew his small handheld device from his pocket. The message he had been typing in response to his mother remained unfinished and unsent. He tried to send it, but the glass was shattered in so many ways that it surprised him that the thing even turned on. Cory wasn't sure if it had been the fall in the burning home or if it had happened during the fight with Justin and his friends that broke it.

"I guess I will have to send my parents a letter once I can. So, they don't worry." Cory sighed. Then he checked if he had received a response from the person he had messaged prior. It took some effort to get the screen to do what he wanted, but it finally did. His lips turned into a frown. "No response...of course. Probably still shaken up and hasn't had a chance to look at their messenger, let alone respond. Or perhaps she lost it. Or maybe..."

"You say something?" Cogeta asked his friend.

Cory shook his head and slipped the handheld back into his pocket. "Nah, man. It's nothing."

"Okay. Come on. Let's see where we were assigned. Oooh, I hope I'm serving under General Zelthia, or dare the gods to be so kind, General Lusta." Cogeta rubbed his hands together as he grinned like a Cheshire cat.

"Yeah, it's a good thing Becky didn't sign up. She'd kick you in the head for acting a fool and drooling over them like a mindless hound. And seriously, you just got done saying how lucky you were to be with Becky."

Cogeta laughed. "I'm just saying they are the best generals we have.

Fierce, intelligent, and oh so hot! I've heard that General Lusta loves to flirt with her troops, get them riled up, and then turn them loose on the enemy once completely devoted to her. I'd love to banter with her and become close. Real close."

"On the flip side, I hear General Zelthia is cold-shouldered."

"I'd warm her up."

"I'm going to send a letter to Becky about how you want to serve under one of the female generals so you can sleep with them."

"Cory, I'm shocked and hurt that you would think that. If General Lusta orders me into her bed chamber to run through aggressive drills, or General Zelthia commands me to join her in her quarters on a chilly night to share body heat, how can I, as a loyal soldier, refuse my commanding officer's orders?"

"You're terrible; you know that?" Cory shook his head in shame.

"Yeah, I know. But that's just part of my overwhelming charm." Cogeta continued to smile. He was doing his best to keep their spirits up. Their lives had just been ripped apart. The only way he could think of to keep himself and his best friend sane was to be positive. To be the clown to make them both smile. Give them both a sense of normalcy in a time where everything around them was no longer the same. "Come on, let's go find our names and see who we got placed with."

The two walked down into the crowd and were separated into lines. Cory looked to his left and right, letting his mind soak in this moment. There were lines on either side of him, and they continued to grow as more men and women who were not already soldiers arrived. Cory imagined the scene was similar in Midstar and other cities. The Emperor's address had been broadcasted worldwide and picked up on all channels and stations. When it was finally Cory's turn, he approached a table where a uniformed soldier sat with his tablet.

"What's your full name, boy? Damn... looking a little rough there."

Cory chuckled softly. "Yeah... umm. Name's Cory Darin Ryker, sir."

"A'ight, place your thumb on the screen there." The man pointed down to a small screen on the table. It scanned his thumb with a green light and then beeped when finished. His entire record then appeared on the man's tablet.

"A'ight kid, going to ask you a few questions to confirm your identity. Age?"

"...16"

"Name your father and mother."

"Father is William Ryker, and mother is Sandy Ryker."

"A'ight then. Damn, you got high marks in your studies. You should be able to advance quickly through the ranks. Welcome to the infantry. You're assigned to General Marrow. Take this," he hands Cory a pamphlet with a sigil marked with bones. "These are your letters of assignment. You'll present them to your commanding officer upon introduction. Go through the gate and find a tent with your general's sigil. Do not attempt to sneak off and hide. Desertion is treated as treason, a slow, painful execution. Do not try to trade assignment orders. You will be severely punished."

"Yes, sir. Umm, quick question..."

"Ugh, what kid? I have a lot of people behind you."

"Is it true we can't go home to see our families?"

"That is correct. We don't have time to say goodbye. We have all you fresh cadets to assign, and we ship off in the morning. Welcome to the infantry. Now get moving."

"Yes, sir." Cory tightened his grip on the pamphlet to avoid losing it as he walked past the soldier and through the gate. He stopped at the top of the hill and saw a sea of tents below. The army had set up tents so the soldiers had somewhere to sleep. Not being allowed home to spend the night with their families or loved ones was hard on everybody. Flags fluttered in the wind. Each general's sigil was marked upon them. It wasn't hard to find his assigned general's designated area. However, he was in no rush to get there. Instead, he headed down the hill searching for Cogeta or even Angel. Everyone was sitting near fires talking. They spent their final free time with their friends. They all knew it might be the last time they saw them. Soon, though, they would disperse, join their generals, and sleep in the tents surrounding his encampment marked by his or her banners. While walking amongst the tents for several minutes, following his friend's aura, he finally found Cogeta sitting in front of one tent. He smiled and walked over, and joined him.

"So, who were you assigned to? I got put with General Marrow." Cory asked as he took a seat.

"Bones? Dang, I hear he is rough. I am with General Barkley. From what I gathered, he never uses an inside voice and always barks out sentences as though each was a command."

"Sounds like he lives up to his name. If he orders you to his bed chamber to keep him warm, remember, as a loyal soldier, you can not refuse."

They had a good little laugh as Cogeta stirred a fire that he had started as the light was fading.

Meanwhile, as the troops chatted amongst themselves, the generals were assigned to go with their officers and ensure the ships were loaded with the armor owned by their soldiers. Many of whom wore the armor of their fathers and grandfathers. Along with the armor, they were gathering the weapons that the soldiers owned, so when they boarded the ships, everything was there, waiting for them on their assigned bunks. It was a lot of work, but they had volunteers and other staff to help. Soldiers with no armor or weapons were given standard issues from the military.

Many mothers broke into tears upon hearing their sons and daughters were going to war and quickly began packing them extra clothes. However, these were denied. All casual wear would be waiting on the ship in their lockers. Everything they needed would be on board come morning. The High Councilman volunteered to make sure of that personally.

As Cory and Cogeta were talking at their fire, a soft feminine voice whispered from behind. "Pst! Hey, I am looking for one handsome man who looks gorgeous in a uniform."

Cogeta turned around and saw a woman's hand motioning for them to enter the tent. He quickly followed the hand, pulling Cory along with him by his arm. Inside the tent were pillows and blankets, two small tables big enough to hold a lantern, and a familiar person sitting back on her legs.

"Becky?! What, I mean, how did you get in here?" Cogeta yelped, scrambling over the covers, hugging her close, and kissing her repeatedly.

Giggling, Becky pushed him back, "I came looking for you when you didn't come back after the sirens went off."

"But the rules…." Cogeta said.

"Cogeta Fairway, don't even talk to me about breaking rules." She smirked, and he started laughing.

"What about the guards?"

"It was a piece of cake! Look whom I bumped into trying to sneak in here too." Behind her was a bump in the covers. Becky raised them to reveal another girl. She had bright pink mid-length hair and bright blue eyes.

Cogeta gasped, "Is that Stone's girl?"

"Yep. By the way, whose tent is this?"

Pointing his thumb to his chest, "It's mine."

"Ah, good. Cory, would you please get Stone to come over here?"

"Sure thing, Becky." Cory crawled out and went looking for their friend. After he had left, Becky looked at Cogeta, her smile gone, and she looked serious.

"Cory is looking rough." She said, concerned.

"Yeah, he says he got jumped by a group of Vampirians. That's what he says, anyway."

"You don't believe him? Honey, we were jumped by a band of Vampirians too. You just had me there to protect you." She smiles.

Cogeta chuckles, "Oh, I am well aware of whom I have to thank for my life on this day. But yeah, no, I believe he fought them for sure. He has some of their blood on him, and I can smell it on him too. But that's not the only thing I smelt on him when I first encountered him."

"Oh?"

"Becky, I smelled Utopian too."

"Yeah, babe, maybe because he's Utopian."

"No, no. I know what my friend's scent smells like. This was not his scent. It was that of others."

Becky's eyes grew narrow. "You think that someone attacked Cory in the middle of a grawfiggin invasion?"

Cogeta tilted and rubbed the back of his head, "I... think so. But he won't tell me. And I'm not sure who it is. I have my suspicions..."

"Justin?"

"Yeah, how'd you guess that?"

"Cory has a crush on his girlfriend. He knows it. Everyone knows it. But I would've never thought someone would use an invasion to cover up an attack on their own before. Then again, Justin isn't exactly above underhanded tactics."

"Right. As I said, I have no concrete proof."

"And Cory would never snitch out someone. Especially if it could come back and, in some form, hurt her."

"Bingo. Damn, you're so smart. What's a girl like you doing with a guy like me?"

Becky smiled as she rested her head on her elbow. "Everyone loves some entertainment."

From behind Becky, a soft voice interrupted their playful banter. "Umm... you two know I'm still here, right?"

Becky looked back over her shoulder and smiled. "Don't worry, Elli. I'm not going to pounce on him in front of you."

"I make no such promises," Cogeta grinned ear to ear.

Becky playfully scoffed, "You're so terrible, Cogeta."

Elsewhere, Cory finally found Stone chugging down a keg of brew.

"HA! I win again. Pay up, Sammy." He roared in victory.

A small guy sitting beside him handed over a small pouch of coins.

"Hey, Stone!" Cory greeted and waved to get his friend's attention.

"Yo, Core, what's up?" Stone looked up while bouncing the small red coin sack in his hand.

"Would you mind coming to Cogeta's tent? He has to tell you something important."

Cory tried to act serious, not wanting to ruin the surprise or get the girls in trouble for sneaking in. Stone shrugged his shoulders and stood up. He told his other friends he'd return and went with Cory. Following him in, he was shocked and overjoyed to see his girlfriend sitting beside Becky and Cogeta. She was even wearing his favorite light blue dress with the silver bracelet he had gotten her for her birthday.

"Elli? What are you doing here?"

"What do you think? I am here to see you off. I won't be seeing you; only Odin knows for how long," she smiled. She spoke in a sweet, tender voice.

"But you could get in serious trouble," Stone was filled with concern, but his face betrayed his excitement at seeing her one last time.

"It's worth the risk to see you." She smiled. The gentle giant crawled over and kissed her. His right hand cupped her head as his left arm wrapped around her. At the same time, she was wrapping her arms around him.

Becky smiled through pursed lips, "And she was concerned about me pouncing on you?"

Cogeta grinned. "Let the young ones have their fun."

"Are you saying we're old?"

Cogeta twisted his smile into a devilish grin. "No, my dear. I am saying our love is ageless." He leaned in and kissed her deeply.

Cory cleared his throat, feeling awkward as the two couples made out. "I.., I should probably go to my tent."

Becky broke the kiss with Cogeta and looked over at Cory. "No, you don't need to leave." She reached out one hand and cradled Cogeta's head in her other arm. "You can come join us."

"Um..uh... I... uh... I couldn't." Cory stuttered and stammered, sweat forming on his brow. His face grew hotter.

Becky smiled brightly, "Oh, I am so going to miss seeing you turn so red." She left Cogeta alone momentarily as she grabbed Cory by the hands, brought him over to her, and sat down with him. She hugged his head against her bosom. While she embraced him, her hands stroked the back of his head and up and down his back. In a whisper, she said, "It's going to be okay. It's all going to be okay."

Cory's arms wrapped around her and embraced her tightly. His shoulders trembled, and he lost emotional control once more.

Becky felt her dear friend break in her arms. She heard his soft sobbing as she held his head against her. She looked over to Cogeta as she began to tear up as well. "It's... It's going to be okay." Cogeta swiftly moved in and embraced them both. She rested her head upon his shoulder and rubbed against him, seeking comfort as he rubbed his cheek against hers.

Elli combed her fingers through his golden locks, finally breaking her kiss with Stone. "My father says to tell you to be careful and not to stand straight up." She giggled after stating that and was joined by the others.

"I will do my best." He cocked a smile and ran his fingers through her hair.

Cogeta, at last, told Becky about Leen's death. She could not hold back the tears and buried her face in his chest, sobbing. Cory moved aside so Becky and Cogeta could fully embrace and comfort one another. He remained beside them. Stone and Elli bowed their heads in mourning while holding each other close. Elli's soft voice broke the silence.

"I first met Leen when she came to my house. The church had sent her over to tend to my great-grandmother. She was so nice and sweet. My grandmother could tell story after story, and it would annoy some of her caretakers, who treated her like she was just ... a burden. But Leen," Elli teared up, "Leen listened to every word. She talked to her and comforted her. She was then so friendly to me and taught me about medicines that I could craft to help my grandmother in case she was in pain and had run out of her medication. My grandmother would ask for her by name. She didn't remember any of her other caretakers. When age took her in her sleep, Leen was there when we laid her to rest and gave me strength."

"Lady Leen," Stone stated, "We had all been friends for a little while.

Elli and I were still a new couple, and her first birthday with us together was coming up. I never told you, but I was a complete wreck trying to figure out what to get you. I asked Leen if she could give me ideas. Something exceptional. Something that you would always cherish. She and I spent a few days shopping together until finally." He rubbed Elli's arm and gently raised her hand to show off the bracelet on her wrist, "I found something that I felt you would most appreciate as a token of my love for you."

Elli threw her arms around his neck and kissed him once more.

After sharing more stories, Cogeta mentioned that Sparticus had selected Angel to lead the armies into battle. This news surprised the girls. However, Becky felt okay with it. This guaranteed his chance to avenge Leen's murder.

"Is it really wise to appoint a new general at a time like this?" Elli asked.

Cory looked down at the ground as he thought about an answer. "He has top marks in his studies. Though, it's true that studies alone cannot teach you all you need to know nor prepare you for real-life application. However, everyone starts somewhere."

"Don't they usually start as a soldier and work their way up?" Elli continued.

"Yeah, that is usually how it goes. I don't know why Sparticus has stepped down now."

"Well, he said he had to because of his child being seriously ill and no one to take care of him. He wants to be there for him. That's understandable." Cogeta added in.

"Oh, really? Wow, but why not just promote another general into the position?" Elli asked.

"I don't know," Cogeta shrugged, "Sparticus' decision. He has the right, as Planetary General, to choose his successor."

"Do you think Angel is up for this?"

Elli watches as Cogeta, Cory, and Stone all share a glance and smile. Stone nodded. "Oh, yeah, he can certainly handle the pressure."

The group of friends went back to sharing more stories. When the sun began to set over the camp, it brought an end to a heartrending day. The two couples started saying their farewells and kissing one last time. Before leaving, Becky turned back to Cogeta, pulling him close to her, and preceded to whisper into his ear.

"I know this goes without saying, my love, but I love you. I truly do, and I know being away from me for a long time," her arms slowly eased their way around his neck as her forehead rested against his, the tips of their noses touching, "A *long* time," she emphasized, "is going to drive you crazy. But remember, I will be here waiting for you to come back, alive or dead. But if you come home with another woman," Cogeta felt her nails dig into his shoulders, and Becky's voice grew darker, "I will tear you limb from limb, piece by piece, until I calm down, and then I will begin the torture."

"Y-yes, dear," He winced from the pain but slowly made eye contact with her, and his face took a seriousness that was rarely seen. "You have nothing to fear from that. You are all I need. Every woman I see out there in the vastness of space will never compare to you." Her hand covered his mouth.

"As long as you get the point," she removed her hand and kissed him one last time.

Elli turned to Stone, "That goes for you, too."

Stone nodded. "Don't you worry, my love. You need not question my loyalty."

Becky smiled and pulled Cogeta to the side, "One other thing, I know that if you see a damsel in distress, you'll jump right in to save her, but be extra careful out there. It being war, if you need to find comfort and solace with someone for a night, I won't hold it against you."

Cogeta laughed, "Becky, come on-"

She once again cut him off with her hand. "I am putting our relationship on hold." His eyes nearly bugged out, and he pulled her hand away.

"What? Why? Do you want to leave your options open in case the worst should happen? Do you have someone in mind?"

"No. Don't be stupid. I am doing this so you don't have to feel guilty if you get caught in a moment of weakness. Not feeling guilty about it won't interfere with your ability to fight and get you killed. You're a male, after all. Plus, I know some generals will not enforce the caging during the Red Moon."

"Becky, what are you saying? This isn't an issue of trust. You have nothing to worry about."

"I know that. I am not doing this because I am worried about your loyalty, nor am I saying I doubt it. I am just covering our bases. It's one more X factor that could bite you, and I want you to come home safely to me. I am still yours, but we are on hold until you return. I will not negotiate this."

"You are still going to write to me, right?"

"Oh, hell yes. Our relationship is on hold, but as far as I am concerned, you are still mine. Hence, you better not bring any of the space girls home."

"And you'll always be mine."

The girls soon left, using the same way they had gotten in. After they had gone, Stone stood up and patted Cogeta and Cory on their backs.

"Take care out there, my friends. Oh, I never asked. Whom are you guys serving under?"

"I got Barkley, and Cory has Marrow. What about you?"

"I am under Angel's command." Stone puffed out his chest proudly at the thought of serving under his friend.

"You lucky bastard. Do us a favor and ensure he stays safe, okay?" Cogeta replied.

"Of course," Stone nodded. As he took his leave, Cory and Cogeta followed him out and watched as he walked back to his tent.

"Well, you better head to your tent. I wouldn't want to make the old dog bark at me so soon," Cogeta jested.

"Farewell, Cogeta. Be safe, friend." Cory had tears forming in his eyes.

"Yo, man, no need for the tears. I will be safe, no worries. These Vampirians, psshhh, they have nothing on me, nor do they on you. Watch yourself out there, nonetheless. Okay?" Cogeta did his best to stay calm and ease his friend's nerves.

Cogeta's parents had died in a war, and he was not looking forward to going off to fight in his own war. He had too much to lose, his girlfriend and his friends. The thought of not coming back gnawed at him deep down. He knew it would be those things that would bring him home safely. He would not let that gnawing overtake him. Still, in the back of his mind, the thought lingered. *What if something happened to him?* He shook his head. He did not want to think about it, especially now. Cory held out his hand to shake Cogeta's in farewell, but Cogeta moved it aside and gave Cory an encouraging hug.

"Until we meet again, keep your head on your shoulders and always watch your back."

"Will do, Cogeta, and you do the same." He could not stop the tears from rolling down his cheeks again. *Damn, it... Stop crying... be strong... You got to be.*

You will be. You are strong. You need to register it in your mind that it's a fact and not a question.

Cory leaned back and looked at Cogeta while they still hugged. Cogeta was smiling. He then nodded at him. Cogeta patted his friend's back and took a step back. Cory was not ready for this, and Cogeta knew it, but he could do nothing. As Cory walked away, he turned back to Cogeta and waved goodbye one last time. He then rejoined his group. Cory found a tent amongst those assigned to his general and entered, wiping the tears from his eyes. Deep down, he knew this would probably be the last time his tears ran. Where he was going, there would be no time for them. *Cogeta is right. I am strong. I need to believe it. I'll need to get stronger from here on out till this war is over. Odin, watch over my friends as well as myself on this journey. Please don't let my parents worry, nor lose confidence that I will return to them. I really hope I am going to be ready for this.* He slipped into a sleeping bag and laid his head on his pillow.

CHAPTER 13

A STRANGER COMES KNOCKING

A few miles away from the military encampment in a lush forest, Angel made his way toward the temple of Gilgamesh. He had been walking for hours now. After he had snuck out the back of the auditorium, he flew in the temple's direction. Upon reaching the forest's edge, he made his way on foot. The events of earlier replayed in his head. It fueled his drive. For in truth, he wasn't fighting this war for his pride. He only said that because he knew that was what the men wanted to hear. Angel was fighting to take the life of the one who killed his true love. He knew they wouldn't follow him if he had told the men the truth. They wouldn't serve a man who only had his interests in his heart, nor should they. He had a great rage building inside of him, and only one thing he felt would put the fire out, standing over Serkuma's corpse. Suddenly, a twig snapped from behind him. He immediately snapped out of his thoughts. Already on edge, Angel twisted around into a fighting stance.

"Who's there? Come out and face me!" A shadowy figure stepped out from behind a tree and stepped forward. "Arieta, is that you?" Angel relaxed and put his fists down to his sides. "What are you doing out here?"

Before him stood Leen's sister. She wore an open black jacket, a light blue short T-shirt underneath, and black leather pants and boots. "I saw you leaving the city away from the camp. I followed you because I have something to tell you." She took a deep breath. "Execute that bastard who murdered my sister. You got that!" She snapped, her anger showing through her reddened eyes. "Leave nothing left of him."

"I was going to do nothing less. You better head back home before your dad worries about you. Sorry, I did not get him and you when I buried her. I was concentrating on one thing at a time. She is beside your mother

251

under the willow. And... honestly, I couldn't face either of you then, especially Vox. Still can't...."

"Thank you. I am sure she would want to be there. I will let Dad know. He's beside himself with grief. Inconsolable. Sis was... meant so much to him. He will be okay. If he could, he would be joining you in battle. But he knows he's needed here. I could take care of myself but... even so. I wish I knew... how to ease his pain. But I'm hurting too. She was my sister! She was like a mother to me...."

Her pain was evident on her face and in her mournful cries. Angel stepped closer, took her into his arms, and held her close. He rubbed the back of her head and ran his fingers through her long blue hair. She sobbed into his shoulder. He didn't know the words to say that would truly take the pain away. Time was the only thing that would help numb her pain into a dull sore scar, forever there as a reminder of this nightmarish event in their lives.

"We fought... together. She refused to seek shelter. She wanted to help protect those who could not defend themselves. Your sister was a great help to me and everyone. She showed no fear as she charged forward to the aid of those around her. Even when the Vampirian soldiers ran toward her, she stood her ground and fought them back. Oh, Arieta, your sister was one of the bravest people I've known...." Speaking of her in the past tense was surreal to him. He hated it. He struggled to keep himself together as he tried to console Arieta. His words seemed to have the desired effect as he felt her slowly nod against his chest.

"Where are you going? Are you not supposed to be in the camp with the rest of the soldiers? It is obvious we mean to go to war. Not deserting and going rogue, are you? You wouldn't get far in that outfit." She pointed at his white garb.

"I would be there, but I have just been given the title of Planetary General. This is my uniform... it's different, but I kind of like it."

"What? Angel… you are too young to be put in charge of such an important status."

"Thanks for the confidence, but Sparticus has already retired. With this power, however, I will have my chance to face the leader of the Vampirians. I will make the man dead for what he did to you, your dad, and me. As I promised," Angel growled.

Arieta smiled, "Well, I know when you set your mind to something, you accomplish it, so I hope you don't stop now. But you still have not told me why you are out here?"

"Well, I have to do some trial thing. To prove I am worthy enough to have the position."

She looked puzzled. "Shouldn't that have come before giving you the title and the uniform?"

"I'd think so too, more fanfare... a celebration... but... things are moving quickly. He decided out of necessity, not because he wanted to."

"What happens if you fail?"

"Then I guess Sparticus has the shortest retirement in history," he smiled.

"Need help?" Deep down, she wanted to be of help. Not being there to help her sister was killing her, and she hoped that if she could help Angel, even a little would help ease her pain. She wasn't ready to face her father.

"Sorry, but I have to do this alone." Angel gave her a small hug. "Thank you, though."

"I understand. I'm sure Sparticus would prefer it that way and all."

She nodded, feeling alone and lost.

Angel pushed her away gently with his hands on her shoulders. Looking at her, he could see the hurt on her face before she turned away and looked down at the ground.

"Ah, what the hell? I could use the company. But only as far as the temple, okay?"

Arieta perked up and smiled at him, "You sure it's okay?"

"I'm the Planetary General. If they don't like how I do things, they should have picked someone else." He jested, "Besides," his voice was somber, "we don't need to be alone right now."

She smiled weakly, "Thank you, Angel. You said temple. The only temple I know of out here is... Gilgamesh."

"Yep. That's where I am headed. I must go inside and bring back proof that I was there." He explained.

Arieta looked at him with a look of confusion. "That's suicide. They are sending you to die. No man who has ever entered the temple has come back."

"Yeah, I know. But the task had to be worthy of the position. An impossible feat for me to prove that I can handle the threats that lie ahead. Or something to that nature, I guess."

"Angel, do you have a plan?"

Angel turned around and faced the sky in thought. "Thinking about taking a page from Thor's playbook. I might need to borrow a dress and a wig..." He looked over his shoulder and smiled at her.

Arieta started laughing. "You would make a lovely Angelina."

"Oh crap, don't pass that around. I'd never hear the end of it." He put his arm around her shoulders as he started laughing with her. Giving her a comforting squeeze. "Let's be off."

Arieta smirked, "Lead the way, oh mighty Angelina."

"Hahaha, stop."

Together, they continued to trek through the woods. Angel led the way. They walked silently for a while, their closeness being enough to ease the pain just a little.

"Do you think she is in a better place?" Arieta's soft voice broke the silence. Angel stopped and glanced back at her. "I'm sorry. Of course, she is."

"She is with your mom right now. Probably telling her how much you've grown and become such a good person."

Arieta smiled, fighting back her tears. A branch snapped in the distance. Angel snapped his head forward. He glanced around quickly as he clenched his fists. They could hear small woodland creatures scurrying past them, hidden by the thick underbrush. Then they felt the ground shake in equal intervals. Something was coming near, something big.

"Stay behind me. Whatever is coming toward us, I won't let it harm you."

Arieta nodded, not wanting to argue. Suddenly, a colossal beast came bursting through the trees. Upon seeing Angel and Arieta, the creature snarled and growled. Angel held his hand in front of Arieta and placed himself before her. The creature's head was covered with light brown fur and was feline-like as it snarled. Sandy hair covered its body. Thick green scales protected its chest and vital organs, and a black frill ran down its back. Its large front claws dug into the dirt, and its hind paws kicked up the ground. Its long, scaly tail swished back and forth. The creature stood eight feet tall and boldly bared its fangs toward the two. With a mighty roar, it made its presence overly known throughout the surrounding woods, scaring off many small animals. Angel stood his ground, glaring at the beast as it glared back.

"A lyzon," He muttered to himself.

He grabbed Arieta and jumped back as the lyzon took a swat at them. Angel shot an energy blast at the beast, burning its face. This only made it more determined to kill the trespassers. Steadying itself, it raised its head and took a deep breath. Then, with a guttural growl, he looked down at Angel and Arieta. It opened its mouth, and out came a raging fire. Angel quickly pushed Arieta down, then covered her and himself with an energy shield as the beast moved its head from side to side, scorching the ground.

"Do you know any spells?" Angel asked as he reinforced his shield.

"I-I'm thinking!" Arieta screamed in a panic.

"Well, think faster!" He ordered.

At last, the fire attack ceased. Angel faced the beast. Rushing in, he jumped over its swatting claws and landed a hard kick to the lyzon's head. Leaping back, he fired several small blasts before hitting the ground and sprinting around the beast. The lyzon followed Angel, repeatedly trying to snatch him in his teeth or claw. Frustrated, the beast raised its head again as it took another deep breath and released a wave of ice. Angel jumped behind a tree as the area he once stood in was frozen with chunks and ice spikes. The beast followed Angel, freezing the tree that he hid behind. The lyzon roared when it finished covering the small area in a blizzard. Angel whipped around the tree and flew forward, hitting the lyzon square in its jaw, snapping its jaw shut, and silencing its mighty roar. Out of the corner of his eye, he saw Arieta standing perfectly still, with her head bowed and her hands together. *Just a little longer*, he thought as he ducked under the beast and struck at the inner sides of its hind legs. The mighty beast stumbled as the muscles in its legs trembled under Angel's strikes.

"Gods of old, gods of power, hear this child's plea. I summon you to strike at this foe before me so that I may pass. In all the heavens, I demand you send forth your righteous SWORD!" Arieta extended her hand toward the beast, and a small star-shaped burst flew and disappeared in the lyzon's fur. The beast didn't appear to notice a thing, as all its attention was on Angel.

The wind suddenly picked up and howled. Then, from behind her, a pair of white arcs of air shot forth and struck the beast where the star had disappeared. The lyzon roared out as his side was slashed repeatedly. It tried to turn around, but the wind blades kept coming and cutting into its hide. At last, the beast gave up and retreated into the jungle. Arieta relaxed her hand, and the surrounding wind returned to normal.

"That was impressive." Angel walked up and patted her shoulder. "I'm glad you came with me." Arieta smiled faintly. The spell had left her feeling drained. "You, okay?"

"Yeah, yeah, just I'm not as great as my sister. Spells like that still take a lot out of me. But it was the only one I could think of to use."

"Well, you did a magnificent job. You just saved both of us. Come on."

He gently pulled her close to give her added support. They continued and, at last, came to their destination. Clearing the brush, they looked at the temple before them. With all the moss growing on the steps and up the sides of the impressive stone structure, it appeared centuries old. It loomed over its surroundings, rising higher and higher in layers of stone, like a guardian of old, watching over the forest and defending its ancient secrets.

"Well, here we are," Angel said as he looked around the clearing.

"It's… kind of spooky as if we are being watched."

A small smile appeared on Angel's face. "We probably are. As the legend goes, an alien god is deep inside those walls." He walked her over to the temple's steps and sat with her.

"Yeah, I know the story. It came from space and landed here. Men throughout history who were brave enough to venture in never returned. The screams echoed out the doorway."

"Yeah, many men never returned from here. However, as the story goes, a maiden…"

"A "virginal" maiden cannot forget that part. They are always virgins in these old stories."

"Ha ha, all right, a virgin maiden came across the continent and braved the temple for the sake of her ailing father and younger brothers. With her, she brought a young warrior and a priest. They protected her on her long journey. Yet they stayed outside the temple when they finally reached it, afraid of the legend. They waited for several long agonizing hours, unsure of her fate, until she finally emerged, carrying a small vial of blue potion. She told the two men that she saw no corpses or spirits, only heard a voice that guided her and told her to take the vial. The voice instructed her to give each of her sick family members one drop from the vial, no more, no less. Upon returning home and doing as instructed, the vial was emptied. A day later, her father and brothers felt better than ever. From then on, word spread about the god who lives here, and the High Councilman supposedly got wind of the tales. He consulted the stars and told the Emperor of that time that it would be in the planet's best interest to perform a yearly ceremony for the new god."

"So every spring, we hold the ceremony, send in two virgin maidens with gifts as an offering. In return, he supposedly gives us his blessings."

Angel nodded, "Right."

"But no man ever goes in there, even now."

"Right again."

"So then… why are you going in there?"

"I told you, it's my trial to prove that I am worthy of the position and title of Planetary General."

"But why would they send you in there knowing that?"

"It's simple. The man who holds the title cannot be afraid of anything. Least of all stories. The men probably just got lost inside there."

"And the women didn't?"

"You women are always saying how much better your sense of direction is."

Arieta narrowed her gaze and stuck out her tongue. "That isn't what I meant."

Angel laughed and stuck his tongue out back at her. "I know that. Don't worry. I will find my way back. I have to. I will for the sake of everyone and for what is at stake. But like I said earlier, I have to go in alone. So, I want you to wait here for me."

"But Angel, I am feeling better. My strength has returned. If you really can't let me go with you, then I can head home."

"No!" Arieta shrunk back from his tone. "I don't want you going back alone. What if you are attacked by another lyzon or something bigger? I cannot be worrying about you, wondering if you made it home safely. I already couldn't protect one Puraday this afternoon. I will not risk losing another. If I did and something were to happen... I..."

Arieta's eyes widened as it donned on her what he must have been feeling. She scooted closer, reached out, and took his hands in hers. "I understand, Angel. I really do." Gently, she brought them up and rubbed them against her soft cheek. "I will remain here and wait for you."

"Promise?"

"I promise. You have my word."

"Thank you. Now, if anything comes out of these woods, I want you to hide."

"Okay. I can do that."

Angel nodded and rose to his feet. As he looked at her sitting on the steps, he felt an eerie sensation creep up on him. The hairs on the back of his neck stood up. Arieta was looking past him with a concerned expression. She raised her hand and pointed. "Angel?" Sensing danger, he spun around, and his eyes gazed upon an open portal.

It was black in the center, with a chaotic red aura moving around the outer side. Tendrils of arcane power danced along the edge of the supernatural doorway. In front of it stood what Angel could clearly define as an undead ghoul. His stomach glowed with an eerie purple hue. What flesh Angel could see was pale grey with hints of blue and purple from decay. His hair was long and black but unkempt and knotted. He wore a small black leather jacket that was tattered. The coat only had a left sleeve and shoulder flaps decorated with metal studs on the left side and spikes on the right. He wore black pants with a chain wrapped around his upper right thigh and around his left shin and burnt black leather boots. He also wore a chain belt with a creepy demonic-looking buckle. Its voice sounded menacing, dark, and otherworldly when it spoke, yet his lips didn't move.

Dark, Dark Angelus Everlast?

"Yes. What is it you want? Who are you?" Angel was already preparing for a fight, standing in front of Arieta.

The ghoul simply laughed at Angel's reaction. *Calm down, tough guy. I am not here to kick your ass. I suppose we have plenty of time later for that if you want a good ass-kicking. Someone special sent me to pick you up, so let's go.*

"I am not going with you. You could be working for that blood-sucking bastard, Serkuma."

If I did, you would have been dead already.

I can hear him… but he isn't actually talking… telepathy? Angel glanced behind him at Arieta. She was shifting her eyes back and forth between the two, confused. *Looks like she isn't hearing him.*

The stranger leaned over to see what Angel turned his attention toward and saw Arieta sitting on the steps. His lips curled into a toothy grin but snapped back to normal as he straightened up when Angel turned toward him.

"How can I hear you speaking, but your lips aren't moving?"

Come on, isn't it obvious? The ghoul pointed to the hole in his neck. *Someone disliked how I talked, so they ripped out my voice box. As you surmised, I am speaking to you through telepathy. Beats passing notes. Speaking of passing notes, I didn't know you'd be bringing a friend. She's cute. But come on, isn't it a bit too soon for you to have a new girlfriend?*

Angel's eyes burned with rage as he launched himself forward. The stranger easily stopped and held Angel's fist while he hung in midair, letting out his anger as he pushed for his fist to connect.

You really shouldn't leave her exposed like that.

His words immediately snapped Angel back to his senses. He looked over his shoulder and saw Arieta being held by grey limbs from the ground. One hand was over her mouth to stop her from crying out for help as she struggled against their grip.

"Arieta!"

Angel turned and flew to her aide, but in mid-flight, he was seized and pulled down to the ground by the same things that had her. He clawed and fought to free himself from their hold.

"AAAGH! Arieta, hang on!"

Power surged around his body as he suddenly snapped free of his bonds, but even more appeared, and once again, he was pulled down to the ground. The stranger uncrossed his arms as purple waves vibrated off his head. Worm-infested bodies popped out of the ground around Angel. The grotesque creatures moaned as they pulled their rotten corpses from the soil. Some had slack jaws, bones piercing through their clothes. However, they all shared the ghostly, empty look in their eyes, the look of death.

You are really like a wild animal. Look at you, clawing at the ground, gnashing your teeth, and growling. Just calm down. We will not harm the girl. We are only after you. Bring him home, boys! The stranger shouted while stepping to the side of the portal.

The foul-smelling undead creatures holding Angel down came out of the ground. With the help of the other undead, they easily lifted his body off the ground and into the air. The four then carried him toward the portal, with the remaining minions acting as escorts.

"Angel!"

Arieta stood frozen with fear as she watched them carry Angel away as he tried to fight them off. The last one through the portal was their leader, who looked back at Arieta with an enormous grin, waggled his eyebrows, and blew her a kiss before vanishing into the portal.

He's gone! They took him, and I could do nothing. What am I going to do? Oh, shit. Shit. SHIT! I'm so frigging worthless. I couldn't help him. If only I were stronger! She fell to her knees. She beat the ground with her fists and pulled out fistfuls of grass in her frustration. *What did those things want with him? Maybe... maybe he will come back. He has to. I told him I would wait here... I'll wait. If he doesn't return by morning, then... then...* "I don't know! Angel! PLEASE, COME BACK! You have to come back!"

CHAPTER 14

QUEEN OF DEATH

On the other side of the portal was a landscape he had never seen before through his studies. The ground was dirt, patches of brown but mostly black, like charcoal. The sky was a depressing gray, and the air was dry and muggy. A revolting combination of scorched earth, rotting meat, and sulfur assaulted his nose. All around him, he saw ruins and tombstones. Some tombstones adorned the ground. Some were fit for a king, while others were mere twigs. The ghoulish leader watched with a smile, holding back his laughter as Angel struggled to break free.

"Where are you taking me?" His fighting spirit raged around him like a beacon; one could see it far away. "When I break free, I will kill every one of you!"

"Will you calm down, Dark? We are not your enemies. You have worse things to fear than us where we are going." The fiendish ghoul laughed, "But seriously, calm down and lower your energy. You are alerting everything around to your presence, and trust me; you don't want that."

What the ghoul said was the truth, for as he was saying it, eyes from all over the land were being drawn to the horizon toward his energy. Most who felt it didn't understand what it meant. They just knew something was amiss. A few, however, knew that the energy didn't belong and knew what it signaled. Angel took deep breaths, slowly calming himself down, and stopped struggling. His attempts had been proven futile, anyway. He paid more attention to his surroundings, making landmarks in his head. The path they were on was winding through the graves. As Angel passed the tombstones, he tried to see whose they were, but he did not recognize any names, something he felt he should be thankful for.

"Where are you taking me?"

"Over the river and through the woods, to grandmother's house, we go," the ghoul sang.

"Don't toy with me, beast."

The ghoul laughed. "I wasn't. Grandma is making little Gretel cookies and Hansel pie for us as we speak. What was that, Sal?" The ghoul turned his head toward one zombie carrying Angel. He heard the zombie groan and garble something. The ghoul nodded his head and laughed. "Yeah, I remember those. Nothing beats those cookies, but you'll never have those again. I hate to tell you, friend, but you're dead."

The zombie's face twisted into a look of shock as if this was news to him. Then the ghoul and other zombies started laughing. The noise sent chills up Angel's spine, but he did his best to remain calm.

"What are you talking about? What's so funny?"

"Oh, sorry. Sal, here was a pirate back when he was alive. He was a wily rascal, chasing skirts up and down the islands, getting all sorts of cookies and pie. That is until a dragon knocked him overboard into Davey Jones' locker."

"A dragon?"

"Oh, right, not an actual dragon. It was a nickname given to a type of old gun. It had a large muzzle and was loaded with nearly anything to do damage. More commonly called a blunderbuss. When it worked, it was quite effective."

The zombie called Sal nodded.

"I see. Well, I've stopped struggling, so could you do me the courtesy of telling me where you are taking me? You said someone sent for me. Who?"

"You will meet them soon enough. As for where we are heading," the ghoul pointed off to the distance.

As they overcame a short hill, Angel saw tall towers rising from the horizon. The closer they got, the higher the towers climbed. At first, Angel thought it was a castle, but as the building became more apparent, he saw it more as a cathedral.

"All right, look, I am clearly stuck here, so why not put me down? I can walk on my own."

"What do you take me for? I am dead, not stupid. Just enjoy the ride."

Angel growled under his breath.

At long last, they stood in the shadow of the massive building. It indeed was a monument in the barren wasteland. As abandoned and worn down as it was, the cathedral still made an impression. Outside, standing guard by the large doors, were two red-hulking beasts that wore simplistic forms of armor. The beasts growled and stepped forward with their pikes crisscrossing the door. The stranger waved his hand for them to stand down. By his command, the two beasts stepped back and opened the doors, allowing them passage inside.

The only light source inside the tremendous old cathedral came from candles in tall stands, but they did not illuminate the room completely. Vast shadows splashed against the walls and danced in the candlelight. However, from his position, he could make out some stairs leading up along the far wall. Then there came a chilly yet commanding feminine voice.

"Put him down. He is no threat."

The zombies set him down on his feet as ordered. Afterward, they slowly shuffled out the door that they then slammed closed behind them. Angel's eyes gazed around the room. He got his bearings as his eyes adjusted to the little light he had to work with. Sniffing the air, he hoped to learn more about what or who was coming. However, this plan backfired on him. Wherever he was smelled slightly less foul than the air outside. The smell of death filled his nostrils, making it nearly impossible to filter out the distinct scents in the room. He shook his head to clear it from his nose to no avail. However, his attention was quickly drawn to the stairs as he heard the faintest of footsteps making their steady pace downward.

Angel's eyes got a glimpse of a ghostly white barefoot as it stepped onto a stair where the light could reach. The soft footsteps stopped on the last stair. Even with his heightened night vision, Angel still could not clearly distinguish the person.

"You are having trouble seeing me, aren't you? It is a spell that obscures the vision of even the most perceptive creatures. I wanted to see you before you saw me." Her voice came to him softer than it had to the undead creatures. "You can relax, Dark. No one here will harm you. I am the ruler of this kingdom. I am known as Lady Deathbringer, Lady of the Damned, Lady of the South, and to those I deem worthy, know me as Lady Exspes."

From where she stood, a sweet perfume filled his nostrils, drowning out any other smell around him. His eyes slowly closed as he took in this fresh smell, his head feeling lighter. It somehow seemed familiar to him, but he didn't know from where. The woman stepped down and walked into the light. Angel cracked his eyes and looked her over—the spell she had cast on him was now broken.

She stood about five-seven. Her skin was a ghostly white and as smooth as that first blanket of snow. She had long, thick, and wavy hair the same color as her skin except for a streak of red in her bangs. Her eyes were void of pupils and were a dark ruby color. The Lady wore a cape made from a giant bat or demon wing, linked by two little claws in front. Underneath, she appeared to be wearing nothing more than a black bodice with gold interlacing designs. She calmly stared at Angel as he stood silently and stared back, his mind racing to figure the situation out.

At last, she spoke softly, but enough to end their silence. "I am sure you have questions."

"You're damn right I do." He snapped. At long last, he would get answers. "For starters, what happened to Arieta? Where are we? Why am I here? ARGH! WHY NOW?" He shouted.

She stood there calmly as he shouted at her. She knew this was going to happen. After all, he had been through a lot in one day for any man. She waited for him to return to a more relaxed pose before answering.

"You are in Hell. South Hell. I brought you here to offer my help in your coming battles. That is why I chose now to bring you here. As for the girl, Arieta, she is safe and will remain so."

His ears picked up two sets of footsteps coming up behind him. One group was heavier than the other. All his training and gut sent signals, warning him that he was quickly entering a dangerous situation. He spun around quickly, preparing for a fight.

"Dark, it's okay. These are my commanders and trustees. Crolarious is my blacksmith and personal bodyguard. Damien, my "recruiter" you have already met, and Vagrant, my "sharp eyes." He keeps me informed of what I want and need to know."

Angel looked at the three men standing in front of him. He relaxed his shoulders and unclenched his fists.

Crolarious stood around eight-five and was muscle from head to toe.

He bore scars all over his chest and a few on his face. He wore a tattered brown leather long coat with a hood. His pants were of raw black leather, with several brown patches sewn in. The boots he wore were old fashion, with the tops rolled down. They were also made from brown leather but had a darker tint. Angel suspected the darker shade was from walking in muddy areas over many years. Around his waist was a thick, dark brown belt with many small throwing daggers attached to straps. On his left hip hung a short sword; strapped to his back was a ginormous axe, whose blade was chipped all to heck from years of use.

The man she called Vagrant stood as the second tallest. He had spiky silver hair and pale skin. He wore black shades and a long black coat with a collar that covered half his face. A zipper ran from the top of the collar to the middle of his chest. Four straps were buttoned, left to right, across his chest, and a belt hung on his hips. The belt buckle had the image of a firing gun imprinted on it. On his shoulders were silver round plate guards. The tall boots he wore also had metal toe guards. He was very lean in stature. Using his previous experience with warriors of similar build, Angel surmised Vagrant had to be agile and extremely fast to compensate for the lack of muscle.

"So what do you want with me?" Angel asked demandingly, not liking that he was in a strange place and now surrounded.

"I only want to help you, Dark, not harm you," the lady's voice remained soft and sincere.

"How can I trust you?" He asked while looking over his shoulder at her.

"Listen to your heart. It knows it can trust me."

Against better judgment, Angel closed his eyes and calmed himself, focusing his senses to seek malicious intent from those around him. She was right. Even though powerful levels of power radiated from those around him, deep down, he felt no danger from her companions or her. Sensing past the cathedral walls was another story. All around, he felt similarly strong levels of power. Some were passive, but most were malevolent. The forces he sensed outside the cathedral made the hairs on his neck stand up and gave him goosebumps. There were two in particular that gave him an icy chill. They were far off, but he had never sensed such darkness radiating off a single person. Their power was beyond what he had encountered, even now with the powerful individuals surrounding him, even stronger than what he had sensed from Serkuma. However, he needn't fear them. He knew he was safe with this woman.

"You see?" The woman finally asked.

"Ok, but how do you plan to help me?" Angel turned back around to face her.

"First, I need you to do battle."

Angel shot her a glare. "What do you mean?" *Of course, I would have to fight. Why can things never go the easy way?*

"I must first see what you can do. Then I will know better what to bestow upon you as my gifts."

She nodded her head at the three men behind him. Angel stepped back into a fighting stance, glancing around at each one, sizing them up. Damien stood behind him, popping his neck, knuckles, and other visible joints. Crolarious walked around to his left glaring at him, and Vagrant strolled to Angel's right. Angel was keeping a close eye on Vagrant as one of his hands slipped into the right side of his long, black coat and pulled out a large silver handgun. From the butt of the gun, a blade shot out. Then three separate blades sprang out of that blade.

Vagrant was the first to attack. Whipping the gun around as his finger pulled the trigger. Angel tried to dive out of the way, but his legs refused to move. The bullet pierced his right shoulder with searing pain. He gritted his teeth, holding back his cry. Glancing down to see why his feet hadn't responded, he saw zombies had grabbed him. Their boney arms crawled up his legs. Angel looked over his shoulder to see Damien raise his hands, calling more zombies. They smashed through the floor and crawled out, each appearing uglier than the next.

As Angel struggled with their hands around his legs, he heard the loud, thunderous bang of the gun going off once again. Instinctively, Angel bent over backward to avoid the speeding bullet. He did so, but when his hands touched the floor, cold, slimy hands grabbed him at the wrists. He once again struggled to break free, to no avail. Then the sound of giant footsteps coming his way filled his ears and shook the ground. He looked over to his left just as Crolarious brought his big boot up, nailing Angel in his back.

Angel yelled as he felt the force of the kick shoot through his spine. With such power behind the kick, Angel soared into the air, taking the zombies with him. Spinning his body around, he tried to shake them off. When that failed, Angel slapped his hands together, causing the two to smash their heads against one another. Their skulls cracked like two eggs before they fell to the ground. Once his hands were free, he knelt forward and blasted the other two off his legs.

Vagrant didn't waste time taking aim once more at the falling Angel and let fly a barrage of bullets. Angel dodged most of them, moving as fast as he could, but a few still found their target. His right shoulder was again hit. Another bullet bore into his left leg, and one clipped his right ear. Angel landed on his feet, but unfortunately, it was on his left leg first. He winced in pain, dropping to one knee right in front of Crolarious' hulking form. Crolarious took no pity on him and struck Angel with a right hook, which sent him sliding across the floor. He came to a sudden stop as he banged his head against the wall. Using it for support, Angel made his way back to his feet. However, he didn't stay on them long, as a flying kick from Damien sent Angel into the air once more. Angel's body slammed into the stone steps, popping his shoulder out of its socket.

Enjoying the spectacle, Exspes strolled to her skull-covered throne, sat down, and crossed her legs, watching the battle playing out before her eyes with intense delight. Angel had gotten back to his feet. He stood his ground as best he could, taking harsh blows from all around while delivering some of his own to each of them. It was a blur of motion as the four fought, but after a lengthy battle, Angel collapsed, coughing up blood on the chilly stone floor.

Exspes stood up and waved her hand. "Enough." The three men obligingly backed away from the wounded body. Angel struggled to stand but fell back into a sitting position and settled for that minor triumph.

"Why stop now?" He spat out some excess blood and wiped the corner of his mouth with his thumb. "I... I was just warming up." He smirked while catching his breath.

"You have heart, Dark, and a reluctant warrior's spirit. That will not be enough to win this war, let alone avenge your lover's death. You must become stronger, for the enemy you face is more powerful than these three. In your current state, you would be crushed in a matter of moments." Her words were bitter but rang with honesty.

Angel slowly got to his feet and looked directly into the eyes of Exspes. "Excuse me a moment." He then sauntered over to the wall on his left. He rested his body against it and took several deep breaths before slamming his shoulder against the stone. "Aaaargh! Son of a...!" He growled and breathed deeply as he put his shoulder back in place. He felt and heard his ribs adjusting and being restored. He momentarily turned around and leaned against the wall as he rubbed his hand over his ribcage, checking their status before pushing off and walking back toward Exspes. Holding onto his shoulder with his right hand, he rotated his arm around. When he was again face to face with her, he smirked, "Don't underestimate me. Being Utopian has its advantages. My body can heal most wounds in moments, and after each fight, I get stronger."

"I know this, Dark. I factored that in already. You know, of course,

273

Utopians aren't the only race to have that advantage. Neither your rapid regeneration nor ability to grow stronger from battle against an enemy will do you any good if you are dead. The enemy ahead of you, Serkuma, has it within his power to kill you as you are now." Her eyes narrowed toward him.

"How do you know his name?" Angel stared back with his piercing eyes.

"His name is vaguely known down here. Not a household name, as I am sure he would prefer, but nonetheless, it is known. Plus, when you questioned Damien's allegiance earlier, it didn't really help matters." She smirked with a calm gaze.

Mimicking her expression, "I see. So then, did I earn your approval?"

"Well, you are much weaker than I expected you would be." Taking a pause, she thought for a moment. "Though you are weak, I might still assist you. The question is, are you willing to accept an outsider's help?"

Angel thought about it, weighing his options. He could refuse and return to his original trial, get this war started and finished sooner, or see what this woman offered. His curiosity got the better of him.

"Sure, why the hell not? How can you be of help to me?"

Her lips curled into a smile. "Well, I can do many things for you if you trust me."

He raised his right eyebrow. "For the moment."

She let out a small laugh, "That being the case, choose of the three men behind you to be your guide. They will lead you where you need to go."

"What? More trials? I have little time, Lady Deathbringer. I cannot go running around doing meaningless tasks! I need to get back to Arieta before she starts to panic. She's been through enough today as it is. And I still have to prove my worth to LEAD the armies into battle!" He snapped, losing his patience.

He knew there was some cause to hurry. Dawn was fast approaching, and he could not be late. Suddenly, his body was overcome by a significant surge of pain. Dropping to his hands and knees, he gasped for air. He could feel his insides being twisted around. His muscles felt as if they were being stripped from his bones. He forced his head up at Exspes, but something was different about her. Her once calm, empty eyes were now alive, sparks of red energy shooting out from the corners as anger filled her.

She snapped back at him with a harshness she hadn't before shown. "Don't get an attitude with me, boy. You have plenty of time, for it flows differently down here. All the time you spend down here will only be a minute at most to what you are used to. If you need more than that, then when you are through, I will have you transported back in time to make up for what you lost. Time is not an issue here! Your survival of this war is!" She took a deep breath and calmed herself. As she did, the pain inside him soon subsided. "Regarding the girl, she will be fine. As I said, time is not an issue, so she will barely notice you are gone. Now choose a guide and be off!"

Angel stood to his feet and turned around slowly to face his choices. His muscles still tingled from the pain they had just experienced, and he worked to regain his balance. He wanted to argue but knew it best not to anger the woman with the title of "Deathbringer" further. After all, she wished to help him.

He turned his attention to the task and looked over at Crolarious. *Big and strong would come in handy with any confrontation that comes along.* He shifted his eyes to Damien. *He is shorter than the other two and can summon armies of zombies, but these trials are centered on me. Those zombies will do me no good. He also seems to know his way around, but…   I don't like his smart mouth. He would probably talk too much. Pester me even. He's already shown he can get past my mental blocks, so I wouldn't be able to ignore him.* He then turned his attention to Vagrant. *"Her sharp eyes" means he must play the role of her scout. That should mean he knows his way around, perhaps more so than the other two. He doesn't seem very talkative, either, which is a plus.* "I choose," he gives all three one last look, "Vagrant."

"Very well. Be off. You have a long journey ahead. Oh wait, one last thing, Dark," she said. Getting his attention, she tossed Angel a black bag from behind her thrown. "Might be best if you didn't go off fighting in that outfit. There is a spare change of clothes." As she spoke, Angel opened the bag and pulled out clothes that belonged to him. "I took the liberty of having Damien pay a visit to your home if you can call it that, to grab you something else to wear before he went after you. You may enter the room down that hallway and into the fifth door on your right." She pointed toward the torch-lit hall to his right.

He took a pause, looking down at the clothes in his hands. "You… knew I would need a spare set of clothes? Confident enough that I would agree to stay and accept your help? What if I had refused?"

Lady Exspes shrugged. "I would've thrown them into the fire. I had a strong faith that you would accept my aide."

"Thank you, Lady Deathbringer. May I leave these in your care until I get back then?" He gestured to his current attire.

"Of course, you may. Just place it back into the bag, and I will be responsible for its safety. I will have it mended while you are gone. Also, feel free to call me Exspes," she smiled.

"Thank you. I appreciate that." He bowed to show her respect and his gratitude. Not a gesture he would typically perform for most, but it felt appropriate. He then walked down the hallway lit by torches set into the walls.

Upon entering the room, his eyes could not believe what he was looking at. The room was filled with red and black candles. Amidst them, all was   this large, round pool. Hanging from above and draping around the pool were red sheer curtains. His sense of smell drew him closer to the pool, and when at its edge, he slowly pushed the curtain aside. The pool was filled to the brim with red water with a strong yet sweet fragrance. Upon dipping a finger in and tasting, he could fully confirm his suspicions.

Blood. A female's, lots of females. His fangs involuntarily took form. *Why is this here? Is this a treat for me because she knows Utopians like the taste of blood? Doubtful. Now isn't the time to indulge.* He consciously forced his fangs away. Licking his finger clean, he returned to his reason for being in this alluring and erotic bath chamber. After finding a table to rest his general's uniform on, he dressed in clean clothes.

A black jacket, a T-shirt, a pair of black jeans, and a pair of boots, the same attire had had on only hours ago before the Vampirian army attacked. He debated whether to take the jacket because of the stories of Hell's climate. However, the weather seemed tolerable in this region.

When he returned to the throne room, he handed her the black bag containing his white uniform. Turning around, he saw Vagrant waiting by the door. Exspes smirked and watched as the two adventurers left her presence.

CHAPTER 15

LET THE TRIALS BEGIN

Angel had no clue where to go outside the cathedral, but his guide sure seemed to. Immediately, Vagrant started walking northward without a word. The gray dirt path they walked led them through a run-down town. Buildings were put together with rotted wood and clay. A few leaned to one side, threatening to fall over with a good push. Others seemed to draw support from the building beside it. Nothing here was reminding him of home. He was just grateful that he didn't live here. Like the path that led them there, it was dreary and gray, with bones of unknown creatures scattered about with other trash and rocks. The air was stuffy and humid. It was filled with the thick scent of sulfur and death that nearly choked Angel. It was a significant change from the warm sunny day of Fall, with its cool breeze, and from the smooth cobble streets and white sidewalks, he left behind. A morbid thought then entered his mind. *If I lost the war, would Utopia turn into this?*

Angel turned his gaze from the rickety buildings to the creatures that called this poor excuse for a townhome. He looked at them in awe. They were all different looking. What surprised him the most was that there were families, women, men, and children. They were doing many things that would be normal. Working, shopping, talking to each other like neighbors, all the things they did above ground. When they saw him, they all stopped what they were doing and stared at him. Not with the same awe as he had for them but with disgust and hatred. They snarled and growled at Angel. Some even clawed in his direction. Mothers pulled their children back and protectively shielded them. Somehow, amongst demons and hellish creatures, they considered him the monster. He ignored them the best he could. However, he could have sworn he heard Vagrant chuckle at their reactions.

When they reached the top of a hill outside the town, Angel's eyes fell on a land scorched black from fire and lava. Geysers were spurting lava at least thirty feet or higher. When it came back down, it scarred the already tortured land. Vagrant walked on and led Angel safely through the bursts. A few he just barely missed.

Angel finally broke the silence, curious about what his trials would entail. "So, where are we going?"

Vagrant remained silent.

"Okay, fine."

Angel sighed, knowing that he would get nothing out of his companion. He picked him because he appeared to be the most silent of the three, but a little information wouldn't have hurt. Hours passed as they traversed the geyser-riddled land. At last, they crossed the land of geysers. Looking back over his shoulder, the hill they had started this journey on was a mere speck on the horizon. Continuing, he was led to a lake of lava, where his silent companion stepped into a small rowboat.

"You are kidding, right?"

In an unfriendly, serious tone, Vagrant finally spoke, "Get in."

Angel listened and got in, not seeing a point in arguing. Once in the boat, Vagrant shoved off with one oar. Maybe it was magic, or the ship was made out of some strange material unknown to Angel, but the lava did not affect it. The immense heat had Angel sweating profusely. His travel companion didn't appear affected. Especially surprising when considering what he was wearing. He was wearing more black than a widow at her husband's funeral. Vagrant looked at Angel and then at the oars. Angel followed the gaze and got the hint. With a heavy sigh, he grabbed them and started rowing out onto the lake. Vagrant casually leaned back to enjoy the ride. Angel shook his head.

Lazy bastard. He could give a hand. *Trying to row through this is like trying to paddle through sludge.*

Somewhere out in the middle, Vagrant motioned him to stop rowing. He then reached over to Angel and placed his hand on his shoulder.

"Good luck."

"What do you mean?"

Before he could get his answer, Angel was shoved overboard.

His body burned and stung as though red-hot needles were piercing every pore. The pain was much worse on his sensitive tail that had become exposed. The lava was only meant to torture those who lived here, not relieve them, something Angel was learning the hard way. However, he was not dead yet, and the lava was slowly, agonizingly, working towards remedying that for him. Below him, Angel could make out a cavern through the harsh burning in his eyes. Figuring that was where he was meant to go. He began swimming with all his strength to get there.

His healing ability was working hard to ensure that the lava did not kill him. However, despite how hard he swam, he was not moving very far. The lava was so thick that it was as if he was swimming in place. *Ah, shit! It frucking burns!* He wanted to cry out, but if he did, then the lava would get into his throat and the softer tissue. *How am I going to make it down there? At this rate, I'm going to be cooked to death. Wait… let's see if this works.* Cupping his hands, he rolled over, facing his hands toward the surface. From his palms, he released a wave of azure energy, propelling him toward the mouth of the cave.

Once he was in front of the opening, he shot another wave, pushing himself inwards, and kept doing this, making his way down the corridor. Some ways in, he finally saw another opening above him. Not wasting any time, he shot a wave of energy downward to propel himself out of the lava and onto the rocky bank. He sighed, lying on the ground, trying to catch his breath.

"Finally, I made it."

His victory was short-lived as a fresh wave of pain coursed throughout his body. First, he looked at his hands. It exposed his fingers down to the bone, the muscles in his arms laid bare. He struggled to look down at his chest, realizing most of his skin had been burned away. Laying on the hot ground, he discovered his legs were half-gone. His tail was nearly gone.

"Well, there is a first," he tried to joke, but the pain was overwhelming and caused him to cry out. He tried to calm himself through deep breaths. "Really glad I don't have a mirror right now. Leen, I hope you aren't seeing this."

He was completely exposed. The ground and the air were in no way a comfort. The hot air simmered his exposed muscles, and the dirt dug and scratched him as he tried to move. Remembering his training, he tried to shut the pain out. *With all the blasting, I wonder if I didn't speed up the process.* He floated up off the ground in an attempt to lessen his anguish. Looking down at his legs again, he knew what must be done. Bending over alone made him want to cry, but he held it back. *My legs have been cauterized… I need to reopen them so I can heal. All this better be frigging worth it. Otherwise, I don't care how strong that woman is or how many undead beasts she has under her control. I am going to throw her into this pit.* Claws grew from his fingernails, and he scratched and clawed at his limbs, trying to remove enough so that his body could regenerate itself. He stopped and hissed in pain; *This is taking too long.* He looked at his bloodied claws. *Only one other way to try.* He closed his eyes to once more try to push the pain aside. He slowly floated back down to the ground as his body transformed into a large black wolf. Lying on the ground, he leaned his head in, gnawed, and chewed away at the partially opened wounds. He chewed fast and ripped flesh away on both legs until the wounds were opened again. Transforming back to his original form, he lay on the ground, huffing.

"There… that should do it. Damn, I hope I never have to go through this sort of thing again." He turned his head and spat out a mouth full of his blood.

His body's regeneration finally kicked in and appeared to work slowly, healing his legs inch by inch. He closed his eyes and focused hard on healing, which increased its rate. After a relatively short time, his legs were as good as new, his tail was once again covered in fine black fur, and the rest of his body was healed. He slowly got to his feet and started bending his knees one at a time, getting the numbness out of them. He could feel the blood rush through his new veins for the first time. As he worked and stretched his new limbs, he looked around where he was. The walls were made of fire rock that illuminated the room and a pathway leading further into this submerged cavern, and the ground he stood on was obsidian rock. He looked back down at himself.

"Well, so much for being decent." He joked. "Nothing I can do about it, I suppose. Good thing Lady Exspes thought ahead to get me this spare set of clothes. I'd hate to explain losing the general's uniform."

With no other option, he headed deeper into the cavern. Deeper and deeper, he explored, wondering where he was going. After many winding turns and climbing up ledges, he finally came to a large chamber. The room was spherical, with a tiny walkway leading off to a cone-shaped chunk of land on which a throne sat. Below was a pit of more bubbling lava. The throne had pillars of flame on either side of it and appeared to be shaped from the ground itself, and upon this throne sat a man. His flesh was red and seemed to be glowing. He had long black hair and wore black armor on his shins, arms, and waist. A small protective covering hid his mouth and nose and went up, encircling his eyes. About his feet were women of the same complexion as himself. They lacked clothing except for small black cloth tied around their waists. Two ladies sat in his lap. One played with his hair, and the other traced the outlines of his chest. Two more girls were massaging his legs. As Angel's eyes gazed upon this creature with his mistresses, the demon's eyes gazed back in a fiery glow.

"Dark Everlast, I presume," the being spoke in a dark voice, deep and powerful.

"Yeah, that's me. I am here for my—"

"Yes, yes, I know. Your trial. Before we get to that. Like what you see? What do you think of these women, huh? Gorgeous, are they not? It would appear part of you certainly does." The demon smirked under his mask as he tilted his head. Angel moved to cover himself, growing more embarrassed by the situation. "No need to be shy. Don't think the girls mind the display. Why not forget the trial and instead join us? They do bite and will gobble you up. I hear you lost yours. Here, choose from my lot to take back with you. They answer to every command, and I mean every command. Whatever your sick mind can imagine, they'll happily indulge. They make fantastic pets." The beast leaned down and scratched the chin of one of the girls at his feet. She cooed and purred at his touch.

"Let's get this over with, demon!" Angel shouted. "I am not here for your sick games."

"Ah, a demon I am. I am one of fire, if you couldn't tell, and of lust."

"Both were pretty obvious. Guess you're Hell's Cupid?"

The demon glared at Angel for a moment, then let out a loud laugh. "Not quite. Cupid has nothing on me. I'm far more powerful. He prances around in his sheet, spreading the flames of love, weak embers. It takes time to build them up into a raging inferno. Those flames still flicker in the wind, even in their full raging glory. On the other hand, the fires of lust burn strongly everywhere you look. The fires of lust have overcome many men and women, warming their souls and beds at least once in their brief life. No one can escape it. I am one of many who bring lust into people's hearts. I am by far the best at it. But anyway, let us get on with business." He stood up from his throne, letting the women slide off his lap. "My name is Inferno."

"I don't care what your name is. I want to get this over with."

Inferno shrugged. "Fine, have it your way. Let us begin our game. You have a lot of guts showing up here as you are."

The girls around Inferno whispered amongst themselves as they stared at Angel.

"Wasn't my choice. Your doormat did away with my clothes."

"Hehe, well, you should've come more prepared. As I mentioned, I don't think the girls mind much. After I am through with you, I may toss you to them, like a chew toy for them to play with. I bet you'd enjoy that too. However, I won't go easy on you. After all, you likened me to a cherub or Cupid himself. I despise both. For that, I will make you BURN!"

Inferno flew at Angel at super speed, fire trailing in his wake. He took hold of Angel by the head in a firm grip. His hands burned and melted Angel's flesh. Inferno flung him off the side and into the lava down below. Laughing evilly, Inferno stood watching the lava intently.

Oh, shit!

"My, that was easy. Ladies, come and please the victor. Your champion!" He held his arms open as the women came to him.

Holy crap, it actually worked! Damn it! Why didn't I think to try this before? All well. No time to worry about that now.

The entire chamber trembled. Large boulders and small rocks shook loose from the walls and fell into the lava. Inferno looked back toward the ledge where he'd thrown Angel and snarled, "Stubborn."

Angel shot up into the air with a shield of energy surging around him. His flesh was slowly regenerating, and he was smiling at Inferno.

"Nice try. Now it's my turn."

Angel dropped from the air and sped towards Inferno, giving him a hard left to his jaw. The force was enough to throw Inferno back to the wall, which cracked and crumbled under the impact. Chunks of rubble splashed into the pool below. Inferno slipped down into the lava, appearing to be unconscious. Angel missed it as Inferno let a slight grin pass his hidden lips. Angel hovered in the air, looking around.

It couldn't have been that easy. No, this fight is just beginning. Now what is he going to do next?

Within the lava, Inferno was growing stronger as he absorbed the energy from the heat. When ultimately charged, he moved through the pool quickly, as if flying through the air. Breaking the surface silently, he moved around behind Angel. Swooping in, he grabbed Angel by his collarbone. Not giving Angel a chance to react, he swung hi ceiling covered with thousands of sharp red-tipped stalactites just waiting to pierce his flesh.

Angel barely stopped himself a mere breath away from the ruby-tipped spikes. Spinning around, he let fly a barrage of blue energy blasts zooming towards Inferno. Occupied by keeping one step ahead of the oncoming onslaught, Inferno was surprised by a harsh blow to his gut. As he hunched, Angel smirked before sending through his hand another bombardment of blasts directly into Inferno's stomach. Each shot exploded upon contact and propelled him all the way back to the wall. The blasts kept coming until Inferno was buried within the side of the cavern. He slowly clawed his way toward the opening. Slamming his hands on either side of the hole, Inferno launched himself free and tackled Angel to the ground. They rolled around, exchanging lefts and rights, fighting violently without remorse to gain the upper hand.

Finally, they broke apart. Rising to their feet, they stared each other down. For a few moments, the only noise within the cavern was the bubbling of the lava. Angel took a deep breath. *I don't know how much longer I can keep going. He's looking worn down himself. I have to finish this quickly—* That stillness ended when they collided again. They met with such fury that their punches made the lake where Vagrant was resting ripple and lightly rocked the boat. Vagrant glanced over the side of the boat. Shaking his head, he snuggled back down into his nap.

Back in the cavern, the two men stood locked in a power struggle, neither losing nor gaining any ground over the other. Red and blue energy sparks crackled about them. Pebbles and stones floated up into the energy field that formed around them. The small rocks were turned to dust as larger stones broke apart into bits before disintegrating.

Inferno gritted his teeth, trying his hardest to overpower Angel. "Damn, kid, you have been eating your vitamins."

"Thanks. I always try to eat right. Eat my vegetables, you know."

"Oh, but of course. Speaking of eating right. Tell me, how did that broad of yours taste? Sweet as one of your, oh what are they, duffins, or as revolting as a rotting boar left in the sun to bake on hot sand for several months?"

Angel's eyes flashed with rage. However, he quickly calmed himself and relaxed his tension. He let himself fall backward, taking Inferno with him. Then, with both his feet, he kicked Inferno skyward. Angel gave chase, flying up and punching him repeatedly. Grabbing Inferno's arm, Angel spun him around faster and faster until releasing him to the ground.

Inferno muttered to himself as he lay on the ground. "Note to self, don't talk about his dead woman anymore during this battle." Pain suddenly ripped through him as Angel descended, burying his knees into Inferno's abdomen.

"Aaahh! Damn! You bitch!" Inferno coughed and spat out what appeared to be green blood.

"Do you yield?"

"HA! You wish!"

Inferno received more hard strikes on his face.

Angel glared at him and growled, "What about now?"

Inferno gazed up at him. Still feeling cocky, he let slip, "I wonder, does your woman like her new home?" *Ah, I couldn't resist.*

Angel's red eyes ignited with rage. It was not until Inferno's face was barely recognizable and his jaw lay crooked. Angel withheld his fists, showing great restraint. Angel growled through his gritted teeth.

"Do you surrender, demon?"

"Man, you are persistent. I like that. I suppose I could yield…." Inferno reviewed his predicament. Battered and defenseless beneath a naked man, "Yeah, I yield. Let's go."

"What do you mean, let's go?"

Inferno laughed as he slammed his hand on Angel's forehead. Concentrating his power, he began to vanish. Angel was screaming in pain, unable to move, though he struggled to break free. His brain felt as though it was engulfed in flame, and the pain traveled throughout his body. When

Inferno was gone, Angel was engulfed in red and white flames. These flames were different, however. They did not hurt him in the least. Instead, they were warming and comforting, almost empowering.

These new flames only lasted a moment before dying away. Angel stood up and looked around. The women had vanished along with their master. He expected as much, however. Something inside him said he had passed his first trial. He looked over his body and saw a new pair of clothes had magically formed. He couldn't help but smirk because he didn't have to worry about being naked for the rest of the trip.

That is until I have to swim back to the surface... damn it.

He returned to the entrance and prepared himself for a rough swim back to the surface. He dived in, ready for the worst. However, instead of feeling as if he was in a pool of agonizing pain, he was surprised to find that the lava no longer affected him. It was as if he was in a warm tropical ocean and could swim unhindered. Best of all, his clothes were also protected from the fiery liquid, to his amazement and relief.

Exiting the cavern, he glided effortlessly through the lava up to the top. Within a minute, he was pulling himself into the boat. He looked over to Vagrant, who still had not moved from his resting place. Without opening an eye, he pointed to the oars and then pointed back toward the shore. Angel shook his head, took hold of the oars, and started rowing back to the black beach.

"Vagrant, I want to know something. Before, did you know for certain that I would survive in the lake?"

"No."

"But you shoved me in any way?"

"Obviously."

"What would have happened if I had died?"

"Then I suppose your story would've been over," Vagrant replied sarcastically.

"Gee… how encouraging."

"Heh, if my Lady didn't think you could have survived, she wouldn't have sent you here," Vagrant said confidently.

"How much about me does she truly know?"

"She knows everything she needs to know about you. The lava here isn't designed to kill because everyone here is already dead. Its sole purpose is to torture and cause immense pain. I did not know how it would affect you, one of the living, nor did I care because I trust in my Lady. She told me to bring you here, so I did."

"Are all the trials going to be as painful?"

"Possibly. I cannot tell you for sure one way or the other. They aren't my trials to take. I will tell you this. However, you have the means to survive. The question is a matter of; do you have the will?"

Their conversation ended as the boat hit land. Vagrant stepped out and walked north once more, leaving Angel quickly behind. Angel jumped out of the ship and ran to keep up with his fleet-footed guide.

CHAPTER 16

WHEN HELL FREEZES

Their journey continued in silence. Vagrant led Angel down into a valley, where a ghostly wind blew. A cool breeze left an icy chill. It made the hairs on the back of his neck rise. Ahead, he saw a long mountain range with ice caps. Snow in Hell? The sight was bewildering. Maybe it was an illusion, but as they came closer, the cold air and falling snowflakes proved it was no mere figment of his imagination.

"Let me guess. My next assessment is a snowball fight with some jotun."

Angel's sarcastic comment got no reply from Vagrant, not even a glance. They trudged through the valley, with the snow getting thicker as they approached the mountains. At last, they reached the base of the largest mountain and climbed. As they ascended, it got colder and colder, and the snow was coming down harder with each step. The surrounding wind whipped and howled, blowing shards of ice so hard that they cut into Angel's flesh and ripped his clothes. Just the wind alone was cutting through his clothes and into his skin. If the combination of flying shards and whipping wind weren't enough to deal with, ice crystals would immediately take root every time he got scratched. Once attached, they would splinter and spread out, completely covering the scratch.

"These trials better be worth all this, Vagrant!"

After a long climb and a few near falls, they'd come to a flat ledge where they stopped. The wintery mix and wind wreaking havoc on Angel were no longer an issue. The wind blew around this ledge as if an invisible barrier kept its rage at bay. Angel took this chance to catch his breath and survey his surroundings as he brushed and broke off the ice crystals that had taken form on his body. About twenty feet away from them was a door on the side of the snow-covered rock face. The door was an icy blue with a unique design shaped on it with frosty white lines. Vagrant looked back at Angel, who was looking at the door.

Vagrant spoke up calmly, "This is your second test."

"… Right. I gathered that. Any idea what it is?"

"No."

"All right, what are we waiting for?"

"For you to get the door."

With an annoyed sigh, Angel walked past Vagrant and tried to force the door open. With all his might, he pushed and shoved. Angel then tried pulling at the door, but it would not give. He then looked back at Vagrant as he leaned into the door, still trying to push it in.

"It won't budge!"

Vagrant shook his head. "It's always polite to knock first before entering someone's home. Don't they teach manners where you came from?"

Angel raised an eyebrow, then turned to the door and knocked. The door opened slowly as if it had a life of its own. A gust of cold air came bursting out. Angel shook his head in disbelief, then walked in. Slipping along the floor, he fell over onto his knees. The pathway was iced over completely. Angel could hear snickering coming from behind him. He looked back at Vagrant quickly, but he stood silent as a statue by the door.

"Go on. I will guard your back."

Angel nodded and began walking slowly deeper into the cave. Still slipping a bit, he had a bright idea. Angel hovered off the ground to avoid falling on his ass again. As he floated quietly down the ice corridor, Angel was unaware of the eyes within the walls observing him from all around. After he had traversed the ice cave for some time, he came to a fork in the path.

Looking down both corridors, he saw no difference between the two. *Left or right? 'Tis be the question of the day. I don't sense a presence from either and smell nothing. Friggit. I'll backtrack if I run into a dead end.* Picking the left path, he continued on his way. While walking down this new corridor, three giant demonic arachnid-like beasts ambushed Angel. They were made of ice shards; some red innards could be partially seen through their outer shell.

"Oh, crud," Angel sighed, "The right path. I should've taken the right path. As Cogeta always says, "Right is right. You always go right." He dashed to the side as one creature lunged at him. Spinning around the beast for a safer position, Angel punched the beast's backside. He cried out in pain as he pulled his fist back to his chest. He examined his fist quickly, seeing shards of ice embedded in his knuckles. Jumping around to avoid being impaled by the spider's front pointed legs as it stomped at him. Frustrated, he stretched out his left hand and fired three large blue energy blasts that exploded on contact. The monster reared up on its four back legs, making a loud, ticking noise.

"Ha! That hurt, didn't it ugly?" Angel celebrated shortly before ducking below one of the other legs as it tried to impale him again.

Quickly, Angel flew up underneath the beast and once again fired several more bursts of energy at the undercarriage of the monster. As he did so, ice shards shattered off. To his amazement, the beast lay in two after the cloud of ice shavings cleared. *So that is your weakness,* he thought as he rolled out of the way of the third monster. It tried to stomp on him with his two front legs.

The ice spider aimed with its spinnerets as Angel got to his feet. Bolts of ice shot out successfully, pinning Angel to a wall by his clothes. He struggled to rip free to no avail. The spider shot two more bolts aimed at its prey's chest.

Angel yelled barbarically, erecting an invisible force field before him, shattering the ice bolts before they could pierce through him. The arachnid moved around to join with the first spider Angel had merely dazed earlier. Angel broke free of his restraints and took an outstretched position. Quickly he summoned his strength. Angel held his ground calmly as the arachnids charged him together. With a satisfying grin, he watched them rushing toward him. They were ignorant of what he had ready for them. When they were just a few feet away, Angel yelled out,

"MEGA BLAST!"

The corridor erupted in a series of explosions and shook the ground all the way back to where Vagrant stood by the door. The aftermath of his devastating attack was apparent on the cracked walls and ceiling. There was no trace left of the spiders.

After taking a few deep breaths, then straightening his jacket, Angel continued down the corridor. Only when he made a turn around a corner did he realize he would have to backtrack. This path was a dead end. Flying back down the hall from where he came, he headed the other way. With no ambushes this time, he arrived at a large square room with columns made of shimmering ice lining a path to the far wall leading to two thrones. As he looked around, Angel placed his feet back on the ground. Unlike the rest of the cavern, this floor was solid blue stone and not slippery.

Of the two thrones, only the left one sat occupied. Angel was taken aback when he first glanced at the person. He looked almost identical to Inferno. The only differences Angel saw right away were that his flesh was a dark blue, not red, and he had cold mist coming off his body instead of glowing. The demon sat with his head down, but upon Angel coming closer, he slowly raised his head to gaze at his visitor.

Sternly, the demon spoke while holding back a hidden smile, "You're late."

"Sorry to keep you waiting. The journey here was not an easy one."

"How do you want to do this?"

"However, you like. But one quick thing, snow in Hell, really?" Angel smirked.

The man smiled under his face guard, "Lady Exspes has been kind to me. She can manipulate all the land in South Hell to make it as she wants. She gave me this valley to decorate as I wanted, and I like the cold. I need little, just this snowcapped mountain with a shield to fend off possible intruders. I hope that you didn't try to eat the snow at the base of my home."

"No, I didn't want to waste time. My guide keeps a quick pace, and I couldn't risk losing him."

"Well, that is good because the snow turns to acid once it melts to prevent those who would quench their thirst. So anyway, let us begin."

The man stood up as he finished talking. Then, with a gesture of his hand, an upsurge of snow and ice raced toward Angel. Unable to dodge it, Angel quickly covered his face from the onslaught. He tried to keep his footing and force his way through the intense snowstorm his enemy had unleashed. He did not hold on to it for long and ultimately lost the struggle, being thrown backward. As he recovered, the storm subsided. Angel engaged the stranger in a stare-down. With fists clenched tightly, he rushed forward, itching to make contact. The stranger quickly sidestepped him and slid around to his backside. When Angel whipped around, what he saw astounded him. Standing before Angel now was a room filled with copies of his opponent.

In unison, the mob spoke. "Come and get me."

Angel growled and rushed into the group. However, no matter how fast he moved or how hard he tried, each one stayed one step ahead of him. Sliding this way and that. To make matters worse, they even began taunting Angel by circling him, laughing, and chatting,

"Missed me. You missed me again. Ha! Ha! Oh, so close that time. Can you not swing faster than that? How pathetic. Surely you can do better."

As Angel continued his assault, he desperately worked on trying to devise a plan so that his attacks would have some effect. Unknown to him, though, all their circling was a distraction. As they circled, they covered the floor with more ice. Frantically, Angel tried to get a hold of one until finally leaping blindly at one of the blue demon clones. He missed it entirely as it dashed to the side. Then they all scattered far out of reach, flying back in all directions.

To make matters worse, when Angel jumped, his foot slipped, making him fall face-first to the floor and slide into the wall. After making the floor so slippery that it was useless to Angel, they all rejoined back into one being and quickly rushed him. Angel started hovering again to avoid being hexed by the floor's disadvantage and successfully blocked the demon's first attack. He was giving it his all. However, with every blow he successfully landed on the demon, his fists would freeze, and sharp pains shot through his knuckles and up his arms.

The demon grinned as he watched Angel grimace as they fought. "You feel that pain going through your arm with each blow you land on me?

That's your blood freezing in your veins. You cannot beat me, Dark. Give up now."

"Watch me, snowman. We're just getting started."

Angel retreated to a safe distance, resorting to power blasts. Unfortunately, they seemed ineffective even as they hit the demon dead on. The battle dragged on, and Angel received much more punishment. Angel's clothes were once again tattered. Angel's ribs were broken in multiple places. The blood from his nose and his lips had frozen. His knuckles were busted open and frostbitten from constant ineffective attempts to hit the demon. Yet he had not even chipped the iceman. Adding to his frustration was the continuous sound of someone laughing close by. He knew it was at his fruitless efforts. It sounded familiar, but he could not place it right offhand.

Then the laughter stopped, and a voice told him, "Why don't you just give up, Dark? You are obviously far too weak to fight him, and I am not even going to talk about the massive gap in brain power."

Suddenly, he realized, or perhaps it was the blow to his head, that the ice demon had gotten in. Angel knew whose voice it was.

Inferno!

"You got it, moron. Took you long enough to figure that one out. I'm in your head. Quite scary in here. Ever thought of cleaning it up a bit?"

In my head? Get out!

"I can't do that. You and I made a pact. You beat me, and I yielded my power to you. In exchange, I got a home here and will be able to leave this dreadful place that I have called home for so long."

Your power? I feel no different.

While mentally conversing with Inferno outside, he was busy flying around the room, doing his best to dodge the ice shards being hurled at him.

"Of course, you feel no different, you dope. You've not asked for any help. These trials are to help you get stronger, and they will also help you by making some new friends on the way, like me," Inferno gave a big toothy grin that his face guard hid.

Can you take control of my body?

"Only when it is necessary. Like NOW!"

Angel's hand shot up without hesitation and deflected a spike of ice that was about to give him a third eye.

Thanks.

"No problem. If you ask nicely, I will help you melt this popsicle."

Will the fire hurt me?

"No, of course not. No flame will ever harm you. Not while I am here, anyway. Just like how the lava didn't bother you after our fight. Are you ready? Just do as I instruct. Put forth your hands with your palms facing him."

Angel did as he was told while floating high above the frozen ground. That's when he felt something inside him stir. It was like the feeling that one gets when the solution to a problem becomes apparent, and they see the answer was with them the entire time. Throughout his body, Angel could feel a power surging through his veins. Lava suddenly shot forth from his hands as if two geysers erupted simultaneously. The instant it touched the ice, it evaporated, filling the room with huge billowing clouds of steam.

The blue stranger backed up to the doorway, all the while using his powers to cool the lava as much as possible to keep it at bay.

"Do you yield?"

The demon smiled as he looked up toward Angel and then slowly vanished. Angel only had a second to recognize the object in front of him before it smashed into his face, sending him to the ground. The demon had moved through the walls and came from the right side with a roundhouse kick.

He looked down at Angel as he lay on the ground. "I am not so easily beaten."

Angel stood back up and looked at him. "Good."

Angel clenched his fists tightly. As he did so, they glowed red, with small flames rising from them. The two charged each other. Angel connected with his right, as the demon found his mark with his left. They fell to the ground, quickly recovered, and collided again. This time around, though, Angel's punches were visibly doing damage. He saw steam come from his enemy's body with each successful hit. The longer they went, the more he saw his opponent being worn down by his newfound ability. However, for every strike he landed, one found its mark on him. Blow for blow, they went at it, neither side gaining a real foothold.

Until Angel came up with an uppercut, clipping the man's chin and sending him backward. As the man did a flip, he caught Angel in the chin with his foot, sending Angel to the ground. Angel quickly got back to his feet and ducked a left hook. Seeing a clear opening, he began drilling into the demon's rib cage with his fist. A bright, reddish glow covered his hand, allowing his fist to sink deeper into the monster with every devastating hit. This onslaught brought the blue devil to his knees. With the last of his strength, he pushed Angel back with his hand on his shoulder.

Taking slow, deep breaths, he looked down at the floor as his body mended. "You have done well, and thus, I yield."

Angel stood there, looking down at his beaten opponent, catching his breath. It was then he heard Inferno's voice inside his head. "Put your hand on his forehead."

A burst of cold air and snow erupted upon doing so, and the blue demon was gone. Just like before, Angel felt the power swell inside himself.

"ARRGHHH!" Angel let out a scream of pain, dropping him to his knees.

A wall of ice shot up around him, encasing his body. A storm of cold sleet and snow raged around him. As quickly as it started, the effects subsided, and Angel slowly exited the cavern.

As he walked down the icy corridor, Angel said, "So, what is your name, stranger?"

The new demon found a comfortable place in Angel's mind and set up his home. In the calm voice of someone of great importance, the demon answered, "Call me, Subzero."

"Nice to meet you." A bit of pride began filling Angel, having bested two demons thus far.

"The pleasure is mine. You don't know how long we have waited to leave." Subzero spoke quietly as he relaxed in his new home.

It wasn't much to speak of compared to the one he had before, but all the same, he crafted a throne made of ice and made himself comfortable. Inferno had done the same with his small area, crafting himself a small pool of lava to soak in.

Angel, at last, came to the entranceway where he had left Vagrant. However, he was no longer there. Stepping outside, Angel saw him waiting near the edge of the ledge with a small vehicle designed for snow terrain. Angel didn't know where he got it from, and at this point, he didn't care. Angel was relieved he did not have to climb back down. He also looked forward to riding this interesting-looking vehicle for the first time.

"Now you are talking! Where's mine?"

"I will meet you at the bottom."

"Sure, unless I beat you there. So where is mine?"

Vagrant smiled and then leaped with the vehicle off the side of the mountain. Angel rushed to the edge and watched in disbelief as Vagrant descended the slope.

"You can't be serious. Damn it! Some guide you are!"

He glanced around, realizing that the snowstorm circling the mountain had stopped. Seeing that there was no other way to get down, Angel decided to have some fun. Walking back to the door, he paused, turned, and sprinted toward the edge, leaping right off the side.

CHAPTER 17

INTO THE PIT

Slowing his descent, he landed on the ground and saw the snowmobile abandoned. Vagrant was walking a little ahead, so Angel ran to catch up. The winds that were blowing in the valley had stopped just as the snowstorm surrounding the mountain had now that the conjurer was no longer sitting on his throne.

"So, what is next?"

Vagrant didn't bother looking back as he spoke. "Just know you are going to be tested in pain."

Angel replied with a sarcastic flare. "Oh goody, sounds like fun. So far, I have been torched, and moments ago, I was thrown into the freezer."

"It gets worse." Vagrant plainly stated, showing no emotion.

After walking for miles in a desolate land of yellow sand heading westward, they avoided many sand traps and ran from a swarm of eight-headed ants that stood ten feet tall with dark color patterns along their bodies. Their pincers dripped with thick green mucus. Vagrant cautioned Angel about fighting them in a group, as their mucus was acidic. Angel could already pick up on that information from the vile smell that permeated off their pincers. Finally, they came to a pit that descended deep into the ground. It seemed bottomless at first glance. Vagrant glanced over his shoulder at Angel, then back to the hole.

"What? Me first?"

Vagrant smirked. "Yep. Not my test. Watch your step. It's a long fall."

Angel nodded. How could he argue? Angel stepped forward and jumped into the pit. He fell for a long time before hitting the bottom with a loud thud that echoed inside the chamber. Straightening himself up, he looked around in the pitch black. Glancing upward, he could barely make out the opening. It now looked like a small round light fixture that had yellowed. Holding his hand in front of him, a flame emerged, covering half his arm, lighting his surroundings.

The ground he stood on crunched and cracked with each subtle movement he made. Looking down to see what he was standing on, holding his flame-engulfed hand downward, Angel saw bones and busted skulls of different sizes and shapes. He leaned down to examine a few. Some looked to belong to the ant beasts Vagrant, and he had run from. From the looks of it, some of these beasts had had a poor landing. While others must have been killed by whatever lived in this cave. Angel's fingers traced several outlines of what were possibly claw or even teeth marks that scarred some remains. A heavy rustling in the wind overhead suddenly caught Angel's attention. He swiftly jumped out of the way as Vagrant came crashing down, landing exactly where Angel had just been standing.

"Darn, I missed," he teased.

"Your coat flapping on the way down gave you away. Besides, I thought you were staying up there?"

Vagrant shrugged, "Got bored."

They shared a small, quick laugh before pressing forward. A tunnel had been dug out through the wall. The ceiling gently brushed against the tips of Vagrant's spiked hair. Angel led the way with his ignited hand. They finally came to a large room after following the narrow path, squeezing their way around tight corners, and ducking under low ledges. He stood at the entrance and scanned the area quietly. Something or someone had filled with many torture devices and spiked metal wheels. Racks with cranks to pull people apart. Chairs with spikes across the back and seat and more across the front where the back of the legs would rest. Straps laid open across the arms and legs of the chairs. Odd pyramid shapes of varying sizes were spread around the room, dried blood staining the tips. Vices, pincers, saws, and knives, big and small, littered the tables around the room. He could also see pear-like decorations of various sizes scattered about. Cages hung from above and over what looked to be old fire pits. Amongst the tables and along the floor, he could see the remains of those who had been before. A decayed foot there, a half-consumed upper torso over there, a severed finger or two on the tables. Other body parts or small decaying creatures were stacked in a far corner. The smell was gut-wrenching, like putrid waste and molting flesh on a hot summer's day. It all disgusted Angel. To add to his unease, he noted that no tool or device was without copious amounts of bloodstains.

"What the heck is this place, the devil's playroom?"

"Close, but even Lucifer has his limits with torture. If you can believe that, sure, he has no problem sentencing one to it, but he doesn't stay and watch for long periods. He's created minions to do the dirty work, and they love it. He enjoys his women, though."

"Who is Lucifer?"

Vagrant looked at Angel, wondering if he was serious. "Are you kidding me?"

"No. You forget I am not from around here."

"Well, Lucifer was once an angel of the Lord. However, he got arrogant, even jealous, because the Lord created humans and given upon them the gift of choice. The choice to worship, to believe, and to serve. They did not give Lucifer and the other angels that gift. It also upset him. He was told he had to serve the humans even though he was created before they were. Figured it should have been the other way around. He was superior to them as far as he could see. So he and one-third of the angels with whom he turned to his ideals began a rebellion. The war took its toll but finally ended. Lucifer and his army lost and were sent to this wonderful summer paradise. He has ruled here ever since, that is until Exspes came and challenged him."

Angel listened intently. "Hard to believe more didn't side with him in the beginning. Freedom of choice, to do as one pleases, feels so commonplace now. Anyone who would impose upon that is usually considered a villain."

"Now, certainly. But this was eons ago. He created the tiers of angels to serve him and help spread his word. He created them for that sole purpose. Lucifer fell because he became narcissistic and thought he was superior and should be in charge."

Angel nodded in understanding. "I guess, strangely, he got his wish. Now he rules over his kingdom. Though have there not been those to challenge him for his crown? Before Exspes, I mean."

"Oh yeah, countless others have tried to seize control but failed. Lady Expses then rose to power. After many years of war between their two great armies, he gave her the southern region of his kingdom to barter a truce.

Thus, South Hell was born. This is one of his many hidden chambers. There are many like this, some even larger, scattered around. Never know when you will need to do some torturing. It Saves having to drag a prisoner back to the capital. Don't worry, in any case. He won't be bothering us. He wouldn't want to break the truce by coming across the border. That was one arrangement. The only way for either to cross the designated line without declaring war is if they are invited. You can imagine how often that happens. The Lady Exspes cannot stand him. Though I'm sure he knows a fleshy is here."

"So I am on E-Earth? Did I pronounce that right?"

"Yes, you did, and in a way, you could say you are, just extremely, far, far, far beneath its surface. Overall, though, yeah, you could say that in some way. It's more of a different plane. If they were to dig and dig and dig, they wouldn't come through our ceiling or anything like that."

"And what does this guy, Lucifer, look like?"

"Well… he can morph his form into whatever he likes, but he is normally seen down here, among us, as a red-skinned man with long black horns, long black hair, and a goatee. Sometimes no goatee. He's powerful and not one to deal with or take lightly. He'll lie to you and promise you your darkest or purist desires, only to have them twisted in some fashion to his liking. Not be trusted at all."

"I have read the book titled the Holy Bible, among other religious scriptures. However, that was a long time ago because of an assignment. I didn't think it was real, however. It was part of a class where we were taught about different planets and their cultures, including their religions. On Earth, you have so many religions. On my planet, we only have one."

Vagrant tilted his head to one side. "What's that?" being genuinely curious.

"We worship Odin and his family. It's called Asgardius or Asgardism. We also have a festival honoring a god known as Gilgamesh once a year. His temple suddenly crashed onto our planet. At least, that is the legend. I was going there when Damien appeared and "escorted" me down here."

"Ah. Well, some humans long ago also worshiped Odin and his lower gods. Now he and the rest are thought of as only myth."

"That's what I thought this place was. Being here, however, kinda punches holes in that theory. Besides, with so many religions on Earth, how can one be so sure if one is better or worse than the other? From an outsider's standpoint, they all speak of the same thing, with varying differences. This one says this, but these two over here say that, while these fifteen say something entirely different from the other three."

Vagrant sighed with a hint of annoyance. "I don't know. Do I look like a scholar to you? I have never seen Heaven, Valhalla, Shangri-La, Mount Olympus, Atlantis, Timbuktu, or home sweet home. Hell is all I have known."

"Okay, fair enough. Changing the subject to what lies ahead. Is the guy I am coming here for a masochist?"

"You could say that."

At that moment, they both caught sight of movement on the back wall. From what Angel could make out, through all the horrible objects obscuring his vision, the motion was coming from an iron maiden. He recognized it from the books in the academy's library. Slowly the door to the iron prison creaked open but was suddenly and forcefully shoved wide open. Angel could not determine what was lurking inside but knew it could not be pleasant.

"Stand your ground," whispered Vagrant.

Angel only had time to nod when out of the maiden leaped a foul beast. He flew over the instruments of pain, a good fifty-foot jump, and landed in front of Angel and Vagrant. The beast was huge and muscular. Its flesh was gray with green tiger stripes. Its eyes glowed solid white. It had teeth that were three inches long. Its claws were twice as long as his fangs and looked stained with blood. It growled and snarled as he stood upright, making himself even more imposing while eyeing the two angrily.

While it glared at the two trespassers, it spoke, its words hissing, "What is it you want?" The beast's tongue licked the air.

Damn, that's a long tongue, Angel thought.

"It can be longer," replied Subzero, "and he can hear your thoughts like most demons that dwell here. I just thought you would like to know."

"But he can't hear us. We are demons, so we know how to block each other." Inferno added.

"Ah crap," Angel mumbled under his breath.

The creature stepped forward and placed his face into Angel's. "What are you looking at?" The beast snapped, showing his fangs for added intimidation.

Angel placed his hands on the creature's chest and shoved him back. "Get   out of my face. Your breath is foul," Angel growled aggressively, not about to give the demon the pleasure of seeing him quiver.

The creature let out a screeching howl. He whipped his left clawed hand around, slashing into Angel's chest. His long talons caught onto Angel's rib cage, sending him into the air. Across the room, he flew right onto a spiked gate strapped to the upper half of the wall. Angel gasped as the agonizing pain from the jagged spikes punctured his body in multiple places, crucifying him on the gate.

He hung helplessly on the gate even as he struggled to free himself. The creature ran across the opposite wall. Slicing a rope with his claws, it released another spiked gate from the ceiling. It swung down, smashing into Angel with an echoing thunderous crash. He was trapped between the two spiked gates. Angel's blood dripped to the floor. He tried to force his body to move, but it wouldn't obey him. The beast jumped from the far wall onto the bottom half of the gate, the added weight stretching Angel's wounds. The beast climbed upward to look Angel in the eyes.

With his ghostly eyes, he stared at Angel through the bars and hissed, "Not so tough now, are you?"

Angel could not reply. One spike from the front gate had gone through his mouth, shattering his teeth. He glared back at the beast as he tried to lift the gates apart once more. However, he could not muster the strength since the vital sinews in his arms had been severed. He was utterly at the mercy of this foul beast as he felt an overwhelming burning of pain shooting through his nerves.

Suddenly, a ricochet bounced off the metal beam beside the demon's head. The creature spun around, still holding onto the gate. His eyes grew wide as shock filled him. He was now looking down the barrel of Vagrant's gun. He was floating in mid-air level with them.

"That was a mistake, pale one," the beast growled with an evil hiss.

"No! What was a mistake was attacking this man without finding out who he is." Snapped Vagrant, unshaken by the demon's hostile behavior.

"And who is this man?"

Vagrant replied, keeping the aggressive tone, "He's the one who would take your foul-smelling self out of here. Why else would I have brought him down to this dump?"

Surprised, the beast squealed, pointing a claw at Angel through the bars. "He is the man?"

"Yes!" Vagrant shouted in annoyance.

"Then who are you?" The beast asked in confusion, cocking his head to the side.

Vagrant's tone softened but still ringed with the demand for respect. "I am Vagrant. I serve the Lady."

"The Lady?" screeched the demon. "She sent this man?"

"Yes," Vagrant answered calmly, lowering his gun.

The beast looked back at Angel with a voice much like that of a child scorned, "My deepest apologies."

The beast jumped off the gate and onto the rope he had severed. With his weight, it raised the top gate back to the ceiling where it had been. As it rose, it brought Angel's limp body with it. He slowly slipped off and fell to the stone floor. The beast once more secured the gate to the wall with a hurried knot and then quickly came to Angel's side.

"My deepest apologies, oh Great One. I didn't know." The creature bowed its head low and his arms out. Angel's body mended itself within moments of being free. The only remaining evidence were the holes in his once again ragged clothes and the soreness he felt. He stood up and faced the still bowing beast.

Taking a deep breath, Angel spoke calmly, still feeling angry, "I am Dark."

"I am known as Scythe. The demon of endurance is me. I can handle any pain, and I wish to serve thee." As he introduced himself, he kept his head very low in shame, pleading for forgiveness, his eyes never leaving the floor as he spoke.

"That is it? You don't want to fight me?"

Until now, he had fought the demons as part of the trials. Vagrant warned him that there was worse to come. However, this one wished to join him just like that. If only the other two had been so straightforward, it could have saved him time, and he would have been back on Utopia by now.

"Oh, no, sir. I would never strike you." Scythe spoke so humbly with his hissing voice.

"I have evidence to the contrary." Angel looked at his clothes.

Scythe lowered his head even lower, nearly touching the floor, his body almost bending in half. "I said I was sorry. If I had known who you were, I would not have acted so hostile."

"It's no big deal now. I have already healed and will live." Angel touched Scythe's forehead, becoming accustomed to the procedure.

With a feeling that was now all too familiar, Angel cried out in pain as Scythe disappeared and made a new home in his mind. Angel dropped and rolled on the ground as barbed chains whipped around him, scratching the floor and lashing up into the air. Spikes shot out of his flesh. After a moment, the pain subsided as quickly as it had come, and the barbed wire and spikes were gone. Angel slowly got to his feet and glanced at his clothes. They were once again fully mended. He looked over to Vagrant.

He spoke half-heartedly with a smile, "That was the easiest one so far."

Vagrant laughed, "He was kicking your butt. If I hadn't stepped in to save you, you would have been stuck there for ages at his mercy."

Angel smirked. "Yeah, whatever. Thanks for the hand."

"The Lady would have been upset if I hadn't intervened. Nevertheless, you are welcome. Now let's get moving. Come this way."

Vagrant walked to the back wall next to the iron maiden. He placed his hand on a stone lump on the wall and pulled it out a little way. Then slowly, he turned it three times to the right, then twice to the left. The rock clicked with each turn, and when he was through, Vagrant pushed the stone back into place.

"A lock? I thought you hadn't been down here." Angel gave Vagrant a confused look.

"Look around, Dark. This is Hell. It has many secrets. As the Lady's scout, it's my job to know each of them. I don't enjoy coming here; it creeps me out, but it was also partly due to Scythe. He is a tad freakish." Scythe, in Angel's mind, looked saddened by this. As if sensing it, Vagrant added, "I was only kidding, Scythe." With that, Scythe perked back up. "Your next trial is beyond here, just a way ahead."

"Knew I had chosen wisely when I picked you," Angel laughed as he watched as part of the wall shook and moved inward, then slid over to reveal a passage. "But if I had chosen Crolarious or Damien…, would they have known about all this?"

"Oh, I would have filled them in on what to do and given them a map of the route that we've taken so far. Crolarious has been here the longest, so he would know where to go more easily, whereas Damien… you may have gotten lost a few times. I am not even sure he knows how to read a map."

That made Angel laugh.

Once again, he had to take the lead, lighting the way with his hand. Meanwhile, in his head, Angel could hear the demons discussing what was recent in their lives before joining him.

Inferno was sitting on a fiery throne, looking at Subzero, who was relaxing on his throne made of ice. "You still see that ice chick?"

"Yeah. Why?"

"Just curious. Are you going to pop the question soon?"

"What? Shut up, Inferno." Subzero snapped.

"Come on, Sub. You and I are practically brothers."

"Including me," Scythe spoke up, trying to join the conversation.

"Yeah, in a very, very distant, barely noticeable, freakish way," Inferno replied with a contorted expression, "So, anyway, Sub, remember that party a few months back at old Tigras' place?" Inferno turned his attention back to Subzero.

"Tigras had a party?" Scythe interrupted again.

"Yes, but you weren't invited. So, what about it?" Subzero answered.

Scythe lowered his head and sat quietly in the spot he had claimed as his. While the two continued talking and laughing about the party, he traced designs on the black floor with his nail. As Scythe wished to join in the conversation, Angel could not stop hearing them, no matter how hard he tried to block them out.

I hate to sound rude, guys, but is there any way to make it so I don't hear you? I am sure some of the stuff you are discussing is between you two and isn't my business.

Inferno smiled, "Well, as nice as that would be, you can't tune us out. We are part of your mind, so you hear loud and clear whatever we say. I know it's weird, but you will get used to it. As long as you don't talk to us aloud in public, no one will ever know we are here. They will just be amazed by all the special powers you have control over."

Well, I hope I get used to it soon. It's rather distracting. Not to mention it's a bit annoying. Angel set his mind back on the task at hand, going through a maze of twists and turns down a steep, slippery walkway.

"That's not completely true, Inferno." Subzero spoke up, "If they can sense demons, they will get the feeling you are one. Good news is that we can make it faint cause we can help hide our presence. We'll also help you block other mind readers. You have some defenses up now, but they are crude at best. We'll fix that and strengthen them so people won't be able to read or hear your thoughts like Scythe did earlier. Vagrant, there can't hear you or us, however, cause we are strengthening your mind. That and he isn't trying to spy."

Awesome. The added protection will come in handy.

Angel turned a bend, entering a mid-size empty chamber. The pathway ended at the edge of an underground lake.

Angel looked at Vagrant with a disbelieving look. "Water, really? Here in Hell?"

Vagrant shrugged. "What's so surprising? You climbed a snowy mountain."

"Good point, it's just…." Angel couldn't think of what more to say.

"I know. Not what you were expecting. It's the same with many others. However, you do not want to drink this water. It doesn't hurt your skin, or if you open your eyes while in it, but if you swallow any, it will slowly eat and dissolve away your insides."

"Well, that sounds like some delicious water."

"I actually hear it is quite tasty. I've heard stories where newly arrived souls have escaped the torturers, come across pools of water, and started drinking. They say it is so sweet that even though it is devouring you from the inside, you can't stop drinking."

"Wow. That would be a horrible way to go. So I assume it's a water demon I'm after next, huh?"

"Obviously. So go fish," Vagrant smirked as he shoved Angel into the water.

Angel came back to the surface and moved the hair from his eyes. "That was uncalled for."

"Did you get any water in your mouth?"

"No, luckily. When I saw the water coming, I immediately closed it tight."

"Well then, what are you waiting for? We have other demons to see. He is at the bottom probably, so hurry up." Vagrant waved on.

After sighing, Angel took a deep breath and dived deep into the crystal blue water. He opened his eyes and scanned the bottom. After some time had passed, he came back for some more air. Twenty times, he did this. Each trip turned up nothing. After his twenty-first try, he came to the surface and turned to Vagrant.

"I cannot find him. Maybe he is out."

"Did you look everywhere?"

"Yes, he isn't here," Angel answered, annoyed.

"Well, that's odd," Vagrant trailed off and started scratching his head until out of his peripheral vision. "Dark, behind you!" Vagrant yelled, pointing over Angel's shoulder to a lump of water.

Angel spun around, only to glimpse the lump returning to the water. Quickly, Angel ducked back under and looked around frantically, but no luck.

Dang it, where is he?

"Allow me," said Subzero.

Angel's body temperature quickly dropped dramatically, and within moments, the enormous underground lake was frozen solid.

Angel then heard Scythe hissing, "There! There! There he is!"

Angel turned around through the solid water and saw a silhouette of a man trapped in a spot of ice.

"Go, quickly. He is boiling his way out," ordered Subzero.

Angel took off through the ice unhindered, as if he were a part of it. He came to a halt inside a hole that the creature had formed. He stood face to face with the demon, each eyeing the other. This one was different from the previous three. He was not a solid being but more of a body of water in the shape of a man. Angel sensed no danger from him as he had with the previous three, which he found most intriguing

"Hello," said the demon in a kind voice, finally breaking the silence. Looking from side to side, then back to Angel, "What's up?"

"Not too much, just been looking for you."

"Really? I just figured you wanted to swim. Gets pretty hot on the surface, I hear. So? What's your name?"

"Dark Everlast, but just call me Dark, and yours?"

"I am the Master of the raging waves, King of the land under the water's surface. The Sovereign of fresh and salt realms. I am the one they call, dramatic pause, Hydro." He spoke with an enthusiastic, theatrical flair, striking poses with each title he announced. "So, what brings you down here?" Hydro asked back in his normally soft voice.

...It's... Cogeta... Angel thought to himself.

"I am proving myself to Lady Exspes, -er Deathbringer. She says she is preparing me for a war against the Vampirian general Serkuma and his armies. She said she had gifts to help me and then sent me on these trials." Angel leaned back against the frozen body of water.

"A-ah, ok, but what do you want with me?"

"Honestly, I don't know. Vagrant is my guide in this strange place. He has been taking me around to each of my so-called trials. Each brings me to a different demon that has entered my mind, and then they have lent me some of their power. So far, I have met Inferno, Subzero, and Scythe, all of which have joined me, or rather, with me, in some sort of pact." Angel answered the best he could, giving Hydro a quick summary of his adventure so far.

"So let me get this straight. You are going around absorbing demons to give you more power to beat this badass flea, and Scythe is with you," Hydro asked, waving his hand in front of Angel. In his mind, Angel could see Scythe waving back.

"Yes, that is about it, and yes, he is with me. He joined after hearing Exspes sent me. Are you two friends?"

"Yes, he was the only one who visited me. Aside from the dark lord himself back when this land was his. Scythe has also been kind enough to guard the door, so no one would try to steal from the chamber you passed through or take control of me."

"Forgive me, but why would they even try? From what I was told, the water here is just as dangerous as everything else."

"It is, but I can create fresh drinking water if I so wanted. I'll show you, have Subzero make you an ice glass."

You can do that?

Subzero nodded. "I can make just about anything you can imagine from ice, just as Inferno could manipulate fire into any shape for his amusement. Hold out your hand."

Angel did as instructed, and ice rose from his palm in a tall glass shape.

Wow!

"Now for my next trick," Hydro joked before holding his hand to the glass. A stream of water flowed from his fingers into it. "Okay, go on and try it."

"This isn't a trick, is it?"

Hydro shrugged, "Maybe."

Angel looked at the glass, then back at Hydro, then back at the glass. Looking into the glass, he swirled the contents around. He gently sniffed it to see if it was a trick, but nothing stood out. He raised the glass and took a sip.

"Wow, that's rather good. I've been aching for something to drink while I've been here."

"Exactly. That's why I am so valuable here. Congratulations, you just passed too."

Angel looked up as he finished the glass. "Hmm?"

"I was seeing if you were willing to trust me, even though I was a demon, and you did. So, I will join you, but first, let me look you over. I don't give myself to anyone swimming in my lake." Hydro said with sarcasm.

He pulled Angel's mouth open with the tip of his fingers. His touch was very cool and gentle. When Hydro opened it wide enough, his legs floated upward toward his head, then flooded into Angel's mouth. Angel hunched over as Hydro went through his system. After a moment, Angel coughed and hacked as Hydro poured out of Angel's mouth and reformed outside his body.

"Well, your insides seem ok. No disease or other nastiness, so I am yours."

Hydro spread his arms out and bowed down, much like Scythe had done, waiting for Angel to place his hand on his head. When Angel went to put his palm on Hydro's forehead, however, he moved his head to the side. When Angel went for it again, Hydro moved once more. Angel put his arm back to his side and looked at him. Hydro laughed and leaned his head toward him. Angel finally placed his hand on Hydro's forehead, and just like that, Hydro was gone.

Angel arched back as Hydro entered his mind. A wave of hot and cold water washed over him and swirled around him in a flashy display, as it had been with all the others. Then, with no warning, the ice returned as it was. Angel was caught in the middle of the lake with no air. However, because Hydro was now one with him, he no longer needed air to be underwater. Amazed by this new ability, he swam about in the lake. He was even more impressed at how fast he could cruise before coming up to the surface and looking over to Vagrant.

Vagrant looked at him, obviously bored. "Are you finally done?"

"Yeah, done here. What is next in our journey?"

"You will see. Now come on, you can dry off on the way." Vagrant walked ahead through the passageway as Angel jumped out of the lake to follow.

Upon exiting the lake, the water swirled violently. It sprang forth suddenly toward Angel in a large burst. Angel turned and outstretched his arm as if by instinct, with his palm facing the oncoming wave. The water was sucked toward his hand, and the lake was gone in moments.

"Couldn't leave that behind for someone to find." Hydro smiled.

When they came to the enormous hole where they entered from, Vagrant squatted down, then using all the strength in his legs, he leaped into the air. He jumped back and forth along the tunnel to the top. Once he was on the surface, he looked back down and laughed.

"Hurry up! Or I will leave you here!"

Angel smirked and took off like a jet flying upward. While on his way, Vagrant decided to tease him. He picked up a few rocks that lay around the pit's opening. He started firing them down with his right arm when he had an arm full. The stones flew toward Angel at speeds exceeding any normal Utopian could throw. His arm moved in a spinning blur as he threw rock after rock into the cave.

Angel was going at a good clip when the first rock hit him between the eyes. The force from the impact sent him flying back, hitting the side of the chasm. This caused him to bounce from wall to wall. All the while still being pelted with the rocks like bullets. Many of the skulls and bones at the bottom shattered under his weight when Angel crash-landed. Some shards scratched and tore into his back. As he lay there in pain, the rocks continued to rain down from above, precisely nailing their target.

Angel lay pinned down under the barrage. Then suddenly, one rock hit his black tail that was lying beside him, no longer hidden as it had been. His red pupils flashed as he lost all his self-control. Instantly, he curled into a ball, yelling and cursing in rage, wallowing in pain.

Angel could not afford to buy a tail guard. In hindsight, having it right about then would have been nice. He was not expecting this to happen. Nor could he have prepared himself for the excruciating pain his entire body was being racked by. He had been in a lot of pain while in the lava pool before, but he was feeling it all over, and as his flesh and bone were eaten away, so were the pain receptors. But this, this was not fading away. He'd rather be back in the lava pool than feel the excruciating pain firing through his tail.

His mind flashed back to years ago, before he had become friends with anyone, before he began seeing Leen, when the city guard had captured him, and they subjugated him to torture. Their so-called punishment in retribution for the disgrace he had brought upon them for outsmarting and making a mockery of them in battle, or so he thought at the time. In a small square room, they had his arms and legs bound outstretched and had his tail stretched out and bound. There they sentenced him to decimation. With a small knife, the torturer, who wore a black robe and hood over his head, cut ten slivers of flesh from his tail, not all at once. He would cut a piece and then fry the meat in front of him, so Angel had to smell his flesh burning. The next day, he would return for another sliver.

Ten days he suffered through a punishment saved for the most despicable criminals. To everyone's horror, however, he did not beg to be set free. Not once did he cry out. He didn't dare give them the satisfaction of victory over him. On the last day, he heard a familiar man's voice talking to his torturer. Looking up, he saw through the bars he saw the unmistakable face of the High Councilman glaring back at him. Later on, he learned through some guards who were on better terms with him that the High Councilman was the one who ordered the punishment to be carried out on account of Angel openly disrespecting his clergymen and for being a blight in his eyes. Angel never spoke of this to anyone, but it forever ignited a hatred for the High Councilman and his ilk. Then his life changed, he gained friends, and Leen was then by his side. All the attacks from the High Councilman stopped.

"THAT'S IT!"

Jumping to his feet, and glared up at the chasm. His eyes burned with rage. All the rocks still coming down from the top were shattered into dust just mere inches away, with the power pulsating from Angel's body. With a mighty shout, Angel thrust his open palm upward toward the entrance to the pit.

A wave of invisible power shot from his hand, rocketing up the passage. As it moved through the tunnel, the walls exploded and cracked. Above, it made the ground rumble and shake like a mighty earthquake. It shook so violently that Vagrant struggled to keep his balance as the wave erupted from the mouth of the hole. He was thrown back onto the ground. Looking up, he saw Angel floating above the pit.

"Getting stronger." Vagrant got back to his feet, brushing himself off as he did.

Angel glared at his companion. "You were throwing rocks at me for what reason?"

"Be happy they weren't bullets," Vagrant replied seriously. "Just a bit of demonic fun."

Angel took a breath and landed beside him. He checked his tail. It was still extremely sore and throbbing in pain, but still in one piece with no broken bones. He wrapped it around his waist before continuing their journey. He remained bitter towards Vagrant for what he did at the pit, but his temper calmed down as they walked, and he dismissed it.

What was done is done. No point in holding a grudge or upsetting the man guiding you. He could decide to leave me in this forsaken land. Besides, what doesn't kill me will only strengthen me.

As they walked, Vagrant told Angel that he had thrown the rocks to see just how much he had gained in power thus far. He was pleased to say that before, Angel couldn't have knocked him down with just a mere energy push. Vagrant told him that the next demon was the furthest away, and it would take them a lengthy amount of time to get there. He was not kidding.

CHAPTER 18

WHEN A DEMON CROSSES YOUR PATH

In what felt like weeks to Angel, they had climbed over jagged mountains, trudged through rivers of black sludge, and followed narrow pathways through murky swamps. They avoided many gruesome creatures and traps before them, with a few very narrow escapes. They were now walking through an eerie and sinister forest. Within these dark woods, Angel glanced from side to side seeing glowing eyes watching as he passed. He listened to their growls and hissing.

"You are strange to them. You aren't dead or smell of absolute sin. They are also hungry."

"What are they?" Inquired Angel as his eyes gazed into the woods, with hundreds of different colored eyes staring back.

"Various beasts. They tear apart anyone who dares come in here alone. Be it escaped sinners from the North or a wandering demon. Very few are strong enough to defend themselves when the creatures of this forest attack. The smaller canine-like ones always swarm in large numbers," Vagrant explained. "Nasty little things, attack from all sides. They are stupid but very bold—the ones you really have to fear most that lurk in here are the Snearagrins. They are around seven feet tall, pale yellowish creatures. Walk on two legs covered with very sharp spines. Their hands have three eight-inch-long claws for slashing and tearing one's flesh from their bones. Their heads are elongated, with three sets of eyes for watching you scream in pain. They have no upper lips, so their razor fangs are always presented in an evil grin."

Angel glanced at Vagrant. "Are you trying to scare me? If you are, it isn't working."

Vagrant laughed, "If I were trying to scare you, I would simply leave you here alone and let these creatures have their way with you. I am just telling you about them because I thought you were interested."

"I just want to get back to Utopia, finish my first quest assigned to me, and kill that son of a—" He stopped, trying to control his anger.

"He's that bad, huh?"

"He murdered my girlfriend right in front of me. I was too weak to do anything, couldn't save her when she needed me most." Angel began watching the ground as he walked.

"Damn, that sucks. Pretty stupid of him to let you live like that. Knowing you will be after him, especially after what you vowed to do. The whole "splattering his blood across the universe" thing was pretty gruesome. Also, kind of funny. Were you planning on taking his corpse from planet to planet and sprinkling his blood around?"

Angel stopped momentarily and looked at Vagrant, who had stopped to look back. "How do you know what I said to him?"

"Oh, um, you know, guys always do that when their girls are slain in front of them. Never seen a cheesy action movie?"

Not buying it, anger built up inside him. He reached out, grabbed Vagrant by the shoulder, and turned him around to look him dead in the eyes. "Were you watching the attacks on Utopia?"

"Calm down," Vagrant said softly, brushing Angel's hand off his coat, "Exspes watches different things through her globe."

"So, you were watching?" Angel's eyes burned with rage, and his fists closed tight.

"Calm down, Dark. I wasn't watching. Damien filled me in later. He was watching with Lady Exspes."

"Well, I hope they enjoyed the show. Glad the death of Leen and the others could be someone's amusement. Explains a comment that Damien made when he stole me away."

Angel was on the verge of snapping. The gall she had to sit back and watch as everything he cared about was ripped away, and now she wanted to help him?

Why didn't she help me then? She could've sent that freak then without waiting to ambush me when I was alone. Why did she just watch? Who does that? Does she get off on watching people suffer?

Angel felt a hand on his shoulder. Without realizing it, he had stopped looking at Vagrant and turned his sights toward the ground. Looking back at Vagrant's pale face, he didn't expect to see a calm smile.

"Why? If she was watching the battle as it happened, why didn't she send me help then? Why couldn't she have sent Damien before Leen... before she..."

Angel's words trailed off as he lowered his head. Resting his forehead on the palm of his right hand, he tried to fight back the tears. The wound her death had made was still very fresh, like an open nerve. It pulsed and sent wave upon wave of pain—an overwhelming pain that gripped and strangled his heart and choked his lungs.

"Those are questions best asked of her when we return. I cannot and will not dare try to speak for her on that matter. I do, however, know she does not possess foresight. Otherwise, she possibly would have sent you aide beforehand if she could. As I was saying before, I wasn't watching events unfold with her. I was away. I recall Damien was wondering where all those dead went if not here since they were not humans. Only the worst humans come here, tortured for their sins repeatedly without mercy. Over time, some are given a choice to continue their punishment or to punish others. If they choose to punish others, over time, their bodies will mutate into demonkin or demons. Mostly, all memories of their past life melt away by the fires of Hell. We don't get other races' evildoers." Vagrant explained matter-of-factly.

"Is that what happened to you? Did you become someone else's torturer?"

"No. I am a special case. In a way, I was born here. It was only by chance or fate that Lady Exspes came upon me during a walk. I was nearly dead, but she still took me in and raised me."

"She has a caring heart. Surprising to find such a thing down here."

"Just because we look as we do, or the fact we are demons, doesn't mean we are all purely evil. We are the odd ones of our kind, the outcasts, and the rotten apples. Every race has its fair share of rotten apples."

"That is true. There is no end to it. And to answer Damien's question—"

"Oh, I don't really care. He was asking," Vagrant shrugged his shoulders and started walking again.

Angel followed behind. "True, but just think how much fun it will be to throw in his face, how much more you know."

"Point taken. Go on."

Angel smiled, the conversation helping him distract himself from the overwhelming emotions boiling inside him. "Our dead go to Valhalla. As far as I know, if they were evil in nature, they don't, and then the goddess Hel gets them. We have four places in our afterlife. First, there is Valhalla. It's where the courageous warriors who died honorably on the battlefield go to meet Odin. Freya usually takes the female warriors to a realm that she rules over. It's said to be a vast meadow with a grand hall, where she trains the women to be Dis."

"Dis?"

"Valkyries."

"Oh, okay. Continue."

"Then, there is the Holy Mountain. Those who die of disease or old age go there. It's a peaceful place for those who don't want to go to war but remain loyal followers. Last, there is Niflheim. It's where Hel rules and takes all those dishonorable in their life."

As they walked further along, a question formed in Angel's mind. He tried to bury it, but it kept coming back to him. Until, at last, he couldn't fight it any longer.

"Why was Lady Exspes watching a planet that has nothing to do with her?"

"Only because she can. Who cares? However, I am now curious about one thing."

"What's that?"

"Is there really a rainbow bridge? It's mentioned in the myths left behind on Earth."

"I don't know. You only see it when you die. Otherwise, you have to be a god to traverse it."

"Ah, okay."

"But I suppose it's possible. I mean, had you told me that Hell existed yesterday, I probably would have had my doubts. Yet here I am. I didn't wholeheartedly put much stock in my world's beliefs, yet... If one is true... Here's another question, if you say that these creatures around us were once human, does that mean their debt is paid? And where are the first demons?"

"Hehe, the first demons were the angels that believed in the ideals started by Lucifer and followed him into battle. Holy warriors have killed some, but quite a few remain. But when a human becomes a demon, it doesn't mean their debt is paid or that they are forgiven for the sins they committed. They will never find forgiveness in this place. It just means they have been down here so long that all their memories of their old lives are gone. Their souls were devoured. All you are left with is the animal. Their outer shell, over time, morphs into something grotesque, a twisted visage of the inner self. I've heard tales that some can come back from it, but they need help from a being strong in the ways of the light. Those who choose to end their torture and become a torturer change quicker than those who don't, only because the darkness seeps into them faster. Harder for them to come back from their transformation because they accepted it willingly. However, a majority of the creatures you see are spawned down here. Like animals, they have no higher thought like you and I, only think of killing and devouring. The people we passed in town when we first started were once human. They were freed from their lives of torture and wished to start again. Lady Exspes accepts all refugees from the North that desire a new life. But these things never were."

Angel absorbed the information, becoming more curious about how this realm functioned. "So then, there is a class system here? Lucifer on top, his underlings, the damned souls... then the beasts?"

Vagrant chuckled, "That's very close. Yes, there is a class system. Where one stands depends on their power. Lady Exspes, for example, is up there with Lucifer and his court. Her other two generals, and I, aren't nearly as strong, but we rival some archdukes or a lord, I would say... Lucifer is indeed the ruler. Below him are the Great Evils, the demons over the seven deadly sins he is also a part of. Then there are the Lesser Evils, then the archdukes. Demonkin are demons who think and act on their own. Beasts are beneath them. They're spawned or crafted. They come in all sorts and comprise most of the higher echelon's armed forces. The bottom tier, damned souls."

"If you don't mind my asking, how did you come to be down here?"

Vagrant paused in his step. "I am a special case. I never had a chance at life. All I can remember now is racing toward a bright light. I was frightened of it. But something inside told me it was what I needed to do. Then I felt something grab me. Then I was falling backward. I fell for so long. Lady Exspes told me she found me on the river Styx. She thought I had been abandoned and took me in. She raised me. She trained me. Molded me into who I am. Had she not done so, a wandering demon could have ended my existence."

"Where do you go if you die here?"

"It all depends on how you die. Most of the time, you go into a state of purgatory or a corporeal form that roams until your body reforms. That's if you die in a fight or something. If you are killed and completely devoured, that's the end for you. They absorb you. That demon grows stronger. On the flip side, if a demon is killed on Earth, it will likely be reborn here. Even lesser demons can be quite difficult to kill for a normal person. Only ones who can truly kill a demon are those of divine origin, are blessed or using a blessed weapon, and there aren't many of those lying around."

"Couldn't they just have a priest bless it?"

Vagrant began walking once more, relieved the topic had changed from himself. "A true blessing is a very time-consuming ritual. It's not as simple as splashing water on an item and reciting a prayer over it. The one doing the ritual has to be a pillar of faith. No doubt. No shadows. Pure of heart. Not many men like that around."

"Okay, but what about exorcisms?"

"I've never possessed someone personally. From what I hear, they are painful and a great annoyance. Because once that demon is cast out, he returns here and has to find someone new. However, it doesn't always end happily, with the demon gone and the person returning to themselves. Damien told me how one demon possessed a child, a little girl, maybe twelve, and how it was fighting the priest. He wouldn't let the child go and, in desperation, forced the child to claw her chest open. I remember being so pissed when Damien told me that, I decked him right out of his chair."

Angel stopped, feeling sick. "That's… Why? Why do that to a child?"

Vagrant stopped and turned to him. "Why do people murder?"

"But you are a demon. I'm… making pacts with demons. Have you or they done anything like that? Do you root for your kind when they do such things?" Angel looked inwardly at the demons that had joined him.

"I told you, I've possessed no one. Many demons haven't. Because they don't know how or don't have the desire to, Damien, Crolarious, Lady Exspes, and a few others that I know don't like it and would never do it. Of the demons I've been taking you to, they all know how, but only Scythe has. He's still made fun of because of it. He possessed a cat and became someone's pet until they died."

Scythe spoke up in a soft, somber tone. "I don't regret it, either. The boy was very kind to me."

"As far as if I root for them, mostly no. If I hate the demon doing it, I hope the priest beats the tar out of him. If he is a friend, sure, I hope he gets a punch in on the priest. There aren't many priests that I've seen that I can say I respect. Some shame their profession and are hypocrites. In North Hell, it is more of a game for them. They enjoy watching the struggle. I've seen them turn on a television; yes, we get that down here too; and watch the struggle and root for their "team." It's like watching a grand event, especially if the possessing demon is well-known. The only thing that comes close to enjoyment here is barbaric games of death. I hate it. It disgusts me, but that's how it is. South Hell is the refuge from it."

"I'm sorry I lost it. It's a lot to take in."

"Dark, I went through the same thing when I first learned about it. It's just how things are down here. It's not pretty, and it really isn't meant to be. But anyway, we still got a long way to go, and if you don't want to meet the Snearagrins, I suggest we get moving along."

"All right, let's go."

They continued on their way. However, Angel was still feeling slightly uneasy about the conversation and about still being watched by the creatures of the forest and this Lady Exspes. He couldn't help but wonder if she was watching him right this minute through her globe.

Once they cleared the woods, Angel felt a bit more comfortable. That is as comfortable as one could get when walking in a place like this. They walked along the beaten path silently. The land had become jagged, with cliffs and deep ravines. The ground was black like charcoal, with scattered patches of brown dirt, and the air was deathly stale and humid. As they turned around the edge of a large brown rock face, Vagrant put his hand in front of Angel to stop him. Curious, Angel cautiously peaked around the corner to see the issue.

Blocking the path ahead were six giant troll-like demons sitting around a fire. A dark reddish one with stringy hair just over his shoulders sat with his back to Angel and Vagrant. Beside him on his right sat a massive dark green troll. He had no hair to speak of on his head but had more than enough to make up for it on his back. Moving around the fire sat an opaque gray troll, picking at his large belly button with his middle finger. He had two large canines growing outward like tusks. He also had just a few strands of hair on his head. To his right was a pale-yellow troll with a long-rounded nose with warts all over it. He sat in the middle, stirring the fire. Next to him were two others, a muddy brown one with two upper and lower teeth growing outward. The last was a dark olive color with blue hair standing up in a mohawk fashion.

Vagrant and Angel were just about to work their way around them quietly. When from between two of the beasts that were facing away from them ran out a small child. As loud as her little lungs could manage, she screamed and yelled for help while running as fast as her tiny twig-like legs could carry her.

The two monstrosities turned around and began trying to catch or perhaps squash the child. Angel could not tell what their true intent was. However, when the hand of the red troll came down on the child, Angel was quickly there to stop it from crushing the poor girl.

"Grrr—Run!" Angel hollered, trying to hold up the massive hand, his knees close to buckling under him.

The child stared up at Angel with tear-filled eyes, alive with terror, before she ran as she was told. However, the hand of the dark green demon blocked her escape this time. The red troll raised his hand off Angel, who quickly turned to face him, ready to fight. Angel froze when he saw the six huge trolls towering over him. He felt like an ant looking up at a skyscraper that challenged the clouds.

Angel could now clearly see what he was up against. They all had many things in common. They were humongous and had different tribal markings painted on like war paint. All were wearing fur loincloths except for the pale-yellow troll demon. Instead, he wore a fur garment with one strap over his right shoulder. They each had their own markings painted on them and had varying scars. Two of them had accessories in their ears. That is unless you include spiders and bugs as an accessory.

"Save me! I don't want to die!" screamed the small child. Angel found he couldn't move. His eyes were transfixed by what the giant trolls wore around their waists.

Over the top of their fur cloths, large rope belts went around. On them, children hung by their limbs in small loops or holes in the ropes. Some hung upright, others upside down, some screaming, others crying, while some hung silently, overcome with death. Angel could not move. He was stricken with horror at what he beheld before him. His mind could not comprehend what he was seeing.

In a gruff voice, the dark olive-colored troll spoke. "What do we have here?"

The green troll, who had blocked the child from escaping, laughed, "Come here, little one. Did you think you could run off my plate? HA! You'll be with your friends yet."

Angel watched as the dark gray demon plucked a few children off his belt. Some came easily, while others left a part of themselves behind. He raised his arm and let them slide from his hand into his gaping mouth. Angel's eyes played witness as the demon chomped and chewed the little bodies within. He saw their blood seeping down his chin, a terrifying scene forever etched into his memories.

"Mmm, maybe he is a new resident of our humble home," the beast spoke as he ate. Bits of his meal fell out of his mouth as he did so.

"I think the little man wet himself. Look, he is too afraid to move," roared the brown troll in the group with laughter.

"About to vomit up his lunch he is!"

Vagrant made his way over to Angel's side. Looking at him, he could see Angel was trembling and twitching with fear. "Dark, let's go. We still have a long way to go."

"We can't just leave… them," Angel replied, stricken with horror yet filled with anger at the same time. He wanted to move, but his body would not obey his commands.

"I don't want to either, but-"

The yellow demon in the group interrupted with a shout, "What, you want to save the children? Want to be a hero? Imagine that! A hero in… Hell!"

Roars of laughter from the giant trolls filled the dry, humid air. Their voices were so loud that they scared smaller creatures away and could be heard for miles. The children, still with their strength, screamed for help. Most just hung there crying, although many no longer had tears. The demons then tormented and goaded Angel with remarks. One even went as far as plucking bodies and limbs off their belt and offering him some. As Angel remained silent, the demon laughed, bringing his hand to his mouth and savagely eating from his palm. He joined the others in their jubilant laughter at Angel's expense. They continued to laugh as they returned to their campfire and plates piled high with bodies drenched in thick, boiling white gravy.

Silence suddenly ripped through the air, taking hold of everyone around after the sharp song of a firearm rang out. The giant trolls watched as their yellow comrade fell backward as blood and brain matter spewed from his forehead. Vagrant stood unfazed, holding his gun. The trolls turned back around quickly. They looked at him and Angel with rage. They were grinding their teeth and showing them furiously as they snarled. Their fists were clenched tight, with their muscles and veins popping out from their arms.

There were no more words exchanged between them. Anger now controlled the surrounding atmosphere, and it demanded action. The red troll was first to strike, swinging his fist downward towards Angel, but he jumped out of the way, safely avoiding the smash.

"Vagrant, shoot their belts! Free the kids!" Angel yelled, taking flight and dodging the demons as they swung their mighty fists at him.

Vagrant's aim was precise. With each ear trembling burst from his gun, he hit the thick ropes, splitting the strands that made it and popping holes into the trolls who seemed unfazed. The belts of children fell as the trolls ignored the pain and tried to squash Angel as he flew around their heads, keeping them busy. As belts fell, Angel quickly flew down, grabbed one end of the rope, and put the children safely onto the ground, out of reach of the demons.

Once the trolls had lost their belts, Angel and Vagrant turned from defense to complete offense. As Vagrant blew holes into their bodies with his powerful demonic weapon, Angel flew around, striking wherever he saw an opening.

Angel dodged one of the red demon's hands, but the other came from behind and caught him by surprise. The troll quickly stuffed Angel into his mouth and started munching. Angel was being batted around by the monster's tongue as it tried to force him down the monster's throat or into his teeth.

Angel smiled inwardly. *Inferno, how hot can you get?*

An evil grin spread across Inferno's face, and he placed his hands on Angel's shoulders within the mind. "Prepare yourselves. Someone just put the wrong type of pepper in their mouth," Inferno teased.

Angel's body began giving off immense heat. So much that when he put his hands on the demon's tongue, it melted through like butter. The monster let out a scream of agony that was heard for miles. Angel covered his ears and cried out as the loud noise hurt his overly sensitive ears. Angel turned around, biting down on his tongue to ignore the pain in his ears as he held out his hands—a stream of lava shot down the giant's throat from them to stop the awful noise. As the fiend tried to scream again, he could only gasp and cough.

Unknown to Angel, the fire had eaten its way through the monster's hide. His remaining two comrades were frightened as his belly melted open, and his molten innards poured out onto the ground.

Vagrant had already gunned down the others with excellent marksmanship. With his incredible agility, none had come close to touching him. He had taken one down by running up its arm, jumping off his shoulder, flipping around, and firing into the back of the troll's head. He took down another by standing on his shoulder and repeatedly firing into his ear. The others had fallen just as quickly to his barrage of gunfire.

The red brute finally dropped to the ground, and Angel flew out of his mouth. Seeing this little man with such powers and unable to stop the mad albino gunman, the last two made for the hills. Something within Angel would not allow them to escape. Using Subzero's power, he shot spears of ice from his palms into the back of their knees, causing them to fall forward.

As they fell, Angel heard Scythe's voice in his mind, "Allow me to finish this, master." Then Scythe put his hand on the side of the black wall of Angel's mind and closed his eyes.

Angel watched as spikes with serrated edges burst out of the ground, ready to catch the giant's heads as they came down. Afterward, the spikes disappeared, and all that remained was the bloody aftermath.

"Endurance, chains, spikes, and such are my gifts and curse," said Scythe quietly.

Angel nodded in his mind and then turned to face Vagrant. "Where are the kids?"

"All gone. Ran away to be caught and killed another day." He answered unemotionally.

"What? Then we did this for nothing?" Angel asked in frustration.

"No, some may survive. However, it is more likely that most will not. Many demons feast on the weak and helpless."

"They weren't demons. What were they, Vagrant?" Angel asked, concerned, as he felt an uneasy feeling creeping over him.

"Another time, Dark. Another time. We still have a great deal of walking to go."

"Another time? Vagrant! Those were not demons! I could smell them. They didn't smell like any of the others here. What were they?!"

"You are in Hell, Dark! This place is filled with horrors such as that. You'd see far worse if you stayed longer. The Lady does not wish you to be longer than you need to, so we must continue. Now."

Vagrant turned away and began walking down the path drenched in troll blood. Unknown to them, a pair of eyes watched them with great interest. These eyes had been watching them since they left Lady Exspes' city. Attentively, they observed, always alert, always out of view.

The journey grew to be longer, as neither of them was talking. Angel was worried about those kids. *What is to come of them in this horrible place? They weren't demons. They didn't smell like demons. Who were they, or rather, what were they?* He wondered to himself. The demons remained silent and didn't want to discuss the subject. Other thoughts weighed heavily on his mind, those of his friends and the war still to come. However, the one thing most present on his mind over all others was Leen.

What he wouldn't give to be out of this appalling place and be back in her father's blistering blacksmith shop, waiting anxiously for her angelic voice as she brought lunch to the two of them. She always seemed to arrive when he wanted her the most. He fondly remembered sneaking off with her often to go up through the lush woods to a cliff that overlooked the shining white palace, the emperor's home, and all the royal officials. It was one of their little spots to set up and enjoy a picnic together. Many a night, they would go to that spot and lay on the grassy ledge, gazing at the twinkling stars and discussing their dreams. One of those peaceful nights stood out to him the most. Especially now, given his current situation.

He and Leen had snuck out after dinner, making their way to their lookout. Once there, they got comfortable on the grass under a large tree. Angel was wearing a soft black sweater with a small cutesy angel in the center that Leen had sewn for him, along with a pair of blue pants and white shoes. Leen was wearing a furry lilac sweater with a white kitten in the middle, white pants, and white shoes.

"Why did you wear those pants? You know you will never get the stains out," he said, lying down, wrapping his arm around her shoulder as she rested her head on his chest.

"Bet me. I am the one who does the laundry around here." She laughed while playfully poking him.

"That's because it is your job. Ouch! What was that for?" Angel laughed as he felt a pinch.

Leen smiled after pinching Angel on his side again. "You have been hanging around Cogeta too much."

He chuckled and then placed a small kiss on her forehead. She smiled and nuzzled her head against his chest. She felt so happy, wrapped in his strong yet warm embrace. Leen tilted her head up, placed small kisses on the exposed skin at the base of his neck, then turned and placed multiple soft, delicate kisses up his neck. She then rolled herself around and rested her back against his chest, ensuring his arms were around her again. She then rested her arms over his.

"Ever wondered what you would be when you grew up," she asked while gazing up into the night sky as a gray cloud passed overhead.

"Nope."

"Hmm, I want to be a healer or a priestess," Leen stated as the stars came back into view.

Angel shifted his gaze from the sky down toward her for a moment. "Are they not the same thing?"

"Yes, and no—"

"That isn't possible. Either they are, or they aren't."

"Well, they are similar, but if I joined the Priestess Sisterhood, I couldn't have a relationship, which would mean no husband, no children, and no you. I do not want to lose you, but I cannot say I wouldn't want to work there either, truthfully. I have been working there part-time, and I really love it. It's just so stunning from the great oak doors with stained-glass windows, white marble floors, and gorgeous architecture. The girls who I work with are so nice and friendly. In addition, I would have to travel a lot, which would be so cool to go to other towns and help people all over the planet. As a healer, I would help people but do it from a more...." She hesitated momentarily, trying to choose her words carefully. "I want to say more like a business-type style. I have worked in a few clinics in town, and it feels so one-sided. They only take care of the physical pains, you know. As a priestess, I could also help the emotional ones."

"Honey, I am behind you, no matter what you decide. But to remind you from a career standpoint, you don't get paid for being a priestess."

"Angel, it isn't about the money. I only want to help people. I thank you and appreciate your support. But if I become a priestess, we cannot be together anymore. Is that what you want?"

She looked at him from his shoulder with her beautiful, dark violet eyes. She was trying to guess what he was thinking, but he wasn't giving her anything to read, and she wasn't about to try reading his mind. That thought never occurred to her, and would never do so.

He gazed back into her eyes. "Of course not, but just 'cause some stupid sisterhood says you cannot have a relationship doesn't mean you have to do as they say. Your dad said we couldn't date at first, but now here we are. We would just have to keep it quiet."

"Angel, the two are nothing alike. It is a requirement of a priestess to be single and pure. I would have to take a vow of celibacy. You know what that means, don't you?" She said seriously.

"Of course I do. I just think it's stupid. As if Odin really cares. Personally, I think it would please him more to see two people in love than someone who has sworn him or herself to be alone for the rest of their lives in his name. Don't they have a program that one can join, an order that sends members out to protect the priestess when she does her travels? I could join them, get assigned to you, and then no one has to know that their best priestess is with her love."

"Angel, first, it is mean of you to say that. It is an honor to serve in the sisterhood or to become a priest. They do a lot of good for the people. So please do not insult it. Second, yes, there is such an order. It's called the Knights of the Cloth. However, I don't think you really would like to join them."

"Why not?"

"They, too, are sworn to celibacy and, well… they are trained not to have such feelings, wants, or desires."

"Well, damn," he laughed, "I guess the High Councilman really made it so he had the only set of balls there, huh?"

"Angel! That isn't nice!" Leen scorned, quickly sitting up and staring at him with hurt written on her face.

"So what? That guy has been hounding me ever since I came here, and it only got worse when I started dating you. Worse than any other guy, and that is saying something when you consider the crap Shaw puts me through simply because Shaw is jealous that you love me instead of him. I think the high and mighty councilman wants you for himself, too."

"That isn't even funny! He is one of the few still alive that have been around since the beginning of our entire race. He has helped many who sought guidance and truth. I look up to him, Angel."

As Leen looked at him, her eyes were becoming watery.

"I know you do, dear, sorry. I just… I do not have an outstanding track record with him. But know I will not come between you and your dreams. I think you would make a great priestess. However, that doesn't mean I will stop being your boyfriend. I do not care what the rules say.

If one has the will, one can change anything, no matter how big or impossible it seems. That's how things get changed. I love you, Leen, and I am more than willing to fight the system to keep you." Angel said, wrapping his arms around her as she lay back down with her head against his chest.

Leen smiled and snuggled closer, wiping the tears away on his shirt. "What about you? What do you want to be when you are through with school?"

He lay there for a moment, thinking, "I don't know."

"Come on. There must be something you want to be."

"I really don't know, Leen. Cogeta talked about becoming a professional fighter. I can see myself doing that. Not many options for me. I like to fight. I like the rush of it. But as far as a job, I don't know."

"Well, my dad said that if you and I stuck together, he could pass ownership of the shop to you. You have grown skillful in there over these years. Then I wouldn't have to watch you put your body through harsh punishment. When you enter those tournaments, I worry about you and wonder if it might be your last. There have been accidental deaths, you know."

"Yes, I know there have been deaths in the past, but I love the rush of a good fight, and it is great training to increase my skills. I probably could handle taking over your old man's shop. I honestly don't know what I would want to be yet."

From time to time after that night, she would ask him that same question, and he never could answer her. Even now, as he walked this road in a foreign land surrounded by unfamiliar objects and creatures, he re-asked himself that same question and still couldn't answer. Everything was happening so fast.

Inferno's calm voice interrupted Angel's chain of thought. "She seems like a significant person."

You can… see my memories? Inside his mind, he looked over his shoulder at Inferno.

Subzero smiled. "Yes, every thought you have, we hear. Everything in your past we can look through like a picture book. Not a lot of privacy on your part, but if there is anything you do not want us to see, there are ways to "lock it up," so to speak. Though asking us not to look is also a suitable way to do it."

"If you don't mind me saying, and I mean this in a heartfelt good-natured way, DAMN, YOUR GIRL IS HOT!" Hydro shouted out.

Angel growled. *Thanks. Now please stop drooling at her. She means a lot to me… and I couldn't save her.*

"Relax, with us on your team; you will get this… wait, is that the guy who killed her? Man, he is ugly!" Inferno exclaimed, laughing, "Makes Scythe look like prince charming!"

Angel could not help smiling and laughing a little to himself.

"Who is prince charming?" Scythe asked, not catching the joke.

I do hope that I can keep my vow.

"Like I said, with us, you will have no problem getting that ugly, long-fanged, butt-sucking, awfully dressed villain. I have one question, however. If things weren't how they are now and were the way you wanted them, what would you want to be, Dark?" Inferno smirked.

I don't know… Angel replied softly.

Hydro spoke up suddenly. "I have a question! Can we call you Angel instead of Dark? Dark is so menacing and evil. If you are supposed to be the good guy, have a good guy name. Dark is, I don't know, evil. I mean, it is Dark… it just makes you feel gloomy." he kept making funny facial expressions and gestures while he spoke.

Yeah, Leen gave me the same reason. Though, why do people always cut my middle name down? It isn't simply Angel. It is Angelus.

"Again, sounds evil, and besides, Angel is so much easier to say in conversation. It only has two syllables, whereas Angelus has three," Hydro lectured.

Fine, you guys can call me Angel.

"Yes, we are friends now! It says here in your mental notes that you only let your friends call you that, so I figured you didn't want to be friends with us. And since we are pretty much roomies. I thought it best we should be friends." smiled Hydro.

Yeah, all right. Angel nodded.

"So, Angel, buddy, pal, what did you say you wanted to be again?" Questioned Hydro once more.

I said I didn't know. Angel sighed.

CHAPTER 19

THE FINAL TRIAL

At last, it seemed they had made it to their destination. Vagrant had stopped in front of the mouth of a large cave. Angel halted beside him and took in the surroundings. The land was still jagged and barren, and the ground was laden with black stones. Bones of assorted creatures littered the place, and a light mist covered the land like a silvery blanket. The fog started from the cave and poured out from its mouth like a flowing stream. The surrounding air smelt like an old, forgotten tomb. The fragrance of old death was also present from the nearby remains. Vagrant, at last, spoke as he gazed into the cave. Angel could hear a hint of sadness in his words.

"I can't go in there with you. I must remain out here."

"Is this the last one?"

"Yes, this is your last test. Good luck."

"Thanks, Vagrant. I hope he is as easy as the last one." Angel joked before walking past Vagrant and into the unknown.

"And just what is that supposed to mean, Angel?" Hydro asked, crossing his arms, "Why, I never in all my years have been called easy."

"Not to your face, you mean," Inferno laughed and was soon joined by everyone but Hydro.

"I don't find that funny," Hydro huffed as he sat down in the waterfall he had created in his corner of Angel's mind.

Angel followed the walls, passing through large webs that clung to his hands as he brushed them aside. The thick mist obscured the ground. His peak vision was only a little help. He could make out the rough edges of the walls, but it only afforded him a couple of feet of advanced warning. Beyond that was complete and eerie darkness. His foot suddenly slipped off to the side. He narrowly stopped himself from going over into a bottomless pit. Angel carefully pulled himself back to solid ground. He continued cautiously, taking slow steps. After some time, the cave opened into a large chamber. This room had a bit more light, allowing his eyes to adjust and his surroundings to become more apparent. He almost immediately wished for the darkness when his eyes opened and saw what lay before him. It was filled with many skeletons of different demons scattered around the jagged stalagmites. Some positions the skeletons were in depicted the story of their last few moments. More than a dozen were lying as though impaled on the sharp rocks. The smell of blood was long gone, but Angel could see the darkened stains left behind.

I'm getting used to seeing skulls everywhere.

He jested as he walked past them, uncaring, until his ears picked up rustling behind him. He turned around and watched as the skeletal remains were reanimating. Angel stood unfazed and just shook his head.

Are those the best this demon offers? This is going to be easy.

Angel effortlessly danced around their blades and weapons. Snatching and breaking one of the skeleton's arms off, he turned it around and began using it to fend off their attacks. As he moved around the room, more and more skeletons came to life and joined the fight. Angel took a second to count them as he stepped back. There were forty-four undead closing in around him. His back was against a wall, and he had two on either side, inching closer with their sword and spear drew back at the ready. Suddenly, the skeleton before him charged forward in a ghostly scream with his sword over his head. How it managed the ghostly wail, Angel didn't know nor care as he tossed the arm aside and stopped the blade with his bare hands before it cleaved his head in two.

"I don't have time for this annoyance."

He flipped the sword out of the skeleton's hands and into his own. Then, using the powers of Inferno, he covered the blade in fire and began slicing metal and bone alike, pushing and cutting his way through the crowd. He weaved and spun, cutting through the mass of warriors and putting his skills to the test. However, now and then, he would feel the sting of one of their blades barely making contact.

This is taking too long. I need to change tactics. Need to thin them out.

He saw an opening and dashed toward the wall. He ran up the side of the cave wall, flipped backward over the growing crowd of skeletal warriors, and unleashed a barrage of energy bolts into them. Angel prolonged his time in the air as he spun around, firing into the group. When he landed on the other side of them, he took a moment to catch his breath and survey the scene. The tunnel was filled with white smoke and mist.

Is it over? Wait... no... Here they come again.

Out of the cloud stepped one, then five skeletons, their teeth chattering as if laughing at his futile attempt to be rid of them. More and more skeletal warriors appeared out of the mist and smoke while others began dropping from the ceiling. For every dozen he destroyed, there seemed to be another twenty to step up.

Oh, you have got to be joking... They just keep coming! I need to end this now.

Growing more frustrated, he switched to Subzero's powers and froze the entire room. Then, with Scythe's, he had chains of barbed wire shoot from the ground and shattered the skeletons into splinters. It filled the room with shattering ice and the screeching of chains as they tore through bone. Angel gritted his teeth but bore the pain in his ears, knowing it would be over quickly.

He sighed once it was over. He looked over the devastation he had wrought before continuing onward. For good measure, while he passed, he blasted the walls with molten lava to ensure there was nothing left for the creatures to reform from. Angel walked along the tunnels, finding more than a few dead ends, until, at last, he came to the belly of the cave. Within, he saw a table with two chairs. Both were made from bone with red velvety cushioned seats and up the backrest. The cushions had a black skull imprinted upon them. Human skulls adorned the ends of the arms and the feet of the chairs. The small round table's legs matched the design. A man's soft voice spoke out to Angel.

"Welcome."

"Hello. You must be the one I am supposed to meet," Angel answered back, looking for the source of the voice.

A hooded figure stepped out from the shadows and, in greeting, bowed toward Angel. "Indeed, I am. My name is Hades."

He wore a long black cloak made of thick wool, with a round hood that covered his face. The hem of the cloak perfectly hid his feet, and the sleeves were so long and wide that they easily hid his hands.

Angel returned the bow respectfully. "I am Dark. So first, I find myself in Hell and am now meeting Hades. It must mean other stories are also true. Where is Cerberus?"

"I am not that Hades. We share a name. Nothing more." Hades said calmly.

"Apologies."

Hades waved his robe-covered hand to the side as if to dismiss the confusion. "Think no more of it. Let's move on. Angel, for my trial, which I believe to be your last, you must defeat me."

Angel narrowed his eyes and stepped into a battle stance. "I said my name was Dark, not Angel."

"Relax, please. This is not a battle of strength to be won in a needless brawl. I dare say your body could not handle much more. May I say your clothes have stayed intact well for someone who has gone through so much? In addition, I called you Angel, for that, is what your friends call you. Since I want to be your friend, I, too, would like to call you Angel." Hades paused as Angel looked himself over, brushing off some of the bone fragments from his earlier encounter. There were several cuts in his jacket and around his pants, but compared to his other trials, particularly his first, he was relieved to arrive in better condition.

"Well, the demons I met repaired my clothes each time I passed their trial. As far as my name, you have not earned my friendship and, therefore, not the right to use that name." Angel stated, looking back at him, unable to make out his face.

"I see. Very well, Dark, I can understand and respect that. As for the demons repairing your clothes, they did it as a sign of respect. Wouldn't want you running around naked down here. You may get a rash or a lava burn, and you wouldn't want to singe anything important." Angel smirked at Hades, who continued, "This trial, Angel- pardon me, Dark- is a strategy battle. You see before you a table and chairs. Please have a seat, and let us begin."

Hades gracefully waved a skeletal hand over to the seat closest to Angel. As they both sat down across from each other, Hades went on,

"Do you like chess? I do, but not that normal white piece versus black piece. How utterly vapid, monotonous, and prosaic that is. Instead, I prefer to liven things up. To do that, I prefer to play with souls. It is much more fun that way. Everything is more entertaining when precious things are on the line, and what is more precious than one's soul? It's always with you, even though you cannot see it, and yet men have died for it, people have sought others who connected with it, and there has been a long war over who gets it. Yet some will willingly trade it for meaningless things because those things at the time seemed meaningful. Now let us see whose souls we shall toy with."

Hades rested his elbows on the table and brought his hands together in front of his face before lowering his head in thought.

"Ah, I got it."

Hades brought his arms to his side and then raised them. As he did so, the mist floated over the table, covering the board and all its pieces. Angel sat somewhat unimpressed until the fog separated, revealing its magic. Angel's face turned to shock at what he saw before him. Some pieces in front of Hades looked identical to his friends. The king was the young emperor. The bishops were the councilman and Spartacus, and the knights were Cory and Cogeta. Some he did not quite recognize. He knew them to be other Utopians as well. As Angel scanned the pieces, he noticed one was missing.

"Nice trick, but you missed your queen."

"Ah, well, let us remedy that." Hades placed his skeletal hand around the unchanged queen piece. After a moment of silence, a bright light shined between his fingers. After it died down, his hand moved away from the small statue.

"Leen!"

"Yes, I thought she would be perfect as the queen. Her soul was wandering around, so I brought her here to play with us."

Angel whispered and shook his head in disbelief. "Is it really her? I mean, that cannot truly be her. It's a trick."

"It is not a trick. It is she. Well, not her true self. That shell died on your home world, but it is her genuine soul. Everything that made Leen, Leen, is here. She sees you as you see her. The only thing different is the shell. Look, she is crying tears of joy to know you are alive." Hades said smoothly.

Angel looked down. And indeed, she was crying. He also noticed that some barrier was keeping her trapped in her square. "What is holding her back?"

"It's a magic field. Don't want her switching sides on me," Hades jested. "Your friends here are also really here, but they will only think of it as a very odd dream when it is over and quickly forget it. So don't worry. What happens here remains between us and us alone." Hades assured him.

"Can she hear me?" Angel looked up from her to Hades with a hopeful expression. He so badly wanted to talk to her once more.

"Oh, yes, she can indeed hear everything you say. They all can. However, let us not waste time with romantics. We have a game to play."

"All right. I just wish to say I love you, Leen." Angel whispered.

The small ivory piece nodded her head and kissed upwards against the field toward him before stepping back to the center.

"Now then, look at your pieces." Hades pointed.

Angel looked down to examine his pieces, picking each one up to look closely at them. He did not recognize any of them except two. He picked up his queen, and it was a man. Someone he used to know, but he could not match the face with a name. When he picked up his king, his eyes filled with hatred.

"Serkuma," he growled and slammed the piece back down.

"Correct, you will play with the souls of your enemies." as Hades told this to Angel, a wicked smile appeared on Angel's face. "Glad to see you like that idea, but here are the rules before you decide to kill or lose on purpose. If I win, your friends, for as long as they live, will never know what happiness is again. They will lose everything they have worked for. Bad luck will follow them as sharks follow the scent of blood. Upon death, their souls will not find peace. Instead, they will be lost forever, never to find rest nor enter the magnificent halls of Valhalla, left to wander purposelessly in limbo.

As for your beloved, since she has already passed on, she will suffer worse than any of the others. She too will not go to Valhalla, she will not go to Heaven, she will not pass go, and she will not collect two hundred dollars. Instead, her spirit, her soul, indeed her very essence, will be destroyed. No one will remember her. Not how she looked, none of the good she had accomplished, lives she may have helped, or even her name. Most importantly, you, who hold her dear, shall not remember her. It shall be as though she never existed, but I will leave you the empty feeling you suffer from now."

Angel knocked over his chair as he leaped to his feet. "What?!"

"Don't raise your voice to me, young Dark. Though the game has not started, I can still give her soul PAIN." Hades spoke with a far darker voice than before, filled with malevolence, shocking Angel.

As Hades spoke, his right hand clenched closed as if to be strangling something. Angel watched in horror as the Leen grasped her throat and fell to her knees, gasping for air. Red strangling marks appeared around her neck as she desperately tried to loosen the invisible grip, though it proved futile.

"Ok! Ok! You made your point! Stop! You made your point!" Angel yelled, almost coming to tears. He could not bear to see Leen in pain, not again. Though some of him believed she was not truly there, he couldn't stand seeing her suffer. Hades smiled underneath his hood and released his grip. Leen remained on her knees, taking deep breaths. Hades returned his voice returned to normal.

"Good. Now, please, Dark, take your seat once more." Angel fixed his chair and sat back down quickly to avoid angering the demon further. Hades continued, "Now, if you win, you save your friends and your darling Leen from all those terrible, horrible, no good, very bad things. However, the Vampirians will be destined to win this coming war. You will ultimately lose no matter how hard you and the armies you command fight. Oh, and Serkuma becomes Utopia's new emperor, ushering its utter downfall."

"So, if I lose, my friends' souls are lost, and my love will practically never have existed, but if I win, the Vampirians will win the war. In both scenarios, my friends are lost. If the Vampirians win, they will enslave my friends and my people or slay them for standing against them."

Hades shrugged his shoulders. "Life's a bitch. Get ready to play. To move the pieces, all you have to do is order a piece into a place. Within its abilities, of course, and it will march there itself."

Angel growled, "Fine, I'll play this twisted game. As if I had a choice."

"Good, glad to hear that. Since I am so fair, I will let you move first."

"Before we begin, one last question. What happens if it's a draw?"

"That's simple, Dark. You lose."

Well, that seems like bullshit. "Technically, if it is a draw, wouldn't you lose, too?”

Hades reached up and rubbed his forehead under his hood, “Have you forgotten already who is in control here?”

“No, no, not at all. I just want to be completely clear on the rules.”

“It’s simple. We play, and either you win, or you lose. There is no middle ground, much as it is with war.”

Angel blindly ordered one of his pawns forward, and Hades followed suit similarly. When either side would take a piece, the two figures would fight it out with various weapons and in a gory fashion. Red or black blood would stain the squares when the battle was over. Hades had slain piece after piece and, at the same time, teased Angel by putting Leen in danger on purpose. Then when Angel refused to take her, Hades forced her to take one of the open pieces, staining her hands in blood. She tried to resist the command at first. However, her body betrayed her by moving independently. No matter if she struggled to stop it, the result was the same.

“Not much of a strategist, are you?” Hades inquired as he removed one of Angel’s dead pieces from the board again.

Angel did not answer and took his turn. His knight took Hades’ rook, which looked like Shaw, only to be taken by the bishop in the next turn. Not liking Shaw that much initially didn’t stop him from feeling some guilt watching some unknown Vampirian behead him. He watched as Cory was knocked from his horse and impaled through the heart by a spear, a part of himself dying with him. Then he felt the same gut-wrenching feeling as Cogeta was sliced in half.

“Still, you use no strategy. Did you think I was joking?” Hades mocked as the game went on, watching Angel closely. “If I didn’t know any better, I would think you wanted to lose.”

Angel did his best to focus. Angel and Hades were down to only two pieces left within another hour. He felt exhausted. His soul drained to the brink of nonexistence. Hades had his king and queen, and Angel only held his king and a bishop. Hades ordered Leen forward by doing so, putting Angel in check, but leaving her wide open to his bishop's attack.

"Do it. Do it, Dark. You have no other course. Unless, of course, you wish to lose and forget all about your beloved." Hades tormented Angel with his words.

"Would you shut up?" He said hollowly.

"Let me ask you this, Dark. Do you think you're sparing her pain by not killing her? Look at her hands, Dark. They are stained with blood. You've forced your beloved to kill again and again. Because you couldn't bear to see her die a second time. Do you think that is right? Is that your idea of protecting her?"

The realization crushed whatever soul he had left. Hades was right. He had just made his beloved murder others. She would've never wanted that. She would've sacrificed herself to save others. He had betrayed her in his attempt to protect her from harm. The thought of betraying her destroyed him inside. He had lost. Angel closed his eyes tightly as tears poured down his face. He gave the order to his bishop to take the queen in a dispirited voice.

"I'm sorry," he whispered in a dreary, defeated tone.

"No! Angel, no!" He thought he heard her scream as the bishop pulled a dagger and drove it into her body repeatedly.

Angel slowly opened his eyes and looked in horror as he saw his love lay dead before him. Once again, he was helpless to save her. Even though it was a simple ivory piece, the sheer thought of seeing her, only to lose her again, pierced him deeply.

Hades laughed cruelly, "Well done, Dark, you killed Leen! My king surrenders, and the Vampirians win the day!" Hades knocked over his king and stood up, smiling under his hood. "Well, now you have one more demon on your team. Thank you for the game. It was quite entertaining, and I hope enlightening to you. I am the demon of bone and, in some areas, of death. I am at your service." Hades said friendlily and bowed once more, but Angel did not reply, nor did he budge.

"I betrayed her. Then I killed her again. I will never see her again. How could I look at her if I could?" Angel said in a nearly inaudible tone, barely above a whisper. He sat with his head hung over the table.

"Did you forget that this was but a dream to them? They will not remember a thing."

"But I will. I will always remember that I made my beloved a murderer in my selfish attempt to avoid seeing her die again."

"A bad dream, Dark. A nightmare. That's all this is. You did nothing wrong." Hades sighs, "It was just an ivory piece. She was never truly here. You did not betray her nor her memory."

"What? But then why?"

"Trial, remember? I had to make you invested in the outcome. There are none more important in your life than your friends and beloved. No higher stakes I could use. You could've given up the game at any time. Instead, you saw it through to the end. Sacrificing it all because I told you that your friends would suffer horrible fates. That Leen's precious memory would be lost to not just you but to everyone. I tested your resolve to see how far you would go and whether you would give up when things were bleak. Whether you'd make the hard choices. Everyone else thus far tested your body. It was my job to test your spirit."

Angel raised his head from looking down at the table for the first time since the game ended. He then turned and looked at Hades. People say that the eyes are the doorways to the soul, and within that moment of eye contact between Hades and Angel, Hades saw someone lost and confused within Angel. While at the same time, he saw bravery, courage, and determination buried deep, covered by the pain he felt now.

Hades moved around the table to Angel, placing his hand on his shoulder. "My friend, you have been through a great tragedy, and many more lay ahead, but you have the strength to overcome. Moreover, the other demons and I will see that you do. Now, let us end all this and get you back to your home."

Angel felt a cold pain take over his shoulder, and it quickly spread. He fell out of his chair and yelled out as a cage of bone engulfed him, breaking through the table and chairs. On the cold ground, he writhed in pain as ghostly figments swirled around and through his body as they let out a ghastly scream of their own. The surrounding cage exploded when the pain finally ceased, sending bone fragments flying everywhere. The haunts faded away into the mist.

Hades spoke up inside Angel, "So now that I am one with you, may I call you Angel, Dark?"

"Sure, but answer me this, if you are the demon of death, is it possible-"

"I know what you are about to ask, Angel and the answer is no. I do not do resurrection. You'll find that though this universe is vast and many possess great powers, very few can truly bring the lost ones back to those who love them. That does not mean you cannot speak to them occasionally. Do you understand?"

"Yeah…" Angel trailed off as he made his way out.

Vagrant could not help but let slip a small smile as Angel appeared in the mist, returning from the cave.

When he spoke, it was even more apparent that he was glad to see Angel successful. "You passed. Good job. You will now have to learn how to work with them. They are there to help you. Don't forget that. Come, let us return to the castle. Lady Exspes will be pleased to learn you succeeded in all your trials."

Angel barely managed a nod as he walked past Vagrant silently. Watching Leen suffer again, real or not, gnawed at him. He also thought he single-handedly ensured that the Vampirians, more precisely, the bastard Serkuma, would be victorious. Though perhaps that, too, was a lie. As he thought more and more on it as he walked silently with Vagrant, he decided that even if Serkuma would win, then he would at least make him work for the victory and go down fighting. Angel wouldn't allow himself or his friends to be captured, just to be enslaved. They'd fight until the very end.

The two only made small talk before Angel opened up and told Vagrant what had happened inside the cave. He listened intently. But as they passed the rocky hill where they fought the giant troll demons, Vagrant stopped.

"Vagrant, what's----" Angel did not have to finish. His sixth sense noticed a powerful feeling of danger. What power... it's incredible. He traced its vibes back over the hill in front of them. Just then, a form stepped over the top and looked down at them. Vagrant took a step in front of Angel protectively and drew his gun.

"What do you want?" He demanded, trying to hold his gun steady.

"Vagrant, who is this guy?" Angel tried to ask.

"Quiet, Dark," Vagrant snapped, keeping his eyes locked onto the unknown threat on the hill.

The stranger slid down the rocky hill and stepped up to the end of the gun barrel. He stood a few inches taller than Vagrant and wore armor Angel recognized from his Earth studies as a samurai fashion, primarily black and red with gold decor. He could make out many draconic designs within his armor. His helmet covered his face, and as Angel looked him over, one of his boots stood out and caught his attention. On his left foot, his boot had an intricate dragon design. As he stared at it, one eye turned to him and glared. Angel quickly looked away, amazed and curious at how it did that. There was much commotion in his head, but he could make none out, only that the demons were gravely concerned.

"What do you want? I won't ask again," demanded Vagrant once more.

The stranger spoke sternly, "Shut up, messenger boy. I only came to see if it was true. I have been tailing you since you left the city ruled by the wench who thinks of herself as a queen. Are you going to shoot me?"

"Step aside so we can get back," Vagrant replied, gritting his teeth and pulling the hammer on his gun back.

"No! You move! I want to see if he is as good as they say." The man quickly shoved Vagrant to the side and moved closer to Angel. "So, you are the host. He's not much of a man, but if it means getting out of this place."

With his last words, he entered Angel's body and joined the others in his mind. Angel immediately felt pain and fell to his knees as surges of dark power flew around him. He pounded the ground as his body buckled and seemed to snap under such malevolent pressure. He opened his eyes wide and yelled in agony as red light glowed from his eye sockets and mouth.

"My name is Lazarus so that you know. I am the demon of power." The new demon announced.

Nice… to… meet you, Angel said to him while struggling with the pain.

"Whatever, save the pleasantries. I want out of here." Lazarus said, taking a spot in Angel's mind. He summoned a large throne and sat down.

Fair enough, Angel agreed. He stood back up after the pain subsided. He took several deep breaths to calm himself, then looked at Vagrant. "Why does that happen each time?"

Vagrant only shrugged as he holstered his gun. "I don't know. Let's get back before anything else happens." Angel nodded and followed behind him.

Inferno said, "It happens because your body isn't used to such powers. It's kind of like a way to awaken it inside you, and for us to be comfortable in here, it must be done."

Ah, okay. Angel nodded to himself.

"Vagrant, are we gonna have to walk all the way back?"

"Oh, heck no!" Vagrant laughed. He extended his arm, and a red and black portal opened.

"If you could've done that, couldn't you have done that to all the trials?"

Vagrant smirked. "Journey was part of the trials."

"How so?"

"Have you never read a hero's journey before? Now come on, the Lady awaits."

Angel chuckled as he walked through the portal with Vagrant right behind him. Unbeknownst to them, a figure sat on top of a massive, hellish steed several hundred yards away on a hill, watching them intently. A red hand stroked the stranger's chin and the hairs of his goatee—a toothy grin spreading across his face.

"Interesting. I thought I felt a strange presence in my domain. Former... domain. Wonder what she is up to."

The red portal opened inside the town Angel had passed through at the beginning of his journey. He was greeted by more scowls and cruel slanders again from the residents. They even threw food scraps at him. However, they never touched him. As the scraps came close, they burst into flames and vanished. Inferno shook his head as he kept the fire shield going until Vagrant and Angel walked past them to the cathedral. Crolarious and Damien were standing guard. The two parties silently greeted and acknowledged the other before entering. Exspes was sitting in her thrown reading from a tome that she was floating in front of her. When she heard the doors open, she looked up and graced them with a smile upon seeing who it was.

"Welcome back, Dark. Tell me, Vagrant, did he pass each assessment?" She asked kindly.

"Indeed, he did, and he even gained an extra," Vagrant announced.

Exspes looked intrigued, "Oh?"

"Yes, my lady. The demon Lazarus intercepted us on our way here. A few words were spoken, but nothing serious. He said that he wanted out of here."

Exspes laughed softly to herself. "I see. Well then, Dark, congratulations. Vagrant, you can leave us now."

Vagrant bowed and departed through the doors.

Looking back at Angel, she smiled. "I have something more to give you." She held up a shimmering crystal.

"What is it?" Angel asked, peering curiously at the beautiful object.

"This you may find unbelievably hard to fathom. But within this crystal is a demon of immense power. He is a demon that has done some horrible things through multiple lifetimes, and he now wishes to find forgiveness and atonement by turning over a new leaf. He came to me because I have been on the same quest for many eons now." As she spoke, Angel looked over the dark blood crystal.

"How am I to help him?"

"By allowing him to become a part of you, much like the demons you have got. He will break from this seal when the situation is most dire. He shall return to his slumber inside it when it is over," she explained.

"All right, I understand." Angel nodded.

"I knew you would. Now come closer, and kneel so that he can move in."

Angel took a breath, walked to the throne, and kneeled. Exspes stood up with the crystal in hand and stepped toward him. She placed the tip of the glass-like object on Angel's forehead and then pushed it down. As it slipped into his mind, Angel felt no pain. When the last bit went in, she retook her seat. Inside his mind, the demons and he watched as the crystal materialized, hanging from the ceiling like a chandelier. They could not make out much of who was inside the red crystal. All they could see was a face of a man, and his arms lain across his naked chest.

"Does he have a name?" Angel asked, looking up at her.

"His name is Angelor, and that is all I can do for you. You have a long journey ahead of you, filled with perils. I hope that the experiences here and the powers you've gained help you through them. I truly do. Damien will see you out. Here are your original clothes, as they were before, unharmed. Just go back into the room you had used before, and then you may leave." Exspes smiled, handing him the black bag.

Angel smiled and nodded. "Thank you. And I am sure everyone inside my head will help me. For demons... they don't seem so bad. And I can say the same for you and Vagrant. Guessing the other two as well."

"We are all looking for ways to redeem ourselves. As the old saying goes, never judge a book by its cover. Now get going."

Angel took the bag and went back down the hall and into the door on the left, as he had done when he had arrived so long ago. The room was still dark, lit only by candles all over the room. The small pool was filled with crystal blue water, slightly misting like a hot spring, surrounded by the red-sheer curtain.

When he turned around from closing the door, three women stood before him. To his utter surprise, they were scarcely covered. The ladies only wore bikini bottoms and a sheer sash tied around their waists.

The girl on the left end was a young, slim bleached blonde with sparkling jade eyes. Black eyeliner accentuated their beauty. Her lips were dressed in bright red lipstick. The woman in the center had fiery red hair. She was also slender with a full-body tan. She had bright blue eyes brought out by red eyeliner and naturally pink lips. The last girl standing before him was a brunette with dark brown eyes, no makeup, and with an hourglass shape.

As he gazed upon them, he noticed they each looked perfectly normal until he spied their pointed ears, the small horns on their heads, and small spikes along the outside of their arms. He was about to protest when the woman in the middle pressed her finger to his lips. The two others stepped around and began peeling off his jacket. The red-headed woman with her finger to his lips smiled seductively and whispered,

"We are to help you clean before you return to your home, as ordered by the Lady Exspes."

"I can bathe myself… honest." Angel tried to say, feeling uncomfortable. The demons in his head were telling him to go for it.

"Relax, sir. Please, don't let us get in trouble for not doing what the Lady wishes," whispered the blonde into his right ear.

"Just relax. We'll take care of you, deary," said the other as her hands slid his shirt over his head.

Once he was nude, the redhead pulled off her sheer pink sash and wrapped it around his neck, holding on to either end. Guided by her, Angel was led into the pool of warm water. The two other girls grabbed a large, round yellow sponge and washed his shoulders. Then they slowly scrubbed down his chest. The red-headed woman slid him forward, slipped behind him, and washed his back. Angel could not stop his eyes from closing, and a small moan of pleasure passed his lips as she washed up the back of his neck.

His breath caught in his throat when the brunette woman began slowly massaging his tail. He bit his lower lip and leaned back into the redhead behind him, who gently wrapped her arms around his neck and caressed his chest, the back of his head resting on her soft shoulder. Meanwhile, the blonde woman scooted back into the water and gently raised his right leg out of the water. Softly, her hands rubbed and stroked his calf down to his foot. She rubbed his sole with her thumbs as her fingers worked on the top.

A nervous smile came over his lips when she caught him staring at her.

She returned the smile with a sultry one of her own, pressed his foot against her bosom, and slowly slid it back into the pool. She retrieved his other leg and started the same treatment on it.

I need to end this. I have to get going. Must avenge Leen. Leen.

"Relax, Angel," Inferno said softly, "you will not have time to relax like this on the road ahead."

"He's unfortunately right," Subzero agreed.

"You just finished a long journey across the lands of Hell. You've earned a moment of rest."

That might be true, but I really shouldn't…

Hades rested his hand on his shoulder. "Pamper yourself this once. You won't get this again."

The words of the demons in his head seemed to echo in his mind. The ladies seemed intent on making him feel completely comfortable. They even serenaded in a hauntingly lovely lullaby. Angel didn't know why, but it wasn't unfamiliar to him. He thought he'd heard it before, but from where he could not say. The combination of their soft caresses, massaging, and echoing lullaby proved too much for him. His eyes grew heavy, and his head drifted. His eyes snapped open, and he sat up with a start.

"H-how, for how long was I asleep?" He asked in a panic.

The red-headed demoness wrapped her arms around his shoulders and hugged him to calm him. "It's not even been an hour."

"You no doubt need a good long sleep after your journey," added the brunette.

"I thank you, ladies, but I must go now," Angel said, trying to get out of the pool.

"What a gentleman, thanking the help," cooed the redhead as she stepped out with Angel and licked his cheek. "Please, allow us to finish."

Angel stood still as each girl began wiping his body with golden towels. When thoroughly dry, they dressed him even though he tried to insist he could do it himself. He had the same amount of success as he had before. He finally gave in and went along with it. The last thing they put on him was a necklace. The brunette demoness tied it on behind his neck.

It had the top half of a snarling wolf's head and curved down into the tip of a crescent moon. The necklace was made from an unfamiliar metal, but as Angel tried to bend it, he could not. A thin brown leather strip held it.

Angel held up the medallion. "What is this?"

"It was in the bag that had your uniform in it. Perhaps a gift from the Lady. We swear we did not put it in there. We mean no harm to you, sir, we swear," replied the brunette with great urgency. The others like her, looking nervous.

Why are they acting so scared all of a sudden? Angel pondered.

"Think about it," said Hades, "You accuse them of trying to harm you, and their lady would kill them."

I wouldn't do that. They've been so kind to me, even though they are demons. No offense.

"All offense taken." Hades replied, "However, we don't blame you for the stereotyping. We've more than earned the reputation as a whole. But try to remember that, like not all Utopians are dumb-witted mongrels brought up to howl at the moon and force breed with anything that catches their fancy, not all demons seek to do you harm, to feast on your soul or drag you to hell. Those in South Hell wish to escape that image and create a new life."

Touché. I understand.

"Relax, I wasn't assuming you did. I will ask Exspes about it." He graciously thanked the women and took his leave. He left behind the clothes he had been wearing as they requested.

When he returned to the throne room, where Exspes sat waiting. "You enjoyed that, I hope. You were in there for a long time. Were the girls to your liking?"

His cheeks turned a little red. "They were very kind and lovely and… thorough with the task given." Angel held out the pendant. "What is this? It is not mine."

Exspes smiled gently. "Think of it as one last gift from me. It was forged during the "Wolf Moon." I thought it would look good on you, which it does. It will bring you some extra luck and protection. Please, accept it."

"You have given me so much already, Lady Exspes. I couldn't accept more. I feel as if I am stealing these from you." Angel stepped forward as he reached behind his neck to untie the necklace. Her hands stopped him from taking it completely off as she stood mere inches from him and grinned.

"Please, accept it, Dark. It goes well with you, and it would please me greatly if… if you would wear it so that you may remember." Her hands slowly tied the straps back together and straightened them out so the medallion lay flat.

He couldn't help but smirk. "I doubt I will ever forget my time here."

"I hope not." Exspes smiled, then stepped back to her throne and sat back down. "Now then, did you enjoy yourself? As I said before, you were there for well over four hours."

Angel was shocked at how long he had spent being pampered. "If you don't mind me asking, why did you order them to bathe me, and why have you helped me? I understand you watched everything that happened on Utopia. Why—"

"Why didn't I help you then?" Lady Exspes cut him off.

Angel nodded, "Yeah." His chest felt tight.

"It's true I watched the events transpire on Utopia. However, I do not possess foresight, so I couldn't have known what would happen. Even had I moved to help you before the fighting was over, such a spell to open a portal from here to your world takes time. It would've been a futile attempt. By the time the ritual would've been completed, the battle would have been over and the damage done. While you've been gone, I've prepared a portal for your return trip. The reason I helped you is that I hate what happened to you. Perhaps by helping you, I can redeem myself from past sins." She looked sad and lost in thought for a moment but then continued. "As far as the ladies in the bathroom, I wanted you to feel refreshed when you left here. Dark, you have been through a lot already. You probably do not realize this, but the last time you entered my cathedral was five months ago. You still have much more to go through, and you will not get such treatment for a while, so I thought it would be a pleasant treat for you," Lady Exspes smiled.

"Five months... wow. I thank you, Lady Exspes. I am surprised to say this, but I did enjoy the adventure down here. Though some parts of it will definitely not leave me anytime soon." Angel bowed, and then as he turned to leave, he looked back at her, "You may call me Angel from now on, Lady

Exspes. If you are ever in need of me, send a portal, and I'll readily assist how I can." He then walked out to where his escort was waiting.

Lady Exspes smiled as she watched him leave and the doors close, "Good luck, Angel." She said to herself quietly. She hadn't felt a swell of emotion building inside of her in years. Sadness. Taking a deep breath and slowly exhaling, she forced the feeling aside.

Damien smiled as Angel came out of the cathedral,

"The portal is ready to be opened once again. Shall I raise the dead to carry you home?"

Angel shook his head. "Haha, I don't think that will be necessary."

Damien nodded, opened the portal for Angel, and waved him through.

Angel stepped forward but stopped and turned to the three demons. "Thank you for all the help you've given."

Crolarious and Vagrant nodded in reply.

"Good luck," noted Damien as Angel walked toward the gateway. Damien and Vagrant looked at each other, and they shared a wolfish grin between themselves. They both rushed forward and gave Angel a hand through the portal by kicking his backside.

CHAPTER 20

HE WHO DWELLS IN THE TEMPLE

Angel fell through the other side of the portal face first. Standing up, he dusted himself off.

"Bastards, and you guys shut up. That wasn't funny!"

"If you say so," Inferno said through his boisterous laughing.

Just then, Angel heard a female voice whisper his name. Looking around, he saw Arieta sitting on her knees. She looked up at him with redness around her eyes, tears running down her pale cheeks.

"Angel? Is it really you?"

"Yes, Arieta. It's really me. I'm back." She didn't respond as she was already off the ground, with her arms around him, and was busy squeezing the life out of him with her bear hug. "It's okay. It's okay. I'm back now." He whispered calmly to her as he held her close and stroked the back of her head and along her back.

"I didn't know what to do. I was so frightened and… GARGH, I am so useless! Couldn't even help you when you needed me."

"Hey," he pulled her head up by the chin so that he could look into her eyes, "you aren't useless in any sense of the word. You helped me take down that lyzon earlier. You were held back by those zombie arms, so you couldn't help me. They covered your mouth so you couldn't cast any spell."

"Angel… good casters don't need to say the wo—," Angel's finger pressed against her lips.

"The point I am trying to make is you aren't useless."

"I thought that you'd never come back. Don't know what I would've done. I was so scared."

"What is it they say about heroes? They always come home. But… I am afraid I still have to go into that temple alone. Would you mind waiting out here for me, as you promised?"

"I will."

"Just out of curiosity, how long was I gone?"

"Well, you were taken through the portal. I guess only ten or fifteen minutes passed before it reopened and you were falling through it. But it felt like eternity."

"You have no idea," Angel mumbled.

"What?"

He shook his head, "Nothing." *Time hasn't really passed at all here. Hell runs on a different plane of time than most, just as Exspes said.* "I need you to remain brave for me. Remain here and guard my backside. Hopefully, nothing will follow me in nor will the door suddenly close behind me. I'll be back as soon as I can."

Arieta nodded. He smiled, kissed Arieta on the cheek, and walked her back to have a seat on the steps before he headed up towards the entrance of the temple of Gilgamesh.

Their attentions were suddenly drawn to the forest from which they came, as they heard branches snapping. Angel quickly moved to stand in front of Arieta and posed himself, ready to attack. Then out of the treeline burst Cory and Cogeta in full flight. Angel relaxed and grinned upon seeing his best friends land on their feet before him.

"What are you two doing here?" Angel asked when he was suddenly hugged by both of them. "Guys?"

"What the hell happened to you?" Cogeta questioned. A look of genuine concern on his face. Angel saw the same look on Cory's as well. "There I am in camp, about to fall asleep, terrified of tomorrow, and then suddenly I feel something strange. Your aura just vanished off the face of the planet. Poof! Gone! Found Cory questioned him."

"I felt it disappear, too. I couldn't explain how it could've happened." Cory put forth his two cents.

"So, we hightailed it this way, where we last sensed your presence. But we ran into an angry lyzon."

"That.. slowed us down a bit." Cory nodded. "Never faced one before."

"But we kicked its ass and made it run back to whatever hovel it calls home because we're awesome. Cory shot it in the eye with lightning!"

"It had you pinned down and was about to bite your head off."

"His timing and aim were perfect! I gave it a taste of my wicked flames and it knew it was outmatched by our skills."

Angel glanced over at the state of his two friends. Their uniforms were in tatters and stained with blood. They had definitely run into a vicious animal. But the encounter didn't go as one sided as Cogeta was making it out to sound. Angel could imagine the horrific battle that his comrades had endured by the battle-damaged clothes they wore, and the wounds upon their bodies that had yet to heal.

Could it have been the same lyzon that Arieta and I faced? Angel wondered.

Cory continued the story, "So the after we fended off the beast. Drowsiness suddenly overcame us and passed out."

"Had a dreadful sleep. Complete with a whacked-out nightmare." Cogeta said.

"As did I," added Cory. "When we came to, we suddenly felt your presence again and flew here as fast as we could."

Angel hugged them both once more. "I'm glad you both are safe. I'll explain everything later. But right now, I have a task that I must complete before the night is over."

Cogeta patted his friend's back. "Well, alright then, let's do this."

Arieta suddenly spoke up, "He has to do it alone."

Cory and Cogeta looked past Angel's shoulders and finally noted Arieta sitting upon the step. So relieved to reunite with their friend they had failed to notice her. Suddenly, they were both stricken with renewed grief. Did she know of Leen's murder? Surely, Angel would not have kept it from her. Should one of them ask?

"Arieta, what are you doing here?" Cogeta hesitatingly asked.

"I brought her along to help me." Angel said.

"Don't lie for me. I insisted on coming, at least as far as I could go." She looked back and forth at Cogeta and Cory, reading their uneasy facial expressions. Their eyes filled with sorrow. She could sense their anxiety.

"Yes, I know what happened to my sister. Angel told me." She was surprised when she suddenly found herself embraced by both of them.

"We're so sorry, Arieta. If you need anything, we'll be right here for you." Cogeta said, kissing the top of her head.

"Don't lie to me. I know you both are leaving to go fight. Just like Angel is. It's fine. You want to do something for me... then kill as many of them as you can. Kill the one who killed my sister."

Cogeta grinned. "Promise."

Cory was a bit more unsure. His hands were no less stained with blood as theirs he knew. He was still struggling with the fact internally. He caught Arieta looking at him. Her two differing jewels for eyes peering deep into his. He forced a smile and nodded.

"Of course."

"So," Angel began, "they want me to go into the temple and bring back evidence. That's how they want me to prove my mettle and right to lead."

"I'm still trying to wrap my head around you being the new general. No offense." Cogeta smiled, "Never would've seen that coming."

"Neither did I. They just sprung it on me. But I won't waste the opportunity that it presents for me to exact my revenge. Certainly beats going at it alone."

Cogeta grinned at his friend. "You wouldn't have been alone."

"Thank you. Thank you both. I best get going."

"Be careful." Cory said as he took a seat beside Arieta. "We'll remain here with Arieta."

"Yeah. We'll keep her safe in case that lyzon or anything else comes this way."

Angel gave a nod and walked up the sacred steps of the temple. He remembered that, according to legend, only women could enter the inner chambers. All the men brave enough to try never came back. Angel smiled, welcoming the unknown. He had powers he never dreamt of having and surely whatever lay ahead was nothing like the horrors he saw in Hell. Dashing up the remaining steps and he walked through the open doorway.

Stepping inside, Angel looked down a seemingly endless hall. Barely any light was visible down the long stretch. His eyes adjusted easily enough to make up for the lack of it. Pictures were etched into the walls and painted with red clay depicting times of old. He traced a few with his fingers, unable to understand the writings that accompanied them. From the pictures, he surmised they told a story, possibly the history of the temple.

Continuing onward, Angel felt a sudden shake. A rumbling noise quickly followed. Suddenly, the floor dropped from beneath him. He tried to hover, but it felt as though the gravity beneath had been increased and was pulling him down. Angel did his best to remain calm, but as he fought the pull. It was becoming stronger.

"Subzero, I need some footing!"

On cue, an ice bridge formed under his feet, allowing him to run across to the other side before the bridge was sucked into the void.

Thank you. Let's make this quick.

He tried to fly off but found that he suddenly could only barely get his feet off the ground. He put his feet back down on the ground and then tried jumping, which he had no problem doing.

A spell that keeps me tethered to the floor? I guess he doesn't want me cheating.
Angel laughed.

He then continued on foot, dodging various other traps hidden in the hallway. He ducked arrows that smelled of poison. Jumped past bursts of acid. Dodged swinging axes and circular razor blades that came shooting out of the walls. He was nearly skewered by spikes and had to bridge his way across more trapped doors that opened into other gravitational voids. He then came across twin gargoyles on either side of the hall. Cautiously, he stepped by them. After taking a few paces past the stone watchers. one then turned its head and fired a beam from its eyes, hitting Angel's right arm. He let out a yell as his right arm turned to stone. Turning around, he dodged another beam. He glanced over his shoulder just in time as the floor where the beam hit melted away.

Whoa, okay, so I can't get hit twice. Damn, this is going to be tough with this arm slowing me down and not being able to fly.

Angel ducked another beam and then rolled out of the way of another. Coming up with a plan quickly, he summoned forth chains from the ground, ensnaring one gargoyle. Then, with the bottom of his boots becoming slippery like ice, he slid toward the other. He leapt onto the wall, out of the way of its beam. Thrusting off the wall, he landed on to the back of the gargoyle and began wrestling it, trying to force it to turn its head. By this time, the other gargoyle had broken free of the chains. It spun into the air with its black wings encompassing its body.

"Angel, six o'clock!" Hydro shouted.

He spun himself and the gargoyle around into the path of the beam and shoved the gargoyle into it. It didn't die quietly. It filled the hall with its painful cries as its body melted away. The other gargoyle, showing compassion for his comrade, flew down to its side and pawed at its companion's remains. Unable to save him, the gargoyle snapped its head around to Angel. Its face more contorted and menacing looking than before.

"Looks like it's a little pissed," commented Hydro.

"No shit!" Angel shouted as he jumped from side to side to avoid the beams that shot forth from the enraged gargoyle's eyes.

Angel fired a mix of fire and ice blasts at the beast. The gargoyle dodged them easily, flying around and firing another beam attack. Angel slid out of the way, throwing bolts of ice back at the gargoyle. It again weaved its way around the attack with ease. Growing tired of this game, Lazarus pushed Angel aside in the mind, taking control of his body. He rushed the beast, jumping off the walls to avoid the beam attacks. Once he was close enough, he jumped over the demon's head, swung Angel's stone arm down, and shattered the skull of the gargoyle.

"There, that's how you do it!" Lazarus then gave control back to Angel.

"Umm… T-thanks," Angel replied, a bit shocked.

Upon defeating the two gargoyles, the walls all around shook and rumbled. Angel heard loud crashes coming from behind him. He turned to look and saw that the passageway was sealing itself. It interchanged how it did so. First, the ceiling shot downward as the floor rose to meet it. Then the side walls would come together. This pattern continued as it transitioned down the passageway. Angel started running. Running as hard as he could, he tried to stay ahead, but the walls kept gaining. The weight of his right arm, growing heavier and heavier the harder he ran. Then, just when he wondered if it was over, he saw a doorway at the end of the stretch. With renewed energy, he pushed himself forward. However, the walls also closed quicker. If he could only fly, he would be in no danger. Thinking quickly, Angel began to spin his right arm around like a windmill. Faster and faster, he spun his arm until it was spinning around in a blur of motion. Then suddenly he flung his arm forward and let the momentum carry him. Flying through the doorway, just as the wall sealed shut behind him, a second more and he would have been flattened. Angel stood up straight, brushed himself off with his left hand, and glanced around, catching his breath.

The room was sparsely decorated. Chandeliers of candles lit the room just enough to keep the darkness at bay. A long wooden dining table aligned the left wall. It was littered with vases and ornaments from foreign lands, and they surrounded a stand holding six unique swords. Along the back wall was a stone throne that appeared to be occupied by a large mass, however Angel could not make it out clearly. Angel paid it no heed and moved closer to the table to examine the swords. An ominous, low voice spoke to him from the direction of the throne.

"So, after eons of living here, a man finally made it past my security. I am impressed, stranger." The man sitting on the throne let out a yawn and stretched in his chair.

Angel glanced over his shoulder and smiled. "Gilgamesh, it's me, Angel."

Gilgamesh let out a sigh, and his voice took a more casual yet still impactful tone. "You mean that little punk who snuck in here through the hidden passageway with that cute girl?"

"I am one and the same. Just too big to sneak through the hole now. Besides, not like it was extremely hard to find. A mere bush hid it. Any kid could find it and make their way into here. The only thing that may deter them would be the thorns and fear from the legends." Angel laughed softly.

"Yes, I know. I don't mind children or women coming here. It is just men that I hate having over. They are the ones who like to start fights and make a mess looking for loot. Now, where is that cute girl, Leen, at?" Gilgamesh asked with a smile.

"Gilgamesh… she is dead. I am here to prove my worth to the

Emperor, the High Councilman, and to all Utopia that I am worthy of leading them to victory over the Vampirians who attacked us this afternoon, and more to the point, to avenge her."

"So that was what the commotion was about. I'm truly sorry for your loss, my young friend. She... she was something special. One in a billion."

Angel looked down at the floor, hand resting on the table. "I know."

"Alright then, let's get you ready."

Gilgamesh stood up and came forward. The candles in the room flared up and illuminated the room entirely. The man towered over Angel at around eight feet tall. He was wearing a long red cloak over a loose-fitting silver shirt with large billowy black pants with gold ornate patterns. A black cloth belt was wrapped around his waist, and red armor covered his otherwise black boots. Angel had not once ever seen his face in all the times he visited. He kept it covered by a scarlet mask. It was wrapped around his face, leaving only his cold black eyes visible, each with a streak of red ran vertically across both, and with a hint of his grey face. Gilgamesh threw his cloak over his shoulders, revealing three large grey arms. All on the right side, with no sign of any arms on his left. The shirt was sewn closed as though not needed.

"What happened? Since when do you have multiple arms? I don't remember ever seeing them."

"That's because I only showed you one arm and kept the rest well hidden. I lost the left three in a battle, a harsh reminder of my past failures. The price I paid for one man's pride. Enough about that. You are here to prove yourself. We shouldn't keep the people waiting for their chance at vengeance, let alone keep you from your prey." Gilgamesh walked over to Angel and brushed his arm, knocking the stone off as if it was mere dust so that Angel could use it once more. As he did so, he spoke softly, "Always fight fairly. Then no one can deny you were the better man. Of course, some still will. However, those are the ones who lack dignity and honor. Those two items are scarce in the universe's vastness. Cherish them, seek them out, and keep them close. They are priceless commodities. Now choose your weapon."

Gilgamesh then moved to the table, selecting three swords off the stand. The first was a katana style blade. It had a jade dragon hand guard, and the handle was wrapped in dark green cloth with rubies evenly spaced down the center on both sides.

As Angel watched him, he couldn't help the urge to ask his friend, "Do your swords have names?"

"Of course, they do. All good weapons deserve a name. This one is called 'Jade Dragon'," The second sword Gilgamesh picked up was a bastard sword. The edges of the blade were jagged menacingly, its hilt was clear and glowed red. "This is, 'Widower'." The last sword to be picked up was a short sword. It was made of wood and emblazoned with dragon teeth all over the blade. The hilt had a picture of a fairy and a dragon etched into it. "And this is one is named 'The Fantasy Killer'."

Angel got into a fighting stance.

"No weapon?" Gilgamesh inquired.

Angel smirked. "Nope."

Gilgamesh raised his eyebrow and smirked under his cloth, "You're going to make it hard on yourself."

"Nah. Just try me. This is a trial to prove myself, after all."

With those words, the battle erupted. Gilgamesh came at Angel, swinging and thrusting the swords in a wild blur. Angel could not help but notice while evading the oncoming attacks that Gilgamesh was amazingly good for only using half of his body. Angel stepped back quickly to get out of range, at the same time freezing one of Gilgamesh's feet to the stone floor.

"Well, that's new. You have been taking your magic skills seriously as of late, I see."

Angel smirked and then dashed forward, hitting Gilgamesh in his chest twice, with one fist of fire and the other covered in spikes and bone.

"You could say that."

Angel smiled before running up Gilgamesh's large frame and flipping back. While in mid-flight, he drove his palms forward, hitting Gilgamesh with a torrent of water that knocked the swords out of his hands. Before he could recover, Angel touched down, and then flew at him. He pulled his fist far back and yelled as loud as he could as he flew through the air. His fist was engulfed into a ball of blue energy before Angel hit Gilgamesh with everything he had.

Gilgamesh was freed from the icy hold and went sliding back along the floor, and then down to one knee. Quickly, Angel back flipped a few feet away, got into position, and began charging his final attack. He knew if the rumors were true and if Gilgamesh was indeed a god, then he had to attack without hesitation.

Move in quickly and hit hard, never giving him a chance to recover. That's what I have to do if I plan to win this fight. If I don't, then the fight could well be over in a split second. I refuse to fail. I cannot!

Gilgamesh lifted his head and smirked. He then flew forward. He broke Angel's guard with his right shoulder and began assaulting him with his three fists. They flew at Angel from multiple angles at blinding speed that he would've sworn he had more arms hidden under his cloak. However, his time in hell had not been a waste, as he found he was able to block and dodge the barrage with moderate ease. The blows he couldn't dodge he could block and did with constructs from Subzero's ice or Hades' bone.

The battle raged for some time. Neither side landing a finishing strike. Their power was obvious from each attack that reverberated off the walls.

Chains shot out from the ground behind Gilgamesh in an attempt to restrain his movements, but this proved futile as he laughed. He whistled and the swords he had dropped came to life and zipped around the room. They then swung down and broke the chains holding him. They floated around Gilgamesh for a moment as he stared down Angel. He raised his right arms and pointed toward him. Angel knew what was coming and began to back up. He then jumped backward as the swords zoomed toward him. He froze one sword in midair. Angel then tried to chain down another. However, the sword Widower swooshed and cut the chains down.

Angel formed a shield of bone on his left arm to deflect the third sword's strike. At the same time, he conjured a long whip of molten lava to strike back. He cracked the whip and snapped it deflecting the Fantasy Killer to the side. Angel swung the whip around his body and turned it into a flaming spear. Widower flew forward and swung multiple times, but Angel used the spear to block the strikes. Then from his right he caught a glimpse of Fantasy Killer's edge coming toward him. He managed to block it with his shield of ice. However, he didn't just block it. Upon impact, the ice grew around the sword and ensnared it. Angel shed the shield from his arm as he turned his entire focus onto the Fantasy Killer. Chains once again shot forth from the ground, but the sword evaded and deflected the attempts to bind it.

Angel suddenly felt the hairs on the back of his neck stand up. He glanced back over his shoulder and saw Gilgamesh looking at him. With a sudden blow to the side of his face, Angel was for the first time, knocked off his feet. Angel quickly got back to his feet and clapped his hands together. When he pulled them a part a wall of bone and ice came forth to shield him from the newly freed Jade Dragon and Fantasy Killer. Their blades becoming stuck in the wall. Angel flew over the construct and delivered a devastating onslaught upon Gilgamesh. Strikes strong enough to bust boulders rained against him as he blocked and guarded himself. Fire and ice, metal and bone; he saw it all come against him. Gilgamesh even thought that Angel had splashed him with water. Gilgamesh suddenly saw Angel vanish, only to re-emerge with a crushing hit his side, that was quickly followed by a thunderous blow that broke through his guard and smashed his chest. Gilgamesh's large frame slammed into the wall. It cracked and splintered. Angel got into position for his final attack.

"Mega——!" Blue energy began to swirl around his body, starting at his legs and making its way violently up.

"That is enough, Angel!" Gilgamesh stated firmly, still kneeling down on one knee, with his three arms holding his chest, where Angel had delivered the last devastating punch.

Angel continued to charge his attack. *What? No, it's a trick. It's got to be. No way that took him down.*

"Of course, it is a trick! Finish him, you fool!" Lazarus yelled at Angel.

Angel looked closely, trying to spot a hint of a trap, but Gilgamesh was showing no signs of moving.

"Are you serious? Are you being serious right now!?"

"Yes. I yield to you. Angel, it appears you have proven yourself. You will make a powerful general." Gilgamesh stood up. He collected his swords and put them back on the stand in their original order. Angel stood back, dumbfounded by the sudden end. He watched him intently, still half expecting for Gilgamesh to drop the facade and renew the bout.

Gilgamesh then picked up the sword that was at the bottom. "A good general must always have a trusty blade at his side. This is the 'Sword of the Phoenix'…," Gilgamesh trailed off, getting lost in thought. As he held the sword, a flood of memories came rushing back. Fond and happy memories, and tragic ones too.

Angel started stepping forward. "Gilgamesh?"

"Hmm? Oh sorry, here you may have it. She will serve you well on the field of battle." He walked over, presented it to Angel, and smiled. "From now on you are one of my knights, as Leen was."

"Leen? How?"

"She came by more often than you. She usually came over while you were working with her father or out training with your friends. We sat and talked about all sorts of different things. A lot of the time about you and what you were up to. I helped her with learning some more advanced forms of magic. She was a natural in the mystic and healing arts. She would have made a fine priestess. I always thought you two would get married. She and I talked about that day often."

Angel's gaze turned to the floor. "In a way, we had a bond similar to that already."

Gilgamesh smiled. "Yes, well, I hoped to be the one to unite you two."

"It would have been an honor to have you bless us."

Gilgamesh felt the warmth in his chest building. He had known them since they were small children and seen them grow over the years. Now one was lost, taken, no stolen was more accurate, and the other stood before him a man.

"Back to the sword. It is unique and possesses amazing powers. For starters, it's indestructible, so you don't have to be afraid to use your full strength. It is capable of traveling any length of distance to reunite with you, a nice security feature, so no one can easily steal it from you. And possibly most importantly, it serves as a link to me. If you ever need my help, hold the blade towards the sky and shout my name. No matter where you are, I will hear you and will come to your aid."

As Gilgamesh talked, Angel listened closely while at the same time was examining the mystical weapon now in his hands. The sheath was white with gold decorative clips at both ends. A gold rope hung from it so he could strap it to his side. The handle was covered in black leather with a gold trigger-like fixture attached.

"Gilgamesh, what is this for?" He held up the sword and pointing to the odd feature.

"Oh, that will fire the blade toward your target. Great for sneak attacks. The blade can return by a mere thought, or you can do it manually. Now, the sheath also has a purpose. It can put up a shield to protect you from such dangerous things like dark magic, or the forces of nature, for instance. Your sword has many other abilities, but to be honest, I do not recall them all. They will come instinctively to you over time as the bond between you and it grows."

Gilgamesh went on to explain as he watched Angel examine the sword, plainly seeing that he was in awe of its beauty and abilities. Much like its previous owner had been when he first received it so many eons ago.

Angel drew the sword out of its scabbard and looked at the steel to see from what it was forged. It was gorgeously adorned with a phoenix at the bottom of the blade on both sides, but also had symbols running partly up the blade. He held it outward and was amazed by the balance and the sheer lightness of it. The steel it was crafted from he had never seen before. Like the metal of the medallion he now wore, it was alien to him.

"What is this steel, Gilgamesh? It's not Utopian in origin."

"No, the greatest metal worker forged it on my old planet, galaxies away from here." Gilgamesh smiled, again seeming to recall old memories.

"Whoever he was, he does superb work." Angel complimented as he re-sheathed the sword.

"Thank you."

Angel looked up at him. "You did this?"

"I collect swords of great history and value, but I also enjoy making swords with a universal uniqueness to them. That sword is my best work. I haven't been able to make anything that can top it, yet." He smirked under his mask as he slanted his head.

"Thank you, again. Tell me, could you possibly identify what this medallion is made of? I um… found it on the way here."

Angel did not want to get into where he actually got the strange necklace. It would probably be hard to believe in the first place, but might mean that Gilgamesh would see it as disproving his worthiness to lead since he was helped along the way. Gilgamesh took the medallion into his hand and felt over the intricately designed trinket.

"It's definitely Utopian in origin, generally speaking." He let it fall back onto Angel's chest. "It's Asgardian metal. Very tough. It will not be broken by any mortal means. You found it, you say?" Gilgamesh looked at Angel, not believing the story.

"I glanced down as I rested, the gleaming metal caught my attention, and there it was. I thought it looked cool, so I kept it." Angel spun his tale. Trying to make it sound believable.

"I see. Well then, you are a very lucky person. First you get the position of Planetary General, then you find this necklace, and sometime between that and making your way through my traps you gained or somehow awoke these amazing powers of fire, water, ice, bone, and spikes. Especially surprising when I recall you were not one to put much stock in the mystical arts. That was Leen's forte. And now you have this amazing blade at your command," Gilgamesh spoke in such a tone that let Angel know he was not fooling him any. He was no fool and Angel felt ashamed for trying to conceal the truth from his friend.

"Listen, Gilgamesh, I mean no disrespect," Angel started, but he stopped when Gilgamesh placed his hand on his shoulder.

"Angel, it doesn't matter how you got these powers, nor how you came upon this necklace. Something tells me it belongs with you. You have been given a chance to punish those who did wrong here today. I don't need to know the details now, but perhaps when this is all over, you will feel more comfortable telling me." Gilgamesh smiled. "Just know that even if you had told me now, I still would have considered you more than worthy to have this sword and lead this army."

"Thank you, and when this is over, I will tell you what happened tonight, but right now, I must go. I have to get back before dawn."

Angel tied the sword to his belt with the gold rope.

"Alright. Well, go through that door. It will take you safely outside," Gilgamesh pointed towards the wall to the right, where a doorway magically appeared.

"Um, Gilgamesh, I don't want to sound rude, but… you didn't put up much of a fight."

Gilgamesh laughed. "Well, Angel, I look at it this way. You have somehow gained powers that technically you shouldn't have. The real test was getting past my traps. I was watching as you did, so you passed. In truth, you proved yourself worthy to me back when we first met. I knew then you had a lot of potential in you. Besides, you had to have something special if you had little Leen falling for you."

"Still, though, you didn't give me much of a challenge. You are, according to legend, a god and yet… I beat you."

"Well, I didn't want to beat you too badly because you do have to get back. The Utopian army needs a worthy leader, which you are. Besides, I just woke up, still a little tired. Now get going. Leen's death needs avenging." Gilgamesh patted Angel's back. "Oh, one more thing. I just remembered, don't ever worry about having to sharpen or clean the blade. It never dulls and it never rusts. Even if you were to forget it at the bottom of an ocean, it would never lose its edge. Though, if you do that, I will hunt you down and kill you," Gilgamesh said teasingly, but with an underlining tone that told Angel he was not completely kidding.

"And, Gilgamesh…"

"Yes?"

"I am sorry for destroying your two gargoyles."

Gilgamesh let out a soft laugh. "Don't concern yourself with them. They've already been restored to life."

Angel nodded and took off through the door and down a brief corridor.

Upon exiting the temple, Angel gripped the hilt of the sword. He could feel its mysterious energies flowing up his arm. He smiled with the sense of pride for accomplishing what he was sent out to do. Coming down the steps, he saw Arieta huddled up against a statue, sound asleep. Cory and Cogeta sat beside her. Upon seeing their friend, they smiled with relief.

Cory moved to wake Arieta, but Angel stopped him. Angel quietly and gently lifted her up into his arms. The group then started back. It wasn't until they were nearly halfway through the woods that she began to stir. Angel had been telling them about what he saw inside the temple, but their conversation came to a pause when Arieta began to wake up.

"Shhh, you don't have to wake up. We're almost home." He said softly in a warm, comforting tone.

"Angel?" Arieta yawned.

"Told you I'd be back. How long was I gone this time?"

"Heh, too long. I got bored and fell asleep. Did you get what you went for?"

"Yep, got my proof." Angel smiled.

"May I see it?" Arieta asked, excited to see what he got.

"Sure." He set her down, released his sword from his belt, and handed carefully over to her. As she looked it over, the other two looked at it as well.

"Wow… it's pretty," As she held the handle, it began to warm up. "Whoa, that's kind of cool. The handle is warming up rather quickly."

"Oh?" Angel took hold of it beneath her hand. As he did, the handle returned to normal.

"Huh, it just went away when you touched it." Arieta said quizzically.

"Might be a defense mechanism. Gilgamesh told me that this sword had a lot of special abilities, but that I would have to learn them for myself.

I'll tell you all about what I saw inside as we walk you home."

Starting once more from when he entered the temple, he regaled his friends about his adventure within and how he won his prize. At last, they came to the front of her house. It was late, though nearly morning, but all were still asleep in the nearby houses. Most importantly, her home appeared quiet, no lights were on, so they hoped her father had been able to get some rest.

"Alright, this is where I have to leave you… again. I have to return to the encampment and show them the sword as proof. This is probably going to be the last time we see each other for a long while, so take care of yourself and your father."

"I will, and you be careful, too. All of you." She looked at each one individually. Wanting to burn their faces in her mind, as this may be the last time she saw them together.

"Of course." Cogeta smiled, trying to be reassuring. Cory joined him with a nod.

"We will, and one other thing I would like to ask you to do while I am gone. Visit Leen a little every day for me. I will try to keep in touch as much as I can, but I need you to do this for me."

"Of course, but you better write often, so I can tell Leen all about your victories and how you are doing."

Angel nodded. "Of course I will."

"May we write you too?" Cogeta asked with a small grin.

Arieta smiled softly and nodded. "Yes, of course. Please do, I'd like that."

She smiled faintly, pushed herself up onto her tiptoes, and kissed Angel's left cheek. She then gave Cogeta and Cory a tight hug. Hating the fact she had to let them leave. She turned around and went inside without another word. Arieta closed the door quietly and leant up against it, holding her arms across her chest. She did not want them to see her tears as they began to flow. Arieta had barely got to know her mother before she passed. She had just lost her sister, now to top it off, the one person who she could relate to was leaving her as well.

Angel was completely unaware of her inner turmoil as he headed off with the others. They went back through the woods towards the encampment. Along the way, he made a quick detour since he still had some time. Unaware where their friend was leading them, Cory and Cogeta followed along. They came out onto a grassy ledge overlooking the campsite and the great white palace of the Emperor. The warm glow of the sun peeked over the horizon as Angel looked on, joined by his best friends on either side. It was there he told them of his adventure in Hell, leaving out the more horrific parts, including the game of chess where he had to order the deaths of his friends. They listened intently, not sure what to say.

Cogeta broke the silence first, as he often was, "So, you made pacts with actual demons. Are they able to control you?"

Angel gave a slight nod. "It's possible for them to take control. They have a time or two to block an attack I didn't see coming. But it doesn't seem an easy feat for them to do. It's a mutual pact. They used me as a ferryman of sorts to get them out of Hell. In return, they give me access to their powers." Angel lifts his left hand engulfed in flame and then his right coated in ice to display just a couple of those powers. When he lowers them a moment later, they are back to normal. His friends stared. A look of some amazement on their faces.

Cory spoke up. "Amazing. I mean, I can sense that your aura has changed some. Certainly more powerful than it was before. How does it feel when you use their powers?" His scientific mind showing itself as he tried to piece what his friend was going through. "Does it hurt when you call on them?"

"No, it doesn't hurt. In fact, their powers give me more resistance to that element. For instance, Cogeta, burn me with your fire." Angel requested, pushing his sleeve up and holding out his arm.

Cogeta looked at his friend but having trust that Angel knew what he was talking about, he obliged. His hand ignited with bright orange flames. He then focused the flames on just the tip of two fingers and held them under his friend's arm. A moment passed, and Angel didn't react. His skin wasn't even turning red.

"See?" Angel asked. "Don't feel a thing. I don't know the limits of it just yet. But these powers will certainly come in handy when I face Serkuma."

Cory grimaced. "They may seem like gifts now, but be careful. They may come at a great price. Over use them and the demons may take control of you more readily... perhaps."

Angel heard the soft chuckling from a few of the demons within. "He's a good friend to worry. But we aren't interested in taking control of your body. I prefer my own just fine." Inferno jested.

"You needn't worry. I'll be careful. I wanted to tell you both about what happened because you two are really the only true friends I have. There has always been an air of distrust around me, and you two never seemed to buy into it. Once I start using these powers, I'm sure rumors will spread. I would rather you knew it from me rather than through idle hearsay."

Cogeta laughed. "You got nothing to worry about. Sure, we've always heard the outlandish tales about you, but we knew the real you. And, if the roles were different, I would gather as much power as I could as well. Wouldn't give much thought to where it was coming from. Thank you for sharing this with us. I'm sure Cory will agree. We'll keep this secret to ourselves." Cogeta over to Cory, who nodded in agreement.

Angel nodded and shook both their hands. "So, who are you two serving under?"

"I got stuck with General Barkley." Cogeta answered first.

"And I'm with General Marrow," Cory replied while slipping his hands into his pockets. His fingers on his right hand slowly tracing some cracks on his handheld.

Angel nodded as he made a mental note of the information. Both generals were well seasoned and had served Sparticus for many an age. He worried about resentment towards him for being chosen so abruptly to become their leader. However, that was what the trial to Gilgamesh's temple was to help resolve. It disappointed him, however, that neither of his closest friends had been put under his direct command. Fear of a conflict of interest. Sure, he could understand to some degree, however, he knew he wouldn't have   treated them any differently than others. Angel felt he treated them as fairly as he treated everyone else in the fighting team.

Cogeta could sense the gears turning in his friend's mind. He reached out and put a hand on Angel's shoulder. "Now don't go getting any ideas about having either of us transferred."

Angel looked at his friend. "The thought crossed my mind."

Cogeta laughed. "Well, let it pass on through. As great as it would be, if you did that, it would undermine the loyalty of others. It would look like to them you were showing favoritism. We got to stand on our own, build our reputations, achieve our own honors, follow our own destinies."

Angel nodded. He understood what his friend was saying. It was every warrior's dream to earn honor and prestige through their deeds. In times of peace, this would've been done through tournaments, or great hunts. In times of war, their bravery and valor would garner them accolades and solidify their name in history. More importantly, to some, it would guarantee a place in Odin's great hall in the afterlife. It would be harder for his friends to achieve this if they were lost in his shadow.

"Besides, our bonds of friendship could never be broken. No matter how far apart we are." Cogeta grinned ear to ear. "Just be sure to stay in touch."

Cory grimaced. He withdrew his small handheld computer from his pocket. "Going to be rather hard to do with this thing in its current state."

"Dang! Dude, what happened? You never break your stuff." Cogeta asked, taking the device from his friend.

"I think it broke when I fell. I managed to send a message out... but... of course, I never got a reply."

Cogeta struggled to get the thing to function. But he managed to flip through some screens. Not trying to be nosey, but he couldn't resist. He saw who the last person he sent a message to was.

Of course it would be to Alisandra. He thought as he saw Cory had asked if she was okay, if she was safe. She hadn't replied. He scrolled through the message logs. More messages sent from Cory showed up on the right side in dark grey bubbles. They ranged from asking how she was, how her day was going, if she had seen the latest episodes of some show he'd never heard of. The messages were spread out between several days and weeks. But not one had been responded to. Then he saw a message from her a few weeks back on the left side of the screen in a blue bubble. She wanted to know if she could borrow his notes for a class. Scrolling up some more, he found other messages from her. Each time she was asking to borrow notes, a textbook, answers to questions from the end of lesson's chapter. *Oh, Cory... she's just using you. Surely you can see that. Of course you can. You're not an idiot. You're smitten with her and can't deny her. You want to be her knight. There to help her.*

"Surprised you had her number. Were you able to sense her aura at least?" Cogeta asked.

Cory nodded. "Yeah, she had given it to me a few years back when she and I were lab partners. Made sense to stay in touch while working on the project. I could sense her aura, so I know she's alive. Just probably very busy with all this craziness."

Angel and Cogeta shared a quick glance. Angel then looked at Cory and smiled. "Are you going to be able to fix that?"

Cory took the device back. "I think I can. Just got to get the parts." Cory turned his gaze back to the encampment. "Perhaps this may be good for me. You guys are always telling me she isn't good for me. Here is my chance. Out of sight, out of mind. Right? Should have no problem with the out of sight part." He halfheartedly laughed.

Cogeta stepped in and threw his arm around Cory. "Who knows, maybe you will find a lovely alien girl. She'll be super smart, beauty to match. Probably tendrils for hair. Tentacles for lips."

"What?!" Cory jerked away and looked at Cogeta in complete bewilderment. "Why she got to have tentacle lips? That's so... just no." He started laughing, joining Angel and Cogeta, who were already chuckling.

The three friends shared what could possibly be their last laugh together. Angel was the first to stop and looked out at the sun. He didn't want to see his friends go. He wished they were going with him, as he knew he would be stronger with them by his side. With a heavy heart, he looked at his friends.

"You two should probably get back to your camps. They will start mobilizing soon, so should try to get some rest. Tomorrow brings a whole new venture for us. You two better keep yourselves safe. Stay alive."

Cogeta smiled. "Of course, man. You better do the same."

Cory, not wanting to show them his fear, put on a smile of his own. Though it wasn't as convincing as Cogeta's. "I will."

"You gotta. You can't go dying, being you find that tentacle girl." Angel jested.

"Agh, shut up!" Cory chuckled. He gave his friends one last hug and started on his way.

Cogeta and Angel both watched as he leapt down from the ledge and began making his trek back. Cogeta was suddenly feeling conflicted. He glanced over at Angel, then back down at Cory. Should he share his concerns with Angel, or keep them to himself, he pondered. He knew Angel already had a lot on his mind and was already going to be stressed out by his new found duties.

Angel could sense something was troubling his otherwise cheery friend by how silent he had become. "Everything okay, Cogeta? Aside from the obvious things that are not. What's troubling you?"

Cogeta let out a sigh and then smiled. "Just preparing for the crap ahead. And it's going to be a lot of crap."

Angel laughed. "Yeah. That's for sure. Just be safe out there, okay? Don't do anything too wild."

"Who? Me? Angel, don't forget that I'm the Greatest. You best be on your guard. You may be the new Planetary General, but legends are about to be made with my name spreading across the galaxy. My enemies will shake in fear, and the ladies will run to my sides upon seeing me." He joked as he reached out and gently bumped Angel's chest with his fist. "Yeah, you best believe I'm going to show everyone my greatness knows no limits."

"Just be sure to keep your head on your shoulders." Angel continued to chuckle.

"Will do. And you do the same, my friend." Cogeta wrapped his arms around his close friend and hugged him tight, then eased off and patted his back. Before Angel could say anymore, he took his leave, jumping down from the ledge and running off in the direction Cory had gone.

After Cogeta had disappeared from view, Angel watched as the light divided the camp, making a bright pathway down the center. Remembering everything he had recently gone through, he took a solemn moment.

"If you're there Odin, watch over my friends." he smirked, feeling a little silly, but then focused his gaze on the path that the light was creating through the camp. "That is the road I must walk now. I wish we could walk it together, Leen. But I know," he paused, his emotions building up and threatening to burst forth. "I know you are with me in spirit and in my heart. No one can truly take you away. We will meet again in Valhalla. I guess I better not keep them waiting. As you used to say,"

"The path to a brighter future begins with only one simple step forward. All you need is the courage to take it." He heard her in voice.

Angel wiped his eyes one last time with his hand and gripped his sword ever so tightly.

From here on, I must be strong. I cannot let the men see me shed these tears or else they will think I was weak and unfit to lead. I will avenge you, Leen, my love.

Without wasting another minute, he jumped off the side of the cliff to begin his journey.

CHAPTER 21

CONQUEST OF BLOOD

Deep somewhere in the black void of space, a huge armada of ships cruised slowly through the sea of stars. Menacing in design, they were black with jagged edges and long points. They were made to strike fear in those who saw them. The sizes of the ships ranged from medium to gigantic, hulking metal beasts. Their smaller ships were used mainly to store spare supplies when there was not room for the others. Their larger size spacecrafts were carriers, home to several hundred well-trained soldiers and two hundred crew members and made up most of the fleet. The largest of the space spacecrafts that housed a couple thousand soldiers, a few hundred crew members, and small squads of bat shaped fighters. On board each ship, there was a grand celebration going on, for they had just left a successful surprise strike on an enemy planet. They had crushed their morale, slaughtered thousands, and crippled their military bases. The soldiers sprayed bottles of a thick red beverage all over themselves and each other. They cheered and guzzled down gallons of the party's refreshments. This was the Vampirian army, and they were celebrating their victory over Utopia.

Their leader was on board his flagship, celebrating with his generals over the successful ambush. They sat at a long dark metallic table within a similar style room. It was dimly lit, but was sparsely decorated. There was a dark red carpet leading to the table with Serkuma's coat of arms. The table itself had a matching tablecloth with a twelve-branch candelabra. Along the wall to the right of the door were several glass panels, giving a scenic view of the black sea outside. However, at the moment, it was also showing the massive fleet at Serkuma's command.

At the head of the table, Serkuma sat in a large chair, decorated ornately to symbolize power, while the other chairs around were visibly less imposing and less decorative. They still, however, were well-crafted pieces. Serkuma sat wearing his dark violet formal attire. As he had a pale woman, scantily clad, pour him another glass of blood, the red beverage that they all drank in excess, one of his generals, a Count, spoke up with a confident young man's voice.

"Lord Serkuma, as great as today was, I cannot help thinking if a few of the men might think of it as a loss. After all, when the Utopian army countered struck, we retreated."

Serkuma grinned, looking out from over the edge of his silver goblet. "My dear Count, it was not a retreat, least of all a loss. We did as we set out to do. We struck their ports, their factories, and their military bases. Those were our targets. The citizens we killed along the way were bonuses, like the rich icing on top of a cake." He took a sip from his goblet of gold and ornately decorated with the designs of his ancestors passed, and jewels.

"And what of this boy you tormented? That you killed his wench right in front of him and not him is troublesome. History has shown that such things have proved catastrophic. It's as if you are testing fate. I know if you had killed my wife, had I one, and assuming I gave two cents about her, I would want you dead as well."

One general at the table looked at the Count when he made that statement, but went back to drinking quietly.

Serkuma just raised an eyebrow before laughing loudly, "Count Victor, as funny as it is to envision you in "love" with a woman let alone care for one, I must truly laugh at your suggestion that I would fall into that catastrophic scenario you speak of. I only allowed the runt to live for fun. This war would grow boring without someone hunting me. Vengeance is a powerful driving force, and I chose him to be my ultimate opponent. I look forward to meeting him again, if for nothing more than to see if history will uphold its unwritten law."

"What law is that, sire?" Spoke one general who sat to the right of Serkuma. His voice was low but clear, and his gaze was chilling.

"Strider, were you not paying attention to Count Victor?" Asked Serkuma sarcastically, looking over to his second in command.

"Only when he has something intelligent to say, this has yet to happen." Strider glanced at Victor, smiling as Victor glared back, while Serkuma laughed.

"Oh, Strider, you are amusing. Victor mentioned that history has shown that those who have a score to settle are victorious. I want to test the law that history repeats itself. With this Dark's help, I will find out. You say I am testing fate? My dear Victor, I am outright challenging it. At the very least, knowing the name of one man out there who has sworn to kill me will keep me entertained. This entire campaign would probably bore me otherwise. Besides, I highly doubt that he will be the only one wishing to drive a dagger through my black heart."

Serkuma grinned. "It was entertaining to see the despair in his eyes. The shattering of his soul as he watched his wench die before him, helpless to save her. I enjoyed it immensely." Serkuma paused and reveled in the pleasure that moment brought back to him. "Now then gentlemen, and my lovely succubi," he smiled over at the only two female generals sitting beside each other at the dining table, "are there any other questions before we move on?" He paused a moment and glanced around the table. When no one spoke up, he continued,

"Alright then, we already have over one-hundred thousand men stationed on the planet Teris. It is close enough to Utopia that it will serve as a nice buffer. We have a strong fortress setup there, left over from the Nebulian-Utopian wars, so it will be a while before those dogs overcome it. I know that it will be lost in time, but they will have served their purpose. Now then, I have been going over star-charts and have decided on the following planets and sectors to attack. Some have strategic value, while some are simply land that can be owned. If nothing else, the latter will make us look bigger, stronger, and ultimately play as somewhat of a decoy for any army to waste their time to regain. The planets I want under my rule are Drax, Stokely, Scatix, Germise, Ravi, Peeris, and Tactis. The two sectors are Sectors 12T, and Q9. Any questions thus far? I have a base already underway on Mardook, but I want more men stationed there. Yes, Lazaar?" Serkuma paused and acknowledged the general that raised his hand at this point.

"Drax is inhabited by an extremely hostile race. They will be a tough one to subdue. Sector 12T is nothing more than an asteroid field. Mardook might as well be considered a death trap. I'm surprised anyone would agree to go there."

"Where do we begin? First off, indeed, Mardook is a barren wasteland, barely inhabited by those who live there now. Nevertheless, it will be and is a suitable location for a communication station. In fact, Count Victor already has some men stationed there, few but enough to keep a town under control while his scientists work sleeplessly on my special project I have him on. The Utopians wouldn't look there because of the extreme heat during the day. They will believe that it would be pointless to station any men there because of our weakness to sunlight, even more reason why I have them hidden there. Men would do anything if you promised them riches and women... but you all know that already."

Serkuma smiled as he looked at each general. A few chuckles were heard, but quickly silenced.

"Sector 12T is an asteroid field," Serkuma continued," and I believe it will be great for camouflage, can easily hide a fleet or two in stealth on a few large asteroids. It's territory and I want it. For Drax, I know those blasted lizards are reluctant to be ruled over, but I want them to know the might of the Vampirian race. We are the superiors. I want them to be my slaves. I am not disillusioned that this will be an easy fight. It will be a hard one. However, I am confident that my armies, that my generals, can handle it. Is that a good enough explanation for you? I realize it is not common for leaders such as I to tell you the purpose of such things, let alone allow you to ask questions, but I want you to see that I am… considerate." Serkuma sat in his massive chair, smiling wickedly.

Lazaar nodded. "Last question, it seems we are spreading ourselves thin —"

"We will not be. We have more than enough men to spare. Besides, I will only have you send a portion of your forces with a few officers, while I send you elsewhere. For the time being, we'll only worry about those planets that have a central city of power. We'll occupy it, fortify ourselves, and control the planet from there. I will worry about the planets that are backwater'd in their ways and have more than a singular seat of power. That's just one headache we can avoid for now. If things go as I plan by the time we aim our sights on them, we will have such a force that none will stand against us."

Count Victor spoke up again, "Pardon me, sire, but it is bugging me. Why didn't we push ahead and seize Utopia when we had a chance?"

"That is simple. I want to savour their defeat. For the longest they have had a reputation of being one of the strongest forces in the universe. I would feel disappointed and feel I missed out on something truly worthwhile if I crushed them in such an underhanded attack. My goal was to cripple them, kick the beehive, and rile them up. I did just that. If at any time you think you are a more competent leader than I, please step up."

"No, sir, I didn't mean it in such a way."

"Of course, you didn't, Victor. I realize it is a bit… foolish of me to not crush them now, but it's still how I wish to go about this. The Utopians will provide me a little more entertainment. They are an arrogant race, and I look forward to smacking them down. Had we pressed forward and conquered them, the victory would've been hollow given the manner in which we achieved it. No, if we are to truly prove that we, the Vampirian race, are superior, we must defeat them in open battle.

Moving on, here are your targets. Pay attention. Grizor, I want you to invade Scatix. Trista, you go to planet Peeris. Lazaar, you will go to the planet Tactis. Count Victor, I want you to send part of your army and take Germise. It should be an easy victory. Send an extra three thousand troops to Mardook. I want that place defended, so send some of your best men. Keep the rest with you and continue working on your project, and report all breakthroughs to me immediately. If the town was larger, I would say send more, but three thousand should do it.

Calwine, send part of your army to Sector Q9 and then go to these people and see if they are willing to join our cause." Serkuma slid him a manila folder, then continued. "Count Laughastein, send part of you army to Sector Q9 as well, the rest set on standby and you may go back to… sharpening your interrogation skills on those in room B9." Count Laughastein grinned to himself at this news while Serkuma continued, "Jackle, I want you to take part of your army, and Creach, part of your army, and send them to the planet Drax. Jackle, you then take the rest of your forces and go "recruit" more "volunteers" from Va-Blood to join our noble cause.

Dista, you, and half your forces will remain at my castle with Victor, the other half joining with half of Monty's men and attack planet Stokely. Monty and Creach, you two will join your partial forces with Sagert's full force and fly together, as you go,make our presence known. Try to make some friends. Anyone willing to bow down to us will do. The main thing is to appear powerful. If they refuse to join, you blow a few buildings up. If that doesn't do it, well... make them regret their decision.

Zeth, I want you and your entire force to go to Sector 12T. Strider, you will head to the outer planets in this direction, looking for easy alliances. As for myself, I will head to the planet Ravi and enslave them personally. I believe that is everyone," Serkuma lightly laughed, "Therefore, finish your last cup and head out. You are to report in when something of importance takes place, otherwise transmission silence. Dismissed." Serkuma gulped down the last of the blood that was in his goblet.

The generals all stood up, placed their right fist over their hearts, and bowed before taking their leave. Only Strider and one other man remained in the room with Serkuma.

"I dislike having no destination of a planet to kill, and what of him?" Strider pointed to a mysterious man who had been standing in the far-left corner the entire time. He had remained silent the entire meeting, nor did he partake of any beverages.

"Do not trouble yourself with him. He is just a left hand, as you are my right hand. As far as not having a precise destination, you will have one soon. I am just not sure which planet to take in that direction. I plan to rule it all. But for now, I must weigh the pros and cons of each, rather bothering and inconvenient, I must say." Serkuma teased, but it satisfied Strider's curious mind and, after saluting, he took his leave.

As the slave girl went to refill Serkuma's goblet, his hand slowly took hers and brought it to his warm lips. Kissing the back of her hand first, he moved down to her wrist. Then turned it over and kissed the inside of her palm. When he had kissed his way back to her wrist, he placed a small peck on her skin before sinking his fangs into her veins. The girl fell to her knees helplessly as Serkuma feasted on her. All the while, the mysterious man dressed in all black stood silently watching. Once he had his fill, Serkuma pushed the girl away.

"I do prefer it fresh from the source. What do you think?"

"I do not need drink or food to live," said the man in black, in a low voice.

"What about women? Do you enjoy them? Let's see, our agreement was you would get the chance to kill that man, wasn't it? Is that truly all you want? I will gladly give you a great discount on stock, my old friend."

"You can keep your women. Sell them off as you intend to do. I don't care. I want my revenge on the one who destroyed my life."

"There is a lot of that going around, it seems." Serkuma took a deep breath, smiling with pride. "I'm going to turn so many lives upside down. To be able to affect so many, that's true power." Serkuma laughed whole-heartedly. "It's going to be glorious. And when it is over, the universe will bow at my feet. Knowing that the Vampirians are superior to all races that exist now, in the past, and that have yet to have been spawned."

The man in black stared at Serkuma, his plans of universal dominance and enslavement mattering little to him. His goal was far simpler, to crush the skull of the man who humiliated him so many years ago.

∅∅1 Ut⊕pia

U t ⊕ p i a n s
The Pe⊕ple

The people from the planet Utopia, although mostly humanoid in appearance, possess incredible strength, speed, agility, intelligence and regenerative capabilities. Along with such inherent attributes, they also can transform into a wolf at will. They have two different transformations: a gestalt form and then a full transformation. These wolves are very large and the color of their fur varies from person to person.

One thing that distinguishes them from humanoids in physical appearance is their long, fine-furred tails. Most either wrap them around their waists like a fur belt, let them freely trail behind, or hide them from view entirely. The tail is a very sensitive part of their anatomy. It contains many nerves within it, making the tail very responsive to such things as pleasure and pain to vast degrees of either. Despite this, it is strong enough to be used to grab or hold things for a lengthy period. Some Utopians have even learned to use it as a weapon during a fight. The tail acts as a separate entity at times, moving on its own as if it had a brain. Training to control one's tail is done at an early age.

Another important thing that is inherent to Utopians is the rate of their growth and aging. Within several months of being born, they will have grown to their full height, and appear to be in either their early or late twenties. From then on, their growth and aging slows down drastically. Allowing an elder Utopian to appear to be merely

in his early fifties, when in actuality he could be well nearing his
fifty-millionth birthday, give or take a few hundred thousand years.
Their years are much longer than Earth's standards, and their
bodies are slow to deteriorate. Being a race that thrives on battle, it
is in their genes to be in their prime for as long as they can.

They are born with the skill to fly without assistance; though not
fast at first. The same force that allows them to fly also gives them
the ability to shoot bursts of energy from their hands. Some have
even learned to channel this energy so that it is usable from other
parts of their body, such as their eyes, and or out their mouth. With
enough time and effort into honing this power, it is possible to
release a blast capable of turning lush landscapes into barren
wastelands. There are stories told of those who are so powerful
that they can destroy planets and solar systems. As destructive as it
is, the energy can also protect one's self or others by forming
shields.

The last ability that I shall mention is the ability to regenerate
their wounds at an accelerated rate. The time varies depending on
the severity of the wound. If one were to lose an arm, it would take
several minutes to grow back if unhindered. However, if one were
unfortunate to lose one's tail in a fight, it would take years for it to
grow back to the length that it was. Through focus and
concentration, one can increase the healing rate, but it causes much
discomfort to rush a major injury.

THE CULTURE

Their culture is based on one monarch ruling over the entire
planet, simply called the Emperor. He has as two official advisors,
the High Councilman and Planetary General. The Emperor is only
chosen through one bloodline and has been through the same blood
since the beginning of the planet's history appointed by the heavens.

If no male heir is obtained during the ruler's reign, then the High Councilman rules until the closest relative in the bloodline is found. If none is found, then the High Councilman will perform a ceremony asking their lord to bring them their next Emperor, though luckily this has not yet been necessary.

The High Councilman handles all matters that deal with religion and law-making. He is part of the jury with other councilmen, who walk the path of righteousness and study diligently in solitude within a temple near the palace. The other councilmen all hope of one day being selected as the next High Councilman should the present one pass on. The judge in court is the Emperor himself. All major cases are brought to the Emperor in the imperial city, while full-fledged council members and those in training are sent out to deal with minor cases that the minor officials cannot handle.

The High Councilman lives inside the palace and is constantly busy with something, either with holy preparations for coming festivals and sacred offerings, or with hearing and helping the citizens with some of their troubles. He gives the Emperor holy advice and tells him what the signs from the heavens say. The same man has held the position as High Councilman since the first Emperor was crowned. Rumors speculate he is only still alive because of science and magic, but these are unconfirmed. However, as a man of high status, many Utopians dislike him for his attitude and unjust, strict actions. These voices are kept quiet in fear of his holy wrath and power. Many others disagree, citing all the good that he has done for the people over the ages and arguing that he passes strict punishments on those who break the laws and endanger others. Those on that side of the debate see him as a wise, holy man who is just trying to do the right thing while others try to make names for themselves by disgracing someone whom they envy.

The Planetary General is the one in charge of all the armies of

Utopia. It is a position of significant responsibility. The Planetary General is honored and respected all over Utopia. He takes his orders from the Emperor directly, but he's also obligated to obey the High Councilman's orders as well. He controls his own army, independent of the armies of the generals ranking below him. Typically, eight generals serve under the Planetary General.

He gives military advice to the Emperor when it is called for when in royal meetings. In the history of Utopia, there have been over twenty different Planetary Generals, the current one being Sparticus. Sparticus has earned respect throughout all Utopia for being general during the longest and most debated war in Utopian history, the Nebulian-Utopian Wars. Ask either side and they will say they won, but the wisest and the ones willing to admit truth know it was a draw, and they made a truce to end the carnage.

The planet has many armies formed and stationed on both major continents, at sea, and even underground with bunkers and other facilities. The Planetary General's army is separate from the primary force, as mentioned before, and is given to the general as a sign of status. Even during times of peace, he can call on them for whatever reason. They act as bodyguards for the Planetary General, a selected few accompanying him on trips, or to public festivals.

The largest Planetary General army to date has been 450,000 strong. This record is held by Sparticus. Normally, Planetary General armies don't exceed 250,000, the same number assigned to them when they are given the position. However, at the approval of a court hearing, one may switch to join another general's army. The reason Sparticus gained so many troops by proving his worth repeatedly in service to the Emperor, who granted him requests of small additions to his forces over the years.

Then there are armies led by his generals, which the Planetary

General controls in times of war by commanding the generals. Typically, their ranks are a minimum of 100,000 soldiers. During times of peace, they place these soldiers on standby and are free to do as they please until called in during wartime. Unlike the planetary army, they cannot be called on at any time to serve during times of peace other than to serve a season of guard duty at a base.

The Emperor and High Councilman have their own armies, though only in dire need may the Planetary General call upon them for service under his command. Their troops are the elite of the elite, outfitted with the latest battle armaments. The Emperor's army exceeds 600,000 men. They rotate from season to season, so that every man serves his time. At any point during the year, the Emperor has 300,000 elite troops at his disposal, ready for action. The High Councilman has roughly 500,000 troops, which are kept on standby and are rarely seen by the public.

Their military strength has been secured and untested since the end of the war with Nebula, the technological tycoon planet. Utopians prefer close combat, specializing in what would be considered a medieval style of warfare. Though they seem old-fashioned, in close quarters combat they are far superior as stronger materials are used to create their weapons and armor. Their spacecrafts are masterfully built and always ready for intergalactic battles. Also, the advanced troops have upgraded to laser and photon-based weapons.

The Utopian forces are not to be trifled with, as many throughout the galaxies already know. In the past, they were very ferocious on the battlefields, taking no prisoners, bathing the ground in the blood of their adversaries without remorse. They left no survivors. However, since the Nebulian-Utopian Wars, and the dawning of a new Emperor, they have reverted their ways and have been living peacefully with their neighboring planets.

The people of Utopia live in homes ranging from small villages to large cities. Their jobs vary from farmers to blacksmiths to teachers and lawyers, much like on Earth. Usually, everyone gets along with one another, and even helps each other if asked. Men tend to hold the higher positions and those requiring the most backbreaking labor, whereas women work as priestesses, nurses, or stay at home to run things there. That is not to say that some women do not have high-status jobs, it is simply not a normal thing, and should a woman gain such status, she is treated with the highest of respect from those around.

Utopians prefer to walk or fly to get to where they need to go, always enjoying the adventure and beauty of their journey. The rich can have a stagecoach prepared for them to travel in. There are no automobiles to congest the streets and pollute the air. To cross bodies of water, there are fusion-powered boats filled with lavish luxuries. Tickets to travel are affordable to the commonest of men. Once the ticket is bought and the person is settled in their room, all the food, drink and entertainment is free, so that one may relax and enjoy one's trip. Airports are typically for trade, while intergalactic travel is reserved for military and business use. Only those with enough money saved have a chance to travel to another planet for a vacation. However, there are special loans and discounts one can get if the trip is for business, study, or for special occasions.

People throughout the planet believe in and worship Odin and his fellow gods throughout the planet. All the young and brash warriors talk about and look forward to going to Valhalla and serving in Odin's army. While women dream of becoming maidens in Odin's court or becoming a part of Freya's Valkyries (also called Dis) to gather the fallen and bring them to Asgard. Festivals, parades, and sacrificial ceremonies are held in honor of the gods several times throughout the year. In the past, female sacrifices were

a normal event at some ceremonies, but with the "New Coming",
such practices have all but ceased in mainstream culture. Though a
few cling to the old ways, they do it far from the public's eyes in
secrecy, in forests and caves. The new tradition is to simply slice the
right hand of the maiden and let her blood pour into the Goblet of
Offers. This goblet is then placed on the altar before a statue of the
god or goddess being honored at the time, with smaller goblet
offerings placed before other deities.

Other than the Asgardian gods, they pay homage to a mysterious
being known as Gilgamesh, whose temple crashed into the forest
north of the capital city Utop many eons ago. It's believed to be the
temple of a god because of the foreign architecture, the alien stone
used, and the fact that it fell from the sky. The Utopians began to
perform a ceremony where they would send two young virgin
maidens into the temple with gifts, ranging from large pearls of the
sea to paintings by the greatest artists to gold and jewels from the
richest mines. The Emperor recites a similar speech each year in
front of the temple with the High Councilmen and other attendees in
hopes of his mercy and his blessings for the gifts. It is well known
that the ceremony was established because, throughout time, brave
men wanting to know who or what was inside the temple have
ventured in, but none has ever returned.

Then one day, as the myth goes, a virgin maiden from a village
from across the continent ventured into the temple. She was seeking
help for her ailing father and younger brothers. A young warrior and
priest went with her to witness if she could do it. The two waited
for her on the steps of the temple, and after several agonizing hours,
she finally emerged, alive and well, with a smile on her face and
tears in her eyes. She neither saw anyone nor encountered any
corpses of past adventurers. However, she heard a voice, and that
voice told her to take the vile of blue potion she saw before her. It
then told her to give a drop of the potion, no more, no less, to each of

her ailing family members. When she returned home with her companions, she quickly did as she was told. After she treated each member with the potion, the vial was empty. A day later, her father and brothers were healthier than they could ever remember being.

Word soon spread throughout the land about a merciful blessed god living in the forest, and when the High Councilman heard such claims, he consulted with the stars. He later told the Emperor of old, informing him it was in the planet's best interest to perform a ceremony to honor this alien god. From then on, each Emperor has done just that, once every year in the spring season.

Speaking of seasons, as I mentioned earlier, a year on Utopia is different from those experienced on Earth. It takes 3,824 days for the planet to make one revolution around its red sun. Years are broken up into sixteen months, with ten days within a week. Names of the months and days are based on various gods and goddesses in their lore. Similar to Earth, where one's birth month dictates a spiritual entity called zodiacs, Utopians also are born with a spirit animal attributed to their month. As with zodiacs, they give an idea of personality or interests and match compatibility.

LAY OF THE LAND

The planet has a large ocean, dividing two landmasses from each other. The Western continent is where the capital city is located. It is called Utop, and it serves as the home of the Emperor's Great White Palace and Utopia University. The land is shrouded in forests and wilderness, with dirt paths or smooth cobbled roads leading to other towns. On the Eastern continent, one can find more forests and vast plains of meadows of wildflowers. Towns and cities are scattered throughout, connected by a web of dirt roads. The East continent is where MidStar University, UU's rival, is located. The temperature stays moderately warm on both continents, with a cool breeze blowing often enough worldwide.

Utopia is also home to many different wild creatures and monsters such as: dragons lurking in abandoned caves, wild boar-like animals (that stand five feet from front shoulders to hoof) roaming through the woods with huge tusks and a raging hunger, large birds of prey soaring through the skies, and monstrous sea creatures gliding through the clear blue water of the deep oceans. Along with the scarier things one could encounter while traveling, there are the more pleasant wildlife such as: small-furry creatures, wild stags, large herds of creatures similar to bison, and wild groups of horses that run along hillsides. The leaders of these herds of horses are easy to spot, as they're always in the lead with long flowing manes and long tails.

FINAL NOTES

There is one other thing particular to Utopia as a whole and that is a yearly occurrence that is scarcely documented. The natives refer to the event as Blood Moon or Red Moon. All I have been able to learn is that once a year the planet's moon, Lunaria, turns red, which affects the behavior of the Utopian people drastically. It, from the stories I have been told, sends them back into the days of their animalistic savagery. The strangest phenomenon is that it affects a person even if they are not insight of or near the red moon when it occurs.

This ends my introductory archival entry for the planet of Utopia. I shall continue my research and record my findings. Once I have finished all other introductions, I shall enter all my findings and notes into the Grand Archive for future reference and posterity. -The Chronicler